THE FIGHTING CHANCE

WORKS OF ROBERT W. CHAMBERS

THE TRACER OF LOST PERSONS
THE RECKONING
IOLE

Cardigan
The Maid at Arms
Lorraine
Maids of Paradise
Ashes of Empire
The Red Republic
The King in Yellow
A Maker of Moons
A King and a Few Dukes
The Conspirators
The Cambric Mask
The Haunts of Men
Outsiders
A Young Man in a Hurry
The Mystery of Choice
In Search of the Unknown
In the Quarter

FOR CHILDREN

Mountain-Land
Forest-Land
River-Land
Orchard-Land
Outdoorland

"There was a little half-hearted struggle, a silence, a breathless moment."

[Page 148.]

THE FIGHTING CHANCE

BY

ROBERT W. CHAMBERS

WITH ILLUSTRATIONS BY

A. B. WENZELL

D. APPLETON AND COMPANY
NEW YORK
1907

Published August, 1906

DEDICATED TO

MY FATHER

CONTENTS

LIST OF ILLUSTRATIONS

THE FIGHTING CHANCE

CHAPTER I

ACQUAINTANCE

The speed of the train slackened; a broad tidal river flashed into sight below the trestle, spreading away on either hand through yellowing level meadows. And now, above the roaring undertone of the cars, from far ahead floated back the treble bell-notes of the locomotive; there came a gritting vibration of brakes; slowly, more slowly the cars glided to a creaking standstill beside a sun-scorched platform gay with the bright flutter of sunshades and summer gowns.

"Shotover! Shotover!" rang the far cry along the cars; and an absent-minded young man in the Pullman pocketed the uncut magazine he had been dreaming over and, picking up gun case and valise, followed a line of fellow-passengers to the open air, where one by one they were engulfed and lost to view amid the gay confusion on the platform.

The absent-minded young man, however, did not seem to know exactly where he was bound for. He stood hesitating, leisurely inspecting the flashing ranks of vehicles—depot wagons, omnibusses, and motor cars already eddying around a dusty gravel drive centred by the conventional railroad flower bed and fountain.

Sunshine blazed on foliage plants arranged geometrically, on scarlet stars composed of geraniums, on thickets of tall flame-tinted cannas. And around this triumph of landscape gardening, phaeton, Tilbury, Mercedes, and Toledo backed, circled, tooted; gaily gowned women, whips aslant, horses dancing, greeted expected guests; laughing young men climbed into dog-carts and took the reins from nimble grooms; young girls, extravagantly veiled, made room in comfortable touring-cars for feminine guests whose extravagant veils were yet to be unpacked; slim young men in leather trappings, caps adorned with elaborate masks or goggles, manipulated rakish steering-gears; preoccupied machinists were fussing with valve and radiator or were cranking up; and, through the jolly tumult, the melancholy bell of the locomotive sounded, and the long train moved out through the September sunshine amid clouds of snowy steam.

And all this time the young man, gun case in one hand, suit case in the other, looked about him in his good-humoured, leisurely manner for anybody or any vehicle which might be waiting for him. His amiable inspection presently brought a bustling baggage-master within range of vision; and he spoke to this official, mentioning his host's name.

"Lookin' for Mr. Ferrall?" repeated the baggage-master, spinning a trunk dexterously into rank with its fellows. "Say, one of Mr. Ferrall's men was here just now—there he is, over there uncrating that there bird-dog!"

The young man's eyes followed the direction indicated by the grimy thumb; a red-faced groom in familiar livery was kneeling beside a dog's travelling crate, attempting to unlock it, while behind the bars an excited white setter whined and thrust forth first one silky paw then the other.

The young man watched the scene for a moment, then:

"Are you one of Mr. Ferrall's men?" he asked in his agreeable voice.

The groom looked up, then stood up:

"Yis, Sorr."

"Take these; I'm Mr. Siward—for Shotover House. I dare say you have room for me and the dog, too."

The groom opened his mouth to speak, but Siward took the crate key from his fingers, knelt, and tried the lock. It resisted. From the depths of the crate a beseeching paw fell upon his cuff.

"Certainly, old fellow," he said soothingly, "*I* know how you feel about it; *I* know you're in a hurry—and we'll have you out in a second—steady, boy!—something's jammed, you see! Only one moment now! . . . There you are!"

The dog attempted to bolt as the crate door opened, but the young man caught him by the leather collar and the groom snapped on a leash.

"Beg pardon, Sorr," began the groom, carried almost off his feet by the frantic circling of the dog—"beg pardon, Sorr, but I'll be afther seein' if anny of Mr. Ferrall's men drove over for you——"

"Oh! Are you not one of Mr. Ferrall's men?"

"Yis, Sorr, but I hadn't anny orders to meet anny wan——"

"Haven't you anything here to drive me in?"

"Yis, Sorr—I'll look to see——"

The raw groom, much embarrassed, and keeping his feet with difficulty against the plunging dog, turned toward the gravel drive where now only a steam motor and a depot-wagon remained. As they looked the motor steamed out, honking hoarsely; the depot-wagon followed, leaving the circle at the end of the station empty of vehicles.

"Didn't Mr. Ferrall expect me?" asked Siward.

"Aw, yis, Sorr; but the gintlemen for Shotover House does ginerally allways coom by Black Fells, Sorr——"

"Oh, Lord!" said the young man, "I remember now. I should have gone on to Black Fells Crossing; Mr. Ferrall wrote me!" Then, amused: "I suppose you have only a baggage-wagon here?"

"No, Sorr—a phayton"—he hesitated.

"Well? Isn't a phaeton all right?"

"Yis, Sorr—if th' yoong lady says so—beg pardon, Sorr, Miss Landis is driving."

"Oh—h! I see. . . . Is Miss Landis a guest at Shotover House?"

"Yis, Sorr. An' if ye would joost ask her—the phayton do be coming now, Sorr!"

The phaeton was coming; the horse, a showy animal, executed side-steps; blue ribbons fluttered from the glittering head-stall; a young girl in white was driving.

Siward advanced to the platform's edge as the phaeton drew up; the young lady looked inquiringly at the groom, at the dog, and leisurely at him.

So he took off his hat, naming himself in that well-bred and agreeable manner characteristic of men of his sort,—and even his smile appeared to be part and parcel of a conventional ensemble so harmonious as to remain inconspicuous.

"You *should* have gone on to Black Fells Crossing," observed Miss Landis, coolly controlling the nervous horse. "Didn't you know it?"

He said he remembered now that such were the directions given him.

The girl glanced at him incuriously, and with more curiosity at the dog. "Is that the Sagamore pup, Flynn?" she asked.

"It is, Miss."

"Can't you take him on the rumble with you?" And, to Siward: "There is room for your gun and suit case."

"And for me?" he asked, smiling.

"I think so. Be careful of that Sagamore pup, Flynn. Hold him between your knees. Are you ready, Mr. Siward?"

So he climbed in; the groom hoisted the dog to the rumble and sprang up behind; the horse danced and misbehaved, making a spectacle of himself and an agreeable picture of his driver; then the pretty little phaeton swung northward out of the gravel drive and went whirling along a road all misty with puffs of yellow dust which the afternoon sun turned to floating golden powder.

"Did you send my telegram, Flynn?" she asked without turning her head.

"I did, Miss."

It being the most important telegram she had ever sent in all her life, Miss Landis became preoccupied,—quite oblivious to extraneous details, including Siward, until the horse began acting badly again. Her slightly disdainful and perfect control of the reins interested the young man. He might have said something civil and conventional about that, but did not make the effort to invade a reserve which appeared to embarrass nobody.

A stacatto note from the dog, prolonged infinitely in hysterical crescendo, demanded comment from somebody.

"What is the matter with him, Flynn?" she asked.

Siward said: "You should let him run, Miss Landis."

She nodded, smiling, inattentive, absorbed in her own affairs, still theorising concerning her telegram. She drove on for a while, and might have forgotten the dog entirely had he not once more lifted his voice in melancholy.

"You say he ought to run for a mile or two? Do you think he'll bolt, Mr. Siward?"

"Is he a new dog?"

"Yes, fresh from the kennels; supposed to be house- and wagon-broken, steady to shot and wing—" She shrugged her pretty shoulders. "You see how he's acting already!"

"Do you mind if I try him?" suggested Siward.

"You mean that you are going to let him run?"

"I think so."

"And if he bolts?"

"I'll take my chances."

"Yes, but please consider my chances, Mr. Siward. The dog doesn't belong to me."

"But he ought to run——"

"But suppose he runs away? He's a horridly expensive creature—if you care to take the risk."

"I'll take the risk," said Siward, smiling as she drew rein. "Now Flynn, give me the leash. Quiet! Quiet, puppy! Everything is coming your way; that's the beauty of patience; great thing, patience!" He took the leader; the dog sprang from the rumble. "Now, my friend, look at me! No, don't twist and squirm and scramble; look me square in the eye; so! . . . Now we know each other and we respect each other—because you are going to be a good puppy . . . and obey . . . Down charge!"

The dog, trembling with eager comprehension, dropped like a shot, muzzle laid flat between his paws. Siward unleashed him, looked down at him for a second, stooped and caressed the silky head, then with a laugh swung himself into the phaeton beside the driver, who, pretty head turned, had been looking on intently.

"Your dog is yard-broken," he said. "Look at him."

"I see. Do you think he will follow us?"

"I think so."

The horse started, Miss Landis looking back over her shoulder at the dog who lay motionless, crouched flat in the road.

Then Siward turned. "Come on, Sagamore!" he said gaily; and the dog sprang forward, circled about the moving phaeton, splitting the air with yelps of ecstasy, then tore ahead, mad with the delight of stretching cramped muscles amid the long rank grass and shrubbery of the roadside.

The girl watched him doubtfully; when he disappeared far away up the road she turned the blue inquiry of her eyes on Siward.

"He'll be back," said the young fellow, laughing; and presently the dog reappeared on a tearing gallop, white flag tossing, glorious in his new liberty, enchanted with the confidence this tall young man had reposed in him—this adorable young man, this wonderful friend who had suddenly appeared to release him from an undignified and abominable situation in a crate.

"A good dog," said Siward; and the girl looked around at him, partly because his voice was pleasant, partly because a vague memory was beginning to stir within her, coupling something unpleasant with the name of Siward.

She had been conscious of it when he first named himself, but, absorbed in thc overwhelming importance of her telegram, had left the analysis of the matter for the future.

She thought again of her telegram, theorised a little, came to no conclusion except to let the matter rest for the present, and mentally turned to the next and far less important problem—the question of this rather attractive young man at her side, and why the name of Siward should be linked in her mind with anything disagreeable.

Tentatively following the elusive mental clews that might awaken something definite concerning her hazy impression of the man beside her, she spoke pleasantly, conventionally, touching idly any topic that might have a bearing; and, under a self-possession so detached as to give an impression of indifference, eyes, ears, and intelligence admitted that he was agreeable to look at, pleasant of voice, and difficult to reconcile with anything unpleasant.

Which gradually aroused her interest—the incongruous usually interesting girls of her age—for he had wit enough to amuse her, sufficient inconsequence to please her, and something listless, at times almost absent-minded, almost inattentive, that might have piqued her had it not inoculated her, as it always does any woman, with the nascent germ of curiosity. Besides, there was, in the hint of his momentary preoccupation, a certain charm.

They discussed shooting and the opening of the season; dogs and the training of dogs; and why some go gun-shy and why some are blinkers. From sport and its justification, they became inconsequential; and she was beginning to enjoy the freshness of their chance acquaintance, his nice attitude toward things, his irrelevancy, his gaiety.

Laughter thawed her; for notwithstanding the fearless confidence she had been taught for men of her own kind, self-possession and reserve, if not inherent, had also been drilled into her, and she required a great deal in a man before she paid him the tribute of one of her pretty laughs.

Apparently they were advancing rather rapidly.

"Don't you think we ought to call the dog in, Mr. Siward?"

"Yes; he's had enough!"

She drew rein; he sprang out and whistled; and the Sagamore pup, dusty and happy came romping back. Siward motioned him to the rumble, but the dog leaped to the front.

"I don't mind," said the girl. "Let him sit here between us. And you might occupy yourself by pulling some of those burrs from his ears—if you will?"

"Of course I will. Look up here, puppy! No! Don't try to lick my face, for that is bad manners. Demonstrations are odious, as the poet says."

"It's always bad manners, isn't it?" asked Miss Landis.

"What? Being affectionate?"

"Yes, and admitting it."

"I believe it is. Do you hear *that*—Sagamore? But never mind; I'll break the rules some day when we're alone."

The dog laid one paw on Siward's knee, looking him wistfully in the eyes.

"More demonstrations," observed the girl. "Mr. Siward! You are hugging him! This amounts to a dual conspiracy in bad manners."

"Awfully glad to admit you to the conspiracy," he said. "There's one vacancy—if you are eligible."

"I am; I was discovered recently kissing my saddle-mare."

"That settles it! Sagamore, give the young lady the grip."

Sylvia Landis glanced at the dog, then impulsively shifting the whip to her left hand, held out the right. And very gravely the Sagamore pup laid one paw in her dainty white gloved palm.

"You darling!" murmured the girl, resuming her whip.

"I notice," observed Siward, "that you are perfectly qualified for membership in our association for the promotion of bad manners. In fact I should suggest you for the presidency——"

"I suppose you think all sorts of things because I gushed over that dog."

"Of course I do."

"Well you need not," she rejoined, delicate nose up-tilted. "I never kissed a baby in all my life—and never mean to. Which is probably more than you can say."

"Yes, its more than I can say."

"That admission elects you president," she concluded. But after a moment's silent driving she turned partly toward him with mock seriousness: "Is it not horridly unnatural in me to feel that way about babies? And about people, too; I simply cannot endure demonstrations. As for dogs and horses—well, I've admitted how I behave; and, being so shamelessly affectionate by disposition, why can't I be nice to babies? I've a hazy but dreadful notion that there's something wrong about me, Mr. Siward."

He scrutinised the pretty features, anxiously; "I can't see it," he said.

"But I mean it—almost seriously. I don't want to be so aloof, but—I don't like to touch other people. It is rather horrid of me I suppose to be like those silky, plumy, luxurious Angora cats who never are civil to you and who always jump out of your arms at the first opportunity."

He laughed—and there was malice in his eyes, but he did not know her well enough to pursue the subject through so easy an opening.

It had occurred to her, too, that her simile might invite elaboration, and she sensed the laugh in his silence, and liked him for remaining silent where he might easily have been wittily otherwise.

This set her so much at ease, left her so confident, that they were on terms of gayest understanding presently, she gossiping about the guests at Shotover House, outlining the diversions planned for the two weeks before them.

"But we shall see little of one another; you will be shooting most of the time," she said—with the very faintest hint of challenge—too delicate, too impersonal to savour of coquetry. But the germ of it was there.

"Do *you* shoot?"

"Yes; why?"

"I am reconciled to the shooting, then."

"Oh, that is awfully civil of you. Sometimes I'd rather play Bridge."

"So should I—sometimes."

"I'll remember that, Mr. Siward; and when all the men are waiting for you to start out after grouse perhaps I may take that moment to whisper: 'May I play?'"

He laughed.

"You mean that you really would stay and play double dummy when every other living man will be off to the coverts? Double dummy—to improve my game?"

"Certainly! I need improvement."

"Then there is something wrong with you, too, Mr. Siward."

She laughed and started to flick her whip, but at her first motion the horse gave trouble.

"The bit doesn't fit," observed Siward.

"You are perfectly right," she returned, surprised. "I ought to have remembered; it is shameful to drive a horse improperly bitted." And, after a moment: "You are considerate toward animals; it is good in a man."

"Oh, it's no merit. When animals are uncomfortable it worries me. It's one sort of selfishness, you see."

"What nonsense," she said; and her smile was very friendly. "Why doesn't a nice man ever admit he's nice when told so?"

It seems they had advanced that far. For she was beginning to find this young man not only safe but promising; she had met nobody recently half as amusing, and the outlook at Shotover House had been unpromising with only the overgrateful Page twins to practise on—the other men collectively and individually boring her. And suddenly, welcome as manna from the sky, behold this highly agreeable boy to play with—until Quarrier arrived. Her telegram had been addressed to Mr. Quarrier.

"*What* was it you were saying about selfishness?" she asked. "Oh, I remember. It was nonsense."

"Certainly."

She laughed, adding: "Selfishness is so simply defined you know."

"Is it? How."

"A refusal to renounce. That covers everything," she concluded.

"Sometimes renunciation is weakness—isn't it?" he suggested.

"In what case for example?"

"Well, suppose we take love."

"Very well, you may take it if you like it."

"Suppose you loved a man!" he insisted.

"Let him beware! What then?"

"—And, suppose it would distress your family if you married him?"

"I'd give him up."

"If you loved him?"

"Love? That is the poorest excuse for selfishness, Mr. Siward."

"So you would ruin your happiness and his——"

"A girl ought to find more happiness in renouncing a selfish love than in love itself," announced Miss Landis with that serious conviction characteristic of her years.

"Of course," assented Siward with a touch of malice, "if you really do find more happiness in renouncing love than in love itself, it would be foolish not to do it——"

"Mr. Siward! You are derisive. Besides, you are not acute. A woman is always an opportunist. When the event takes place I shall know what to do."

"You mean when you want to marry the man you mustn't?"

"Exactly. I probably shall."

"Marry him?"

"Wish to!"

"I see. But you won't, of course."

She drew rein, bringing the horse to a walk at the foot of a long hill.

"We are going much too fast," said Miss Landis, smiling.

"Driving too fast for——"

"No, not driving, *going*—you and I."

"Oh, you mean——"

"Yes I do. We are on all sorts of terms, already."

"In the country, you know, people——"

"Yes I know all about it, and what old and valued friends one makes at a week's end. But it has been a matter of half-hours with us, Mr. Siward."

"Let us sit very still and think it over," he suggested. And they both laughed.

It was perhaps the reaction of her gaiety that recalled to her mind her telegram. The telegram had been her promised answer after she had had time to consider a suggestion made to her by a Mr. Howard Quarrier. The last week at Shotover permitted reflection; and while her telegram was no complete answer to the suggestion he had made, it contained material of interest in the eight words: "I will consider your request when you arrive."

"I wonder if you know Howard Quarrier?" she said.

After a second's hesitation he replied: "Yes—a little. Everybody does."

"You *do* know him?"

"Only at—the club."

"Oh, the Lenox?"

"The Lenox—and the Patroons."

Preoccupied, driving with careless, almost inattentive perfection, she thought idly of her twenty-three years, wondering how life could have passed so quickly leaving her already stranded on the shoals of an engagement to marry Howard Quarrier. Then her thoughts, errant, wandered half the world over before they returned to Siward; and when at length they did, and meaning to be civil, she spoke again of his acquaintance with Quarrier at the Patroons Club—the club itself being sufficient to settle Siward's status in every community.

"I'm trying to remember what it is I have heard about you," she continued amiably; "you are——"

An odd expression in his eyes arrested her—long enough to note their colour and expression—and she continued, pleasantly; "—you are Stephen Siward, are you not? You see I know your name perfectly well—" Her straight brows contracted a trifle; she drove on, lips compressed, following an elusive train of thought which vaguely, persistently, coupled his name with something indefinitely unpleasant. And she could not reconcile this with his appearance. However, the train of unlinked ideas which she pursued began to form the semblance of a chain. Coupling his name with Quarrier's, and with a club, aroused memory; vague uneasiness stirred her to a glimmering comprehension. Siward? Stephen Siward? One of the New York Siwards then;—one of that race——

Suddenly the truth flashed upon her,—the crude truth lacking definite detail, lacking circumstance and colour and atmosphere,—merely the raw and ugly truth.

Had he looked at her—and he did, once—he could have seen only the unruffled and very sweet profile of a young girl. Composure was one of the masks she had learned to wear—when she chose.

And she was thinking very hard all the while; "So *this* is the man? I might have known his name. Where were my five wits? Siward!—Stephen Siward! . . . He is very young, too . . . much too young to be so horrid. . . . Yet—it wasn't so dreadful, after all; only the publicity! Dear me! I knew we were going too fast."

"Miss Landis," he said.

"Mr. Siward?"—very gently. It was her way to be gentle when generous.

"I think," he said, "that you are beginning to remember where you may have heard my name."

"Yes—a little—" She looked at him with the direct gaze of a child, but the lovely eyes were troubled. His smile was not very genuine, but he met her gaze steadily enough.

"It was rather nice of Mrs. Ferrall to ask me," he said, "after the mess I made of things last spring."

"Grace Ferrall is a dear," she replied.

After a moment he ventured: "I suppose you saw it in the papers."

"I think so; I had completely forgotten it; your name seemed to——"

"I see." Then, listlessly: "I couldn't have ventured to remind you that—that perhaps you might not care to be so amiable——"

"Mr. Siward," she said impulsively, "you are nice to *me!* Why shouldn't I be amiable? It was—it was—I've forgotten just how dreadfully you did behave——"

"Pretty badly."

"Very?"

"They say so."

"And what is your opinion Mr. Siward?"

"Oh, I ought to have known better." Something

about him reminded her of a bad small boy; and suddenly in spite of her better sense, in spite of her instinctive caution, she found herself on the very verge of laughter. *What* was it in the man that disarmed and invited a confidence—scarcely justified it appeared? What was it now that moved her to overlook what few overlook—not the fault, but its publicity? Was it his agreeable bearing, his pleasant badinage, his amiably listless moments of preoccupation, his youth that appealed to her—aroused her charity, her generosity, her curiosity?

And had other people continued to accept him, too? What would Quarrier think of his presence at Shotover? She began to realise that she was a little afraid of Quarrier's opinions. And his opinions were always judgments. However Grace Ferrall had thought it proper to ask him, and that meant social absolution. As far as that went she also was perfectly ready to absolve him if he needed it. But perhaps he didn't care!—She looked at him, furtively. He seemed to be tranquil enough in his abstraction. Trouble appeared to slide very easily from his broad young shoulders. Perhaps he was already taking much for granted in her gentleness with him. And gradually speculation became interest and interest a young girl's innocent curiosity to learn something of a man whose record it seemed almost impossible to reconcile with his personality.

"I was wondering," he said looking up to encounter her clear eyes, "whose house that is over there?"

"Beverly Plank's shooting-box; Black Fells," she replied nodding toward the vast pile of blackish rocks against the sky, upon which sprawled a heavy stone house infested with chimneys.

"Plank? Oh yes."

He smiled to remember the battering blows rained upon the ramparts of society by the master of Black Fells.

But the smile faded; and, glancing at him, the girl was surprised to see the subtle change in his face—the white worn look, then the old listless apathy which, all at once to her, hinted of something graver than preoccupation.

"Are we near the sea?" he asked.

"Very near. Only a moment to the top of this hill. . . . Now look!"

There lay the sea—the same grey-blue crawling void that had ever fascinated and repelled him—always wrinkled, always in flat monotonous motion, spreading away, away to the sad world's ends.

"Full of menace—always," he said, unconscious that he had spoken aloud.

"The sea!"

He spoke without turning: "The sea is a relentless thing for a man to fight. . . . There are other tides more persistent than the sea, but like it—like it in its menace."

His face seemed thinner, older; she noticed his cheek bones for the first time. Then, meeting her eyes, youth returned with a laugh and a touch of colour; and, without understanding exactly how, she was aware, presently, that they had insensibly slipped back to their light badinage and gay inconsequences—back to a footing which, strangely, seemed to be already an old footing, familiar, pleasant, and natural to return to.

"Is that Shotover House?" he asked as they came to the crest of the last hillock between them and the sea.

" At last, Mr. Siward," she said mockingly; " and now your troubles are nearly ended."

" And yours, Miss Landis? "

" I don't know," she murmured to herself, thinking of the telegram with the faintest misgiving.

For she was very young, and she had not had half enough out of life as yet; and besides, her theories and preconceived plans for the safe and sound ordering of her life appeared to lack weight—nay, they were dwindling already into insignificance.

Theory had almost decided her to answer Mr. Quarrier's suggestion with a 'Yes.' However, he was coming from the Lakes in a day or two. She could decide definitely when she had discussed the matter with him.

" I wish that I owned this dog," observed Siward, as the phaeton entered the macadamised drive.

" I wish so, too," she said, " but he belongs to Mr. Quarrier."

CHAPTER II

IMPRUDENCE

A HOUSE of native stone built into and among weather-scarred rocks, one massive wing butting seaward, others nosing north and south among cedars and outcropping ledges—the whole silver-grey mass of masonry reddening under a westering sun, every dormer, every leaded diamond pane aflame; this was Shotover as Siward first beheld it.

Like the craggy vertebræ of a half-buried fossil splitting the sod, a ragged line of rock rose as a barrier to inland winds; the foreland, set here and there with tiny lawns and pockets of bright flowers, fell away to the cliffs; and here, sheer wet black rocks fronted the eternal battering of the Atlantic.

As the phaeton drew up under a pillared porte-cochère, one or two servants appeared; a rather imposing specimen bowed them through the doors into the hall where, in a wide chimney place, the embers of a drift-wood fire glimmered like a heap of dusty jewels. Bars of sunlight slanted on wall and rug, on stone floor and carved staircase, on the bronze foliations of the railed gallery above, where, in the golden gloom through a high window, sun-tipped tree tops against a sky of azure stirred like burnished foliage in a tapestry.

"There is nobody here, of course," observed Miss Landis to Siward as they halted in front of the fireplace; "the season opens to-day in this county, you see." She shrugged her pretty shoulders: "And the women who don't shoot make the first field-luncheon a function."

She turned, nodded her adieux, then, over her shoulder, casually: "If you haven't an appointment with the Sand-Man before dinner you may find me in the gun-room."

"I'll be there in about three minutes," he said; "and what about this dog?"—looking down at the Sagamore pup who stood before him, wagging, attentive, always the gentleman to the tips of his toes.

Miss Landis laughed. "Take him to your room if you like. Dogs have the run of the house."

So he followed a servant to the floor above where a smiling and very ornamental maid preceded him through a corridor and into that heavy wing of the house which fronted the sea.

"Tea is served in the gun-room, sir," said the pretty maid, and disappeared to give place to a melancholy and silent young man who turned on the bath, laid out fresh raiment, and whispering, "Scotch or Irish, sir?" presently effaced himself.

Before he quenched his own thirst Siward filled a bowl and set it on the floor, and it seemed as though the dog would never finish gulping and slobbering in the limpid icy water.

"It's the salt air, my boy," commented the young man, gravely refilling his own glass as though accepting the excuse on his own account.

Then man and beast completed ablutions and grooming and filed out through the wide corridor, around the gallery, and down the broad stairway to the gun-room—an oaken vaulted place illuminated by the sun, where mellow lights sparkled on glass-cased rows of fowling pieces and rifles, on the polished antlers of shaggy moose heads.

Miss Landis sat curled up in a cushioned corner under the open casement panes, offering herself a cup of tea. She looked up, nodding invitation; he found a place beside her. A servant whispered, " Scotch or Irish, sir," then set the crystal paraphernalia at his elbow.

He said something about the salt air, casually; the girl gazed meditatively at space.

The sound of wheels on the gravel outside aroused her from a silence which had become a brown study; and, to Siward, presently, she said: " Here endeth our first rendezvous."

" Then let us arrange another immediately," he said, stirring the ice in his glass.

The girl considered him with speculative eyes: " I shouldn't exactly know what to do with you for the next hour if I didn't abandon you."

" Why bother to do anything with me? Why even give yourself the trouble of deserting me? That solves the problem."

" I really don't mean that you are a problem to me, Mr. Siward," she said, amused; " I mean that I am going to drive again."

" I see."

" No you don't see at all. There's a telegram; I'm not driving for pleasure——"

She had not meant that either, and it annoyed her that she had expressed herself in such terms. As a matter of fact, at the telegraphed request of Mr. Quarrier, she was going to Black Fells Crossing to meet his train from the Lakes and drive him back to Shotover. The drive, therefore, was of course a drive for pleasure.

" I see," repeated Siward amiably.

"Perhaps you do," she observed, rising to her graceful height. He was on his feet at once, so carelessly, so good-humouredly acquiescent that without any reason at all she hesitated.

"I had meant to show you about—the cliffs—the kennels and stables; I'm sorry," she concluded, lingering.

"I'm awfully sorry," he rejoined without meaning anything in particular. That was the trouble, whatever he said, apparently meant so much.

With the agreeable sensation of being regretted, she leisurely gloved herself, then walked through the gun-room and hall, Siward strolling beside her.

The dog followed them as they turned toward the door and passed out across the terraced veranda to the driveway where a Tandem cart was drawn up, faultlessly appointed. Quarrier's mania was Tandem. She thought it rather nice of her to remember this.

She inspected the *ensemble* without visible interest for a few moments; the wind freshened from the sea, fluttering her veil, and she turned toward the east to face it. In the golden splendour of declining day the white sails of yachts crowded landward on the last leg before beating westward into Blue Harbour; a small white cruiser, steaming south, left a mile long stratum of rose-tinted smoke hanging parallel to the horizon's plane; the westering sun struck sparks from her bright-work.

The magic light on land and water seemed to fascinate the girl; she had walked a little way toward the cliffs, Siward following silently, offering no comment on the beauty of sky and cliff. As they halted once more the enchantment seemed to spread; a delicate haze enveloped the sea; hints of rose colour tinted the waves; over the uplands a pale mauve bloom grew; the sunlight turned redder, slanting on the rocks, and every kelp-covered reef became a spongy golden mound, sprayed with liquid flame.

They had turned their backs to the Tandem; the grooms looked after them, standing motionless at the horses' heads.

"Mr. Siward, this is too fine to miss," she said. "I will walk as far as the headland with you. . . . Please smoke if you care to."

He did care to; several matches were extinguished by the wind until she spread her skirts as a barrier; and kneeling in their shelter he got his light.

"Tobacco smoke diluted with sea breeze is delicious," she said, as the wind whirled the aromatic smoke of his cigarette up into her face. "Don't move, Mr. Siward; I like it; there is to me always a faint odour of sweet-brier in the mélange. Did you ever notice it?"

The breeze-blown conversation became fragmentary, veering as capriciously as the purple wind-flaws that spread across the shoals. But always to her question or comment she found in his response the charm of freshness, of quick intelligence, or of a humourous and idle perversity which stimulates without demanding.

Once, glancing back at the house where the T-cart and horses stood, she said that she had better return; or perhaps she only thought she said it, for he made no response that time. And a few moments later they reached the headland, and the Atlantic lay below, flowing azure from horizon to horizon—under a universe of depthless blue. And for a long while neither spoke.

With her the spell endured until conscience began to stir. Then she awoke, uneasy as always, under the shadow of restraint or pressure, until her eyes fell on him and lingered.

A subtle change had come into his face; its leanness struck her for the first time; that, and an utter detachment from his surroundings, a sombre oblivion to everything—and to her.

How curiously had his face altered, how shadowy it had grown, effacing the charm of youth in it.

The slight amusement with which she had become conscious of her own personal exclusion grew to an interest tinged with curiosity.

The interest continued, but when his silence became irksome to her she said so very frankly. His absent eyes, still clouded, met hers, unsmiling.

"I hate the sea," he said.

"You—*hate* it!" she repeated, too incredulous to be disappointed.

"There's no rest in it; it tires. A man whc plays with it must be on his guard every second. To spend a lifetime on it is ridiculous—a whole life of intelligent effort, against perpetual, brutal, inanimate resistance—one endless uninterrupted fight—a ceaseless human manœuvre against senseless menace; and then the counter attack of the lifeless monster, the bellowing advance, the shock—and no battle won—nothing final, nothing settled, no! only the same eternal nightmare of surveillance, the same sleepless watch for stupid treachery."

"But—*you* don't have to fight it!" she said, astonished.

"No; but it is no secret—what it does to those who do. . . . Some escape; but only by dying ashore before it gets them. That is the way some of us reach Heaven; we die too quick for the Enemy to catch us."

He was laughing when she said: "It is not a fight with the sea; it is the battle of Life itself you mean."

"Yes, in a way, the battle of Life."

"Oh, you *are* morbid then. Is there anybody ever born who has not a fight on his hands?"

"No; only I have known men tired out, unfairly, before life had declared war on them."

"Just what do you mean?"

"Oh, something about fair play—what our popular idol summarises as a 'square deal'." He laughed again, easily, his face clearing.

"Nobody worth a square deal ever laments because he hasn't had it," she said.

"I dare say that's true, too," he admitted listlessly.

"Mr. Siward, exactly what did you mean?"

"I was thinking of men I knew; for example a man who through generations has inherited every impulse and desire that he should not harbour—a man with intellect enough to be aware of it, with decency enough to desire decency. . . . What chance has he with the storms which have been brewing for him even before he opened his eyes on earth? Is *that* a square deal?"

The troubled concentration of her face was reflected now in his own; the wind came whipping and flicking at them from league-wide tossing wastes; the steady thunder of the sea accented the silence.

She said: "I suppose everybody has infinite capacity for decency or mischief. I know that I have. And I fancy that this capacity always remains, no matter how moral one's life may be. 'Watch and pray' was not addressed to the guilty alone, Mr. Siward."

"Oh, yes, of course. As for the balanced capacity for good and evil, how about the inherited desire for the latter?"

"Who is free from that, too? Do you suppose anybody really desires to be good?"

"You mean most people are so afraid not to be, that virtue becomes a habit?"

"Perhaps. It's a plain business proposition anyway. It pays."

"Celestial insurance?" he asked, laughing.

"I don't know, Mr. Siward; do you?"

But he, turning to the sea, had become engrossed in his own thoughts again; and again she was first curious, then impatient at the ease with which he excluded her. She remembered, too, that the cart was waiting; that she had scarcely time now to make the train.

She stood irresolute, inert, disinclined to bestir herself. An inborn aptitude for drifting, which threatened to become a talent for indecision, had always alternated in her with sudden impulsive conclusions; and when her pride was involved, in decisions which sometimes scarcely withstood the analysis of reason.

Physically healthy, mentally unawakened, sentimentally incredulous, totally ignorant of any master passion, and conventionally drilled, her beauty and sweet temper had carried her easily on the frothy crest of her first season, over the eligible and ineligible alike, leaving her at Lenox, a rather tired and breathless girl, in love with pleasure and the world which treated her so well.

The death of her mother abroad had made little impression upon her—her uncle, Major Belwether, having cared for her since her father's death when she was ten years old. So, although the scandal of her mother's self-exile had been in a measure condoned by a tardy marriage to the man for whom she had left everything, her daughter had grown up ignorant of any particular feeling for a mother she could scarcely remember.

However, she wore black and went nowhere for the

second winter, during which time she learned a great deal concerning the unconventional proclivities of the women of her race and family, enough to impress her so seriously that on an exaggerated impulse she had come to one of her characteristic decisions.

That decision was to break the unsavoury record at the first justifiable opportunity. And the opportunity came in the shape of Quarrier. As though wedlock were actually the sanctuary which an alarmed nation pretends it to be!

Now, approaching the threshold of a third and last season, and having put away her almost meaningless mourning, there had stolen into her sense of security something irksome in the promise she had made to give Quarrier a definite answer before winter.

Perhaps it had been the lack of interest in the people at Shotover, perhaps a mental review of her ancestors' capricious records—perhaps a characteristic impulse that had directed a telegram to Quarrier after a midnight confab with Grace Ferrall.

However it may have been, she had summoned him. And now he was on his way to get his answer, the best whip, the most eagerly discussed, and one of the wealthiest unmarried men in America.

Lingering irresolutely, considering with idle eyes the shadows lengthening across the sun-shot moorland, the sound of Siward's even voice aroused her from a meditation bordering on lassitude.

She answered vaguely. He spoke again; all the agreeable, gentle, humourous charm dominant once more—releasing her from the growing tension of her own thoughts, absolving her from the duty of immediate decision.

"I feel curiously lazy," she said; "perhaps from

"The conversation veered again toward the mystery of heredity."

our long drive." She seated herself on the turf. "Talk to me, Mr. Siward—in that lazy way of yours."

What he had to say proved inconsequent enough, an irrelevant suggestion concerning the training of field-dogs for close covert work and the reasons for not breaking such dogs on quail. Then the question of cross-breeding came up, and he gave his opinion on the qualities of "droppers." To which she replied, sleepily; and the conversation veered again toward the mystery of heredity, and the hopelessness of escape from its laws as illustrated now by the Sagamore pup, galloping nose in the wind, having scented afar the traces of the forbidden rabbit.

"His ancestors turned 'round and 'round to flatten the long reeds and grasses in their lairs before lying down," observed Siward. "He does it, too, where there is nothing to flatten out. Did you ever notice how many times a dog turns around before lying down? . . . And there goes the carefully schooled Sagamore, chasing rabbits! Why? Because his wild ancestors chased rabbits. . . . Heredity? It's a steady, unseen, pulling, dragging force. Like lightning, too, it shatters, sometimes, where there is resistance."

"Do you mean, Mr. Siward, that heredity is an excuse for moral weakness?"

"I don't know. Those inheriting nothing of evil say it is no excuse."

"It *is* no excuse."

"You speak with authority," he said.

"With more than you are aware of," she murmured, not meaning to say it.

She stood up impulsively, her fresh face turned to the distant house, her rounded young figure poised in relief against the sky.

"Inherited or not, idleness, procrastination, are my besetting sins. Can't you suggest the remedy, Mr. Siward?"

"But they are only the thieves of Time; and we kill the poor old gentleman."

"Leagued assassins," she repeated pensively.

Her gown had caught on the cliff briers; he knelt to release it, she looking down, noting an ugly tear in the fabric.

"Payment for my iniquities—the first instalment," she said, still looking down over his shoulder and watching his efforts to release her. "Thank you, Mr. Siward. I think we ought to start, don't you?"

He straightened up, smiling, awaiting her further pleasure. Her pleasure being capricious, she seated herself again, saying: "What I meant to say was this: evils that spring from heredity are no excuse for misconduct in people of our sort. Environment, not heredity, counts. And it's our business, who have every chance in the world, to make good!"

He looked down, amused at the piquant incongruity of voice and vernacular.

"What time is it?" she asked irrelevantly.

He glanced at his watch. She turned her eyes toward the level sun, conscious, and a little conscience-stricken that it was too late for her to drive to Black Fells Crossing—unless she started at once.

The sun hung low over the pines; all the scrubby foreland ran molten gold in every tufted furrow; flock after flock of twittering little birds whirled into the briers and out again, scattering inland into undulating flight.

The zenith turned shell pink; through clotted shoals of clouds spread spaces of palest green like calm lakes in the sky.

It grew stiller; the wind went down with the sun.

Doubtless he had forgotten to tell her the time; she had almost forgotten that she had asked him. With the silence of sunset a languor, the indolence of content, crept over her; she saw him close his watch with the absent-minded air which she already associated with him, and she let the question go from sheer disinclination for the effort of repetition—let the projected drive go—acquiescent, content that matters shape themselves without any interference from her. The sense of ease, of physical well-being invaded her with an agreeable relaxation as though tension somewhere had slackened.

They chatted on, casually, impersonally, in rather subdued tones. The dog returned now and then to see that all was well. All was well enough, it appeared, for she sat beside Siward, quite content, knees clasped in her hands, exchanging impressions of life with a man who so far had been sympathetically considerate in demanding from her no intellectual effort.

The conversation drifted illogically; sometimes he stirred her to amusement, even a hushed laughter; sometimes she smilingly agreed with his views, sometimes she let them go, uncriticised; or, intent on her own ideas, shook her small head in amused disapproval.

The stillness over all, the deepening mellow light, the blessed indolence of the young world—and their few years in it—Youth! That was perhaps the key to it all, after all.

"To-morrow," she mused aloud, knees cradled in her clasped fingers, "to-morrow they'll shoot—with great circumstance and fuss—a few native woodcock—there's no flight yet from the north!—a few grouse, fewer snipe, a stray duck or two. Others will drive motor cars over bad roads; others will ride, sail, golf—anything to kill the eternal enemy."

"And you?"

"Je n'en sais rien, monsieur."

"Mais je voudrais savoir."

"Pourquoi?"

"To lay a true course by the stars"; he looked at her blue eyes and she laughed easily under the laughing flattery.

"You must seek another compass—to-morrow," she said. Then it occurred to her that nobody could guess her decision in regard to Quarrier; and she partly raised her eyes, looking at him, indolent speculation under the white lids.

She liked him already; in fact she had liked few men as well on such brief acquaintance.

"You know the majority of the people here, or coming, don't you?" she inquired.

"Who are they?"

She began: "The Leroy Mortimers?"

"Oh, yes."

"Lord Alderdene and Captain Voucher, and the Page twins and Marion?"

"Yes."

"Rena Bonnesdel, the Tassel girl, Agatha Caithness, Mrs. Vendenning—all sorts, all sets." And, with an effort: "If I'm to drive, I should like—to—to know what time it is?"

He informed her; and she, too indolent to pretend surprise, and finding reproach easier, told him that he had no business to permit her to forget.

His smiling serenity under the rebuke aroused in her a slight resentment as though he had taken something for granted.

Besides, she had grown uneasy; she had wired Quarrier, saying she would meet him and drive him over. He had replied at once, naming his train. He was an exact man and expected method and precision in others. She didn't exactly know how it might affect him if his reasonable demand was unsatisfied. She did not know him very well yet, only well enough to be aware that he was a gentleman so precisely, so judiciously constructed, that, contemplating his equitable perfections, her awe and admiration grew as one on whom dawns the exquisite adjustments of an almost human machine.

And, thinking of him now, she again made up her mind to give him the answer which he now had every reason to expect from her. This decision appeared to lubricate her conscience; it ran more smoothly now, emitting fewer creaks.

"You say that you know Mr. Quarrier?" she began thoughtfully.

"Not well."

"I—hope you will like him, Mr. Siward."

"I do not think he likes me, Miss Landis. He has reasons not to."

She looked up, suddenly remembering: "Oh—since that scrape? What has Mr. Quarrier to do—" She did not finish the sentence. A troubled silence followed; she was trying to remember the details—something she had paid small attention to at the time—something so foreign to her, so distant from her comprehension that it had not touched her closely enough for her to remember exactly what this young man might have done to forfeit the good-will of Howard Quarrier.

She looked at Siward; it was impossible that anything very bad could come from such a man. And, pursuing her reasoning aloud: "It couldn't have been very awful," she argued; "something foolish about an actress, was it not? And that could not concern Mr. Quarrier."

"I thought you *did* know; I thought you—remembered—while you were driving me over from the station—that I was dropped from my club."

She flushed up: "Oh!—but—what had Mr. Quarrier to do with that?"

"He is a governor of that club."

"You mean that Mr. Quarrier had you—dropped?"

"What else could he do? A man who is idiot enough to risk making his own club notorious, must take the consequences. And they say I took that risk. Therefore Mr. Quarrier, Major Belwether—all the governors did their duty. I—I naturally conclude that no governor of the Patroons Club feels very kindly toward me."

Miss Landis sat very still, her small head bent, a flush still brightening her fair face.

She recalled a few of the details now—the scandal—something of the story. Which particular actress it was she could not remember; but some men who had dined too freely had made the wager, and this boy sitting beside her had accepted it—and won it, by bringing into the sacred precincts of the Patroons Club a foolish, shameless girl disguised in a man's evening dress.

That was bad enough; that somebody promptly discovered it was worse; but worst of all was the publicity, the club's name smirched, the young man expelled from one of the two best clubs in the metropolis.

To read of such things in the columns of a daily paper had meant little to her except to repell her; to hear it mentioned among people of her own sort had left her incurious and indifferent. But now she saw it in a new light, with the man who had figured in it seated beside her. Did such men as he—such attractive, well-bred, amusing men as he—do that sort of thing?

There he sat, hat off, the sun touching his short, thick hair which waved a little at the temples—a boyish mould to head and shoulders, a cleanly outlined cheek and chin, a thoroughbred ear set close—a *good* face. What sort of a man, then, was a woman to feel at ease with? What eye, what mouth, what manner, what bearing was a woman to trust?

"*Is* that the kind of man you are, Mr. Siward?" she said impulsively.

"It appears that I was; I don't know what I am—or may be."

"The pity of it!" she said, still swayed by impulse. "*Why* did you do—didn't you know—realize what you were doing—bringing discredit on your own club?"

"I was in no condition to know, Miss Landis."

The crude brutality of the expression might merely have hurt or disgusted her had she been less intelligent. Nor, as it was, did she fully understand why he chose to use it—unless that he meant it in self-punishment.

"It's rather shameful!" she said hotly.

"Yes," he assented; "it's a bad beginning."

"A—*beginning!* Do you mean to go on?"

He did not reply; his head was partly turned from her. She sat silent for a while. The dog had returned to lie at Siward's feet, its brown eyes tirelessly watching the man it had chosen for its friend; and the man, without turning his eyes, dropped one hand on the dog's head, caressing the silky ears.

Some sentimentalist had once said that no man who cared for animals could be wholly bad. Inexperience inclined her to believe it. Then too, she had that inclination for overlooking offences committed against precept, which appears to be one of those edifying human traits peculiar to neither sex and common to both. Besides, her knowledge of such matters was as vague as her mind was healthy and body wholesome. Men who dined incautiously were not remarkable for their rarity; the actress habit, being incomprehensible to her, meant nothing; and she said, innocently: "What men like you can find attractive in a common woman I do not understand; there are plenty of pretty women of your own sort. The actress cult is beyond my comprehension; I only know it is generally condoned. But it is not for such things that we drop men, Mr. Siward. You know that, of course."

"For what do you drop men?"

"For falsehood, deception, any dishonesty."

"And you don't drop a man when you read in the papers that one of the two best clubs in town has expelled him?"

She gave him a troubled glance; and, naïvely: "But you are still a member of the other, are you not?" Then hardening: "It was common! common!—thoroughly disgraceful and incomprehensible!"—and with every word uttered insensibly warming in her heart toward him whom she was chastening; "it was not even bad—it was worse than being simply bad; it was stupid!"

He nodded, one hand slowly caressing the dog's head where it lay across his knees.

She watched him a moment, hesitated, then smiling a little: "So now I know the worst about you; do I not?" she concluded.

He did not answer; she waited, the smile still curving her red mouth. Had she been *too* severe? She wondered. "You may help me to my feet," she said sweetly. She was *very* young.

He rose at once, holding out his hands to aid her in that pleasantly impersonal manner so suited to him; and now they stood together in the purple dusk of the uplands—two people young enough to take one another seriously.

"Let me tell you something," she said, facing him, white hands loosely linked behind her. "I don't exactly understand how it has happened, but you know as well as I do that we have formed a—an acquaintance—the sort that under normal conditions requires a long time and several conventional and preliminary chapters. . . . I should like to know what *you* think of our performance."

"I think," he said laughing, "that it is charming."

"Oh, yes; men usually find the unconventional agreeable. What I want to know is why I find it so, too?"

"Do you?" A dull colour stained his cheek-bones.

"Certainly I do. Is it because I've had a delightful chance to admonish a sinner—and be—just a little sorry—that he had made such a silly spectacle of himself?"

He laughed, wincing a trifle.

"Hence this agreeably righteous glow suffusing me," she concluded. "So now that I have answered my own question, I think that we had better go. . . . Don't you?"

They walked for a while, subdued, soberly picking their path through the dusk. After a few moments she began to feel doubtful, a little uneasy, partly from a reaction which was natural, partly because she was not at all sure what either Quarrier or Major Belwether would think of the terms she was already on with Siward. Suppose they objected? She had never thwarted either of these gentlemen. Besides she already had a temporary interest in Siward—the interest that women always cherish, quite unconsciously, for the man whose shortcomings they have consented to overlook.

As they crossed the headland, through the deepening dusk the acetylene lamps on a cluster of motor cars spread a blinding light across the scrub. The windows of Shotover House were brilliantly illuminated.

"Our shooting-party has returned," she said.

They crossed the drive through the white glare of the motor lamps; people were passing, grooms with dogs and guns and fluffy bunches of game-birds, several women in motor costumes, veils afloat, a man or two in shooting-tweeds or khaki.

As they entered the hall together, she turned to him, an indefinable smile curving her lips; then, with a little nod, friendly and sweet, she left him standing at the open door of the gun-room.

CHAPTER III

SHOTOVER

THE first person he encountered in the gun-room was Quarrier, who favoured him with an expressionless stare, then with a bow, quite perfunctory and non-committal. It was plain enough that he had not expected to meet Siward at Shotover House.

Kemp Ferrall, a dark, stocky, active man of forty, was in the act of draining a glass, when, through the bottom he caught sight of Siward. He finished in a gulp, and advanced, one muscular hand outstretched: "Hello, Stephen! Heard you'd arrived, tried the Scotch, and bolted with Sylvia Landis! That's all right, too, but you should have come for the opening day. Lots of native woodcock—eh, Blinky?" turning to Lord Alderdene; and again to Siward: "You know all these fellows—Mortimer yonder—" There was the slightest ring in his voice; and Leroy Mortimer, red-necked, bulky, and heavy eyed, emptied his glass and came over, followed by Lord Alderdene blinking madly through his shooting-goggles and showing all his teeth like a pointer with a "tic." Captain Voucher, a gentleman with the vivid colouring of a healthy groom on a cold day, came up, followed by the Page boys, Willis and Gordon, who shook hands shyly, enchanted to be on easy terms with the notorious Mr. Siward. And last of all Tom O'Hara arrived, reeking of the saddle and clinking a pair of trooper's spurs over the floor—relics of his bloodless Porto Rico campaign with Squadron A.

It was patent to every man present that the Kemp Ferralls had determined to ignore Siward's recent foolishness, which indicated that he might reasonably expect the continued good-will of several sets, the orbits of which intersected in the social system of his native city. Indeed, the few qualified to snub him cared nothing about the matter, and it was not likely that anybody else would take the initiative in being disagreeable to a young man, the fortunes and misfortunes of whose race were part of the history of Manhattan Island. Siwards, good or bad, were a matter of course in New York.

So everybody in the gun-room was civil enough, and he chose Scotch and found a seat beside Alderdene, who sat biting at a smoky pipe and fingering a tumbler of smokier Scotch, blinking away like mad through his shooting-goggles at everybody.

" These little brown snipe you call woodcock," he began; " we bagged nine brace, d'you see? But of all the damnable bogs and covers——"

" Rotten," said Mortimer thickly; " Ferrall, you're all calf and biceps, and it's well enough for you to go floundering into bogs——"

" Where do you expect to find native woodcock? " demanded Ferrall, laughing.

" On the table hereafter," growled Mortimer.

" Oh, go and pot Beverly Plank's tame pheasants," retorted Ferrall amiably; " Captain Voucher had a blank day, but he isn't kicking."

" Not I," said Voucher; " the sport is capital—if one can manage to hit the beggars——"

" Oh, everybody misses in snap-shooting," observed Ferrall; " that is, everybody except Stephen Siward with his unholy left barrel. Crack! and," turning to

Alderdene, " it's like taking money from you, Blinky—which reminds me that we've time for a little Preference before dressing."

His squinting lordship declined and took an easier position in his chair, extending a pair of little bandy legs draped in baggy tweed knickerbockers and heather-spats. Mortimer, industriously distending his skin with whiskey, reached for the decanter. The aromatic perfume of the spirits aroused Siward, and he instinctively nodded his desire to a servant.

" This salt air keeps one thirsty," he observed to Ferrall; then something in his host's expression arrested the glass at his lips. He had already been using the decanter a good deal; except Mortimer, nobody was doing that sort of thing as freely as he.

He set his glass on the table thoughtfully; a tinge of colour had crept into his lean cheeks.

Ferrall, too, suddenly uncomfortable, stood up saying something about dressing; several men arose a trifle stiffly, feeling in every joint the result of the first day's shooting after all those idle months. Mortimer got up with an unfeigned groan; Siward followed, leaving his glass untouched.

One or two other men came in from the billiard-room. All greeted Siward amiably—all excepting one who may not have seen him—an elderly, pink, soft gentleman with white downy chop-whiskers and the profile of a benevolent buck rabbit.

" How do you do, Major Belwether? " said Siward in a low voice without offering his hand.

Then Major Belwether saw him, bless you! yes indeed! And though Siward continued *not* to offer his hand, Major Belwether meant to have it, bless your heart! And he fussed and fussed and beamed cordiality until he secured it in his plump white fingers and pressed it effusively.

There was something about his soft, warm hands which had always reminded Siward of the temperature and texture of a newly hatched bird. It had been some time since he had shaken hands with Major Belwether; it was apparent that the bird had not aged any.

"And now for the shooting!" said the Major with an arch smile. "Now for the stag at bay and the winding horn—

'Where sleeps the moon
On Mona's rill——'

Eh, Siward?

'And here's to the hound
With his nose upon the ground——'

Eh, my boy? That reminds me of a story—" He chuckled and chuckled, his lambent eyes suffused with mirth; and slipping his arm through the pivot-sleeve of Lord Alderdene's shooting-jacket, hooking the other in Siward's reluctant elbow, and driving Mortimer ahead of him, he went garrulously away up the stairs, his lordship's bandy little legs trotting beside him, the soaking gaiters and shoes slopping at every step.

Mortimer, his mottled skin now sufficiently distended, greeted the story with a yawn from ear to ear; his lordship, blinking madly, burst into that remarkable laugh which seemed to reveal the absence of certain vocal cords requisite to perfect harmony; and Siward smiled in his listless, pleasant way, and turned off down his corridor, unaware that the Sagamore pup was following close at his heels until he heard Quarrier's even, colourless voice: "Ferrall, would you be good enough to send Sagamore to your kennels?"

" Oh—he's your dog! I forgot," said Siward turning around.

Quarrier looked at him, pausing a moment.

" Yes," he said coldly, " he's my dog."

For a fraction of a second the two men's eyes encountered; then Siward glanced at the dog, and turned on his heel with the slightest shrug. And that is all there was to the incident—an anxious, perplexed puppy lugged off by a servant, turning, jerking, twisting, resisting, looking piteously back as his unwilling feet slid over the polished floor.

So Siward walked on alone through the long eastern wing to his room overlooking the sea. He sat down on the edge of his bed, glancing at the clothing laid out for him. He felt tired and disinclined for the exertion of undressing. The shades were up; night quicksilvered the window-panes so that they were like a dark mirror reflecting his face. He inspected his darkened features curiously; the blurred and sombre-tinted visage returned the stare.

" Not a man at all—the shadow of a man," he said aloud—" with no will, no courage—always putting off the battle, always avoiding conclusions, always skulking. What chance is there for a man like that? "

As one who raises a glass to drink wine and unexpectedly finds water, he shrugged his shoulders disgustedly and got up. A bath followed; he dressed leisurely, and was pacing the room, fussing with his collar, when Ferrall knocked and entered, finding a seat on the bed.

" Stephen," he said bluntly, " I haven't seen you since that break of yours at the club."

" Rotten, wasn't it? " commented Siward, tying his tie.

" Perfectly. Of course it doesn't make any difference to Grace or to me, but I fancy you've already heard from it."

"Oh, yes. All I care about is how my mother took it."

"Of course; she was cut up I suppose?"

"Yes, you know how she would look at a thing of that sort; not that any of the nine and seventy jarring sets would care, but those few thousands invading the edges, butting in—half or three-quarters inside—are the people who can't afford to overlook the victim of a fashionable club's displeasure—those, and a woman like my mother, and several other decent-minded people who happen to count in town."

Ferrall, his legs swinging busily, thought again; then: "*Who* was the girl, Stephen?"

"I don't think the papers mentioned her name," said Siward gravely.

"Oh—I beg your pardon; I thought she was some notorious actress—everybody said so. . . . Who were those callow fools who put you up to it? . . . Never mind if you don't care to tell. But it strikes me they are candidates for club discipline as well as you. It was up to them to face the governors I think——"

"No, I think not."

Ferrall, legs swinging busily, considered him.

"Too bad," he mused; "they need not have dropped you——"

"Oh, they had to. But as long as the Lenox takes no action I can live that down."

Ferrall nodded: "I came in to say something—a message from Grace—confound it! what was it? Oh—*could* you—before dinner—*now*—just sit down and with that infernal facility of yours make a sketch of a man chasing a gun-shy dog?"

"Why yes—if Mrs. Ferrall wishes——"

He walked over to the desk in his shirt-sleeves, sat down, drew a blank sheet of paper toward him, and, dipping his pen, drew carelessly a gun-shy setter dog rushing frantically across the stubble, and after him, bare-headed, gun in hand, the maddest of men.

"Put a Vandyke beard on him," grinned Ferrall over his shoulder. "There! O Lord! but you *have* hit it! Put a ticked saddle on the cur—there!"

"Who is this supposed to be?" began Siward, looking up. But "Wait!" chuckled his host, seizing the still wet sketch, and made for the door.

Siward strolled into the bath-room, washed a spot or two of ink from his fingers, returned and buttoned his waistcoat, then, completing an unhurried toilet, went out and down the stairway to the big living-room. There were two or three people there—Mrs. Leroy Mortimer, very fetching with her Japanese-like colouring, black hair and eyes that slanted just enough; Rena Bonnesdel, smooth, violet-eyed, blonde, and rather stunning in a peculiarly innocent way; Miss Caithness, very pale and slimly attractive; and the Page boys, Willis and Gordon, delightfully shy and interested, and having a splendid time with any woman who could afford the intellectual leisure.

Siward spoke pleasantly to them all. Other people drifted down—Marion Page who looked like a schoolmarm and rode like a demon; Eileen Shannon, pink and white as a thorn blossom, with the deuce to pay lurking in her grey eyes; Kathryn Tassel and Mrs. Vendenning whom he did not know, and finally his hostess Grace Ferrall with her piquant, almost boyish, freckled face and sweet frank eyes and the figure of an adolescent.

She gave Siward one pretty sun-browned hand and

laid the other above his, holding it a moment in her light clasp.

"Stephen! Stephen!" she said under her breath, "it's because I've a few things to scold you about that I've asked you to Shotover."

"I suppose I know," he said.

"I should hope you do. I've a letter to-night from your mother."

"From my mother?"

"I want you to go over it—with me—if we can find a minute after dinner." She released his hand, turning partly around: "Kemp, dinner's been announced, so cut that dog story in two! Will you give me your arm Major Belwether? Howard!"—to her cousin, Mr. Quarrier, who turned from Miss Landis to listen—"will you please try to recollect whom you are to take in—and do it?" And, as she passed Siward, in a low voice, mischievous and slangy: "Sylvia Landis for yours—as she says she didn't have enough of you on the cliffs."

The others appeared to know how to pair according to some previous notice. Siward turned to Sylvia Landis with the pleasure of his good fortune so plainly visible in his face, that her own brightened in response.

"You see," she said gaily, "you cannot escape me. There is no use in looking wildly at Agatha Caithness"—he wasn't—"or pretending you're pleased," slipping her rounded, bare arm through the arm he offered. "You can't guess what I've done to-night—nobody can guess except Grace Ferrall and one other person. And if you try to look happy beside me, I may tell you—somewhere between sherry and cognac—Oh, yes; I've done two things: I have your dog for you!"

"Not Sagamore?" he said incredulously as he was seating her.

"Certainly Sagamore. I said to Mr. Quarrier, 'I want Sagamore,' and when he tried to give him to me, I made him take my cheque. Now you may draw another for me at your leisure, Mr. Siward. Tell me, are you pleased?"—for she was looking for the troubled hesitation in his face and she saw it dawning.

"Mr. Quarrier doesn't like me, you know——"

"But *I* do," she said coolly. "I told him how much pleasure it would give me. That is sufficient—is it not?—for everybody concerned."

"He knew that you meant to——"

"No, that concerns only you and me. *Are* you trying to spoil my pleasure in what I have done?"

"I can't take the dog, Miss Landis——"

"Oh," she said, vexed; "I had no idea you were vindictive——"

There was a silence; he bent forward a trifle, gravely scrutinising a "hand-painted" name card, though it might not have astonished him to learn that somebody's foot had held the brush. Somewhere in the vicinity Grace Ferrall had discovered a woman who supported dozens of relatives by painting that sort of thing for the summer residents at Vermillion Point down the coast. So being charitable she left an order, and being thrifty, insisted on using the cards, spite of her husband's gibes.

People were now inspecting them with more or less curiosity; Siward found his "hand-painting" so unattractive that he had just tipped it over to avoid seeing it, when a burst of laughter from Lord Alderdene made everybody turn. Mrs. Vendenning was laughing; so was Rena Bonnesdel looking over Quarrier's shoulder at a card he was holding—not one of the "hand"-decorated, but a sheet of note-paper containing a drawing of a man rushing after a gun-shy dog.

The extraordinary cackling laughter of his lordship obliterated other sounds for a while; Rena Bonnesdel possessed herself of the drawing and held it up amid a shout of laughter. And, to his excessive annoyance, Siward saw that, unconsciously, he had caricatured Quarrier—Ferrall's malicious request for a Vandyke beard making the caricature dreadfully apparent.

Quarrier had at first flushed up; then he forced a smile; but his symmetrical features were never cordial when he smiled.

"Who on earth did *that?*" whispered Sylvia Landis apprehensively. "Mr. Quarrier dislikes that sort of thing—but of course he'll take it well."

"*Did* he ever chase his own dog?" asked Siward, biting his lip.

"Yes—so Blinky says—in the Carolinas last season. It's Blinky!—that's his notion of humour. Did you ever hear such a laugh? No wonder Mr. Quarrier is annoyed."

The gay uproar had partly subsided, renewed here and there as the sketch was passed along, and finally, making the circle, returned like a bad penny to Quarrier. He smiled again, symmetrically, as he received it, nodding his compliments to Alderdene.

"Oh, no," cackled his lordship; "I didn't draw it, old chap!"

"Nor I! I only wish I could," added Captain Voucher.

"Nor I—nor I—who did it?" ran the chorus along the table.

"*I* didn't do it!" said Sylvia gravely, looking across at Quarrier. And suddenly Quarrier's large, handsome eyes met Siward's for the briefest fraction of a second, then were averted. But into his face there crept an expressionless pallor that did not escape Siward—no, nor Sylvia Landis.

Presently under cover of a rapid fire of chatter she said: " *Did* you draw that? "

" Yes; I had no idea it was meant for him. You may imagine how likely I'd be to take any liberty with a man who already dislikes me."

" But it resembles him—in a very dreadful way."

" I know it. You must take my word for what I have told you."

She looked up at him: " I do." Then: " It's a pity; Mr. Quarrier does not consider such things humourous. He—he is very sensitive. . . . Oh, I wish that fool Englishman had been in Ballyhoo! "

" But *he* didn't do it! "

" No, but he put you up to it—or Grace Ferrall did. I wish Grace *would* let Mr. Quarrier alone; she has always been perfectly possessed to plague him; she seems unable to take him seriously and he simply hates it. I don't think he'd tolerate her if she were not his cousin."

" I'm awfully sorry," was all Siward said; and for a while he gloomily busied himself with whatever was brought to him.

" *Don't* look that way," came a low voice beside him.

" Do I show everything as plainly as that? " he asked, curiously.

" I seem to read you—sometimes."

" It's very nice of you," he said.

" Nice? "

" To look at me—now and then."

" Oh," she cried resentfully, " don't be grateful."

" I—really am not you know," he said laughing.

" That," she rejoined slowly, " is the truth. You

say conventional things in a manner—in an agreeably personal manner that interests women. But you are *not* grateful to anybody for anything; you are indifferent, and you can't help being nice to people, so—some day—some girl will think you *are* grateful, and will have a miserable time of it."

"Miserable time?"

"Waiting for you to say what never will enter your head to say."

"You mean I—I——"

"Flirt? No, I mean that you don't flirt; that you are always dreamily occupied with your own affairs, from which listlessly congenial occupation, when drawn, you are so unexpectedly nice that a girl immediately desires to see how nice you can be."

"What a charming indictment you draw!" he said, amused.

"It's a grave one I assure you. I've been talking about you to Grace Ferrall; I asked to be placed beside you at dinner; I told her I hadn't had half enough of you on the cliff. Now what do you think of yourself for being too nice to a susceptible girl? *I* think it's immoral."

They both were laughing now; several people glanced at them, smiling in sympathy. Alderdene took that opportunity to revert to the sketch, furnishing a specimen of his own inimitable laughter as a running accompaniment to the story of Quarrier and his dog in North Carolina, until he had everybody, as usual, laughing, not at the story but at him. All of which demonstration was bitterly offensive to Quarrier. He turned his eyes once on Miss Landis and on Siward, then dropped them.

The hostess arose; a rustle and flurry of silk and lace

and the scraping of chairs, a lingering word or laugh, and the colour vanished from the room leaving a circle of men in black standing around the table.

Here and there a man, lighting a cigarette, bolted his coffee and cognac and strolled out to the gun-room. Ferrall, gesticulating vigorously, resumed his pre-prandial dog story to Captain Voucher; Belwether buttonholed Alderdene and bored him with an interminably facetious tale until that nobleman, threatened with maxillary dislocation, fairly wrenched himself loose and came over to Siward, squinting furiously.

" Old ass! " he muttered; " his chop whiskers look like the chops of a Southdown ram—and he's got the wits of one. Look here, Stephen, I hear you fell into no end of a scrape in town——"

" *Tu quoque*, Blinky? Oh, read the newspapers and let it go at that! "

" Just as you like old chap! " returned his lordship unabashed. " All I meant was—anything Voucher and I can do—of course——"

" You're very good. I'm not dead you know."

" ' Not dead, you know '," repeated Major Belwether coming up behind them with his sprightly step; " that reminds me of a good one—" He sat down and lighted a cigar, then, vainly attempting to control his countenance as though roguishly anticipating the treat awaiting them, he began another endless story.

Tradition had hallowed the popular notion that Major Belwether was a wit. The sycophant of the outer world seldom even awaited his first word before bursting into premature mirth. Besides he was very wealthy.

Siward watched him with mixed emotions; the lambent-eyed, sheepy expression had given place to the buck rabbit; his smooth baby-pink skin and downy white side whiskers quivered in premature sympathy with his listener's overwhelming hilarity.

The Page boys, very callow, very much delighted, and a little in awe of such a celebrated personage, laughed heartily. And altogether there was sufficient attention and sufficient laughter to make a very respectable noise. This, being the major's cue for an exit, he rose, one sleek hand raised in sprightly protest as though to shield the invisible ladies, to whose bournes he was bound, from an uproar too masculine and mighty for the ears of such a sex.

"Ass!" muttered Alderdene, getting up and pattering about the room in his big, shiny pumps. "Give me a peg—somebody!"

Mortimer swallowed his brandy, lingered, lifted the decanter, mechanically considering its remaining contents and his own capacity; then:

"Bridge, Captain?"

"Certainly," said Captain Voucher briskly.

"I'll go and shoo the major into the gun-room," observed Ferrall—"unless—" looking questioningly at Siward.

"I've a date with your wife," observed that young man, strolling toward the hall.

The Page boys, Rena Bonnesdel, and Eileen Shannon were seated at a card table together, very much engaged with one another, the sealed pack lying neglected on the green cloth, a vast pink box of bon-bons beside it, not neglected.

O'Hara and Quarrier with Marion Page and Mrs. Mortimer were immersed in the game, already stony faced and oblivious to outer sounds.

About the rooms were distributed girls en tête-à-tête, girls eating bon-bons and watching the cards—

among them Sylvia Landis, hands loosely clasped behind her, standing at Quarrier's elbow to observe and profit by an expert performance.

As Siward strolled in she raised her dainty head for an instant, smiled in silence, and resumed a study of her fiancé's game.

A moment later, when Quarrier had emerged brilliantly from the mêlée, she looked up again, triumphantly, supposing Siward was lingering somewhere waiting to join her. And she was just a trifle surprised and disappointed to find him nowhere in sight. She had wished him to observe the brilliancy of Mr. Quarrier's game.

But Siward, outside on the veranda, was saying at that moment to his hostess: "I shall be very glad to read my mother's letter at any time you choose."

"It must be later, Stephen. I'm to cut in when Kemp sends for me. He has a lot of letters to attend to. . . . Tell me, what do you think of Sylvia Landis?"

"I like her, of course," he replied pleasantly.

Grace Ferrall stood thinking a moment: "That sketch you made proved a great success, didn't it?" And she laughed under her breath.

"Did it? I thought Mr. Quarrier seemed annoyed——"

"Really? What a muff that cousin of mine is. He's such a muff, you know, that the very sight of his pointed beard and pompadour hair and his complacency sets me in fidgets to stir him up."

"I don't think you'd best use me for the stick next time," said Siward. "He's not *my* cousin you know."

Mrs. Ferrall shrugged her boyish shoulders: "By the way"—she said curiously—"who *was* that girl?"

"*What* girl," he asked coolly, looking at his hostess, now the very incarnation of delicate mockery with her pretty laughing mouth, her boyish sunburn and freckles.

"You won't tell me I suppose?"

"I'm sorry——"

"*Was* she pretty, Stephen?"

"Yes," he said sulkily; "I wish you wouldn't——"

"Nonsense! Do you think I'm going to let you off without some sort of confession? If I had time now—but I haven't. Kemp has business letters: he'll be furious; so I've got to take his cards or we won't have any pennies to buy gasoline for our adored and shrieking Mercedes."

She retreated backward with a gay nod of malice, turned to enter the house, and met Sylvia Landis face to face in the hallway.

"*You* minx!" she whispered; "aren't you ashamed?"

"Very much, dear. What for?" And catching sight of Siward outside in the starlight, divined perhaps something of her hostess' meaning, for she laughed uneasily, like a child who winces under a stern eye.

"You don't suppose for a moment," she began, "that I have——"

"Yes I do. You *always* do."

"Not with that sort of man," she returned naïvely; "he *won't*."

Mrs. Ferrall regarded her suspiciously: "You always pick out exactly the wrong man to play with——"

They had moved back side by side into the hall, the hostess' arm linked in the arm of the younger girl.

"The wrong man?" repeated Sylvia, instinctively freeing her arm, her straight brows beginning to bend inward.

"I didn't mean that—exactly. You know how much I care for his mother—and for him." The obstinate downward trend of the brows, the narrowing blue gaze signalled mutiny to the woman who knew her so well.

"What is so wrong with Mr. Siward?" she asked.

"Nothing. There was an affair——"

"This spring in town. I know it. Is that all?"

"Yes—for the present," replied Grace Ferrall uncomfortably; then: "For goodness' sake, Sylvia, don't cross examine me that way! I care a great deal for that boy——"

"So do I. I've made him take my dog."

There was an abrupt pause, and presently Mrs. Ferrall began to laugh.

"I mean it—really," said Sylvia quietly; "I like him immensely."

"Dearest, you mean it generously—with your usual exaggeration. You have heard that he has been foolish, and because he's so young, so likable, every instinct, every impulse in you is aroused to—to be nice to him——"

"And if that were true——"

"There is no harm, dear—" Mrs. Ferrall hesitated, her grey eyes softening to a graver revery. Then looking up: "It's rather pathetic," she said in a low voice. "Kemp thinks he's foredoomed—like all the Siwards. It's an hereditary failing with him,—no, it's hereditary damnation. Siward after Siward, generation after generation you know—" She bit her lip, thinking a moment. "His grandfather was a friend of my grandparents, brilliant, handsome, generous, and—doomed! His own father was found dying in a dreadful resort in London where he had wandered when stupefied—a

Siward! Think of it! So you see what that outbreak of Stephen's means to those whose families have been New Yorkers since New York was. It is ominous, it is more than ominous—it means that the master-vice has seized on one more Siward. But I shall never, *never* admit it to his mother."

The younger girl sat wide-eyed, silent; the elder's gaze was upon her, but her thoughts, remote, centred on the hapless mother of such a son.

"Such indulgence was once fashionable; moderation is the present fashion. Perhaps he will fall into line," said Mrs. Ferrall thoughtfully. "The main thing is to keep him among people, not to drop him. The gregarious may be shamed, but if anything, any incident, happens to drive him outside by himself, if he should become solitary, there's not a chance in the world for him. . . . It's a pity. I know he meant to make himself the exception to the rule—and look! Already one carouse of his has landed him in the daily papers!"

Sylvia flushed and looked up: "Grace, may I ask you a plain question?"

"Yes, child," she answered absently.

"Has it occurred to you that what you have said about this boy touches me very closely?"

Mrs. Ferrall's wits returned nimbly from woolgathering, and she shot a startled, inquiring glance at the girl beside her.

"You—you mean the matter of heredity, Sylvia?"

"Yes. I think my uncle Major Belwether chose you as his august mouthpiece for that little sermon on the dangers of heredity—the danger of being ignorant concerning what women of my race had done—before I came into the world they found so amusing."

"I told you several things," returned Mrs. Ferrall

composedly. "Your uncle thought it best for you to know."

"Yes. The marriage vows sat lightly upon some of my ancestors, I gather. In fact," she added coolly, "where the women of my race loved they usually found the way—rather unconventionally. There was, if I understood you, enough of divorce, of general indiscretion and irregularity to seriously complicate any family tree and coat of arms I might care to claim——"

"Sylvia!"

The girl lifted her pretty bare shoulders. "I'm sorry, but could *I* help it? Very well; all I can do is to prove a decent exception. Very well; I'm doing it, am I not?—practically scared into the first solidly suitable marriage offered — seizing the unfortunate Howard with both hands for fear he'd get away and leave me alone with only a queer family record for company! *Very* well! Now then, I want to ask you why everybody, in my case, didn't go about with sanctimonious faces and dolorous mien repeating: 'Her grandmother eloped! Her mother ran away. Poor child, she's doomed! doomed!'"

"Sylvia, I——"

"Yes—why didn't they? That's the way they talk about that boy out there!" She swept a rounded arm toward the veranda.

"Yes, but *he* has already broken loose, while you——"

"So did I—nearly! Had it not been for you, you know well enough I might have run away with that dreadful Englishman at Newport! For I adored him —I did! I did! and you know it. And look at my endless escapes from compromising myself! Can you count them?—all those indiscretions when mere living seemed to intoxicate me that first winter—and only my uncle and you to break me in!"

"In other words," said Mrs. Ferrall slowly, "you don't think Mr. Siward is getting what is known as a square deal?"

"No, I don't. Major Belwether has already hinted—no, not even that—but has somehow managed to dampen my pleasure in Mr. Siward."

Mrs. Ferrall considered the girl beside her—now very lovely and flushed in her suppressed excitement.

"After all," she said, "you are going to marry somebody else. So why become quite so animated about a man you may never again see?"

"I shall see him if I desire to!"

"Oh!"

"I am not taking the black veil, am I?" asked the girl hotly.

"Only the wedding veil, dear. But after all your husband ought to have something to suggest concerning a common visiting list——"

"He may suggest—certainly. In the meantime I shall be loyal to my own friends—and afterward, too," she murmured to herself, as her hostess rose, calmly dropping care like a mantle from her shoulders.

"Go and be good to this poor young man then; I adore rows—and you'll have a few on your hands I'll warrant. Let me remind you that your uncle can make it unpleasant for you yet, and that your amiable fiancé has a will of his own under his pompadour and silky beard."

"What a pity to have it clash with mine," said the girl serenely.

Mrs. Ferrall looked at her: "Mercy on us! Howard's pompadour would stick up straight with horror if he could hear you! Don't be silly; don't for an impulse, for a caprice, break off anything desirable on account of a man for whom you really care nothing—whose amiable exterior and prospective misfortune merely enlist a very natural and generous sympathy in you."

"Do you suppose that I shall endure interference from anybody?—from my uncle, from Howard?"

"Dear, you are making a mountain out of a mole-hill. Don't be emotional; don't let loose impulses that you and I know about, knew about in our school years, know all about now, and which you and I have decided must be eliminated——"

"You mean subdued; they'll always be there."

"Very well; who cares, as long as you have them in leash?"

Looking at one another, the excited colour cooling in the younger girl's cheeks, they laughed, one with relief, the other a little ashamed.

"Kemp will be furious; I simply must cut in!" said Mrs. Ferrall, hastily turning toward the gun-room. Miss Landis looked after her, subdued, vaguely repentant, the consciousness dawning upon her that she had probably made considerable conversation about nothing.

"It's been so all day," she thought impatiently; "I've exaggerated; I've worked up a scene about a man whose habits are not the slightest concern of mine. Besides that I've neglected Howard shamefully!" She was walking slowly, her thoughts outstripping her errant feet, but it seemed that neither her thoughts nor her steps were leading her toward the neglected gentleman within; for presently she found herself at the breezy veranda door, looking rather fixedly at the stars.

The stars, shining impartially upon the just and the unjust, illuminated the person of Siward, who sat alone, rather limply, one knee crossed above the other. He looked up by chance, and, seeing her star-gazing in the doorway, straightened out and rose to his feet.

Aware of him apparently for the first time, she stepped across the threshold meeting his advance half-way.

"Would you care to go down to the rocks?" he asked. "The surf is terrific."

"No—I don't think I care——"

They stood listening a moment to the stupendous roar.

"A storm somewhere at sea," he concluded.

"Is it very fine—the surf?"

"Very fine—and very relentless—" he laughed; "it *is* an unfriendly creature, the sea, you know."

She had begun to move toward the cliffs, he fell into step beside her; they spoke little, a word now and then.

The perfume of the mounting sea saturated the night with wild fragrance; dew lay heavy on the lawns; she lifted her skirts enough to clear the grass, heedless that her silk-shod feet were now soaking. Then at the cliffs' edge, as she looked down into the white fury of the surf, the stunning crash of the ocean saluted her.

For a long while they watched in silence; once she leaned a trifle too far over the star-lit gulf and, recoiling, involuntarily steadied herself on his arm.

"I suppose," she said, "no swimmer could endure that battering."

"Not long."

"Would there be no chance?"

"Not one."

She bent farther outward, fascinated, stirred, by the splendid frenzy of the breakers.

"I—think—," he began quietly; then a firm hand fell over her left hand; and, half encircled by his arm she found herself drawn back. Neither spoke; two things she was coolly aware of, that, urged, drawn by something subtly irresistible she had leaned too far out from the cliff, and would have leaned farther had he not taken matters into his own keeping without apology. Another thing; the pressure of his hand over hers remained a sensation still—a strong, steady, masterful imprint lacking hesitation or vacillation. She was as conscious of it as though her hand still tightened under his—and she was conscious, too, that nothing of his touch had offended; that there had arisen in her no tremor of instinctive recoil. For never before had she touched or suffered a touch from a man, even a gloved greeting, that had not in some measure subtly repelled her, nor, for that matter, a caress from a woman without a reaction of faint discomfort.

"Was I in any actual danger?" she asked curiously.

"I think not. But it was too much responsibility for me."

"I see. Any time I wish to break my neck I am to please do it alone in future."

"Exactly—if you don't mind," he said smiling.

They turned, shoulder to shoulder, walking back through the drenched herbage.

"*That,*" she said impulsively, "is not what *I* said a few moments ago to a woman."

"What did you say a few moments ago to a woman?"

"I said, Mr. Siward, that I would not leave a—a certain man to go to the devil alone!"

"Do you know any man who is going to the devil?"

"Do you?" she asked, letting herself go swinging out upon a tide of intimacy she had never dreamed of risking—nor had she the slightest idea whither the current would carry her.

They had stopped on the lawn, ankle deep in wet grass, the stars overhead sparkling magnificently, and in their ears the outcrash of the sea.

"You mean me," he concluded.

"Do I?"

He looked up into the lovely face; her eyes were very sweet, very clear—clear with excitement—but very friendly.

"Let us sit here on the steps a little while, will you?" she asked.

So he found a place beside her, one step lower, and she leaned forward, elbows on knees, rounded white chin in her palms, the starlight giving her bare arms and shoulders a marble lustre and tinting her eyes a deeper amethyst.

And now, innocently untethered, mission and all, she laid her heart quite bare—one chapter of it. And, like other women-errant who believe in the influence of their sex individually and collectively, she began wrong by telling him of her engagement—perhaps to emphasise her pure disinterestedness in a crusade for principle only. Which naturally dampened in him any nascent enthusiasm for being ministered to, and so preoccupied him that he turned deaf ears to some very sweet platitudes which might otherwise have impressed him as discoveries in philosophy.

Officially her creed was the fashionable one in town; privately she had her own religion, lacking some details truly enough, but shaped upon youthful notions of right and wrong. As she had not read very widely, she supposed that she had discovered this religion for herself; she was not aware that everybody else had passed that way—it being the first immature moult in young people after rejecting dogma.

And the ripened fruit of all this philosophy she helpfully dispensed for Siward's benefit as bearing directly on his case.

Had he not been immersed in the unexpected proposition of her impending matrimony, he might have been impressed, for the spell of her beauty counted something, and besides, he had recently formulated for himself a code of ethics, tinctured with Omar, and slightly resembling her own discoveries in that dog-eared science.

So it was, when she was most eloquent, most earnestly inspired—nay in the very middle of a plea for sweetness and light and simple living, that his reasonings found voice in the material comment:

"I never imagined *you* were engaged!"

"Is *that* what you have been thinking about?" she asked, innocently astonished.

"Yes. Why not? I never for one instant supposed——"

"But, Mr. Siward, why should you have concerned yourself with supposing anything? Why indulge in any speculation of *that* sort about *me?*"

"I don't know, but I didn't," he said.

"Of course you didn't; you'd known me for about three hours—there on the cliff——"

"But—Quarrier——!"

Over his youthful face a sullen shadow had fallen—flickering, not yet settled. He would not for anything on earth have talked freely to the woman destined to be Quarrier's wife. He had talked too much anyway. Something in her, something about her had loosened his tongue. He had made a plain ass of himself—that was all,—a garrulous ass. And truly it seemed that the girl beside him, even in the starlight, could follow and divine what he had scarcely expressed to himself; or her instincts had taken a shorter cut to forestall his own conclusion.

"Don't think the things you *are* thinking!" she said in a fierce little voice, leaning toward him.

"What do you mean?" he asked, taken aback.

"You know! Don't! It is unfair—it is—is faithless—to me. I *am* your friend; why not? Does it make any difference to you whom I marry? Cannot two people remain in accord anyway? Their friendship concerns each other and—nobody else!" She was letting herself go now; she was conscious of it, conscious that impulse and emotion were the currents unloosed and hurrying her onward. And with it all came exhilaration, a faint intoxication, a delicate delight in daring to let go all and trust to impulse and emotions.

"Why should you feel hurt because for a moment you let me see—gave me a glimpse of yourself—of life's battle as you foresee it? What if there is always a reaction from all confidences exchanged? What if that miserable French cynic did say that never was he more alone than after confessing to a friend? He died crazy anyhow. Is not a rare moment of confidence worth the reaction—the subsidence into the armored shell of self? Tell me truly, Mr. Siward, isn't it?"

Breathless, confused, exhilarated by her own rapid voice she bent her face, brilliant with colour, and very sweet; and he looked up into it, expectant, uncertain.

"If such a friendship as ours is to become worth anything to you—to me, why should it trouble you that I know—and am thinking of things that concern you? Is it because the confidence is one-sided? Is it because you have given and I have listened and given nothing in return to balance the account? I do give—interest, deep interest, sympathy if you ask it; I give confidence in return—if you desire it!"

"What can a girl like you need of sympathy?" he said smiling.

"You don't know! you don't know! If heredity is a dark vista, and if you must stare through it all your life, sword in hand, always on your guard, do you think you are the only one?"

"Are *you*—one?" he said incredulously.

"Yes"—with an involuntary shudder—"not *that* way. It is easier for me; I think it is—I know it is. But there are things to combat—impulses, a recklessness, perhaps something almost ruthless. What else I do not know, for I have never experienced violent emotions of any sort—never even deep emotion."

"You are in love!"

"Yes, *thoroughly*," she added with conviction, "but not violently. I—" she hesitated, stopped short, leaning forward, peering at him through the dusk; and: "Mr. Siward! *are* you laughing?" She rose and he stood up instantly.

There was lightning in her darkening eyes now; in his something that glimmered and danced. She watched it, fascinated, then of a sudden the storm broke and they were both laughing convulsively, face to face there under the stars.

"Mr. Siward," she breathed, "I *don't* know what I am laughing at; do you? Is it at you? At myself? At my poor philosophy in shreds and tatters? Is it some infernal mirth that you seem to be able to kindle in me —for I never knew a man like you before?"

"You don't know what you were laughing at?" he repeated. "It was something about love——"

"No I don't know why I laughed! I—I don't wish to, Mr. Siward. I do not desire to laugh at anything you have made me say—anything you may infer——"

"I don't infer——"

"You do! You made me say something—about my being ignorant of deep, of violent emotion, when I had just informed you that I am thoroughly, *thoroughly* in love——"

"Did I make you say all that, Miss Landis?"

"You did. Then you laughed and made me laugh too. Then you——"

"What did I do then?" he asked, far too humbly.

"You—you infer that I am either not in love or incapable of it, or too ignorant of it to know what I'm talking about. That, Mr. Siward, is what you have done to me to-night."

"I—I'm sorry——"

"*Are* you?"

"I ought to be anyway," he said.

It was unfortunate; an utterly inexcusable laughter seemed to bewitch them, hovering always close to his lips and hers.

"How *can* you laugh!" she said. "How *dare* you! I don't care for you nearly as violently as I did, Mr. Siward. A friendship between us would not be at all good for me. Things pass too swiftly—too intimately. There is too much mockery in you—" She ceased suddenly, watching the sombre alteration of his face; and, "*Have* I hurt you?" she asked penitently.

"No."

"Have I, Mr. Siward? I did not mean it." The

attitude, the words, slackening to a trailing sweetness, and then the moment's silence, stirred him.

"I'm rather ignorant myself of violent emotion," he said. "I suspect normal people are. You know better than I do whether love is usually a sedative."

"Am I normal—after what I have confessed?" she asked. "Can't love be well-bred?"

"Perfectly I should say—only perhaps you are not an expert——"

"In what?"

"In self-analysis, for example."

There was a vague meaning in the gaze they exchanged.

"As for our friendship, we'll do the best we can for it, no matter what occurs," he added, thinking of Quarrier. And, thinking of him, glanced up to see him within ear-shot and moving straight toward them from the veranda above.

There was a short silence; a tentative civil word from Siward; then Miss Landis took command of something that had a grotesque resemblance to a situation. A few minutes later they returned slowly to the house, the girl walking serenely between Siward and her preoccupied affianced.

"If your shoes are as wet as my skirts and slippers you had better change, Mr. Siward," she said, pausing at the foot of the staircase.

So he took his *congé*, leaving her standing there with Quarrier, and mounted to his room.

In the corridor he passed Ferrall, who had finished his business correspondence and was returning to the card-room.

"Here's a letter that Grace wants you to see," he said. "Read it before you turn in, Stephen."

"All right; but I'll be down later," replied Siward passing on, the letter in his hand. Entering his room he kicked off his wet pumps and found dry ones. Then moved about, whistling a gay air from some recent vaudeville, busy with rough towels and silken foot-gear, until, reshod and dry, he was ready to descend once more.

The encounter, the suddenly informal acquaintance with this young girl had stirred him agreeably, leaving a slight exhilaration. Even her engagement to Quarrier added a tinge of malice to his interest. Besides he was young enough to feel the flattery of her concern for him—of her rebuke, of her imprudence, her generous emotional and childish philosophy.

Perhaps, as like recognises like, he recognised in her the instincts of the born drifter, momentarily at anchor—the temporary inertia of the opportunist, the latent capacity of an unformed character for all things and anything. Add to these her few years, her beauty, and the wholesome ignorance so confidently acknowledged, what man could remain unconcerned, uninterested in the development of such possibilities? Not Siward, amused by her sagacious and impulsive prudence, worldliness, and innocence in accepting Quarrier; and touched by her profitless, frank, and unworldly friendliness for himself.

Not that he objected to her marrying Quarrier; he rather admired her for being able to do it, considering the general scramble for Quarrier. But let that take care of itself; meanwhile, their sudden and capricious intimacy had aroused him from the morbid reaction consequent upon the cheap notoriety which he had brought upon himself. Let him sponge his slate clean and begin again a better record, flattered by the solicitude she had so prettily displayed.

Whistling under his breath the same gay, empty

"She was standing beside the fire with Quarrier, one foot on the fender."

melody, he opened the top drawer of his dresser, dropped in his mother's letter, and locking the drawer, pocketed the key. He would have time enough to read the letter when he went to bed; he did not just now feel exactly like skimming through the fond, foolish sermon which he knew had been preached at him through his mother's favourite missionary, Grace Ferrall. What was the use of dragging in the sad old questions again—of repeating his assurances of good behaviour, of reiterating his promises of moderation and watchfulness, of explaining his own self-confidence? Better that the letter await his bed time—his prayers would be the sincerer the fresher the impression; for he was old-fashioned enough to say the prayers that an immature philosophy proved superfluous. For, he thought, if prayer is any use, it takes only a few minutes to be on the safe side.

So he went down-stairs leisurely, prepared to acquiesce in any suggestion from anybody, but rather hoping to saunter across Sylvia Landis' path before being committed.

She was standing beside the fire with Quarrier, one foot on the fender, apparently too preoccupied to notice him; so he strolled into the gun-room, which was blue with tobacco smoke and aromatic with the volatile odours from decanters.

There were a few women there, and the majority of the men. Lord Alderdene, Major Belwether, and Mortimer were at a table by themselves; stacks of ivory chips and five cards spread in the centre of the green explained the nature of their game; and Mortimer, raising his heavy inflamed eyes and seeing Siward unoccupied, said wheezily: " Cut out that ' widow,' and give Siward his stack! Anything above two pairs for a jack triples the ante. Come on, Siward, there's a decent chap! "

So he seated himself for a sacrifice to the blind goddess balanced upon her winged wheel; and the cards ran high—so high that stacks dwindled or toppled within the half-hour, and Mortimer grew redder and redder, and Major Belwether blander and blander, and Alderdene's face wore a continual nervous snicker, showing every white hound's tooth, and the ice in the tall glasses clinked ceaselessly.

It was late when Quarrier "sat in," with an expressionless acknowledgment of Siward's presence, and an emotionless raid upon his neighbour's resources with the first hand dealt, in which he participated without drawing a card.

And always Siward, eyes on his cards, seemed to see Quarrier before him, his overmanicured fingers caressing his silky beard, the symmetrical pompadour dark and thick as the winter fur on a rat, tufting his smooth blank forehead.

It was very late when Siward first began to be aware of his increasing deafness, the difficulty, too, that he had in making people hear, the annoying contempt in Quarrier's woman-like eyes. He felt that he was making a fool of himself, very noiselessly somehow—but with more racket than he expected when he miscalculated the distance between his hand and a decanter.

It was time for him to go—unless he chose to ask Quarrier for an explanation of that sneer which he found distasteful. But there was too much noise, too much laughter.

Besides he had a matter to attend to—the careful perusal of his mother's letter to Mrs. Ferrall.

Very white, he rose. After an indeterminate interval he found himself entering his room.

The letter was in the dresser: several things seemed

to fall and break, but he got the letter, sank down on the bed's edge and strove to read,—set his teeth grimly, forcing his blurred eyes to a focus. But he could make nothing of it—nor of his toilet either, nor of Ferrall, who came in on his way to bed having noticed the electricity still in full glare over the open transom, and who straightened out matters for the stunned man lying face downward across the bed, his mother's letter crushed in his nerveless hand.

CHAPTER IV

THE SEASON OPENS

Breakfast at Shotover, except for the luxurious sluggards to whom trays were sent, was served in the English fashion—any other method or compromise being impossible.

Ferrall, reasonable in most things, detested customs exotic, and usually had an Englishman or two about the house to tell them so, being unable to jeer in any language except his own. Which is partly why Alderdene and Voucher were there. And this British sideboard breakfast was a concession wrung from him through force of sheer necessity, although the custom had already become practically universal in American country houses where guests were entertained.

But at the British breakfast he drew the line. No army of servants, always in evidence, would he tolerate, either; no highly ornamented human bric-à-brac decorating halls and corners; no exotic pheasants hustled into covert and out again; no fusillade at the wretched, frightened, bewildered aliens dumped by the thousand into unfamiliar cover and driven toward the guns by improvised beaters.

"We walk up our game or we follow a brace of good dogs in this white man's country," he said with unnecessary emphasis whenever his bad taste and his wife's absence gave him an opportunity to express to the casual foreigner his personal opinions on field sport. "You'll load your own guns and you'll use your own legs if you shoot with me; and your dogs will do their own retrieving, too. And if anybody desires a Yankee's opinion on shooting driven birds from rocking-chairs or potting tame deer from grand-stands, they can have it right now!"

Usually nobody wanted his further opinion; and sometimes they got it and sometimes not, if his wife was within earshot. Otherwise Ferrall appeared to be a normal man, energetically devoted to his business, his pleasures, his friends, and comfortably in love with his wife. And if some considered his vigour in business to be lacking in mercy, that vigour was always exercised within the law. He never transgressed the rules of war, but his headlong energy sometimes landed him close to the dead line. He had already breakfasted, when the earliest risers entered the morning room to saunter about the sideboards and investigate the simmering contents of silver-covered dishes on the warmers.

The fragrance of coffee was pleasantly perceptible; men in conventional shooting attire roamed about the room, selected what they cared for, and carried it to the table. Mrs. Mortimer was there consuming peaches that matched her own complexion; Marion Page, always more congruous in field costume and belted jacket than in anything else, and always, like her own hunters, minutely groomed, was preparing a breakfast for her own consumption with the leisurely precision characteristic of her whether in the saddle, on the box, or grassing her brace of any covey that ever flushed.

Captain Voucher and Lord Alderdene discussed prospects between bites, attentive to the monosyllabic opinions of Miss Page. Her twin brothers, Gordon and Willis, shyly consuming oatmeal, listened respectfully and waited on their sister at the slightest lifting of her thinly arched eyebrows.

Into this company sauntered Siward, apparently no worse for wear. For as yet the Enemy had set upon him no proprietary insignia save a rather becoming pallor and faint bluish shadows under the eyes. He strolled about, exchanging amiable greetings, and presently selected a chilled grape fruit as his breakfast. Opposite him Mortimer, breakfasting upon his own dreadful bracer of an apple soaked in port, raised his heavy inflamed eyes with a significant leer at the iced grape fruit. For he was always ready to make room upon his own level for other men; but the wordless grin and the bloodshot welcome were calmly ignored, for as yet that freemasonry evoked no recognition from the pallid man opposite, whose hands were steady as though that morning's sun had wakened him from pleasant dreams.

"The most difficult shot in the world," Alderdene was explaining, "is an incoming pheasant, sailing on a slant before a gale."

"A woodcock in alders doing a jack-snipe twist is worse," grunted Mortimer, drenching another apple in port.

"Yes," said Miss Page tersely.

"Or a depraved ruffed cock-grouse in the short pines; isn't that the limit?" asked Mortimer of Siward.

But Siward only shrugged his comment and glanced out through the leaded casements into the brilliant September sunshine.

Outside he could see Major Belwether, pink skinned, snowy chop whiskers brushed rabbit fashion, very voluble with Sylvia Landis, who listened absently, head partly averted. Quarrier in tweeds and gaiters, his morning cigar delicately balanced in his gloved fingers, strolled near enough to be within ear-shot; and when

Sylvia's inattention to Major Belwether's observations became marked to the verge of rudeness, he came forward and spoke. But whatever it was that he said appeared to change her passive inattention to quiet displeasure, for, as Siward rose from the table, he saw her turn on her heel and walk slowly toward a group of dogs presided over by some kennel men and gamekeepers.

She was talking to the head gamekeeper when he emerged from the house, but she saw him on the terrace and gave him a bright nod of greeting, so close to an invitation that he descended the stone steps and crossed the dew-wet lawn.

"I am asking Dawson to explain just exactly what a 'Shotover Drive' resembles," she said, turning to include Siward in an animated conference with the big, scraggy, head keeper. "You know, Mr. Siward, that it is a custom peculiar to Shotover House to open the season with what is called a Shotover Drive?"

"I heard Alderdene talking about it," he said, smilingly inspecting the girl's attire of khaki with its buttoned pockets, gun pads, and Cossack cartridge loops, and the tan knee-kilts hanging heavily pleated over gaiters and little thick-soled shoes. He had never cared very much to see women afield, for, in a rare case where there was no affectation, there was something else inborn that he found unpleasant—something lacking about a woman who could take life from frightened wild things, something shocking that a woman could look, unmoved, upon a twitching, blood-soiled heap of feathers at her feet.

Meanwhile Dawson, dog-whip at salute, stood knee deep among his restless setters, explaining the ceremony with which Mr. Ferrall ushered in the opening of each shooting season:

"It's our own idee, Miss Landis," he said proudly; "onc't a season Mr. Ferrall and his guests likes it for a mixed bag. 'Tis a sort of picnic, Miss; the guns is in pairs, sixty yards apart in line, an' the rules is, walk straight ahead, dogs to heel until first cover is reached; fire straight or to quarter, never blankin' nor wipin' no eyes; and ground game counts as feathers for the Shot-over Cup."

"Oh! It's a skirmish line that walks straight ahead?" said Siward, nodding.

"Straight ahead, Sir. No stoppin', no turnin' for hedges, fences, water or rock. There is boats f'r deep water and fords marked and corduroy f'r to pass the Seven Dreens. Luncheon at one, Miss—an hour's rest—then straight on over hill, valley, rock, and river to the rondyvoo atop Osprey Ledge. You'll see the poles and the big nests, Sir. It's there they score for the cup, and there when the bag is counted, the traps are ready to carry you home again." . . . And to Siward: "Will you draw for your lady, Sir? It is the custom."

"Are you my 'lady'?" he asked, turning to Sylvia. "Do you want me?"

In the smiling lustre of her eyes the tiniest spark flashed out at him—a hint of defiance for somebody, perhaps for Major Belwether who had taken considerable pains to enlighten her as to Siward's condition the night before; perhaps also for Quarrier, who had naturally expected to act as her gun-bearer in emergencies. But the gaily veiled malice of the one had annoyed her, and the cold assumption of the other had irritated her, and she had, scarcely knowing why, turned her shoulder to both of these gentlemen with an indefinite idea of escaping a pressure, amounting almost to critical importunity.

"I'm probably a poor shot?" she said, looking smilingly, straight into Siward's eyes. "But if you'll take me——"

"I will with pleasure," he said; "Dawson, do we draw for position? Very well then"; and he drew a slip of paper from the box offered by the head keeper.

"Number seven!" said Sylvia, looking over his shoulder. "Come out to the starting line, Mr. Siward. All the positions are marked with golf-discs. What sort of ground have we ahead, Dawson?"

"Kind o' stiff, Miss," grinned the keeper. "Pity your gentleman ain't drawed the meadows an' Sachem Hill line. Will you choose your dog, Sir?"

"You *have* your dog, you know," observed Sylvia demurely. And Siward, glancing among the impatient setters, saw one white, heavily feathered dog, straining at his leash, and wagging frantically, brown eyes fixed on him.

The next moment Sagamore was free, devouring his master with caresses, the girl looking on in smiling silence; and presently, side by side, the man, the girl, and the dog were strolling off to the starting line where already people were gathering in groups, selecting dogs, fowling-pieces, comparing numbers, and discussing the merits of their respective lines of advance.

Ferrall, busily energetic, and in high spirits, greeted them gaily, pointing out the red disc bearing their number, seven, where it stood out distinctly above the distant scrub of the foreland.

"You two are certainly up against it!" he said, grinning. "There's only one rougher line, and you're in for thorns and water and a scramble across the backbone of the divide!"

"Is it any good?" asked Siward.

"Good—if you've got the legs and Sylvia doesn't play baby——"

"I?" she said indignantly. "Kemp, you annoy me. And I will bet you now," she added, flushing, "that your old cup is ours."

"Wait," said Siward, laughing, "we may not shoot straight."

"*You* will! Kemp, I'll wager whatever you dare!"

"Gloves? Stockings?—against a cigarette case?" he suggested.

"Done," she said disdainfully, moving forward along the skirmish line with a nod and smile for the groups now disintegrating into couples, the Page boys with Eileen Shannon and Rena Bonnesdel, Marion Page followed by Alderdene, Mrs. Vendenning and Major Belwether and the Tassel girl convoyed by Leroy Mortimer. Farther along the line, taking post, she saw Quarrier and Miss Caithness, Captain Voucher with Mrs. Mortimer, and others too distant to recognise, moving across country with glitter and glint of sunlight on slanting gun barrels.

And now Ferrall was climbing into his saddle beside his pretty wife, who sat her horse like a boy, the white flag lifted high in the sunshine, watching the firing line until the last laggard was in position.

"All right, Grace!" said Ferrall briskly. Down went the white flag; the far-ranged line started into motion straight across country, dogs at heel.

From her saddle Mrs. Ferrall could see the advance, strung out far afield from the dark spots moving along the Fells boundary, to the two couples traversing the salt meadows to north. Crack! A distant report came faintly over the uplands against the wind.

"Voucher," observed Ferrall; "probably a snipe. Hark! he's struck them again, Grace."

Mrs. Ferrall, watching curiously, saw Siward's gun fly up as two big dark spots floated up from the marsh and went swinging over his head. Crack! Crack! Down sheered the black spots, tumbling earthward out of the sky.

"Duck," said Ferrall; "a double for Stephen. Lord Harry! how that man can shoot! Isn't it a pity that——"

He said no more; his pretty wife astride her thoroughbred sat silent, grey eyes fixed on the distant figures of Sylvia Landis and Siward, now shoulder deep in the reeds.

"Was it—very bad last night?" she asked in a low voice.

Ferrall shrugged. "He was not offensive; he walked steadily enough up-stairs. When I went into his room he lay on the bed as if he'd been struck by lightning. And yet—you see how he is this morning?"

"After a while," his wife said, "it is going to alter him some day—dreadfully—isn't it, Kemp?"

"You mean—like Mortimer?"

"Yes—only Leroy was *always* a pig."

As they turned their horses toward the high-road Mrs. Ferrall said: "Do you know why Sylvia isn't shooting with Howard?"

"No," replied her husband indifferently; "do you?"

"No." She looked out across the sunlit ocean, grave grey eyes brightening with suppressed mischief. "But I half suspect."

"What?"

"Oh, all sorts of things, Kemp."

"What's one of 'em?" asked Ferrall, looking around at her; but his wife only laughed.

"You don't mean she's throwing her flies at Siward—now that you've hooked Quarrier for her! I thought she'd played him to the gaff——"

"Please don't be coarse, Kemp," said Mrs. Ferrall, sending her horse forward. Her husband spurred to her side, and without turning her head she continued: "Of course Sylvia won't be foolish. If they were only safely married; but Howard is such a pill——"

"What does Sylvia expect with Howard's millions? A man?"

Grace Ferrall drew bridle. "The curious thing is, Kemp, that she liked him."

"*Likes* him?"

"No, *liked* him. I saw how it was; she took his silences for intellectual meditation, his gallery, his library, his smatterings for expressions of a cultivated personality. Then she remembered how close she came to running off with that cashiered Englishman, and that scared her into clutching the substantial in the shape of Howard. . . . Still, I wish I hadn't meddled."

"Meddled how?"

"Oh, I told her to do it. We had talks until daylight. . . . She may marry him—I don't know—but if you think any live woman could be contented with a muff like *that!*"

"That's immoral."

"Kemp, I'm not. She'd be mad not to marry him; but I don't know what I'd do to a man like that, if I were his wife. And you know what a terrific capacity for mischief there is in Sylvia. Some day she's going to love somebody. And it isn't likely to be Howard. And, oh, Kemp! I do grow so tired of that sort of thing.

Do you suppose anybody will ever make decency a fashion?"

"You're doing your best," said Ferrall, laughing at his wife's pretty, boyish face turned back toward him over her shoulder; "you're presenting your cousin and his millions to a girl who can dress the part——"

"Don't, Kemp! I don't know why I meddled! . . . I wish I hadn't——"

"I do. You can't let Howard alone! You're perfectly possessed to plague him when he's with you, and now you've arranged for another woman to keep it up for the rest of his lifetime. What does Sylvia want with a man who possesses the instincts and intellect of a coachman? She is asked everywhere, she has her own money. Why not let her alone? Or is it too late?"

"You mean let her make a fool of herself with Stephen Siward? That is where she is drifting."

"Do you think——"

"Yes, I do. She has a perfect genius for selecting the wrong man; and she's already sorry for this one. I'm sorry for Stephen, too; but it's safe for me to be."

"She might make something of him."

"You know perfectly well no woman ever did make anything of a doomed man. He'd kill her—I mean it, Kemp! He would literally kill her with grief. She isn't like Leila Mortimer; she isn't like most girls of her sort. You men think her a rather stunning, highly tempered, unreasonable young girl, with a reserve of sufficiently trained intelligence to marry the best our market offers—and close her eyes;—a thoroughbred with the caprices of one, but also with the grafted instinct for proper mating."

"Well, that's all right, isn't it?" asked Ferrall. "That's the way I size her up. Isn't it correct?"

"Yes, in a way. She has all the expensive training of the thoroughbred—and all the ignorance, too. She is cold-blooded because wholesome; a trifle sceptical because so absolutely unawakened. She never experienced a deep emotion. Impulses have intoxicated her once or twice—as when she asked my opinion about running off with Cavendish, and that boy and girl escapade with Rivington; nothing at all except high mettle, the innocent daring lurking in all thoroughbreds, and a great deal of very red blood racing through that superb young body. But," Ferrall reined in to listen, "but if ever a man awakens her—I don't care who he is—you'll see a girl you never knew, a brand-new creature emerge with the last rags and laces of conventionality dropping from her; a woman, Kemp, heiress to every generous impulse, every emotion, every vice, every virtue of all that brilliant race of hers."

"You seem to know," he said, amused and curious.

"*I* know. Major Belwether told me that he had thought of Howard as an anchor for her. It seemed a pity—Howard with all his cold, heavy negative inertia. . . . I said I'd do it. I did. And now I don't know; I wish, almost wish I hadn't.

"What has changed your ideas?"

"I don't know. Howard *is* safer than Stephen Siward, already in the first clutches of his master-vice. Would you mate what *she* inherits from her mother and her mother's mother, with what is that poor boy's heritage from the Siwards?"

"After all," observed Ferrall dryly, "we're not in the angel-breeding business."

"We ought to be. Every decent person ought to be. If they were, inherited vice would be as rare in this country as smallpox!"

"People don't inherit smallpox, dear."

"Never mind! You know what I mean. In our stock farms and kennels, we weed out, destroy, exterminate hereditary weakness in everything. We pay the greatest attention to the production of all offspring except our own. Look at Stephen! How dared his parents bring him into the world? Look at Sylvia! And now, suppose *they* marry!"

"Dearest," said Ferrall, "my head is a whirl and my wits are spinning like five toy tops. Your theories are all right; but unless you and I are prepared to abandon several business enterprises and take to the lecture platform, I'm afraid people are going to be wicked enough to marry whom they like, and the human race will be run as usual with money the favourite, and love a case of 'also-ran.' . . . By the way, how dared you marry me, knowing the sort of demon I am?"

The gathering frown on Mrs. Ferrall's brow faded; she raised her clear grey eyes and met her husband's gaze, gay, humourous, and with a hint of tenderness—enough to bring the colour into her pretty face.

"You *know* I'm right, Kemp."

"Always, dear. And now that we have the world off our hands for a few minutes, suppose we gallop?"

But she held her horse to a walk, riding forward, grave, thoughtful, preoccupied with a new problem, only part of which she had told her husband.

For that night she had been awakened in her bed to find standing beside her a white, wide-eyed figure, shivering, limbs a-chill beneath her clinging lace. She had taken the pallid visitor to her arms and warmed her and soothed her and whispered to her, murmuring the thousand little words and sounds, the breathing magic mothers use with children. And Sylvia lay there, chilled, nerveless, silent, ignorant why her sleeplessness had turned to restlessness, to loneliness, to an awakening perception of what she lacked and needed and began to desire. For that sad void, peopled at intervals through her brief years with a vague mother-phantom, had, in the new crisis of her career, become suddenly an empty desolation, frightening her with her own utter isolation. Fill it now she could not, now that she needed that ghost of child-comfort, that shadowy refuge, that sweet shape she had fashioned out of dreams to symbolise a mother she had never known.

Driven she knew not why, she had crept from her room in search of the still, warm, fragrant nest and the whispered reassurance and the caress she had never before endured. Yes, now she craved it, invited it, longed for safe arms around her, the hovering hand on her hair. Was this Sylvia?

And Grace Ferrall, clearing her sleepy eyes, amazed, incredulous of the cold, child-like hands upon her shoulders, caught her in her arms with a little laugh and sob and drew her to her breast, to soothe and caress and reassure, to make up to her all she could of what is every child's just heritage.

And for a long while Sylvia, lying there, told her nothing—because she did not know how—merely a word, a restless question half ashamed, barely enough to shadow forth the something stirring her toward an awakening in a new world, where with new eyes she might catch glimpses of those dim and splendidly misty visions that float through sunlit silences when a young girl dreams awake.

And at length, gravely, innocently, she spoke of her engagement, and the worldly possibilities before her; of the man she was to marry, and her new and unexpected sense of loneliness in his presence, now that she had seen him again after months.

She spoke, presently, of Siward—a fugitive question or two, offered indifferently at first, then with shy persistence and curiosity, knowing nothing of the senseless form flung face downward across the sheets in a room close by. And thereafter the murmured burden of the theme was Siward, until one, heavy eyed, turned from the white dawn silvering the windows, sighed, and fell asleep; and one lay silent, head half buried in its tangled gold, wide awake, thinking vague thoughts that had no ending, no beginning. And at last a rosy bar of light fell across the wall, and the warm shadows faded from corner and curtain; and, turning on the pillow, her face nestled in her hair, she fell asleep.

. . . . .

Nothing of this had Mrs. Ferrall told her husband.

For the first time in her life had Sylvia suffered the caresses most women invite or naturally lavish; for the first time had she attempted confidences, failing because she did not know how, but curiously contented with the older woman's arms around her.

There was a change in Sylvia, a great change stealing in upon her as she lay there, breathing like a child, flushed lips scarcely parted. Through the early slanting sunlight the elder woman, leaning on one arm, looked down at her, grey eyes very grave and tender—wise, sweet eyes that divined with their pure clairvoyance all that might happen or might fail to come to pass in this great change stealing over Sylvia.

. . . . .

Nothing of this could her husband understand had she words to convey it. There was nothing he need understand except that his wife, meaning well, had meddled and regretted.

And now, turning in her saddle with a pretty gesture of her shoulders:

"I meddle no more! Those who need me may come to me. Now laugh at my tardy wisdom, Kemp!"

"It's no laughing matter," he said, "if you're going to stand back and let this abandoned world spin itself madly to the bow-wows——"

"Don't be horrid. I repent. The mischief take Howard Quarrier!"

"Amen! Come on, Grace."

She gathered bridle. "*Do* you suppose Stephen Siward is going to make trouble?"

"How can he unless she helps him? Nonsense! All's well with Siward and Sylvia. Shall we gallop?"

. . . .

All was very well with Siward and Sylvia. They had passed the rabbit-brier country scathless, with two black mallard, a jack-snipe, and a rabbit to the credit of their score, and were now advancing through that dimly lit enchanted land of tall grey alders where, in the sudden twilight of the leaves, woodcock after woodcock fluttered upward twittering, only to stop and drop, transformed at the vicious crack of Siward's gun to fluffy balls of feather whirling earthward from mid-air.

Sagamore came galloping back with a soft, unsoiled mass of chestnut and brown feathers in his mouth. Siward took the dead cock, passed it back to the keeper who followed them, patted the beautiful eager dog and signalled him forward once more.

"You should have fired that time," he said to Sylvia —"that is, if you care to kill anything."

"But I don't seem to be able to," she said. "It

isn't a bit like shooting at clay targets. The twittering whirr takes me by surprise—it's all so charmingly sudden—and my heart seems to stop in one beat, and I look and look and then—whisk! the woodcock is gone, leaving me breathless——"

Her voice ceased; the white setter, cutting up his ground ahead, had stopped, rigid, one leg raised, jaws quivering and locking alternately.

"Isn't that a stunning picture!" said Siward in a low voice. "What a beauty he is—like a statue in white and blue-veined marble. You may talk, Miss Landis; woodcock don't flush at the sound of the human voice as grouse do."

"See his brown eyes roll back at us! He wonders why we don't do something!" whispered the girl. "Look, Mr. Siward! Now his head is moving—oh so gradually to the left!"

"The bird is moving on the ground," nodded Siward; "now the bird has stopped."

"I do wish I could see a woodcock on the ground," she breathed. "Do you think we might by any chance?"

Siward noiselessly sank to his knees and crouched, keen eyes minutely busy among the shadowy browns and greys of wet earth and withered leaf. And after a while, cautiously, he signalled the girl to kneel beside him, and stretched out one arm, forefinger extended.

"Sight straight along my arm," he said, "as though it were a rifle barrel."

Her soft cheek rested against his shoulder; a stray strand of shining hair brushing his face.

"Under that bunch of fern," he whispered; "just the colour of the dead leaves. Do you see? . . . *Don't* you see that big woodcock squatted flat, bill pointed straight out and resting on the leaves?"

After a long while she saw, suddenly, and an exquisite little shock tightened her fingers on Siward's extended arm.

"Oh, the feathered miracle!" she whispered; "the wonder of its cleverness to hide like that! You look and look and stare, seeing it all the while and not knowing that you see it. Then in a flash it is there, motionless, a brown-shaped shadow among shadows. . . . The *dear* little thing! . . . Mr. Siward, do you think—are you going to——"

"No, I won't shoot it."

"Thank you. . . . Might I sit here a moment to watch it?"

She seated herself soundlessly among the dead leaves; he sank into place beside her, laying his gun aside.

"Rather rough on the dog," he said with a grimace.

"I know. It is very good of you, Mr. Siward . . . to do this for my pleasure. Oh—h! Do you see! Oh, the little beauty!"

The woodcock had risen, plumage puffed out, strutting with wings bowed and tail spread, facing the dog. The sudden pigmy defiance thrilled her. "Brave! Brave!" she exclaimed, enraptured; but at the sound of her voice the bird crouched like a flash, large dark liquid eyes shining, long bill pointed straight toward them.

"He'll fly the way his bill points," said Siward. "Watch!"

He rose; she sprang lightly to her feet; there came a whirring flutter, a twittering shower of sweet notes, soft wings beating almost in their very faces, a distant shadow against the sky, and the woodcock was gone.

Quieting the astounded dog, gun cradled in the hollow of his left arm, he turned to the girl beside him: "That sort of thing wins no cups," he said.

"It wins something else, Mr. Siward,—my very warm regard for you."

"There is no choice between that and the Shotover Cup," he admitted, considering her.

"I—do you mean it?"

"Of course I do, vigorously!"

"Then you are much nicer than I thought you. . . . And after all, if the price of a cup is the life of that brave little bird, I had rather shoot clay pigeons. Now you will scorn me I suppose. Begin!"

"My ideal woman has never been a life-taker," he said coolly. "Once, when I was a boy, there was a girl—very lovely—my first sweetheart. I saw her at the traps once, just after she had killed her seventh pigeon straight, 'pulling it down' from overhead, you know—very clever—the little thing was breathing on the grass, and it made sounds—" He shrugged and walked on. "She killed her twenty-first bird straight; it was a handsome cup, too."

And after a silence, "So you didn't love her any more, Mr. Siward?"—mockingly sweet.

They laughed, and at the sound of laughter the tall-stemmed alders echoed with the rushing roar of a cock-grouse thundering skyward. Crack! Crack! Whirling over and over through a cloud of floating feathers, a heavy weight struck the springy earth. There lay the big mottled bird, splendid silky ruffs spread, dead eyes closing, a single tiny crimson bead twinkling like a ruby on the gaping beak.

"Dead!" said Siward to the dog who had dropped to shot; "Fetch!" And, signalling the boy behind, he relieved the dog of his burden and tossed the dead weight of ruffled plumage toward him. Then he broke his gun, and, as the empty shells flew rattling backward, slipped in fresh cartridges, locked the barrels, and walked forward, the flush of excitement still staining his sunburnt face.

"You deal death mercifully," said the girl in a low voice. "I wonder what your ci-devant sweetheart would think of you."

"A bungler had better stick to the traps," he assented, ignoring the badinage.

"I am wondering," she said thoughtfully, "what *I* think of men who kill."

He turned sharply, hesitated, shrugged. "Wild things' lives are brief at best—fox or flying-tick, wet nests or mink, owl, hawk, weasel or man. But the death man deals is the most merciful. Besides," he added, laughing, "ours is not a case of sweethearts."

"My argument is purely in the abstract, Mr. Siward. I am asking you whether the death men deal is more justifiable than a woman's gift of death?"

"Oh, well, life-taking, the giving of life—there can be only one answer to the mystery; and I don't know it," he replied smiling.

"I do."

"Tell me then," he said, still amused.

They had passed swale after swale of silver birches. waist deep in perfumed fern and brake; the big timber lay before them. She moved forward, light gun swung easily across her leather-padded shoulder; and on the wood's sunny edge she seated herself, straight young back against a giant pine, gun balanced across her flattened knees.

"You are feeling the pace a little," he said, coming up and standing in front of her.

"The pace? No, Mr. Siward."

"Are you a trifle—bored?" She considered him

in silence, then leaned back luxuriously, rounded arms raised, wrists crossed to pillow her head.

"This is charmingly new to me," she said simply.

"What? Not the open?"

"No; I have camped and done the usual roughing it with only three guides apiece and the champagne inadequately chilled. I have endured that sort of hardship several times, Mr. Siward. . . . What is that furry bunch up there in that tall thin tree?"

"A raccoon," he said presently. "Can you see the foxy head peeping so slyly down at us? Look at Sagamore nosing the air in that droll blind mole-like way. He knows there's something furry up aloft somewhere; and he knows it's none of his business."

They watched the motionless ball of fur in the crotch of a slim forest elm. Presently it uncurled, cautiously; a fluffy ringed tail unfolded; the rounded furry back humped up, and the animal, moving slowly into the tangent foliage of an enormous oak, vanished amid bronzing leafy depths.

In the silence the birds began to reappear. A jay screamed somewhere deep in the yellowing woods; black-capped chickadees dropped from twig to twig, cheeping inquiringly.

She sat listening, bright head pillowed in her arms, idly attentive to his low running comment on beast and bird and tree, on forest stillness and forest sounds, on life and the wild laws of life and death governing the great out-world 'twixt sky and earth. Sunlight and shadows moving, speech and silence, waxed and waned. A listless contentment lay warm upon her, weighting the heavy white lids. The blue of her eyes was very dark now—almost purple like the colour of the sea when the wind-flaws turn the blue to violet.

"Did you ever hear of the 'Lesser Children'?" she asked. "Listen then:

"'Multitudes, multitudes, under the moon they stirred!
The weaker brothers of our earthly breed; . . .
. . . All came about my head and at my feet
A thousand thousand sweet,
With starry eyes not even raised to plead:
Bewildered, driven, hiding, fluttering, mute!
. . . . .
And I beheld and saw them one by one
Pass, and become as nothing in the night.'

"Do you know what it means?

"'Winged mysteries of song that from the sky
Once dashed long music down—'

"Do you understand?" she asked, smiling.

"'Who has not seen in the high gulf of light
What, lower, was a bird!'"

She ceased, and, raising her eyes to his: "Do you know that plea for mercy on the lesser children who die all day to-day because the season opens for your pleasure, Mr. Siward?"

"Is it a woodland sermon?" he inquired, too politely.

"The poem? No; it is the case for the prosecution. The prisoner may defend himself if he can."

"The defence rests," he said. "The prisoner moves that he be discharged."

"Motion denied," she interrupted promptly.

Somewhere in the woodland world the crows were

holding a noisy session, and she told him that was the jury debating the degree of his guilt.

"Because you're guilty of course," she continued. "I wonder what your sentence is to be?"

"I'll leave it to you," he suggested lazily.

"Suppose I sentenced you to slay no more?"

"Oh, I'd appeal——"

"No use; I am the tribunal of last resort."

"Then I throw myself upon the mercy of the court."

"You do well, Mr. Siward. This court is very merciful. . . . How much do you care for bird murder? *Very* much? Is there anything you care for more? Yes? And could this court grant it to you in compensation?"

He said, deliberately, roused by the level challenge of her gaze: "The court is incompetent to compensate the prisoner or offer any compromise."

"Why, Mr. Siward?"

"Because the court herself is already compromised in her future engagements."

"But what has my—engagement to do with——"

"You offered compensation for depriving me of my shooting. There could be only one adequate compensation."

"And that?" she asked, coolly enough.

"Your continual companionship."

"But you have it, Mr. Siward——"

"I have it for a day. The season lasts three months you know."

"And you and I are to play a continuous vaudeville for three months? Is that your offer?"

"Partly."

"Then *one* day with me is not worth those many days of murder?" she asked in pretended astonishment.

"Ask yourself why those many days would be doubly empty," he said so seriously that the pointless game began to confuse her.

"Then"—she turned lightly from uncertain ground—"then perhaps we had better be about that matter of the cup you prize so highly. Are you ready, Mr. Siward? There is much to be killed yet—including time, you know."

But the hinted sweetness of the challenge had aroused him, and he made no motion to rise. Nor did she.

"I am not sure," he reflected, "just exactly what I should ask of you if you insist on taking away—" he turned and looked about him through the burnt gold foliage, "—if you took away all this out of my life."

"I shall not take it; because I have nothing in exchange to offer . . . you say," she answered imprudently.

"I did not say so," he retorted.

"You did—reminding me that the court is already engaged for a continuous performance."

"Was it necessary to remind you?" he asked with deliberate malice.

She flushed up, vexed, silent, then looked directly at him with beautiful hostile eyes. "*What* do you mean, Mr. Siward? Are you taking our harmless, idle badinage as warrant for an intimacy unwarranted?"

"Have I offended?" he asked, so impassively that a flash of resentment brought her to her feet, angry and self-possessed.

"How far have we to go?" she asked quietly.

He rose to his feet, turned, hailing the keeper, repeating the question. And at the answer they both started forward, the dog ranging ahead through a dense growth of beech and chestnut, over a high brown ridge, then down, always down along a leafy ravine to the water's edge—a forest pond set in the gorgeous foliage of ripening maples.

"I don't see," said Sylvia impatiently, "how we are going to obey instructions and go straight ahead. There must be a stupid boat somewhere!"

But the game-laden keeper shook his head, pulled up his hip boots, and pointed out a line of alder poles set in the water to mark a crossing.

"Am I expected to wade?" asked the girl anxiously.

"This here," observed the keeper, "is one of the most sportin' courses on the estate. Last season I seen Miss Page go through it like a scared deer—the young lady, sir, that took last season's cup"—in explanation to Siward, who stood doubtfully at the water's edge, looking back at Sylvia.

Raising her dismayed eyes she encountered his; there was a little laugh between them. She stepped daintily across the stones to the water's edge, instinctively gathering her kilts in one hand.

"Miles and I could chair you over," suggested Siward.

"Is that fair—under the rules?"

"Oh, yes, Miss; as long as you go straight," said the keeper.

So they laid aside the guns and the guide's game-sack, and formed a chair with their hands, and, bearing the girl between them, they waded out along the driven alder stakes, knee-deep in brown water.

Before them herons rose into heavy flapping flight, broad wings glittering in the sun; a diver, distantly afloat among the lily pads, settled under the water to his eyes as a submarine settles till the conning-tower is awash.

Her arm, lightly resting around his neck, tightened a trifle as the water rose to his thighs; then the faint pressure relaxed as they thrashed shoreward through the shallows, ankle deep once more, and landed among the dry reeds on the farther bank.

Miles, the keeper, went back for the guns. Siward stamped about in the sun, shaking the drops from water-proof breeches and gaiters, only to be half drenched again when Sagamore shook himself vigorously.

"I suppose," said Sylvia, looking sideways at Siward, "your contempt for my sporting accomplishments has not decreased. I'm sorry; I *don't* like to walk in wet shoes . . . even to gain your approval."

And, as the keeper came splashing across the shallows: "Miles, you may carry my gun. I shall not need it any longer——"

The upward roar of a bevey of grouse drowned her voice; poor Sagamore, pointing madly in the blackberry thicket all unperceived, cast a dismayed glance aloft where the sunlit air quivered under the winnowing rush of heavy wings. Siward flung up his gun, heading a big quartering bird; steadily the glittering barrels swept in the arc of fire, hesitated, wavered; then the possibility passed; the young fellow lowered the gun, slowly, gravely; stood a moment motionless with bent head until the rising colour in his face had faded.

And that was all, for a while. The astonished and disgusted keeper stared into the thicket; the dog lay quivering, impatient for signal. Sylvia's heart, which had seemed to stop with her voice, silenced in the gusty thunder of heavy wings, began beating too fast. For the ringing crack of a gun shot could have spoken no louder to her than the glittering silence of the suspended barrels; nor any promise of his voice sound as the startled stillness sounded now about her. For he had made something a trifle more than mere amends for his rudeness. He was overdoing everything—a little.

He stood on the thicket's edge, absently unloading the weapon, scarcely understanding what he had done and what he had not done.

A moment later a far hail sounded across the uplands, and against the sky figures moved distantly.

"Alderdene and Marion Page," said Siward. "I believe we lunch yonder, do we not, Miles?"

They climbed the hill in silence, arriving after a few minutes to find others already at luncheon—the Page boys, eager, enthusiastic, recounting adventure by flood and field; Rena Bonnesdel tired and frankly bored and decorated with more than her share of mud; Eileen Shannon, very pretty, very effective, having done more execution with her eyes than with the dainty fowling-piece beside her.

Marion Page nodded to Sylvia and Siward with a crisp, business-like question or two, then went over to inspect their bag, nodding approbation as Miles laid the game on the grass.

"Eight full brace," she commented. "We have five, and an odd cock-pheasant—from Black Fells, I suppose. The people to our left have been blazing away like Coney Island, but Rena's guide says the ferns are full of rabbits that way, and Major Belwether can't hit fur afoot. You," she added frankly to Siward, "ought to take the cup. The birches ahead of you are full of woodcock. If you don't, Howard Quarrier will. He's into a flight of jack-snipe I hear."

Siward's eyes had suddenly narrowed; then he

laughed, patting Sagamore's cheeks. "I don't believe I shall shoot very steadily this afternoon," he said, turning toward the group at luncheon under the trees. "I wish Quarrier well—with the cup."

"Nonsense," said Marion Page curtly; "you are the cleanest shot I ever knew." And she raised her glass to him, frankly, and emptied it with the precision characteristic of her: "Your cup! With all my heart!"

"I also drink to your success, Mr. Siward," said Sylvia in a low voice, lifting her champagne glass in the sunlight. "To the Shotover Cup—if you wish it." And as other glasses sparkled aloft amid a gay tumult of voices wishing him success, Sylvia dropped her voice, attuning it to his ear alone: "Success for the cup, if you wish it—or, whatever you wish—success!" and she meant it very kindly.

His hand resting on his glass he sat, smiling silent acknowledgment to the noisy generous toasts; he turned and looked at Sylvia when her low voice caught his ear—looked at her very steadily, unsmiling.

Then to the others, brightening again, he said a word or two, wittily, with a gay compliment well placed and a phrase to end it in good taste. And, in the little gust of hand-clapping and laughter, he turned again to Sylvia, smilingly, saying under his breath: "As though winning the cup could compensate me now for losing it!"

She leaned involuntarily nearer: "You mean that you will not try for it?"

"Yes."

"That is not fair—to me!"

"Why not?"

"Because—because I do not ask it of you."

"You need not, now that I know your wish."

"Mr. Siward, I—my wish——"

But she had no chance to finish; already Rena Bonnesdel was looking at them, and there was a hint of amused surprise in Eileen Shannon's mischievous eyes, averted instantly, with malicious ostentation.

Then Marion Page took possession of him so exclusively, so calmly, that something in her cool certainty vaguely irritated Sylvia, who had never liked her. Besides, the girl showed too plainly her indifference to other people; which other people seldom find amusing.

"Stephen," called out Alderdene, anxiously counting the web loops in his khaki vest, "what do you call fair shooting at these damnable ruffed grouse? You needn't be civil about it, you know."

"Five shells to a bird is *good* shooting," answered Siward. "Don't you think so, Miss Page?"

"*You* have a better score, Mr. Siward," said Marion Page with a hostile glance at Alderdene, who had not made good.

"That was chance—and this year's birds. I've taken ten shells to an old drummer in hard wood or short pines." He smiled to himself, adding: "A drove of six in the open got off scot free a little while ago. Miss Landis saw it."

That he was inclined to turn it all to banter relieved her at once. "It was pitiable," she nodded gravely to Marion; "his nerve left him when they made such a din in the briers."

Miss Page glanced at her indifferently.

"What I need is practice like the chasseurs of Tarascon," admitted Siward.

"I willingly offer my hat, monsieur," said Sylvia.

Marion Page, impatient to start, had turned her tailor-made back to the company, and was instructing his crestfallen lordship very plainly: "You fire too quickly, Blinky; two seconds is what you must count when a grouse flushes. You must say 'Mark! Right!' or 'Mark! Left! Bang!'"

"I might as well *say* 'Bang!' for all I've done to-day," he muttered, adjusting his shooting-goggles and snapping his eyes like fury. Then exploding into raucous laughter he moved off southward with Marion Page, who had exchanged a swift handshake with Siward; the twins followed, convoying Eileen and Rena, neither maiden excitedly enthusiastic. And so the luncheon party, lord and lady, twins and maidens, guides and dogs, trailed away across the ridge, distant silhouettes presently against the sky, then gone. And after a little while the far, dry, accentless report of smokeless powder announced that the opening of the season had been resumed and the Lesser Children were dying fast in the glory of a perfect day.

"Are you ready, Mr. Siward?" She stood waiting for him at the edge of the thicket; Miles resumed his game sack and her fowling-piece; the dog came up, looking him anxiously in the eyes.

So he walked forward beside her into the dappled light of the thicket.

Within a few minutes the dog stood twice; and twice the whirring twitter of woodcock startled her, echoed by the futile crack of his gun.

"Beg pardon, sir——"

"Yes, Miles," with a glint of humour.

"Overshot, sir,—excusin' the liberty, Mr. Siward. Both marked down forty yard to the left if you wish to start 'em again."

"No," he said indifferently, "I had my chance at them. They're exempt."

Then Sagamore, tail wildly whipping, came smack on the trail of an old stager of a cock-grouse—on, on over rock, log, wet gully, and dry ridge, twisting, doubling, circling, every wile, every trick employed and met, until the dog crawling noiselessly forward, trembled and froze, and Siward, far to left, wheeled at the muffled and almost noiseless rise. For an instant the slanting barrels wavered, grew motionless; but only a stray sunbeam glinting struck a flash of cold fire from the muzzle, only the feathery whirring whisper broke the silence of suspense. Then far away over sunny tree tops a big grouse sailed up, rocketing into the sky on slanted wings, breasting the height of green; dipped, glided downward with bowed wings stiffened, and was engulfed in the misty barriers of purpling woods.

"*Vale!*" said Siward aloud, "I salute you!"

He came strolling back across the crisp leaves, the dappled sunshine playing over his face like the flicker of a smile.

"Miles," he said, "my nerve is gone. Such things happen. I'm all in. Come over here, my friend, and look at the sun with me."

The discomfited keeper obeyed.

"Where ought that refulgent luminary to scintilate when I face Osprey Ledge?"

"Sir?"

"The sun. How do I hold it?"

"On the p'int of your right shoulder, sir. . . . You ain't quittin', Mr. Siward, sir!" anxiously; "that Shotover Cup is easy yours, sir!" eagerly; "Wot's a miss on a old drummer, Mr. Siward? Wot's twice overshootin' cock, sir, when a blind dropper can see you are the cleanest, fastest, hard-shootin' shot in the hull county!"

But Siward shook his head with an absent glance at the dog, and motioned the astonished keeper forward.

"Line the easiest trail for us," he said; "I think we are already a trifle tired. Twigs will do in short cover; use a hatchet in the big timber. . . . And go slow till we join you."

And when the unwilling and perplexed keeper had started, Siward, unlocking his gun, drew out the smooth yellow cartridges and pocketed them.

Sylvia looked up as the sharp metallic click of the locked breech rang out in the silence.

"*Why* do you do this, Mr. Siward?"

"I don't know; really I am honest; I don't know."

"It could not be because I——"

"No, of course not," he said, too seriously to reassure her.

"Mr. Siward," in quick displeasure.

"Yes?"

"What you do for your amusements cannot concern me."

"Right as usual," he said so gaily that a reluctant smile trembled on her lips.

"Then why have you done this? It is unreasonable—if you don't feel as I do about killing things that are having a good time in the world."

He stood silent, absently looking at the fowling-piece cradled in his left arm. "Shall we sit here a moment and talk it over?" he suggested listlessly.

Her blue gaze swept him; his vague smile was indifferently bland.

"If you are determined not to shoot, we might as well start for Osprey Ledge," she suggested; "otherwise, what reason is there for our being here together, Mr. Siward?"

Awaiting his comment—perhaps expecting a counter-proposition—she leaned against the tree beside which he stood. And after a while, as his absent-minded preoccupation continued:

"Do you think the leaves are dry enough to sit on?"

He slipped off his shooting-coat and placed it at the base of the tree. She waited for a second, uncertain how to meet an attitude which seemed to take for granted matters which might, if discussed, give her at least the privilege of yielding. However, to discuss a triviality meant forcing emphasis where none was necessary. She seated herself; and, as he continued to remain standing, she stripped off her shooting-gloves and glanced up at him inquiringly: "Well, Mr. Siward, I am literally at your feet."

"Which redresses the balance a little," he said, finding a place near her.

"That is very nice of you. Can I always count on you for civil platitudes when I stir you out of your day-dreams?"

"You can always count on stirring me without effort."

"No, I can't. Nobody can. You are never to be counted on; you are too absent-minded. Like a veil you wrap yourself in a brown study, leaving everybody outside to consider the pointed flattery of your withdrawal. What happens to you when you are inside that magic veil? Do you change into anything interesting?"

He sat there, chin propped on his linked fingers, elbows on knees; and, though there was always the hint of a smile in his pleasant eyes, always the indefinable charm of breeding in voice and attitude, something now was lacking. And after a moment she concluded that it was his attention. Certainly his wits were wool-gathering again; his eyes, edged with the shadow of a smile, saw far beyond her, far beyond the sunlit shadows where they sat.

In his preoccupation she had found him negatively attractive. She glanced at him now from time to time, her eyes returning always to the beauty of the subdued light where all about them silver-stemmed birches clustered like slim shining pillars, crowned with their autumn canopy of crumpled gold.

"Enchantment!" she said under her breath. "Surely an enchanted sleeper lies here somewhere."

"You," he observed, "unawakened."

"Asleep? I?" She looked around at him. "*You* are the dreamer here. Your eyes are full of dreaming even now. What is your desire?"

He leaned on one arm, watching her; she had dropped her ungloved hand, searching among the newly fallen gold of the birch leaves drifted into heaps. On the third finger a jewel glittered; he saw it, conscious of its meaning—but his eyes followed the hand idly heaping up autumn gold, a white slim hand, smoothly fascinating. Then the little, restless hand swept near to his, almost touching it; and then instinctively he took it in his own, curiously, lifting it a little to consider its nearer loveliness. Perhaps it was the unexpectedness of it, perhaps it was sheer amazement that left her hand lying idly relaxed like a white petalled blossom in his. His bearing, too, was so blankly impersonal that for a moment the whole thing appeared inconsequent. Then, as her hand lay there, scarcely imprisoned, their eyes encountered,—and hers, intensely blue now, considered him without emotion, studied him impersonally without purpose, incuriously acquiescent, indifferently expectant.

After a little while the consciousness of the contact disconcerted her; she withdrew her fingers with an involuntary shiver.

"Is there no chance?" he asked.

Perplexed with her own emotion, the meaning of his low-voiced question at first escaped her; then, like its own echo, came ringing back in her ears, re-echoed again as he repeated it:

"Is there no chance for me, Miss Landis?"

The very revulsion of self-possession returning chilled her; then anger came, quick and hot; then pride. She deliberated, choosing her words coolly enough: "What chance do you mean, Mr. Siward?"

"A fighting chance. Can you give it to me?"

"A fighting chance? For what?"—very low, very dangerous.

"For you."

Then, in spite of her, her senses became unsteady; a sudden ringing confusion seemed to deafen her, through which his voice, as if very far away, sounded again:

"Men who are worth a fighting chance ask for it sometimes—but take it always. I take it."

Her pallor faded under the flood of bright colour; the blue of her eyes darkened ominously to velvet.

"Mr. Siward," she said, very distinctly and slowly, "I am not—even—sorry—for you."

"Then my chance is desperate indeed," he retorted coolly.

"Chance! Do you imagine—" Her anger choked her.

"Are you not a little hard?" he said, paling under his tan. "I supposed women dismissed men more gently—even such a man as I am."

For a full minute she strove to comprehend,

"Such a man as you!" she repeated vaguely; "you mean—" a crimson wave dyed her skin to the temples and she leaned toward him in horror-stricken contrition; "I didn't mean *that*, Mr. Siward! I—I never thought of that! It had no weight, it was not in my thoughts. I meant only that you had assumed what is unwarranted —that you—your question humiliated me, knowing that I am engaged—knowing me so little—so——"

"Yes, I knew everything. Ask yourself why I risk everything to say this to you? There can be only one answer."

Then after a long silence: "Have I ever—" she began tremblingly—"ever by word or look——"

"No."

"Have I even——"

"No. I've simply discovered how I feel. That's what I was dreaming about when you asked me. I was afraid I might do this too soon; but I meant to do it anyway before it became too late."

"It was too late from the very moment we met, Mr. Siward." And, as he reddened painfully again, she added quickly: "I mean that I had already decided. *Why* will you take what I say so dreadfully different from the way I intend it? Listen to me. I—I believe I am not very experienced yet; I was a—astonished—quite stunned for a moment. Then it hurt me—and I said that I was not sorry for you . . . I *am* sorry, now."

And, as he said nothing: "You were a little rough, a little sudden with me, Mr. Siward. Men have asked me that question—several times; but never so soon, so unreasonably soon—never without some preliminary of some sort, so that I could foresee, be more or less prepared. . . . But you gave me *no* warning. I—if you had, I would have known how to be gentle. I—I wish to be now. I like you—enough to say this to you, enough to be seriously sorry; if I could bring myself to really believe this—feeling——"

Still he said nothing; he sat there listlessly studying the sun spots glowing, waxing, waning on the carpet of dead leaves at his feet.

"As for—what you have said," she added, a little smile curving the sensitive mouth, "it is impulsive, unconsidered, a trifle boyish, Mr. Siward. I pay myself the compliment of your sincerity; it is rather nice to be a girl who can awaken the romance in a man within a day or two's acquaintance. . . . And that is all it is—a romantic impulse with a pretty girl. You see I am frank; I am really glad that you find me attractive. Tell me so, if you wish. We shall not misunderstand each other again. Shall we?"

He raised his head, considering her, forcing the smile to meet her own.

"We shall be better friends than ever," she asserted confidently.

"Yes, better than ever."

"Because what you have done means the nicest sort of friendship, you see. You can't escape its duties and responsibilities now, Mr. Siward. I shall expect you to spend the greater part of your life in devotedly doing things for me. Besides, I am now privileged to worry you with advice. Oh, you have invested me with all sorts of powers now!"

He nodded.

She sprang to her feet, flushed, smiling, a trifle excited.

"Is it *all* over, and are we the very ideals of friends?" she asked.

"The very ideals."

"You *are* nice!" she said impulsively, holding out both gloveless hands. He held them, she looking at him very sweetly, very confidently.

"*Allons!* Without malice?" she asked.

"Without malice."

"Without afterthoughts?"

"Without afterthoughts."

"And—you are content?" persuasively.

"Of course not," he said.

"Oh, but you must be."

"I must be," he repeated obediently.

"And you are! Say it!"

"But it does not make me unhappy not to be contented——"

"Say it, please; or—do you desire me to be unhappy?"

Her small, smooth hands lying between his, they stood confronting one another in the golden light. She might easily have brought the matter to an end; and why she did not, she knew no more than a kitten waking to consciousness under its first caress.

"Say it," she repeated, laughing uncertainly back into his smiling eyes of a boy.

"Say what?"

"That you are contented."

"I can't."

"Mr. Siward, it is unkind, it is shameless——"

"I know it; I am that sort."

"Then I am sorry for you. Look at that!" turning her left hand in his so that the jewel on the third finger caught the light.

"I see it."

"And yet—"

" And yet."

" That," she observed with composure, " is sheer obstinacy. . . . Isn't it? "

" It is what I said it was: a hopeful discontent."

" How can it be? " impatiently now, for the long, unaccustomed contact was unnerving her—yet she made no motion to withdraw her hands. " How can you really care for me? Do you actually believe that—devotion—comes like that? "

" Exactly like that."

" So suddenly? It is impossible! " with a twist of her pretty shoulders.

" How did it come—to *you*? " he asked between his teeth.

Then her face grew scarlet and her eyes grew dark, and her hands contracted in his—tightened, twisted fingers entangled, until, with a little sob, she swayed toward him and he caught her. An instant, a minute—more, perhaps, she did not know—she half lay in his arms, her untaught lips cold against his. Lassitude, faint consciousness, then tiny shock on shock came the burning revulsion; and her voice came back, too, sounding strangely to her, a colourless, monotonous voice.

He had freed her; she remembered that somebody had asked him to—perhaps herself. That was well; she needed to breathe, to summon strength and common-sense, find out what had been done, what reasonless madness she had committed in the half-light of the silver-stemmed trees clustering in shameful witness on every hand.

Suddenly the hot humiliation of it overwhelmed her, and she covered her face with her hands, standing, almost swaying, as wave on wave of incredulous shame seemed to sweep her from knee to brow. That phase passed after a while; out of it she emerged, flushed, outwardly composed, into another phase, in full self-possession once more, able to understand what had happened without the disproportion of emotional exaggeration. After all, she had only been kissed. Besides she was a novice, which probably accounted, in a measure, for the unreasonable emotion coincident with a caress to which she was unaccustomed. Without looking up at him she found herself saying coolly enough to surprise herself: "I never supposed I was capable of that. It appears that I am. I haven't anything to say for myself . . . except that I feel fearfully humiliated. . . . Don't say anything now . . . I do not blame you, truly I do not. It was contemptible of me—to do it—wearing this—" she stretched out her slender left hand, not looking at him; "it was contemptible!" . . . She slowly raised her eyes, summoning all her courage to face him.

But he only saw in the pink confusion of her lovely face the dawning challenge of a coquette saluting her adversary in gay acknowledgment of his fleeting moment of success. And as his face fell, then hardened into brightness, instantly she divined how he rated her, and in a flash realized her weapons and her security, and that the control of the situation was hers, not in the control of this irresolute young man who stood so silently considering her. Strange that she should be ashamed of her own innocence, willing that he believe her accomplished in such arts, enchanted that he no longer perhaps suspected genuine emotion in the swift, confused sweetness of her first kiss. If only all that were truly hidden from him, if he dare not in his heart convict her of anything save perfection in a gay, imprudent rôle, what a weight lifted, what relief, what hot self-contempt cooled! What vengeance, too, she would take on him for the agony of her awakening—the dazed chagrin, the dread of his wise, amused eyes—eyes that she feared had often looked upon such scenes; eyes no doubt familiar with such unimportant details as the shamed demeanour of a novice.

"Why do you take it so seriously?" she said, laughing and studying him, certain now of herself in this new disguise.

"Do you take it lightly?" he asked, striving to smile.

"I? Ah, I must, you know. You don't expect to marry me . . . do you, Mr. Siward?"

"I—" He choked up at that, grimly for a while.

Walking slowly forward together she fell into step frankly beside him, near him—too near. "Try to be sensible," she was saying gaily; "I like you so much—and it would be horrid to have you mope, you know. And besides, even if I cared for you, there are reasons, you know—reasons for any girl to marry the man I am going to marry. Does my cynicism shock you? What am I to do?" with a shrug. "Such marriages are reasonable, and far likelier to be agreeable than when fancy is the sole motive—certainly far more agreeable than an ill-considered yielding to abstract emotion with nothing concrete in view. . . . So, you see, I could not marry you even if I—" her voice was inclined to tremble, but she controlled it. *Would* she never learn her rôle? "even if I loved you——"

Then her tongue stumbled and was silent; and they walked on, side by side, through the fading splendour of the year, exchanging no further speech.

Toward sunset their guide hailed them, standing high among the rocks, a silhouette against the sky. And beyond him they saw the poles crowned with the huge nests of the fish-hawks, marking the last rendezvous at Osprey Ledge.

She turned to him as they started up the last incline, thanking him in a sweet, natural voice for his care of her—quite innocently—until in the questioning, unconvinced gaze that met hers she found her own eyes softening and growing dim; and she looked away suddenly, lest he read her ere she had dared turn the first page in the book of self—ere she had studied, pried, probed among the pages of a new chapter whose familiar title, so long meaningless to her, had taken on a sudden troubling significance. And for the first time in her life she glanced uneasily at the new page in the book of self, numbered according to her years with the figures 23, and headed with the unconvincing chapter title, "Love."

CHAPTER V

A WINNING LOSER

THE week passed swiftly, day after day echoing with the steady fusillade from marsh to covert, from valley to ridge. Guns flashed at dawn and dusk along the flat tidal reaches haunted of black mallard and teal; the smokeless powder cracked through alder swamp and tangled windfall where the brown grouse burst away into noisy blundering flight; where the woodcock, wilder now, shrilled skyward like feathered rockets, and the big northern hares, not yet flecked with snowy patches of fur, loped off into swamps to the sad undoing of several of the younger setters.

There was a pheasant drive at Black Fells to which the Ferralls' guests were bidden by Beverly Plank—a curious scene, where ladies and gentlemen stood on a lawn, backed by an army of loaders and gun-bearers, while another improvised army of beaters drove some thousands of frightened, bewildered, homeless foreign pheasants at the guns. And the miserable aliens that escaped the guns were left to perish in the desolation of a coming winter which they were unfitted to withstand.

So the first week of the season sped gaily, ending on Saturday with a heavy flight of northern woodcock and an uproarious fusillade among the silver birches.

Once Ferrall loaded two motor cars with pioneers for a day beyond his own boundaries; and one day was spent ingloriously with the beagles; but otherwise the

Shotover estate proved more than sufficient for good bags or target practice, as the skill of the sportsmen developed.

Lord Alderdene, good enough on snipe and cock, was driven almost frantic by the ruffed grouse; Voucher did better for a day or two, and then lost the knack; Marion Page attended to business in her cool and thorough style, and her average on the gun-room books was excellent, and was also adorned with clever pen-and-ink sketches by Siward.

Leroy Mortimer had given up shooting and established himself as a haunter of cushions in sunny corners. Tom O'Hara had gone back to Lenox; Mrs. Vendenning to Hot Springs. Beverly Plank, master of Black Fells, began to pervade the house after a tentative appearance; and he and Major Belwether pottered about the coverts, usually after luncheon—the latter doing little damage with his fowling-piece, and nobody knew how much with his gossiping tongue. Quarrier appeared in the field methodically, shot with judgment, taking no chances for a brilliant performance which might endanger his respectable average. As for the Page boys, they kept the river ducks stirring whenever Eileen Shannon and Rena Bonnesdel could be persuaded to share the canoes with them. Otherwise they haunted the vicinity of those bored maidens, suffering snubs sorrowfully, but persistently faithful. They were a great nuisance in the evening, especially as their sister did not permit them to lose more than ten dollars a day at cards.

Cards—that is Bridge and Preference—ruled as usual; and the latter game being faster suited Mortimer and Ferrall, but did not aid Siward toward recouping his Bridge losses.

Noticing this, late in the week, Major Belwether kindly suggested Klondyke for Siward's benefit, which proved more quickly disastrous to him than anything yet proposed; and he went back to Bridge, preferring rather to "carry" Agatha Caithness at intervals than crumble into bankruptcy under the sheer deadly hazard of Klondyke.

Two matters occupied him; since "cup day" he had never had another opportunity to see Sylvia Landis alone; that was the first matter. He had touched neither wine nor spirits nor malt since the night Ferrall had found him prone, sprawling in a stupor on his disordered bed. That was the second matter, and it occupied him, at times required all his attention, particularly when the physical desire for it set in, steadily, mercilessly, mounting inexorably like a tide. . . . But, like the tide, it ebbed at last, particularly when a sleepless night had exhausted him.

He had gone back to his shooting again after a cool review of the ethics involved. It even amused him to think that the whimsical sermon delivered him by a girl who had cleverness enough to marry many millions, with Quarrier thrown in, could have so moved him to sentimentality. He had ceded the big cup of antique silver to Quarrier, too—a matter which troubled him little, however, as in the irritation of the reaction he had been shooting with the brilliancy of a demon; and the gun-room books were open to any doubting guests' inspection.

Time, therefore, was never heavy on his hands, save when the tide threatened—when at night he stirred and awoke, conscious of its crawling advance, aware of its steady mounting menace. Moments at table, when the aroma of wine made him catch his breath, moments in the gun-room redolent of spicy spirits; a maddening volatile fragrance clinging to the card-room, too! Yes, the long days were filled with such moments for him.

But afield the desire faded; and even during the day, indoors, he shrugged desire aside. It was night that he dreaded—the long hours, lying there tense, stark-eyed, sickened with desire.

As for Sylvia, she and Grace Ferrall had taken to motoring, driving away into the interior or taking long flights north and south along the coast. Sometimes they took Quarrier, sometimes, when Mrs. Ferrall drove, they took in ballast in the shape of a superflous Page boy and a girl for him. Once Grace Ferrall asked Siward to join them; but no definite time being set, he was scarcely surprised to find them gone when he returned from a morning on the snipe meadows. And Sylvia, leagues away by that time, curled up in the tonneau beside Grace Ferrall, watched the dark pines flying past, cheeks pink, eyes like stars, while the rushing wind drove health into her and care out of her—cleansing, purifying, overwhelming winds flowing through and through her, till her very soul within her seemed shining through the beauty of her eyes. Besides, she had just confessed.

. . . .

"He *kissed* you!" repeated Grace Ferrall incredulously.

"Yes—a number of times. He was silly enough to do it, and I let him."

"Did—did he say——"

"I don't know what he said; I was all nerves—confused—scared—a perfect stick in fact! . . . I don't believe he'd care to try again."

Then Mrs. Ferrall deliberately settled down in her furs to extract from the girl beside her every essential detail; and the girl, frank at first, grew shy and silent—reticent enough to worry her friend into a silence which lasted a long while for a cheerful little matron of her sort.

Presently they spoke of other matters—matters interesting to pretty women with much to do in the coming winter between New York, Hot Springs, and Florida; surmises as to dinners, dances, and the newcomers in the younger sets, and the marriages to be arranged or disarranged, and the scandals humanity is heir to, and the attitude of the bishop toward divorce.

And the new pavillion to be built for Saint Berold's Hospital, and the various states of the various charities each was interested in, and the chances of something new at the opera, and the impossibility of saving Fifth Avenue from truck traffic, and the increasing importance of Washington as a social centre, and the bad manners of a foreign ambassador, and the better manners of another diplomat, and the lack of discrimination betrayed by our ambassador to a certain great Power in choosing people for presentation at court, and the latest unhappy British-American marriage, and the hopelessness of the French as decent husbands, and the recent accident to the Claymores' big yacht, and the tendency of well-born young men toward politics, and the anything but distinguished person of Lord Alderdene, which was, however, vastly superior to the demeanour and person of others of his rank recently imported, and the beauty of Miss Caithness, and the chance that Captain Voucher had if Leila Mortimer would let him alone, and the absurdity of the Page twins, and the furtive coarseness of Leroy Mortimer and his general badness, and the sadness of Leila Mortimer's lot when she had always been in love with other people,—and a little scandalous surmise concerning Tom O'Hara, and the new house on Seventy-ninth Street building for Mrs. Vendenning, and that charming widow's success at last year's horse show—and whether the fashion of the function was reviving, and whether Beverly Plank had completely broken into the social sets he had besieged so long, or whether a few of the hunting and shooting people merely permitted him to drive pheasants for them, and why Katharyn Tassel made eyes at him, having sufficient money of her own to die unwed, and—and—and then, at last, as the big motor car swung in a circle at Wenniston Cross-Roads, and poked its brass and lacquer muzzle toward Shotover, the talk swung back to Siward once more—having travelled half the world over to find him.

"He is the sweetest fellow with his mother," sighed Grace; "and that counts heavily with me. But there's trouble ahead for her—sorrow and trouble enough for them both, if he is a true Siward."

"Heredity again!" said Sylvia impatiently. "Isn't he man enough to win out? I'll bet you he settles down, marries, and——"

"Marries? Not he! How many girls do you suppose have believed that—were justified in believing he meant anything by his attractive manner and nice ways of telling you how much he liked you? He had a desperate affair with Mrs. Mortimer—innocent enough I fancy. He's had a dozen within three years; and in a week Rena Bonnesdel has come to making eyes at him, and Eileen gives him no end of chances which he doesn't see. As for Marion Page, the girl had been on the edge of loving him for years! You laugh? But you are wrong; she is in love with him now as much as she ever can be with anybody."

"You mean——"

"Yes I do. Hadn't you suspected it?"

And as Sylvia had suspected it she remained silent.

"If any woman in this world could keep him to the mark, she could," continued Mrs. Ferrall. "He's a perfect fool not to see how she cares for him."

Sylvia said: "He is indeed."

"It would be a sensible match, if she cared to risk it, and if he would only ask her. But he won't."

"Perhaps," ventured Sylvia, "she'll ask him. She strikes me as that sort. I do not mean it unkindly—only Marion is *so* tailor-made and cigaretteful——"

Mrs. Ferrall looked up at her.

"*Did* he propose to you?"

"Yes—I think so."

"Then it's the first time for him. He finds women only too willing to play with him as a rule, and he doesn't have to be definite. I wonder what he meant by being so definite with you?"

"I suppose he meant marriage," said Sylvia serenely; yet there was the slightest ring in her voice; and it amused Mrs. Ferrall to try her a little further.

"Oh, you think he really intended to commit himself?"

"Why not?" retorted Sylvia, turning red. "Do you think he found me over-willing, as you say he finds others?"

"You were probably a new sensation for him," inferred Mrs. Ferrall musingly. "You mustn't take him seriously, child—a man with his record. Besides, he has the same facility with a girl that he has with everything else he tries; his pen—you know how infernally clever he is; and he can make good verse, and write witty jingles, and he can carry home with him any opera and play it decently, too, with the proper harmonies. Anything he finds amusing he is clever with—dogs, horses, pen, brush, music, women"—that was too malicious, for Sylvia had flushed up painfully, and Grace Ferrall dropped her gloved hand on the hand of the girl beside her: "Child, child," she said, "he is *not* that sort; no decent man ever is unless the girl is too."

Sylvia, sitting up very straight in her furs, said: "He found me anything but difficult—if that's what you mean."

"I don't. Please don't be vexed, dear. I plague everybody when I see an opening. There's really only one thing that worries me about it all."

"What is that?" asked Sylvia without interest.

"It's that you *might* be tempted to care a little for him, which, being useless, might be unwise."

"I am . . . tempted."

"Not seriously!"

"I don't know." She turned in a sudden nervous impatience foreign to her. "Howard Quarrier is too perfectly imperfect for me. I'm glad I've said it. The things he knows about and doesn't know have been a revelation in this last week with him. There is too much surface, too much exterior admirably fashioned. And inside is all clock-work. I've said it; I'm glad I have. He seemed different at Newport; he seemed nice at Lenox. The truth is, he's a horrid disappointment—and I'm bored to death at my brilliant prospects."

The low whizzing hum of the motor filled a silence that produced considerable effect upon Grace Ferrall. And, after mastering her wits, she said in a subdued voice:

"Of course it's my meddling."

"Of course it isn't. I asked your opinion, but I

knew what I was going to do. Only, I did think him personally possible—which made the expediency, the mercenary view of it easier to contemplate."

She was becoming as frankly brutal as she knew how to be, which made the revolt the more ominous.

"You don't think you could endure him for an hour or two a day, Sylvia?"

"It is not that," said the girl almost sullenly.

"But——"

"I'm afraid of myself—call it inherited mischief if you like! If I let a man do to me what Mr. Siward did when I was only engaged to Howard, what might I do——"

"You are not *that* sort!" said Mrs. Ferrall bluntly. "Don't be exotic, Sylvia."

"How do you know—if *I* don't know? Most girls are kissed; I—well I didn't expect to be. But I was! I tell you, Grace, I *don't* know what I am or shall be. I'm unsafe; I know that much."

"It's moral and honest to realize it," said Mrs. Ferrall suavely; "and in doing so you insure your own safety. Sylvia dear, I wish I hadn't meddled; I'm meddling some more I suppose when I say to you, *don't* give Howard his *congé* for the present. It is a horridly common thing to dwell upon, but Howard is too *materially* important to be cut adrift on the impulse of the moment."

"I know it."

"You are too clever not to. Consider the matter wisely, dispassionately, intelligently, dear; then if by April you simply can't stand it—talk the thing over with me again," she ended rather vaguely and wistfully; for it had been her heart's desire to wed Sylvia's beauty and Quarrier's fortune, and the suitability of the one for the other was apparent enough to make even sterner moralists wobbly in their creed. Quarrier, as a detail of modern human architecture, she supposed might fit in somewhere, and took that for granted in laying the corner stone for her fairy palace which Sylvia was to inhabit. And now!—oh, vexation!—the neglected but essentially constructive detail of human architecture had buckled, knocking the dream palace and its princess and its splendour about her ears.

"Things *never* happen in real life," she observed plaintively; "only romances have plots where things work out. But we people in real life, we just go on and on in a badly constructed, plotless sort of way with no villains, no interesting situations, no climaxes, no ensemble. No, we grow old and irritable and meaner and meaner; we lose our good looks and digestions, and we die in hopeless discord with the unity required in a dollar and a half novel by a master of modern fiction."

"But some among us amass fortunes," suggested Sylvia, laughing.

"But we don't live happy ever after. Nobody ever had enough money in real life."

"Some fall in love," observed Sylvia, musing.

"And they are not content, silly!"

"Why? Because nobody ever had enough love in real life," mocked Sylvia.

"You have said it, child. That is the malady of the world, and nobody knows it until some pretty ninny like you babbles the truth. And *that* is why we care for those immortals in romance, those fortunate lovers who, in fable, are given and give *enough* of love; those magic shapes in verse and tale whose hearts are satisfied when the mad author of their being inks his last period and goes to dinner."

Sylvia laughed awhile, then, chin on wrist, sat musing there, muffled in her furs.

"As for love, I think I should be moderate in the asking, in the giving. A little—to flavour routine—would be sufficient for me I fancy."

"You know so much about it," observed Mrs. Ferrall ironically.

"I am permitted to speculate, am I not?"

"Certainly. Only speculate in sound investments, dear."

"How can you make a sound investment in love? Isn't it always sheerest speculation?"

"Yes, that is why simple matrimony is usually a safer speculation than love."

"Yes, but—love isn't matrimony."

"Match that with its complementary platitude and you have the essence of modern fiction," observed Mrs. Ferrall. "Love is a subject talked to death, which explains the present shortage in the market I suppose. You're not in love and you don't miss it. Why cultivate an artificial taste for it? If it ever comes naturally, you'll be astonished at your capacity for it, and the constant deterioration in quantity and quality of the visible supply. Goodness! my epigrams make me yawn—or is it age and the ill humour of the aged when the porridge spills over on the family cat?"

"I am the cat, I suppose," asked Sylvia, laughing.

"Yes you are—and you go tearing away, back up, fur on end, leaving me by the fire with no porridge and only the aroma of the singeing fur to comfort me. . . . Still there's one thing to comfort me."

"What?"

"Kitty-cats come back, dear."

"Oh, I suppose so. . . . Do you believe I could induce him to wear his hair any way except pompadour? . . . and, dear, his beard is so dreadfully silky. Isn't there anything he could take for it?"

"Only a razor I'm afraid. Those long, thick, soft, eyelashes of his are ominous. Eyes of that sort ruin a man for my taste. He might just as reasonably wear my hat."

"But he can't follow the fashions in eyes," laughed Sylvia. "Oh, this is atrocious of us—it is simply horrible to sit here and say such things. I am cold-blooded enough as it is—material enough, mean, covetous, contemptible——"

"Dear!" said Grace Ferrall mildly, "you are not choosing a husband; you are choosing a career. To criticise his investments might be bad taste; to be able to extract what amusement you can out of Howard is a direct mercy from Heaven. Otherwise you'd go mad, you know."

"Grace! *Do* you wish me to marry him?"

"What is the alternative, dear?"

"Why, nothing—self-respect, dowdiness, and peace."

"Is that all?"

"All I can see."

"*Not* Stephen Siward?"

"To marry? No. To enjoy, yes. . . . Grace, I *have* had such a good time with him; you don't know! He *is* such a boy—sometimes; and I—I believe that I am rather good for him. . . . Not that I'd ever again let him do that sort of thing. . . . Besides, his curiosity is quenched; I *am* the sort he supposed. Now he's found out he will be nice. . . . It's been days since I've had a talk with him. He tried to, but I wouldn't. Besides, the major has said nasty things about him when Howard was present; nothing definite, only hints, smiling silences, innuendoes on the verge of matters rather unfit; and I had nothing definite to refute. I could not even appear to understand or notice—it was all done in such a horridly vague way. But it only made me like him; and no doubt that actress he took to the Patroons is better company than he finds in nine places out of ten among his own sort."

"Oh," said Grace Ferrall slowly, "if that is the way you feel, I don't see why you shouldn't play with Mr. Siward whenever you like."

"Nor I. I've been a perfect fool not to. . . . Howard hates him."

"How do you know?"

"What a question! A woman knows such things. Then, you remember that caricature—so dreadfully like Howard? Howard has no sense of humour; he detests such things. It was the most dreadful thing that Mr. Siward could have done to him."

"Meddled again!" groaned Grace. "Doesn't Howard know that *I* did that?"

"Yes, but nothing I can say alters his conviction that the likeness was intended. You know it was a likeness! And if Mr. Siward had not told me that it was not intended, I should never have believed it to be an accident."

After a prolonged silence Sylvia said, overcarelessly: "I don't quite understand Howard. With me anger lasts but a moment, and then I'm open to overtures for peace . . . I think Howard's anger lasts."

"It does," said Grace. "He was a muff as a boy—a prig with a prig's memory under all his shallow, showy surface. I'm frank with you; I never could take my cousin either respectfully or seriously, but I've known him to take his own anger so seriously that years after he has visited it upon those who had really wronged him. And he is equipped for retaliation if he chooses. That fortune of his reaches far. . . . Not that I think him capable of using such a power to satisfy a mere personal dislike. Howard has principles, loads of them. But—the weapon is there."

"Is it true that Mr. Siward is interested in building electric roads?" asked Sylvia curiously.

"*I* don't know, child. Why?"

"Nothing. I wondered."

"Why?"

"Mr. Mortimer said so."

"Then I suppose he is. I'll ask Kemp if you like. Why? Isn't it all right to build them?"

"I suppose so. Howard is in it somehow. In fact Howard's company is behind Mr. Siward's, I believe."

Grace Ferrall turned and looked at the girl beside her, laughing outright.

"Oh, Howard doesn't do mysterious financial things to nice young men because they draw impudent pictures of him running after his dog—or for any other reason. That, dear, is one of those skilfully developed portions of an artistic plot; and plots exist only in romance. So do villains; and besides, my cousin isn't one. Besides that, if Howard is in that thing, no doubt Kemp and I are too. So your nice young man is in very safe company."

"You draw such silly inferences," said Sylvia coolly; but there was a good deal of colour in her cheeks; and she knew it and pulled her big motor veil across her face, fastening it under her chin. All of which amused Grace Ferrall infinitely until the subtler significance of the girl's mental processes struck her, sobering her own thoughts. Sylvia, too, had grown serious in her preoccupation; and the *partie-à-deux* terminated a few minutes later in a duet of silence over the tea-cups in the gun-room.

The weather had turned warm and misty; one of those sudden sea-coast changes had greyed the blue in the sky, spreading a fine haze over land and water, effacing the crisp sparkle of the sea, dulling the westering sun.

A few moments later Sylvia, glancing over her shoulder, noticed that a fine misty drizzle had clouded the casements. That meant that her usual evening stroll on the cliffs with Quarrier, before dressing for dinner, was off. And she drew a little breath of unconscious relief as Marion Page walked in, her light woollen shooting-jacket, her hat, shoes, and the barrels of the fowling-piece tucked under her left arm-pit, all glimmering frostily with powdered rain drops.

She said something to Grace Ferrall about the mist promising good point-shooting in the morning, took the order book from a servant, jotted down her request to be called an hour before sunrise, filled in the gun-room records with her score—the species and number bagged, and the number of shells used—and accepting the tea offered, drew out a tiny cigarette-case of sweet-bay wood heavily crusted with rose-gold.

"With whom were you shooting?" asked Grace, as Marion dropped one well-shaped leg over the other and wreathed her delicately tanned features in smoke.

"Stephen Siward and Blinky. They're at it yet, but I had some letters to write." She glanced leisurely at Sylvia and touched the ash-tray with the whitening end of her cigarette. "That dog you let Mr. Siward have is a good one. I'm taking him to Jersey next week for the cock-shooting."

Sylvia returned her calm gaze blankly.

An unreasonable and disagreeable shock had passed through her.

"My North Carolina pointers are useless for close work," observed Marion indifferently; and she leaned back, watching the blue smoke curling upward from her cigarette.

Sylvia, distrait, but with downcast eyes on fire under the fringed lids, was thinking of the cheque Siward had given her for Sagamore. The transaction, for her, had been a business one on the surface only. She had never meant to use the cheque. She had laid it away among a few letters, relics, pleasant souvenirs of the summer. To her the affair had been softened by a delicate hint of intimacy,—the delight he was to take in something that had once been hers had given her a faint taste of the pleasure of according pleasure to a man. And *this* is what he had done!

The drizzle had turned to fog, through which rain was now pelting the cliffs; people were returning from the open; a motor-car came whizzing into the drive, and out of it tumbled Rena and Eileen and the faithful Pages, the girls irritable and ready for tea, and the boys like a pair of eager, wagging, setter puppies, pleased with everything and everybody, utterly oblivious to the sombre repose brooding above the tea-table.

Their sister calmly refused them the use of her cigarettes. Eileen presented her pretty shoulder, Rena nearly yawned at them, but, nothing dampened, they recounted a number of incidents with reciprocal enthusiasm to Sylvia, who was too inattentive to smile, and to Grace Ferrall, who smiled the more sweetly through sheer inattention.

Then Alderdene came in, blinking a greeting through

his foggy goggles, sloppy, baggy, heavy shoes wheezing, lingered in the vicinity long enough to swallow his "peg" and acquire a disdainful opinion of his shooting from Marion, and then took himself off, leaving the room noisy with his laugh, which resembled the rattle of a startled kingfisher.

In ones and twos the guests reported as the dusk-curtained fog closed in on Shotover. Quarrier came, dry as a chip under his rain-coat, but his silky beard was wet with rain, and moisture powdered his long, soft eyelashes and white skin; and his flexible, pointed fingers, as he drew off his gloves, seemed startling in their whiteness through the gathering gloom.

"I suppose our evening walk is out of the question," he said, standing by Sylvia, who had nodded a greeting and then turned her head rather hastily to see who had entered the room. It was Siward, only a vague shape in the gloom, but perfectly recognisable to her. At the same moment Marion Page rose leisurely and strolled toward the billiard-room.

"Our walk?" repeated Sylvia absently—"it's raining, you know." Yet only a day or two ago she had walked to church with Siward through the rain, the irritated Major feeling obliged to go with them. Her eyes followed Siward's figure, suddenly dark against the door of the lighted billiard-room, then brilliantly illuminated, as he entered, nodded acceptance to Mortimer's invitation, and picked up the cue just laid aside by Agatha Caithness, who had turned to speak to Marion. Then Mortimer's bulk loomed nearer; voices became gay and animated in the billiard-room. Siward's handsome face was bent toward Agatha Caithness in gay challenge; Mortimer's heavy laugh broke out; there came the rattle of pool-balls, and the dull sound of cue-butts striking the floor; then, crack! and the game began, with Marion Page and Siward fighting Mortimer and Miss Caithness for something or other.

Quarrier had been speaking for some time before Sylvia became aware of it—something about a brisk walk in the morning somewhere; and she nodded impatiently, watching Marion's supple waist-line as she bent far over the illuminated table for a complicated shot at the enemy.

His fiancée's inattention was not agreeable to Quarrier. A dozen things had happened since his arrival which had not been agreeable to him: her failure to meet him at the Fells Crossing, and the reason for her failure; and her informal acquaintance with Siward, whose presence at Shotover he had not looked for, and her sudden intimacy with the man he had never particularly liked, and whom within six months he had come to detest and to avoid.

These things—the outrageous liberty Siward had permitted himself in caricaturing him, the mortifying caprice of Sylvia for Siward on the day of the Shotover cup-drive—had left indelible impressions in a cold and rather heavy mind, slow to waste effort in the indulgence of any vital emotion.

In a few years indifference to Siward had changed to passive disapproval; that, again, to an emotionless dislike; and when the scandal at the Patroons Club occurred, for the first time in his life he understood what it was to fear the man he disliked. For if Siward had committed the insane imprudence which had cost him his title to membership, he had also done something, knowingly or otherwise, which awoke in Quarrier a cold, slow fear; and that fear was dormant, but present, now, and it, for the time being, dictated his attitude and bearing toward the man who might or might not be capable of using viciously a knowledge which Quarrier believed that he must possess.

For that reason, when it was not possible to avoid Siward, his bearing toward him was carefully civil; for that reason he dampened Major Belwether's eagerness to tell everybody all he knew about the shamelessly imprudent girl who had figured with Siward in the scandal, but whose identity the press had not discovered.

Silence was always desirable to Quarrier; silence concerning all matters was a trait inborn and congenially cultivated to a habit by him in every affair of life —in business, in leisure, in the methodical pursuits of such pleasures as a limited intellect permitted him, in personal and family matters, in public questions and financial problems.

He listened always, but never invited confidences; he had no opinion to express when invited. And he became very, very rich.

And over it all spread a thin membrane of vanity, nervous, not intellectual, sensitiveness; for all sense of humour was absent in this man, whose smile, when not a physical effort, was automatically and methodically responsive to certain fixed cues. He smiled when he said "Good morning," when declining or accepting invitations, when taking his leave, when meeting anybody of any financial importance, and when everybody except himself had begun to laugh in a theatre or a drawing-room. This limit to any personal manifestation he considered a generous one. And perhaps it was.

. . . . .

A sudden rain-squall, noisy against the casements, had darkened the room; then the electric lights broke out with a mild candle-like lustre, and Quarrier, standing beside Sylvia's chair, discovered it to be empty.

It was not until he had dressed for dinner that he saw her again, seated on the stairs with Marion Page—a new appearance of intimacy for both women, who heretofore had found nothing except a passing civility in common.

Marion was discussing dog-breeding with that cool, crude, direct insouciance so unpleasant to some men. Sylvia was attentive, curious, and instinctively shrinking by turns, secretly dismayed at the overplainness of terms employed in kennel lore by the girl at her side.

The conversation veered toward the Sagamore pup. Marion explained that Siward was too busy to do any Southern shooting, which was why he was glad to have her polish Sagamore on Jersey woodcock.

"I thought it was not good for a dog to be used by anybody except his master," said Sylvia carelessly.

"Only second-raters suffer. Besides, I have shot enough, now, with Mr. Siward to use his dog as he does."

"He *is* an agreeable shooting companion," smiled Sylvia.

"He is perfect," answered Marion coolly. "The only test for a thoroughbred is the field. He rings true."

They exchanged carefully impersonal views on Siward's good qualities for a moment or two; then Marion said bluntly: "Do you know anything in particular about that Patroons Club affair?"

"No," said Sylvia, "nothing in particular."

"Neither do I; and I don't care to; I mean, that I don't care what he did; and I wish that gossiping old Major would stop trying to hint it to me."

"My uncle!"

"Oh! I forgot. Beg your pardon, you know, but——"

"I'm not offended," observed Sylvia, with a shrug of her pretty, bare shoulders.

Marion laughed. "Such a gadabout! Besides, I'm no prude, but he and Leroy Mortimer have no business to talk to unmarried women the way they do. No matter how worldly wise we are, men have no right to suppose we are."

"Pooh!" shrugged Sylvia. "I have no patience to study out *double-entendre*, so it never shocks me. Besides——"

She was going to add that she was not at all versed in doubtful worldly wisdom, but decided not to, as it might seem to imply disapproval of Marion's learning. So she went on: "Besides, what have innuendoes to do with Mr. Siward?"

"I don't know whether I care to understand them. The Major hinted that the woman—the one who figured in it—is—rather exclusively Mr. Siward's 'property.'"

"Exclusively?" repeated Sylvia curiously. "She's a public actress, isn't she?"

"If you call the manœuvres of a newly fledged chorus girl acting, yes, she is. But I don't believe Mr. Siward figures in *that* unfashionable rôle. Why, there are too many women of his own sort ready for mischief." Marion turned to Sylvia, her eyes hard with a cynicism quite lost on the other. "That sort of thing might suit Leroy Mortimer, but it doesn't fit Mr. Siward," she concluded, rising as their hostess appeared from above and the butler from below.

And all through dinner an indefinitely unpleasant remembrance of the conversation lingered with Sylvia, and she sat silent for minutes at a time, returning to actualities with a long, curious side-glance across at Siward, and an uncomprehending smile of assent for whatever Quarrier or Major Belwether had been saying to her.

Cards she managed to avoid after dinner, and stood by Quarrier's chair for half an hour, absently watching the relentless method and steady adherence to rule which characterised his Bridge-playing, the eager, unslaked brutality of Mortimer, the set, selfish face of his pretty wife, the chilled intensity of Miss Caithness.

And Grace Ferrall's phrase recurred to her, "Nobody ever has enough money!"—not even these people, whose only worry was to find investment for the surplus they were unable to spend. Something of the meanness of it all penetrated her. Were these the real visages of these people, whose faces otherwise seemed so smooth and human? Was Leila Mortimer aware of the shrillness of her voice? Did Agatha Caithness realise how pinched her mouth and nose had grown? Did even Leroy Mortimer dream how swollen the pouches under his eyes were; how red and puffy his hands, shuffling a new pack; how pendulous and dreadful his red under-lip when absorbedly making up his cards?

Instinctively she moved a step forward for a glimpse of Quarrier's face. The face appeared to be a study in blankness. His natural visage was emotionless and inexpressive enough, but this face, from which every vestige of colour had fled, fascinated her with its dead whiteness; and the hair brushed high, the long, black lashes, the silky beard, struck her as absolutely ghastly, as though they had been glued to a face of wax.

She turned on her heel, restless, depressed, inclined for companionship. The Page boys had tempted Rena and Eileen to the billiard-room; Voucher, Alderdene, and Major Belwether were huddled over a table, immersed in Preference; Katharyn Tassel and Grace Ferrall sat together looking over the announcements of Sylvia's engagement in a batch of New York papers just arrived; Ferrall was writing at a desk, and Siward and Marion were occupied in the former's sketch for an ideal shooting vehicle, to be built on the buckboard principle, with a clever arrangement for dogs, guns, ammunition, and provisions. Siward's profile, as it bent in the lamplight over the paper, was very engaging. The boyish note predominated as he talked while he drew, his eyes now smiling, now seriously intent on the sketch which was developing so swiftly under his facile pencil.

Marion's clean-cut blond head was close to his, her supple body twisted in her seat, one bare arm hanging over the back of the chair. Something in her attitude seemed to exclude intrusion; her voice, too, was hushed in comment, though his was pitched in his naturally agreeable key.

Sylvia had taken a hesitating step toward them, but halted, turning irresolutely; and suddenly over her crept a sensation of isolation—something of that feeling which had roused her at midnight from her bed and driven her to Grace Ferrall for a refuge from she knew not what.

The rustle of her silken dinner gown was scarcely perceptible as she turned. Siward, moving his head slightly, glanced up, then brought his sketch to a brilliant finish.

"Don't you think something of this sort is practicable?" he asked pleasantly, including Mrs. Ferrall and Katharyn Tassel in a general appeal which brought them into the circle of two. Grace Ferrall leaned forward, looking over Marion's shoulder, and Siward rose and stepped back, with a quick glance into the hall—in time to catch a glimmer of pale blue and lace on the stairs.

"I suppose my cigarettes are in my room as usual," he said aloud to himself, wheeling so that he could not have time to see Marion's offer of her little gold-encrusted case, or notice her quickly raised eyes, bright with suspicion and vexation. For she, too, had observed Sylvia's distant entrance, had been perfectly aware of Siward's cognisance of Sylvia's retreat; and when Siward went on sketching she had been content. Now she could not tell whether he had deliberately and skillfully taken his *congé* to follow Sylvia, or whether, in his quest for his cigarettes, chance might meddle, as usual. Even if he returned, she could not know with certainty how much of a part hazard had played on the landing above, where she already heard the distant sounds of Sylvia's voice mingling with Siward's, then a light footfall or two, and silence.

. . . . .

He had greeted her in his usual careless, happy fashion, just as she had reached her chamber door; and she turned at the sound of his voice, confused, unsmiling, a little pale.

"Is it headache, or are you too in quest of cigarettes?" he asked, as he stopped in passing her where she stood, one slender hand on the knob of her door.

"*I* don't smoke, you know," she said, looking up at him with a cool little laugh. "It isn't headache either. I was—boring myself, Mr. Siward."

"Is there any virtue in me as a remedy?"

"Oh, I have no doubt you have lots of virtues. . . . Perhaps you might do as a temporary remedy

—first aid to the injured." She laughed again, uncertainly. "But you are on a quest for cigarettes."

"And you?"

"A rendezvous—with the Sand-Man. . . . Good night."

"Good night . . . if you must say it."

"It's polite to say something . . . isn't it?"

"It would be polite to say, 'With pleasure, Mr. Siward!'"

"But you haven't invited me to do anything—not even to accept a cigarette. Besides, you didn't expect to meet me up here?"

The trailing accent made it near enough a question for him to say, "Yes, I did."

"How could you?"

"I saw you leave the room."

"You were sketching for Marion Page. Do you wish me to believe that you noticed me and——"

"—And followed you? Yes, I did follow you."

She looked at him, then past him toward a corner of the wide hall where a maid in cap and apron sat pretending to be sewing. "Careful!" she motioned with smiling lips, "servants gossip. . . . Good night, again."

"Won't you——"

"Oh, dear! you mustn't speak so loud," she motioned, with her fresh, sweet lips curving on the edge of that adorable smile once more.

"Couldn't we have a moment——"

"No——"

"One minute——"

"Hush! I must open my door"—lingering. "I might come out again, if you have anything particularly important to communicate to me."

"I have. There's a big bay-window at the end of the other corridor. Will you come?"

But she opened her door, with a light laugh, saying "good night" again, and closed it noiselessly behind her.

He walked on, turning into his corridor, but kept straight ahead, passing his own door, on to the window at the end of the hall, then north along a wide passageway which terminated in a bay-window overlooking the roof of the indoor swimming tank.

Rain rattled heavily against the panes and on the lighted roof of opalescent glass below, through which he could make out the shadowy fronds of palms.

It appeared that he had cigarettes enough, for he lighted one presently, and, leaving his chair, curled up in the cushioned and pillowed window-seat, gathering his knees together under his arm.

The cigarette he had lighted went out. He had bitten into it and twisted it so roughly that it presently crumbled; and he threw the rags of it into a metal bowl, locking his jaws in silence. For the night threatened to be a bad one for him. A heavy fragrance from his neighbour's wine-glass at dinner had stirred up what had for a time lain dormant; and, by accident, something—some sweetmeat he had tasted—was saturated in brandy.

Now, his restlessness at the prospect of a blank night had quickened to uneasiness, with a hint of fever tinting his skin, but, as yet, the dull ache in his body was scarcely more than a premonition.

He had his own devices for tiding him over such periods—reading, tobacco, and the long, blind, dogged tramps he took in town. But here, to-night, in the rain, one stood every chance of walking off the cliffs; and he was sick of reading himself sightless over the sort of books sent wholesale to Shotover; and he was already too ill at ease, physically, to make smoking endurable.

Were it not for a half-defiant, half-sullen dread of the coming night, he might have put it from his mind in spite of the slowly increasing nervous tension and the steady dull consciousness of desire. He drew another *Sirdar* from his case and sat staring at the rain-smeared night, twisting the frail fragrant cigarette to bits between his fingers.

After a while he began to walk monotonously to and fro the length of the corridor, like a man timing his steps to the heavy ache of body or mind. Once he went as far as his own door, entered, and stepping to the wash-basin, let the icy water run over hands and wrists. This sometimes helped to stimulate and soothe him; it did now, for a while—long enough to change the current of his thoughts to the girl he had hoped might have the imprudence to return for a tryst, innocent enough in itself, yet unconventional and unreasonable enough to prove attractive to them both.

Probably she wouldn't come; she had kept her fluffy skirts clear of him since Cup Day—which simply corroborated his vague estimate of her. Had she done the contrary, his estimate would have been the same; for, unconsciously but naturally, he had prejudged her. A girl who could capture Quarrier at full noontide, and in the face of all Manhattan, was a girl equipped for anything she dared—though she was probably too clever to dare too much; a girl to be interested in, to amuse and be amused by; a girl to be reckoned with. His restlessness and his fever subdued by the icy water, he stood drying his hands, thinking, coolly, how close he had come to being seriously in love with this young girl, whose attitude was always a curious temptation, whose smile was a charming provocation, whose youth and beauty were to him a perpetual challenge. He admitted to himself, calmly, that he had never seen a woman he cared as much for; that for the brief moment of his declaration he had known an utterly new emotion, which inevitably must have become the love he had so quietly declared it to be. He had never before felt as he felt then, cared as he cared then. Anything had been possible for him at that time—any degree of love, any devotion, any generous renunciation. Clear-sighted, master of himself, he saw love before him, and knew it when he saw it; recognised it, was ready for it, offered it, emboldened by her soft hands so eloquent in his.

And in his arms he held it for an instant, he thought, spite of the sudden inertia, spite of the according of cold lips and hands still colder, relaxed, inert; held it until he doubted. That was all; he had been wise to doubt such sudden miracles as that. She, consummate and charming, had soon set him right. And, after all, she liked him; and she had been sure enough of herself to permit the impulse of a moment to carry her with him—a little way, a very little way—merely to the formal symbol of a passion the germ of which she recognised in him.

Then she had become intelligent again, with a little laughter, a little malice, a becoming tint of hesitation and confusion; all the sense, all the arts, all the friendly sweetness of a woman thorough in training, schooled in self-possession, clear enough to be audacious and perverse without danger to herself, to the man, or to the main chance.

Standing there alone in his lighted room, he wondered whether, had her trained and inbred policy been less precise, less worldly, she might have responded to such a man as he. Perfectly conscious that he had been capable of loving her; aware, too, that his experience had left him on that borderland only through his cool refusal to cross it and face a hopeless battle already lost, he leisurely and mentally took the measure of his own state of mind, and found all well, all intact; found himself still master of his affections, and probably clear-minded enough to remain so under the circumstances.

To such a man as he, impulse to love, capacity to love, did not mean instant capsizing with a flop into sentimental tempests, where swamped, ardent and callow youth raises a hysterically selfish clamour for reciprocity or death. His nature partly, partly his character, accounted for this balance; and, in part, a rather wide experience with women of various degrees counted more.

So, by instinct and experience, normally temperate, only what was abnormal and inherited might work a mischief in this man. His listlessness, his easy acquiescence, were but consequent upon the self-knowledge of self-control. But mastery of the master-vice required something different; he was sick of a sickness; and because, in this sickness, will, mind, and body are tainted too, reason and logic lack clarity; and, to the signals of danger his reply had always been either overconfident or weak—and it had been always the same reply: "Not yet. There is time." And now, this last week, it had come upon him that the time was now; the skirmish was already on; and it had alarmed him suddenly to find that the skirmish was already a battle, and a rough one.

. . . . .

As he stood there he heard voices on the stairs. People had already begun to retire, because late cards and point-shooting at dawn do not agree. And a point-shooting picnic in snugly elaborate blinds was popular with women—or was supposed to be.

He could distinguish by their voices, by their laughter and step, the people who were mounting the stairway and lingering for gossip or passing through the various corridors to court the sleep denied him; he heard Mortimer's heavy tread and the soft shuffling step of Major Belwether as they left the elevator; and the patter of his hostess's satin slippers, and her gay "good night" on the stairs.

Little by little the tumult died away. Quarrier's measured step came, passed; Marion Page's cool, crisp voice and walk, and the giggle and amble of the twins, and Rena and Eileen,—the last laggards, with Ferrall's brisk, decisive tones and stride to close the procession.

He turned and looked grimly at his bed, then, shutting off the lights, he opened his door and went out into the deserted corridor, where the elevator shaft was dark and only the dim night-lights burned at angles in the passage-ways.

He had his rain-coat and cap with him, not being certain of what he might be driven to; but for the present he found the bay-window overlooking the swimming tank sufficient to begin the vigil.

Secure from intrusion, as there were no bedrooms on that corridor, he tossed coat and cap into the window-seat, walked to and fro for a while listening to the rain, then sat down, his well-shaped head between his hands. And in silence he faced the Enemy.

How long he had sat there he did not know. When he raised his face, all gray and drawn with the tension of conflict, his eyes were not very clear, nor did the figure standing there in the dim light from the hall mean anything for a moment.

"Mr. Siward?" in an uncertain voice, almost a whisper.

He stood up mechanically, and she saw his face.

"Are you ill? What is it?"

"Ill? No." He passed his hand over his eyes. "I fancy I was close to the edge of sleep." Some colour came back into his face; he stood smiling now, the significance of her presence dawning on him.

"*Did* you really come?" he asked. "This isn't a very lovely but impalpable astral vision, is it?"

"It's horridly imprudent, isn't it?" she murmured, still considering the rather drawn and pallid face of the man before her. "I came out of pure curiosity, Mr. Siward."

She glanced about her. He moved a big bunch of hothouse roses so she could pass, and she settled down lightly on the edge of the window-seat. When he had piled some big downy cushions behind her back, she made a quick gesture of invitation.

"I have only a moment," she said, as he seated himself beside her. "Part of my curiosity is satisfied in finding you here; I didn't suppose you so faithful."

"I can be fairly faithful. What else are you curious about?"

"You said you had something important——"

"—To tell you? So I did. That was bribery, perjury, false pretences, robbery under arms, anything you will! I only wanted you to come."

"That is a shameful confession!" she said; but her smile was gay enough, and she noiselessly shook out her fluffy skirts and settled herself a trifle more deeply among the pillows.

"Of course," she observed absently, "you are dreadfully mortified at yourself."

"Naturally," he admitted.

The patter of the rain attracted her attention; she peered out through the blurred casements into the blackness. Then, picking up his cap and indicating his raincoat, "Why?" she asked.

"Oh—in case you hadn't come——"

"A walk? By yourself? A night like this on the cliffs! You are not perfectly mad, are you?"

"Not perfectly."

Her face grew serious and beautiful.

"What *is* the matter, Mr. Siward?"

"Things."

"Do you care to be more explicit?"

"Well," he said, with a humourous glance at her, "I haven't seen you for ages. That's not wholesome for me, you know."

"But you see me now; and it does not seem to benefit you."

"I feel much better," he insisted, laughing; and her blue eyes grew very lovely as the smile broke from them in uncertain response.

"So you had nothing really important to tell me, Mr. Siward?"

"Only that I wanted you."

"Oh! . . . I said *important*."

But he did not argue the question; and she leaned forward, broke a rose from its stem, then sank back a little way among the cushions, looking at him, idly inhaling the hothouse perfume.

"Why have you so ostentatiously avoided me, Mr. Siward?" she asked languidly.

"Well, upon my word!" he said, with a touch of irritation.

"Oh, you are so dreadfully literal!" she shrugged,

brushing her straight, sensitive nose with the pink blossom; "I only said it to give you a chance. . . . If you are going to be stupid, good night!" But she made no movement to go. . . . "Yes, then; I *have* avoided you. And it doesn't become you to ask why."

"Because I kissed you?"

"You hint at the true reason so chivalrously, so delicately," she said, "that I scarcely recognise it." The cool mockery of her voice and the warm, quick colour tinting neck and face were incongruous. He thought with slow surprise that she was not yet letter-perfect in her rôle of the material triumphant over the spiritual. A trifle ashamed, too, he sat silent, watching the silken petals fall one by one as she slowly detached them with delicate, restless lips.

"I am sorry I came," she said reflectively. "You don't know why I came, do you? Sheer loneliness, Mr. Siward; there is something of the child in me still, you see. I am not yet sufficiently resourceful to take it out in a quietly tearful obligato; I never learned how to produce tears. . . . So I came to you." She had stripped the petals from the rose, and now, tossing the crushed branch from her, she leaned forward and broke from its stem a heavy, perfumed bud, half unfolded.

"It seems my fate to pass my life in bidding you good night," she said, straightening up and turning to him with the careless laughter touching mouth and eyes again. Then, resting her weight on one hand, her smooth, white shoulder rounded beside her cheek, she looked at him out of humourous eyes:

"What is it that women find so attractive in you? The man's experienced insouciance? The boy's unconscious cynicism? The mystery of your self-sufficiency?

The faulty humanity in you? The youth in you already showing traces of wear that hint of future scars? What will you be at thirty-five? At forty? . . . Ah," she added softly, "what are you now? For I don't know, and you cannot tell me if you would. . . . Out of these little windows called eyes we look at one another, and study surfaces, and try to peep into neighbours' windows. But all is dark behind the windows—always dark, in there where they tell us souls hide."

She laid the shell-pink bud against her cheek that matched it, smiling with wise sweetness to herself.

"What counts with you?" he asked after a moment.

"Counts? How?"

"In your affections. What prepossesses you?"

She laughed audaciously: "Your traits—some of them—all of them that you reveal. You must be aware of that much already, considering everything——"

"Then, what is it I lack? Where do I fail?"

"But you don't lack—you don't fail! I ask nothing more of you, Mr. Siward."

"A man from whom a woman desires nothing is already convicted of insufficiency. . . . You would recognise this very quickly if I made love to you."

"Is that the *only* way I am to discover your insufficiency, Mr. Siward?"

"Or my sufficiency. . . . Have you enough curiosity to try?"

"Oh! I thought *you* were to try." Then, quickly: "But I think you have already experimented; and I did not notice your shortcomings. So there is no use in pursuing that line of investigation any farther—is there?"

And always with her the mischief lay in the trailing

upward inflection; in the confused sweetness of her eyes, and their lovely uncertainty.

One slim white hand held the rose against her cheek; the other lay idly on her knee, fresh and delicate as a fallen petal; and he laid both hands over it and lifted it between them.

"Mr. Siward, I am afraid this is becoming a habit with you." The gay mockery was not quite genuine; the curve of lips too sensitive for a voice so lightly cynical.

He smiled, bending there, considering her hand between his; and after a moment her muscles relaxed, and bare round arm and hand lay abandoned to him.

"Quite flawless—perfect," he said aloud to himself.

"Do you—read hands?"

"Vaguely." He touched the smooth palm: "Long life, clear mind, and"—he laughed—"heart supreme over reason! There is written a white lie—but a pretty one."

"It is no lie."

He laughed again, unconvinced.

"It is the truth," she said, seriously insisting and bending sideways above her own hand where it lay in his. "It is a miserable confession to admit it, but I'm afraid intelligence would fight a losing battle with heart if the conflict ever came. You see, I know, having nobody to study except myself all these years. . . . There is the proof of it—that selfish, smooth contour, where there should be generosity. Then, look at the tendency of imagination toward mischief!" She laid her right forefinger on the palm of the left hand which he held, and traced the developments arising in the Mount of Hermes. "Is it not a horrid hand, Mr. Siward? I don't know how much you know about palms, but—" She suddenly flushed, and attempted to close her hand, doubling the thumb over. There was a little half-hearted struggle, freeing one of his arms, which fell, settling about her slender waist; a silence, a breathless moment, and he had kissed her. Her lips were warm, this time.

She recovered herself, avoiding his eyes, and moved backward, shielding her face with pretty upflung elbows out-turned. "I told you it was becoming a habit with you!" The loud beating of her pulses marred her voice. "Must I establish a dead-line every time I commit the folly of being alone with you?"

"I'll draw that line," he said, taking her in his arms.

"I—I beg you will draw it quickly, Mr. Siward."

"I do; it passes through your heart and mine!"

"Is—do you mean a declaration—again? You are compromising yourself, you know. I warn you that you are committing yourself."

"So are you. Look at me!"

In his arms, her own arms pressed against his breast, resisting, she raised her splendid youthful eyes; and through and through her shot pulse on pulse, until every nerve seemed aquiver.

"While I'm still sane," he said with a dry catch in his throat, "before I tell you that I love you, look at me."

"I will, if you wish," she said with a trembling smile, "but it is useless——"

"That is what I shall find out in time. . . . You *must* meet my eyes. That is well; that is frank and sweet——"

"And useless—truly it is. . . . Please don't tell me—anything."

"You will not listen?"

"There is no chance for you—if you mean love.

I—I tell you in time, you see. . . . I am utterly frivolous—quite selfish and mercenary."

"I take my chance!"

"No, I give you none! Why do you interfere! A—a girl's policy costs her something if it be worth anything; whatever it costs it is worth it to me. . . . And I do not love you. In so short a time how could I?"

Then in his arms she fell a-trembling. Something blinded her eyes, and she turned her head sharply, only to encounter his lips on hers in a deep, clinging embrace that left her dazed, still resisting with the fragments of breath and voice.

"Not again—I beg—you. Let me go now. It is not best. Oh! truly, truly it is all wrong with us now." She bent her head, blinded with tears, swaying, stunned; then, with a breathless sound, turned in his arms to meet his lips, her hands contracting in his; and, confronting, they paused, suspending the crisis, young faces close, and hearts afire.

"Sylvia, I love you."

For an instant their lips clung; she had rendered him his kiss. Then, tremblingly, "It is useless . . . even though I loved you."

"Say it!"

"I do."

"*Say* it!"

"I—I cannot! . . . And it is no use—no use! I do not know myself—this way. My eyes—are wet. It is not like me; there is nothing of me in this girl you hold so closely, so confidently. . . . I do care for you—how can I help it? How could any woman help it? Is not that enough?"

"Until you are a bride, yes."

"A bride? Stephen!—I cannot——"

"You cannot help it, Sylvia."

"I must! I have my way to go."

"My way lies that way."

"No! no! I cannot do it; it is not best for me—not best for you. . . . I do care for you; you have taught me how to say it. But—you know what I have done—and mean to do, and must carry through. . . . Then, *how* can you love a girl like that?"

"Dear, I know the woman I love."

"Silly, she is what her life has made her—material, passionately selfish, unable to renounce the root of all evil. . . . Even if this—this happiness were ours always—I mean, if this madness could last our wedded life—I am not good enough, not noble enough, to forget what I might have had, and put away. . . . Is it not dreadful to admit it? Do you not know that self-contempt is part of the price? . . . I have no money. I know what you have. . . . I asked. And it is enough for a man who remains unmarried. . . . For I cannot 'make things do'; I cannot 'contrive'; I will not cling to the fringe of things, or play that heartbreaking rôle of the shabby expatriated on the Continent. . . . No person in this world ever had enough. I tell you I could find use for every flake of metal ever mined! . . . You see you do not know me. From my pretty face and figure you misjudge me. I am intelligent—not intellectual, though I might have been, might even be yet. I am cultivated, not learned; though I care for learning—or might, if I had time. . . . My rôle in life is to mount to a security too high for any question as to my dominance. . . . Can you take me there?"

"There are other heights, Sylvia."

"Higher?"

"Yes, dear."

"The spiritual; I know. I could not breathe there, if I cared to climb. . . . And I have told you what I am—all silk and lace and smooth-skinned selfishness." She looked at him wistfully. "If you can change me, take me." And she rose, facing him.

"I do not give you up," he said, with a savage note hardening his voice; and it thrilled her to hear it, and every drop of blood in her body leaped as she yielded to his arms again, heavy-lidded, trembling, confused, under the piercing sweetness of contact.

The perfume of her mouth, her hair, the consenting fingers locked in his, palm against palm, the lips, acquiescent, then afire at last, responsive to his own; and her eyes opening from the dream under the white lids—these were what he had of her till every vein in him pulsed flame. Then her voice, broken, breathless:

"Good night. Love me while you can—and forgive me! . . . Good night. . . . Where are we? All—all this must have stunned me, blinded me. . . . Is this my door, or yours? Hush! I am half dead with fear—to be here under the light again. . . . If you take me again, my knees will give way. . . . And I *must* find my door. Oh, the ghastly imprudence of it! . . . Good night . . . good night. I—I love you!"

CHAPTER VI

MODUS VIVENDI

After the first few days of his arrival at Shotover time had threatened to hang heavily on Mortimer's mottled hands. After the second day afield he recognised that his shooting career was practically over; he had become too bulky during the last year to endure the physical exertion; his habits, too, had at length made traitors of his eyes; a half hour's snipe-shooting in the sun, and the veins in his neck swelled ominously. Panting, eyes inflamed, fat arms wobbly, he had scored miss after miss, and laboured onward, sullenly persistent to the end. But it was the end. That cup day finished him; he recognised that he was done for. And, following the Law of Pleasure, which finishes us before we are finished with it, he did not experience any particular sense of deprivation in the prospect. Only the wholesome dread caging. But Mortimer, not yet done with self-indulgence in more convenient forms, cast about him within his new limits for occupation between those hours consecrated to the rites of the table and the card-room.

He drove four, but found that it numbed his arms, and that the sea air made him sleepy. Motor-cars agreed with him only when driving with a pretty woman. Forced through *ennui* to fish off the rocks, he soon tired of the sea-perch and rock-cod and the malodours of periwinkle and clam.

Then he frankly took to Major Belwether's sunny side of the gun-room, with illustrated papers and apples and decanter. But Major Belwether, always as careful of his digestion as of his financial secrets, blandly dodged the pressing invitations to rum and confidence, until Mortimer sulkily took up his headquarters in the reading-room, on the chance of his wife's moving elsewhere. Which she did, unobtrusively carrying Captain Voucher with her in a sudden zeal for billiard practice on rainy mornings now too frequent along the coast.

Mortimer possessed that mysterious talent, so common among the financially insolvent, for living lavishly on an invisible income. But, plan as he would, he had never been able to increase that income through confidential gossip with men like Quarrier or Belwether, or even Ferrall. What information his pretty wife might have extracted he did not know; her income had never visibly increased above the vanishing point, although, like himself, she denied herself nothing. One short, lively interview with her had been enough to drive all partnership ideas out of his head. If he wanted to learn anything financially advantageous to himself he must do it without her aid; and as he was perpetually in hopes of the friendly hint that never came, he still moused about when opportunity offered; and this also helped to kill time.

Besides, he was always studying women. Years before, Grace Ferrall had snapped her slim fingers in his face; and here, at Shotover, the field was limited. Mrs. Vendenning had left; Agatha Caithness was still a pale and reticent puzzle; Rena, Katharyn, and Eileen tormented him; Marion Page, coolly *au fait*, yawned in his face. There remained Sylvia, who, knowing nothing about his species, met him half-way with the sweet and sensitive deference due a somewhat battered and infirm gentleman of forty-eight—until a sleek aside from Major Belwether spoiled everything, as usual, for her, leaving her painfully conscious and perplexed between doubt and disgust.

Meanwhile, the wealthy master of Black Fells, Beverly Plank, had found encouragement enough at Shotover to venture on tentative informality. There was no doubt that ultimately he must be counted on in New York; but nobody except him was impatiently cordial for the event; and so, at the little house party, he slipped and slid from every attempt at closer quarters, until, rolling smoothly enough, he landed without much discomfort somewhere between Mr. and Mrs. Leroy Mortimer. And it was not a question as to "which would be good to him," observed Major Belwether, with his misleading and benevolent mirth; "it was, which would be goodest quickest!"

And Mrs. Mortimer, abandoning Captain Voucher by the same token, displayed certain warning notices perfectly comprehensive to her husband. And at first he was inclined to recognise defeat.

But the general insuccess which had so faithfully attended him recently had aroused the long-dormant desire for a general review of the situation with his wife—perhaps even the furtive hope of some conjugal arrangement tending toward an exchange of views concerning possible alliance.

The evening previous, to his intense disgust, host, hostess, and guests had retired early, in view of the point-shooting at dawn. For not only was there to be no point-shooting for him, but he had risen from the card-table heavily hit; and besides, for the first time his apples and port had disagreed with him.

As he had not risen until mid-day he was not sleepy. Books were an aversion equalled only by distaste for his own company. Irritated, bored, he had perforce sulkily entered the elevator and passed to his room, where there was nothing on earth for him to do except to thumb over last week's sporting periodicals and smoke himself stupid.

But it required more than that to ensnare the goddess of slumber. He walked about the room, haunted of slow thoughts; he stood at the rain-smeared pane, fat fingers resting on the glass. The richly flavoured cigar grew distasteful; and if he could not smoke, what, in pity's name, was he to do?

Involuntarily his distended eyes wandered to his wife's locked and bolted door; then he thought of Beverly Plank, and his own failure to fasten himself upon that anxiously over-cordial individual with his houses and his villas and his yachts and his investments!

He stepped to the switch and extinguished the lights in his room. Under the door, along the sill, a glimmer came from his wife's bed-chamber. He listened; the maid was still there; so he sat down in the darkness to wait; and by-and-by he heard the outer bedroom door close, and the subdued rustle of the departing maid.

Then, turning on his lights, he moved ponderously and jauntily to his wife's door and knocked discreetly.

Leila Mortimer came to the door and opened it; her hair was coiled for the night, her pretty figure outlined under a cascade of clinging lace.

"What is the matter?" she asked quietly.

"Are you point-shooting to-morrow?"

"No."

"I wanted to chat with you."

"I'm sorry. I'm driving to Wenniston, after breakfast, with Beverly Plank, and I need sleep."

"I want to talk to you," he repeated doggedly.

She regarded him for a moment in silence, then, with an assenting gesture, turned away into her room; and he followed, heavily apprehensive but resolved.

She had seated herself among a pile of cushions, one knee crossed over the other, her slim white foot half concealed by the silken toe of her slipper. And as he pulled a chair forward for himself, her pretty black eyes, which slanted a little, took his measure and divined trouble.

"Leila," he said, "why can't we have——"

"A cigarette?" she interrupted, indicating her dainty case on the table.

He took one, savagely aware of defiance somewhere. She lighted her own from a candle and settled back, studying the sequence of blue smoke-rings jetting upward to the ceiling.

"About this man Plank," he began, louder than he had intended through sheer self-mistrust; and his wife made a quick, disdainful sign of caution, which subdued his voice instantly. "Why can't we take him up—together, Leila?" he ended lamely, furious at his own uneasiness in a matter which might concern him vitally.

"I see no necessity of your taking him up," observed his wife serenely. "I can do what may be useful to him in town."

"So can I. There are clubs where he ought to be seen——"

"I can manage such matters much better."

"You can't manage everything," he insisted sullenly. "There are chances of various sorts——"

"Investments?" asked Mrs. Mortimer, with bright malice.

"See here, Leila, you have your own way too much. I say little; I make damned few observations; but I could, if I cared to. . . . It becomes you to be civil at least. I want to talk over this Plank matter with you; I want you to listen, too."

A shade of faint disgust passed over her face. "I am listening," she said.

"Well, then, I can see several ways in which the man can be of use to me. . . . I discovered him before you did, anyway. And what I want to do is to have a frank, honourable——"

"A—*what?*"

"—An honourable understanding with you, I said," he repeated, reddening.

"Oh!" She snapped her cigarette into the grate. "Oh! I see. And what then?"

"What then?"

"Yes; what then?"

"Why, you and I can arrange to stand behind him this winter in town, can't we?"

"And then?"

"Then—damn it!—the beggar can show his gratitude, can't he?"

"How?" she asked listlessly.

"By making good. How else?" he retorted savagely. "He can't welch because there's little to climb for beyond us; and even if he climbs, he can't ignore us. I can do as many things for him in my way as you can in yours. What is the use of being a pig, Leila? Anything he does for me isn't going to cancel his obligations to you."

"I know him better than you do," she observed, bending her head and pleating the lace on her knee. "There is Dutch blood in him."

"Not good Hollander, but common Dutch," sneered Mortimer. "And you mean he'll squeeze a dollar till the eagle screams—don't you?"

She sat silent, pleating her lace with steady fingers.

"Well, that's all right, too," laughed Mortimer easily; "let the Audubon Society worry over the eagle. It's a perfectly plain business proposition; we can do for him in a couple of winters what he can't do for himself in ten. Figure it out for yourself, Leila," he said, waving a mottled fat hand at her.

"I—have," she said under her breath.

"Then, is it settled?"

"Settled—how?"

"That we form ourselves into a benevolent society of two in behalf of Plank?"

"I—I don't want to, Roy," she said slowly.

"Why not?"

She did not say why not, seated there nervously pleating the fragile stuff clinging to her knee.

"Why not?" he repeated menacingly. Her unexpectedly quiescent attitude had emboldened him to a bullying tone—something he had not lately ventured on.

She raised her eyes to his: "I—rather like him," she said quietly.

"Then, by God! he'll pay for that!" he burst out, mask off, every inflamed feature shockingly congested.

"Roy! You dare not——"

"I tell you I——"

"You *dare* not!"

The palpitating silence lengthened; slowly the blood left the swollen veins. Heavy pendulous lip hanging, he stared at her from distended eyes, realising that he had forgotten himself. She was right. He dared not. And she held the whip-hand as usual.

For every suspicion he could entertain, she had evidence of a certainty to match it; for every chance that he might have to prove anything, she had twenty proven facts. And he knew it. Why they had, during all these years, made any outward pretence of conjugal unity they alone knew. The *modus vivendi* suited them better than divorce; that was apparent, or had been until recently. Recently Leila Mortimer had changed —become subdued and softened to a degree that had perplexed her husband. Her attitude toward him lacked a little of the bitterness and contempt she usually reserved for him in private; she had become more prudent, almost cautious at times.

"I'll tell you one thing," he said with a sudden snarl: "You'd better be careful there is no gossip about you and Plank."

She reddened under the insult.

"Now we'll see," he continued venomously, "how far you can go alone."

"Do you suppose," she asked calmly, "that I am afraid of a divorce court?"

The question so frankly astonished him that he sat agape, unable to reply. For years he had very naturally supposed her to be afraid of it—afraid of not being qualified to obtain it. Indeed, he had taken that for granted as the very corner-stone of their mutual toleration. Had he been an ass to do so? A vague alarm took possession of him; for, with that understanding, he had not been at all careful of his own behaviour, neither had he been at any particular pains to conceal his doings from her. His alarm increased. What had he against her, after all, except ancient suspicions, now so confused and indefinite that memory itself outlawed the case, if it ever really existed. What had she against him? Facts—unless she was more stupid than any of her sex he had ever encountered. And now, this defiance, this increasing prudence, this subtle change in her, began to make him anxious for the permanency of the small income she had allowed him during all these years—doled out to him, as he believed, though her dormant fear of him.

"What are you talking about?" he said harshly.

"I believe I mentioned divorce."

"Well, cut it out! D'ye see? Cut it, I say. You'd stand as much chance before a referee as a snowball in hell."

"There's no telling," she said coolly, "until one tries."

He glared at her, then burst into a laugh. "Rot!" he said thickly. "Talk sense, Leila! And keep this hard-headed Dutchman for yourself, if you feel that way about it. *I* don't want to butt in. I only thought—for old times' sake—perhaps you'd——"

"Good night," she managed to say, her disgust almost strangling her.

And he went, furtively, heavy-footed, perplexed, inwardly cursing his blunder in stirring up a sleeping lioness whom he had so long mistaken for a dozing cat.

For hours he sat in his room, or paced the four walls, doubtful, chagrined, furious by turns. Once he drew out a memorandum-book and stood under a lighted sconce, studying the figures. His losses at Shotover staggered him, but he had looked to his wife heretofore in such emergencies.

Certainly the time had come for him to do something. But what?—if his wife was going to strike such attitudes in the very face of decency? Certainly a husband in these days was without honour in his own household.

His uneasiness had produced a raging thirst. He punched an electric button with his fleshy thumb, and prowled around, waiting. Nobody came; he punched again, and looked at his watch. It astonished him to find the hour was three o'clock in the morning. That discovery, however, only appeared to increase his thirst. He opened the hall door, prepared to descend into the depths of the house and raid a sideboard; and as he thrust his heavy head out into the lighted corridor his eyes fell upon two figures standing at the open door of a bedroom. One was Siward; that was plain. *Who* was the girl he had kissed? One of the maids? Somebody's wife? Who?

Every dull pulse began to hammer in Mortimer's head. In his excitement he stepped half-way into the corridor, then skipped nimbly back, closing his door without a sound.

"Sylvia Landis, by all that's holy!" he breathed to himself, and sat down rather suddenly on the edge of the bed.

After a while he rose and crept to the door, opened it, glued his eyes to the crack, in time to catch a glimpse of Siward entering his own corridor alone.

And that night, Mortimer, lying awake in bed, busy with schemes, became conscious of a definite idea. It took shape and matured so suddenly that it actually shocked his moral sense. Then it scared him.

"But—but *that* is blackmail!" he whispered aloud. "A man can't do that sort of thing. What the devil ever put it into my head? . . . And there *are* men I know—women, too—scoundrelly blackguards, who'd use that information somehow; and make it pay, too. . . . The scoundrels!"

He squirmed down among the bedclothes with a sudden shiver; but the night had turned warm.

"Scoundrels!" he said, with milder emphasis. "Blackmailers! Contemptible pups!"

He fell asleep an hour later, muttering something incoherent about scoundrels and blackmail.

And meanwhile, in the darkened house, from all round came the noise of knocking on doors, sounds of people stirring—a low voice here and there, lights breaking out from transoms, the thud of rubber-shod heels, the rattle of cartridges from the echoing gun-room. For the guests at Shotover were awaking, lest the wet sky, whitening behind the east, ring with the whimpering wedges of wild-fowl rushing seaward over empty blinds.

. . . . .

The unusual stillness of the house in the late morning sunshine was pleasant to Miss Landis. She had risen very late, unconscious of the stir and movement before dawn; and it was only when a maid told her, as she came from her bath, that she remembered the projected point-shooting, and concluded, with an odd, happy sense of relief, that she was almost alone in the house.

A little later, glancing from her bedroom window for a fulfilment of the promise of the sun which a glimpse of blue sky heralded, she saw Leila Mortimer settling herself in the forward seat of a Mercedes, and Beverly Plank climbing in beside her; and she watched Plank steer the big machine across the wet lawn, while the machinist swung himself into the tonneau; and away they rolled, faster, faster, rushing out into the misty hinterland, where the long streak of distant forest already began to brighten, edged with the first rays of watery sunshine.

So she had the big house to herself—every bit of it!—and with it freedom from obligation, from comment, from demand or exaction; freedom from restraint; liberty to roam about, to read, to dream, to idle, to remember! Ah, that was what she needed—a quiet interval in this hurrying youth of hers to catch her breath once more, and stand still, and look back a day or two and remember.

So, to breakfast all alone was delicious; to stroll, unhurried, to the sideboard and leisurely choose among the fresh cool fruits; to loiter over cream-jug and cereal; to saunter out into the freshness of the world and breathe it, and feel the sun warming cheek and throat, and the little breezes from a sunlit sea stirring the bright strands of her hair.

In the increasing brilliancy of the sunshine she stretched out her hands, warming them daintily as she might twist them before the fire on the hearth. And here, at the fragrant hearth of the world, she stood, sweet and fresh as the morning itself, untroubled gaze intensely blue with the tint of the purple sea, sensitive lips scarcely parting in the dreaming smile that made her eyes more wonderful.

As the warmth grew on land and water, penetrating her body, a faintly delicious glow responded in her heart,—nothing at first wistful in the serene sense of well-being, stretching her rounded arms skyward in the unaccustomed luxury of a liberty which had become the naïvely unconscious licence of a child. The poise of sheer health stretched her to tiptoe; then the graceful tension relaxed, and her smooth fingers uncurled, tightened, and fell limp as her arms fell and her superb young figure straightened, confronting the sea.

Out over the rain-wet, odorous grass she picked her way, skirts swung high above the delicate contour of ankle and limb, following a little descending path she knew full of rocky angles, swept by pendant sprays of blackberry, and then down under the jutting rock, south through thickets of wild cherry along the crags, until, before her the way opened downward again where a tiny crescent beach glimmered white hot in the sun.

From his bedroom window Mortimer peeped forth, following her progress with a leer.

As she descended, noticing the rifts of bronzing sea-weed piled along the tide mark, her foot dislodged a tiny triangle of rock, which rolled clattering and ringing below; and as she sprang lightly to the sand, a man, lying full length and motionless as the heaped sea-weed, raised himself on one arm, turning his sun-dazzled eyes on her.

The dull shock of surprise halted her as Siward rose to his feet, still dazed, the sand running from his brown shooting-clothes over his tightly strapped puttees.

"Have you the faintest idea that I supposed you were here?" she asked briefly. Then, frank in her disappointment, she looked up at the cliffs overhead, where her line of retreat lay.

"Why did you not go with the others?" she added, unsmiling.

"I—don't know. I will, if you wish." He had coloured slowly, the frank disappointment in her face penetrating his surprise; and now he turned around, instinctively, also looking for the path of retreat.

"Wait," she said, aware of her own crude attitude and confused by it; "wait a moment, Mr. Siward. I don't mean to drive you away."

"It's self-exile," he said quietly; "quite voluntary, I assure you."

"Mr. Siward!"

And, as he looked up coolly, "Have you nothing more friendly to say to me? Is your friendship for me so limited that my first caprice oversteps the bounds? Must I always be in dread of wounding you when I give you the privilege of knowing me better than anybody ever knew me—of seeing me as I am, with all my faults, my failings, my impulses, my real self? . . . I don't know why the pleasure of being alone to-day should have meant exclusion for you, too. It was the unwelcome shock of seeing anybody—a selfish enjoyment of myself—that surprised me into rudeness. That is all. . . . Can you not understand?"

"I think so. I meant no criticism——"

"Wait, Mr. Siward!" as he moved slowly toward the path. "You force me to say other things, which you have no right to hear. . . . After last night"—the vivid tint grew in her face—"after such a night, is it not—natural—for a girl to creep off somewhere by herself and try to think a little?"

He had turned full on her; the answering colour crept to his forehead.

"Is *that* why?" he asked slowly.

"Is it not a reason?"

"It was my reason—for being here."

She bit her bright lip. This trend to the conversation was ominous, and she had meant to do her drifting alone in still sun-dreams, fearing no witness, no testimony, no judgment save her own self in court with herself.

"I—I suppose you cannot go—*now*," she reflected innocently.

"Indeed I can, and must."

"And leave me here to dig in the sand with my heels? *Merci!*"

"Do you mean——"

"I certainly do, Mr. Siward. I don't want to dream, now; I don't care to reflect. I did, but here you come blundering into my private world and upset my calculations and change my intentions! It's a shame, especially as you've been lying here doing what I wished to do for goodness knows how long!"

"I'm going," he said, looking at her curiously.

"Then you are very selfish, Mr. Siward."

"We will call it that," he said with an odd laugh.

"Very well." She seated herself on the sand and calmly shook out her skirts.

"About what time would you like to be called?" he asked smilingly.

"Thank you, I shall do no sun-dreaming."

"Please. It is good for you."

"No, it isn't good at all. And I *am* grateful to you for waking me," she retorted with a sudden gay malice that subdued him. And she, delicate nose in the air, laughingly watching him, went on with her punishment: "You see what you've done, don't you?—saved me from an entire morning wasted in sentimental reverie over what might have been. Now you can appreciate it, can't you?—your wisdom in appearing in the flesh to save a silly girl the effort of evoking you in the spirit! Ah, Mr. Siward, I am vastly obliged to you! Pray sit here beside me in the flesh, for fear that in your absence I might commit the folly that tempted me here."

His low running laughter accompanying her voice had stimulated her to a gay audacity, which for the instant extinguished in her the little fear of him she had been barely conscious of.

"Do you know," he said, "that you also aroused me from my sun-dreams?"

"Did I? And can't you resume them?"

"You save me the necessity."

"Oh, that is a second-hand compliment," she said disdainfully—"a weak plagiarism on what I conveyed very wittily. You were probably really asleep, and dreaming of bird-murder."

He waited for her to finish, then, amused eyes searching, he roamed about until high on a little drifted sand dune he found a place for himself; and while she watched him indignantly, he curled up in the sunshine, and, dropping his head on the hot sand, calmly closed his eyes.

"Upon—my—word!" she breathed aloud.

He unclosed his eyes. "Now you may dream; you can't avoid it," he observed lazily, and closed his eyes; and neither taunts nor jeers nor questions, nor fragments of shells flung with intent to hit, stirred him from his immobility.

She tired of the attempt presently, and sat silent, elbows on her thighs, hands propping her chin. Thoughts, vague as the fitful breeze, arose, lingered, and, like the breeze, faded, dissolved into calm, through which, cadenced by the far beat of the ebb tide, her heart echoed, beating the steady intervals of time.

She had not meant to dream, but as she sat there, the fine-spun golden threads flying from the whirling loom of dreams floated about her, settling over her, entangling her in unseen meshes, so that she stirred, groping amid the netted brightness, drawn onward along dim paths and through corridors of thought where, always beyond, vague splendours seemed to beckon.

Now lost, now restless, conscious of the perils of the shining path she followed, the rhythm of an ocean soothing her to false security, she dreamed on awake, unconscious of the tinted sea and sky which stained her eyes to hues ineffable. A long while afterward a small cloud floated across the sun; and, in the sudden shadow on the world, doubt sounded its tiny voice, and her ears listened, and the enchantment faded and died away.

Turning, she looked across the sand at the man lying there; her eyes considered him—how long she did not know, she did not heed—until, stirring, he looked up; and she paled a trifle and closed her eyes, stunned by the sudden clamour of pulse and heart.

When he rose and walked over, she looked up gravely, pouring the last handful of white sand through her stretched fingers.

"Did you dream?" he asked lightly.

"Yes."

"Did you dream true?"

"Nothing of my dream can happen," she said. "*You* know that, . . . don't you?"

"I know that we love . . . and that we dare not ignore it."

She suffered his arm about her, his eyes looking deeply into hers—a close, sweet caress, a union of lips, and her dimmed eyes' response.

"Stephen," she faltered, "how can you make it so hard for me? How can you force me to this shame!"

"Shame?" he repeated vaguely.

"Yes—this treachery to myself—when I cannot hope to be more to you—when I dare not love you too much!"

"You must dare, Sylvia!"

"No, no, no! I know myself, I tell you. I cannot give up what is offered—for *you!*—dearly, dearly as I do love you!" She turned and caught his hands in hers, flushed, trembling, unstrung. "I cannot—I simply cannot! How can you love me and listen to such wickedness? How can you still care for such a girl as I am—worse than mercenary, because I have a heart—or had, until you took it! Keep it; it is the only part of me not all ignoble."

"I will keep it—in trust," he said, "until you give yourself with it."

But she only shook her head wearily, withdrawing her hands from his, and for a time they sat silent, eyes apart.

Then—"There is another reason," she said wistfully.

He looked up at her, hesitated, and—"My habits?" he asked simply.

"Yes."

"I have them in check."

"Are you—certain?"

"I think I may be—now."

"Yet," she said timidly, "you lost one fight—since you knew me."

The dull red mantling his face wrung her heart. She turned impulsively and laid both hands on his shoulders. "*That* chance I would take, with all its uncertainty, all the dread inheritance you have come into. I love you enough for that; and if it turned out that—that you could not stem the tide, even with me to face it with you; and if the pity of it, the grief of it, killed me, I would take that chance—if you loved me through it all. . . . But there is something else. Hush; let me have my say while I find the words—something else you do not understand. . . . Turn your face a little; please don't look at me. This is what you do *not* know—that, in three generations, every woman of my race has—gone wrong. . . . *Every one!* and I am beginning—with such a marriage! . . . deliberately, selfishly, shamelessly, perfectly conscious of the frivolous, erratic blood in me, aware of the race record behind me.

"Once, when I knew nothing—before I—I met you—I believed such a marriage would not only permit me mental tranquillity, but safely anchor me in the harbour of convention, leaving me free to become what I am fashioned to become—autocrat and arbiter in my own world. And now! and now! I don't know—truly I don't know what I may become. Your love forces my hand. I am displaying all the shallowness, falseness, pettiness, all the mean, and cruel and callous character which must be truly my real self. . . . Only I shall not marry you! *You* are not to run the risk of what I might prove to be *when I remember in bitterness all I have renounced.* If I married you I should remember, unreconciled, what you cost me. Better for you and for me that I marry him, and let him bear with me when I remember that he cost me *you!*"

She bent over, almost double, closing her eyes with small clenched hands; and he saw the ring shimmering in the sunshine, and her hair, heavily, densely gold, and the white nape of her neck, and the tiny close-set ears, and the curved softness of cheek and chin; every smooth, childlike contour and mould—rounded arms, slim, flowing lines of body and limb—all valued at many millions by her as her own appraiser.

Suddenly, deep within him, something seemed to fail, die out—perhaps a tiny newly lighted flame of unaccustomed purity, the dawning flicker of aspiration to better things. Whatever it was, material, spiritual, was gone now, and where it had glimmered for a night, the old accustomed twilit doubt crept in—the same dull acquiescence—the same uncertainty of self, the familiar lack of will, of incentive, the congenial tendency to drift;

and with it came weariness—perhaps reaction from the recent skirmishes with that master-vice.

"I suppose," he said in a dull voice, "you are right."

"No, I am wrong—wrong!" she said, lifting her lovely face and heavy eyes. "But I have chosen my path. . . . And *you* will forget."

"I hope so," he said simply.

"If you hope so, you will."

He nodded, unconvinced, watching a flock of sandpipers whirling into the cove like a gray snow-squall and fearlessly settling on the beach.

After a while, with a long breath: "Then it is settled," she concluded.

If she expected corroboration from him she received none; and perhaps she was not awaiting it. She sat very still, her eyes lost in thought.

And Mortimer, peeping down at them over the thicket above, yawned impatiently and glanced about him for the most convenient avenue of self-effacement when the time arrived.

CHAPTER VII

PERSUASION

THE days of the house-party at Shotover were numbered. A fresh relay of guests was to replace them on Monday, and so they were making the most of the waning week on lawn and marsh, in covert and blind, or motoring madly over the State, or riding in parties to Vermillion Light. Tennis and lawn bowls came into fashion; even water polo and squash alternated on days too raw for more rugged sport.

And during all these days Beverly Plank appeared with unflagging persistence and assiduity, until his familiar, big, round head and patient, delft-blue, Dutch eyes became a matter of course at Shotover, indoors and out.

It was not that he was either accepted, tolerated, or endured; he was simply there, and nobody took the trouble to question his all-pervading presence until everybody had become too much habituated to him to think about it at all.

The accomplished establishment of Beverly Plank was probably due as much to his own obstinate and good-tempered persistence as to Mrs. Mortimer. He was a Harvard graduate—there are all kinds of them—enormously wealthy, and though he had no particular personal tastes to gratify, he was willing and able to gratify the tastes of others. He did whatever anybody else did, and did it well enough to be amusing; and as lack of intellectual development never barred anybody from any section of the fashionable world, it seemed fair to infer that he would land where he wanted to, sooner or later.

Meanwhile, Mrs. Mortimer led him about with the confidence that was her perquisite; and the chances were that in due time he would have house-parties of his own at Black Fells—not the kind he had wisely denied himself the pleasure of giving, with such neighbours as the Ferralls to observe, but the sort he desired. However, there were many things to be accomplishd for him and by him before he could expect to use his great yacht and his estates and his shooting boxes and the vast granite mansion recently completed and facing Central Park just north of the new palaces built on the edges of the outer desert where Fifth Avenue fringes the hundreds.

Meanwhile, he had become in a measure domesticated at Shotover, and Shotover people gradually came to ride, drive, and motor over the Fells, which was a good beginning, though not necessarily a promise for anything definite in the future.

Mortimer, riding a huge chestnut—he could still wedge himself into a saddle—had now made it a regular practice to affect the jocular early-bird squire, and drag Plank out of bed. And Plank, in no position to be anything but flattered by such *sans gêne,* laboriously and gratefully splashed through his bath, wallowed amid the breakfast plates, and mounted a hunter for long and apparently aimless gallops with Mortimer.

His acquaintance among people who knew Mortimer being limited, he had no means of determining the latter's social value except through hearsay and a toadying newspaper or two. Therefore he was not yet aware of Mortimer's perennial need of money; and when Mortimer laughingly alluded to his poverty, Plank accepted the proposition in a purely comparative sense, and laughed, too, his thrifty Dutch soul untroubled by misgivings.

Meanwhile, Mortimer had come, among other things, on information; how much, and precisely of what nature, he was almost too much ashamed to admit definitely, even to himself. Still, the idea that had led him into this sudden intimacy with Plank, vague or not, persisted; and he was always hovering on the edge of hinting at something which might elicit a responsive hint from the flattered master of Black Fells.

There was much about Plank that was unaffected, genuine, even simple, in one sense; he cared for people for their own sakes; and only stubborn adherence to a dogged ambition had enabled him to dispense with the society of many people he might easily have cultivated and liked—people nearer his own sort; and that, perhaps, was the reason he so readily liked Mortimer, whose coarse fibre soon wore through the polish when rubbed against by a closer, finer fibre. And Plank liked him aside from gratitude; and they got on famously on the basis of such mutual recognition. Then, one day, very suddenly, Mortimer stumbled on something valuable—a thread, a mere clew, so astonishing that for an instant it absolutely upset all his unadmitted theories and calculations.

It was nothing—a vague word or two—a forced laugh—and the scared silence of this man Plank, who had blundered on the verge of a confidence to a man he liked.

A moment of amazement, of half-incredulous suspicion, of certainty; and Mortimer pounced playfully upon him like a tiger—a big, fat, friendly, jocose tiger:

"Plank, is *that* what you're up to!"

"Up to! Why, I never thought of such a——"

"Haw! haw!" roared Mortimer. "If you could only see your face!"

And Beverly Plank, red as a beet, comfortably suffused with reassurance under the reaction from his scare, attempted to refute the other's conclusions: "It doesn't mean anything, Mortimer. She's just the handsomest girl I ever saw. I know she's engaged. I only admired her a lot."

"You're not the only man," said Mortimer blandly, still striving to reconcile his preconceived theories with the awkward half-confession of this great, red-fisted, hulking horseman riding at his stirrup.

"I wouldn't have her dream," stammered Plank, "that I had ever thought of such a——"

"Why not? It would only flatter her."

"Flatter a woman who is engaged to marry another man!" gasped Plank.

"Certainly. Do you think any woman ever had enough admiration in this world?" asked Mortimer coolly. "And as for Sylvia Landis, she'd be tickled to death if anybody hinted that you had ever admired her."

"Good Lord!" exclaimed Plank, alarmed; "You wouldn't make a joke of it! you wouldn't be careless about such a thing! And there's Quarrier! I'm not on joking terms with him; I'm on most formal terms."

"Quarrier!" sneered the other, flicking at his stirrup with his crop. "He's on formal terms with everybody, including himself. He never laughed on purpose in his life; once a month only, to keep his mouth in; that's his limit. Do you suppose any woman would stand for him if a better man looked sideways at her?" And, reversing his riding crop, he deliberately poked Mr. Plank in the ribs.

"A—a better man!" muttered Plank, scarce crediting his ears.

"Certainly. A man who can *make* good, *is* good; but a man who can make *better* is *it* with the ladies—God bless 'em!" he added, displaying a heavy set of teeth.

Beverly Plank knew perfectly well that, in the comparison so delicately suggested by Mortimer, his material equipment could be scarcely compared to the immense fortune controlled by Howard Quarrier; and as he thought it, his reflections were put into words by Mortimer, airily enough:

"Nobody stands a chance in a show-down with Quarrier. But——"

Plank gaped until the tension became unbearable.

"But—what?" he blurted out.

"Plank," said Mortimer solemnly, and his voice vibrated with feeling, "Let me do a little thinking before I ask you a—a vital question."

But Plank had become agitated again, and he said something so bluntly that Mortimer wheeled on him, glowering:

"Look here, Plank: you don't suppose I'm capable of repeating a confidence, do you?—if you choose to make me understand it's a confidence."

"It isn't a confidence; it isn't anything; I mean it *is* confidential, of course. All there's in it is what I said—or rather what you took me up on so fast," ended Plank, abashed.

"About your being in love with Syl——"

"Confound it!" roared Plank, crimson to his hair; and he set his heavy spurs to his mount and plunged forward in a storm of dust. Mortimer followed, silent, profoundly immersed in his own thoughts and deductions; and as he pounded along, turning over in his mind all the varied information he had so unexpectedly obtained in these last few days, a dull excitement stirred him, and he urged his huge horse forward in a thrill of rising exhilaration such as seizes on men who hunt, no matter what they hunt—the savage, swimming sense of intoxication which marks the man who chases the quarry not for its own value, but because it is his nature to chase and ride down and enjoy spoils.

And all that afternoon, having taken to his room on pretence of neuralgia, he lay sprawled on his bed, thinking, thinking. Not that he meant harm to anybody, he told himself very frequently. He had, of course, information which certain degraded men might use in a contemptible way, but he, Mortimer, did not resemble such men in any particular. All he desired was to do Plank a good turn. There was nothing disreputable in doing a wealthy man a favour. . . . And God knew a wealthy man's gratitude was necessary to him at that very moment—gratitude substantially acknowledged. . . . He liked Plank—wished him well; that was all right, too; but a man is an ass who doesn't wish himself well also. . . . Two birds with one stone. . . . Three! for he hated Quarrier. Four! . . . for he had no love for his wife. . . . Besides, it would teach Leila a wholesome lesson—teach her that he still counted; serve her right for her disgusting selfishness about Plank.

No, there was to be nothing disreputable in his proceedings; that he would be very careful about. . . . Probably Major Belwether might express his gratitude substantially if he, Mortimer, went to him frankly and volunteered *not* to mention to Quarrier the scene he had witnessed between Sylvia Landis and Stephen Siward at three o'clock in the morning in the corridor; and if, in playful corroboration, he displayed the cap and raincoat and the big fan, all crushed, which objects of interest he had discovered later in the bay-window. . . . Yes, probably Major Belwether would be very grateful, because he wanted Quarrier in the family; he needed Quarrier in his business. . . . But, faugh! that was close enough to blackmail to rub off! . . . No! . . . *No!* He wouldn't go to Belwether and promise any such thing! . . . On the contrary, he felt it his duty to inform Quarrier! Quarrier had a right to know what sort of a girl he was threatened with for life! . . . A man ought not to let another man go blindly into such a marriage. . . . Men owed each other something, even if they were not particularly close friends. . . . And he had always had a respect for Quarrier, even a sort of liking for him—yes, a distinct liking! . . . And, anyhow, women were devils! and it behooved men to get together and stand for one another!

Quarrier would give her her walking papers damned quick! . . . And, in her humiliation, is there anybody mad enough to fancy that she wouldn't snap up Plank in such a fix? . . . And make it look like a jilt for Quarrier? . . . But Plank must do his part on the minute; Plank must step up in the very nick of time; Plank, with his millions and his ambitions, was bound to be a winner anyway, and Sylvia might as well be his pilot and use his money. . . . And Plank would be very, very grateful—very useful, a very good friend to have. . . . And Leila would learn at last that he, Mortimer, had cut his wisdom teeth, by God!

As for Siward, he amounted to nothing; probably was one of that contemptible sort of men who butted in and kissed a pretty girl when he had the chance. He, Mortimer, had only disgust for such amateurs of the social by-ways; for he himself kept to the highways, like any self-respecting professional, even when a tour of the highways sometimes carried him below stairs. There was no romantic shilly-shallying fol-de-rol about him. Women learned what to expect from him in short order. *En garde, Madame!—ou Mademoiselle—tant pis!*

He laughed to himself and rolled over, digging his head into the pillows and stretching his fat hands to ease their congestion. And most of all he amused himself with figuring out the exact degree of his wife's astonishment and chagrin when, without consulting her, he achieved the triumph of Quarrier's elimination and the theatrical entry of Beverly Plank upon the stage. He laughed when he thought of Major Belwether, too, confounded under the loss of such a nephew-in-law, humiliated, crushed, all his misleading jocularity, all his sleek pink-and-white suavity, all his humbugging *bonhomie* knocked out of him, leaving only a rumpled, startled old gentleman, who bore an amusing resemblance to a very much mussed-up buck-rabbit.

"Haw! haw!" roared Mortimer, rolling about in his bed and kicking the slippers from his fat feet. Then, remembering that he was supposed to be suffering silently in his room, he hunched up to a sitting posture and regarded his environment with a subdued grin.

Everything seems easy when it seems funny. After all, the matter was simple—absurdly simple. A word to Quarrier, and crack! the match was off! Girl mad as a hornet, but staggered, has no explanation to offer; man frozen stiff with rage, mute as an iceberg. Then, zip! Enter Beverly Plank—the girl's rescuer at a pinch—her preserver, the saviour of her "face," the big, highly coloured, leaden-eyed *deus ex machina*. Would she take fifty cents on the dollar? *Would* she? to buy herself a new "face"? And put it all over Quarrier? And live happy ever after? *Would* she? Oh, not at all!

And Mortimer rolled over in another paroxysm; which wasn't good for him, and frightened him enough to lie still awhile and think how best he might cut down on his wine and spirits.

The main thing, after all, was to promise Plank his opportunity, but not tell him how he was to obtain it; for Mortimer had an uneasy idea that there was something of the Puritan deep planted under the stolid young man's hide, and that he might make some absurd and irrelevant objection to the perfectly proper methods employed by his newly self-constituted guide and mentor. No; that was no concern of Plank's. All he had to do was to be ready. As for Quarrier, anybody could forecast his action when once convinced of Sylvia's behaviour.

He lay there pondering several methods of imparting the sad but necessary information to Quarrier. One thing was certain: there was not now time enough before the house-party dissolved to mould Plank into acquiescent obedience. That must be finished in town—unless Plank invited him to stay at the Fells after his time was up at Shotover. By Heaven! That was the idea! And there'd be a chance for him at cards! . . . Only, of course, Plank would ask Leila too. . . . But what did he care! He was no longer afraid of her; he'd soon be independent of her and her pittance. Let her go to the courts for her divorce! Let her——

He sat up rather suddenly, perplexed with a new idea which, curiously enough, had not appealed to him before. The astonishing hint so coolly dropped by his wife concerning her fearlessness of divorce proceedings had only awakened him to the consciousness of his own vulnerability and carelessness of conduct.

Now it occurred to him, for the first time, that if it were not a mere bluff on Leila's part, this sudden coquetting with the question of divorce might indicate an ulterior object. Was Leila considering his elimination in view of this ulterior object? *Was* there an ulterior gentleman somewhere prepared to replace him? If so, where? And who?

His wife's possible indiscretions had never interested him; he simply didn't care—had no curiosity, as long as appearances were maintained. And she had preserved appearances with a skill which required all the indifferent and easy charity of their set to pretend completely deceived everybody. Yes, he gave her credit for that; she had been clever. Nobody outside of the social register knew the true state of affairs in the house of Leroy Mortimer—which, after all, was all anybody cared about.

And so, immersed in the details of his dirty little drama, he pondered over the possibility of an ulterior gentleman as he moved heavily to and fro, dressing himself—his neuralgia being much better—and presently descended the stairs to find everybody absent, engaged, as a servant explained, in a game of water basket-ball in the swimming pool. So he strolled off toward the north wing of the house, which had been built for the squash-courts and swimming pool.

There was a good deal of an uproar in the big gymnasium as Mortimer walked in, threading his way through the palms and orange-trees; much splashing in the pool, cries and stifled laughter, and the quick rattle of applause from the gallery of the squash-courts.

The Page boys and Rena and Eileen on one side

were playing the last match game against Sylvia, Marion Page, Siward, and Ferrall on the other; the big, slippery, glistening ball was flying about through storms of spray. Marion caught it, but her brother Gordon got it away; then Ferrall secured it and dived toward the red goal; but Rena Bonnesdel caught him under water; the ball bobbed up, and Sylvia flung both arms around it with a little warning shout and hurled it back at Siward, who shot forward like an arrow, his opponents gathering about him in full cry, amid laughter and excited applause from the gallery, where Grace Ferrall and Captain Voucher were wildly offering odds on the blue, and Alderdene and Major Belwether were thriftily booking them.

Mortimer climbed the slippery, marble stairway as fast as his lack of breath permitted, anxious for his share of the harvest if the odds were right. He ignored his wife's smilingly ironical offer, seeing no sense in bothering about money already inside the family; but he managed to make several apparently desirable wagers with Katharyn Tassel and one with Beverly Plank, who was also obstinately backing the blues, the losing side. Sylvia played forward for the blues.

Agatha Caithness, sleeves rolled up, tall and slim and strangely pale in her white flannels, came from the squash-court with Quarrier to watch the finish; and Mortimer observed her sidewise, blinking, irresolute, for he had never understood her and was always a trifle afraid of her. A pair of icicles, she and Quarrier, with whom he had never been on betting terms; so he made no suggestions in that direction, and presently became absorbed in the splashing battle below. Indeed, such a dashing of foam and showering of spray was taking place that the fronds of the big palms hung dripping amid drenched blossoms overweighted and prone on the wet marble edges of the pool.

Suddenly, through the confused blur of foam and spray, the big, glistening ball shot aloft and remained.

"Blue! Blue!" exclaimed Grace Ferrall, clapping her hands; and a little whirlwind of cries and hand clapping echoed from the gallery as the breathless swimmers came climbing out of the pool, with scarcely wind enough left for a word or strength for a gesture toward the laughing crowd above.

Mortimer, disgusted, turned away, already casting about him for somebody to play cards with—it being his temperament and his temper to throw good money after bad. But Quarrier and Miss Caithness had already returned to the squash-courts, the majority of the swimmers to their several dressing-rooms, and Grace Ferrall's party, equipped for motoring, to the lawn, where they lost little time in disappearing into the golden haze which a sudden shift of wind had spun out of the cloudless afternoon's sunshine.

However, he got Marion, and also, as usual, the two men who had made a practice of taking away his money—Major Belwether and Lord Alderdene. He hadn't particularly wanted them; he wanted somebody he could play with, like Siward, for example, or even the two ten-dollar Pages; not that their combined twenty would do him much good, but it would at least permit him the pleasures of the card-table without personal loss.

But the Pages had retired to dress, and Voucher was for motoring, and he had no use for his wife, and he was afraid of Plank's game, and Siward, seated on the edge of the pool and sharing a pint of ginger-ale with Sylvia Landis, shook his head at the suggestion and resumed his division of the ginger-ale.

Plank and Leila Mortimer came down to congratulate them. Sylvia, always instinctively and particularly nice to people of Plank's sort whom she occasionally encountered, was so faultlessly amiable, that Plank, who had never before permitted himself the privilege of monopolising her, found himself doing it so easily that it kept him in a state of persistent mental intoxication.

That slow, sweet, upward training inflection to a statement which instantly became a confided question was an unconscious trick which had been responsible, in Sylvia's brief life, for more mistakes than anything else. Like others before him, Beverly Plank made the mistake that the sweetness of voice and the friendliness of eyes were particularly personal to him, in tribute to qualities he had foolishly enough hitherto not suspected in himself. Now he suspected them, and whatever of real qualities desirable had been latent in him also appeared at once, confirming his modest suspicions. Certainly he was a wit! Was not this perfectly charming girl's responsive and delicious laughter proof enough? Certainly he was epigrammatic! Certainly he could be easy, polished, amusing, sympathetic, and vastly interesting all the while. Could he not divine it in her undivided attention, the quick, amused flicker of recognition animating her beautiful face when he had turned a particularly successful phrase or taken a verbal hurdle without a cropper? And above all, her kindness to him impressed him; her natural and friendly pleasure in being agreeable. Here he was already on an informal footing with one of the persons of whom he had been most shy and uncertain. If people were going to be as considerate of him as she had proved, why—why——

His dull, Dutch-blue eyes returned to her, fascinated. The conquest of what he desired and meant to have became merged in a vague plan which included such a marriage as he had dreamed of.

Somebody had once told him that a man who could afford to dress for dinner could go anywhere; meaning that, being a man, nature had fitted his feet with the paraphernalia for climbing as high as he cared to climb.

There was just enough truth in the statement to determine him to use his climbing irons; and he had done so, carrying his fortune with him, which had proved neither an impediment nor an aid so far. But now he had concluded that neither his god-sent climbing irons, his amiability, his obstinacy, his mild, tireless persistency, nor his money counted. It had come to a crisis where personal worth and sterling character must carry him through sheer merit to the inner temple—that inner temple of raw gold whose altars are served by a sexless skeleton in cap and bells!

. . . . .

Siward, inclined to be amused by the duration of the trance into which Plank had fallen, watched the progress of that bulky young man's infatuation as he sat there on the pool's marble edge, exchanging trivial views on trivial subjects with Mrs. Leroy Mortimer.

But her conversation, even when inconsequential, was never wearisome except when she made it so for her husband's benefit. Features, person, personality, and temperament were warmly exotic; her dark eyes with their slight Japanese slant, the clear olive skin with its rose bloom, the temptation of mouth and slender neck, were always provocative of the audacity in men which she could so well meet with amusement or surprise, or at times with a fascinating audacity of her own wholly charming because of its setting.

Once, in their history, during her early married life,

Siward had been very sentimental about her; but neither he nor she had approached the danger line closer than to make daring eyes at one another across the frontiers of good taste. And their youthful enchantment had faded so naturally, so pleasantly, that always there had remained to them both an agreeable after-taste—a sort of gay understanding which almost invariably led to mutual banter when they encountered. But now something appeared to be lacking in their rather listless badinage—something of the usual flavour which once had salted even a laughing silence with significance. Siward, too, had ceased to be amused at the spectacle of Plank's calf-like infatuation; and Leila Mortimer's bored smile had lasted so long that her olive-pink cheeks were stiff, and she relaxed her fixed features with a little shrug that was also something of a shiver. Then, looking prudently around, she encountered Siward's eyes; and during a moment's hesitation they considered one another with an increasing curiosity that slowly became tentative intelligence. And her eyes said very plainly and wickedly to Siward's: "Oho, my friend! So it bores you to see Mr. Plank monopolising an engaged girl who belongs to Howard Quarrier!"

And his eyes, wincing, denying, pretending ignorance too late, suddenly narrowed in vexed retaliation: "Speak for yourself, my lady! You're no more pleased than I am!"

The next moment they both regretted the pale flash of telepathy. There had been something wounded in his eyes; and she had not meant that. No; a new charity for the hapless had softened her wonderfully within a fortnight's time, and a self-pity, not entirely ignoble, had subdued the brilliancy of her dark eyes, and made her tongue more gentle in dealing with all failings. Besides, she was not yet perfectly certain what ailed her, never having really cared for any one man before. No, she was not at all certain. . . . But in the meanwhile she was very sorry for herself, and for all those who drained the bitter cup that might yet pass from her shrinking lips. Who knows! "Stephen," she said under her breath, "I didn't mean to hurt you. . . . Don't scowl. Listen. I have already entirely forgotten the nature of my offense. *Pax,* if you please."

He refused to understand; and she understood that, too; and she gazed critically upon Sylvia Landis as a very young mother might inspect a rival infant with whom her matchless offspring was coquetting.

Then, without appearing to, she took Plank away from temptation; so skilfully that nobody except Siward understood that the young man had been incontinently removed. He, Plank, never doubting that he was a perfectly free agent, decided that the time had arrived for triumphant retirement. It had; but Leila Mortimer, not he, had rendered the decision, and so cleverly that it appeared even to Plank himself that he had dragged her off with him rather masterfully. Clearly he was becoming a devil of a fellow!

Sylvia turned to Siward, glanced up at him, hesitated, and began to laugh consciously:

"What do you think of my latest sentimental acquisition?"

"He'd be an ornament to a stock farm," replied Siward, out of humour.

"How brutal you *can* be!" she mused, smiling.

"Nonsense! He's a plain bounder, isn't he?"

"I don't know. . . . Is he? He struck me a trifle appealingly—even pathetically; they usually do, that sort. . . . As though the trouble they took could ever be worth the time they lose! . . . There are dozens of men I know who are far less presentable than this highly coloured and robust young human being; and yet they are part of the accomplished scheme of things—like degenerate horses, you know—always pathetic to me; but they're still horses, for all that. *Quid rides?* Species of the same genus can cross, of course, but I had rather be a donkey than a mule. . . . And *if* I were a donkey I'd sing and cavort with my own kind, and let horses flourish their own heels inside the accomplished scheme of things. . . . Now *I* have been brutal. But—I'm easily coloured by my environment."

She sat, smiling maliciously down at the water, smoothing out the soaked skirt of her swimming suit, and swinging her legs reflectively.

"Are you reconciled?" she asked presently.

"To what?"

"To leaving Shotover. To-day is our last day, you know. To-morrow we all go; and next day these familiar walls will ring with other voices, my poor friend:

"'Yon rising moon that looks for us again—
How oft hereafter will she wax and wane;
How oft hereafter, rising, look for us
Through this same mansion—and for *one* in vain!'"

"That is I—the *one*, you know. *You* may be here again; but I—*I* shall not be I if I ever come to Shotover again."

Her stockinged heels beat the devil's tattoo against the marble sides of the pool. She reached up above her head, drawing down a flowering branch of Japanese orange, and caressed her delicate nose with the white blossoms, dreamily, then, mischievously: "I'm accustoming myself to this most significant perfume," she said, looking at him askance. And she deliberately hummed the wedding march, watching the colour rise in his sullen face.

"If you had the courage of a sparrow you'd make life worth something for us both," he said.

"I know it; I haven't; but I seem to possess the remainder of his lordship's traits—inconsequence, self-centred selfishness, the instinct for Fifth Avenue nest-building—all the feathered vices, all the unlovely personality and futility and uselessness of my prototype. . . . Only, as you observe, I lack the quality of courage."

"I don't know how much courage it requires to do what you're going to do," he said sulkily.

"Don't you? Sometimes, when you wear a scowl like that, I think that it may require no more courage than I am capable of. . . . And sometimes—I don't know."

She crossed her knees, one slender ankle imprisoned in her hand, leaning forward thoughtfully above the water.

"Our last day," she mused; "for we shall never be just you and I again—never again, my friend, after we leave this rocky coast of Eden. . . . I shall have hints of you in the sea-wind and the sound of the sea; in the perfume of autumn woods, in the whisper of stirring leaves when the white birches put on their gold crowns next year." She smiled, turning to him, a little gravely: "When the Lesser Children return with April, I shall not forget you, Mr. Siward, nor forget your mercy of a day on them; nor your comradeship, nor your sweetness to me. . . . Nor your charity for me, nor all that you overlook so far in me,—under the glamour of a spell that seems to hold you still, and that still holds me.

. . . I can answer for my constancy so far, until one more spring and summer have come and gone—until one more autumn comes, and while it lasts—as long as any semblance of the setting remains which had once framed you; I can answer for my constancy as long as that. . . . Afterwards, the snow!—symbol of our separation. I am to be married a year from November first."

He looked up at her in dark surprise, for he had heard that their wedding date had been set for the coming winter.

"A year's engagement?" he repeated, unconvinced.

"It was my wish. I think that is sufficient for everybody concerned." Then, averting her face, which had suddenly lost a little of its colour: "A year is little enough," she said impatiently. "I—what has happened to us requires an interval—a decent interval for its burial. . . . Death is respectable in any form. What dies between you and me can have no resurrection . . . under the snow. . . . So I bring to the burial my tribute—a year of life, a year of constancy, my friend; symbol of an eternity I could have given you had I been worth it." She looked up, flushed, the forced smile stamped on lips still trembling. "Sentiment in such a woman as I! 'A spectacle for Gods and men,' you are saying—are you not? And perhaps sentiment with me is only an ancient instinct, a latent ancestral quality for which I, ages later, have no use." She was laughing easily. "No use for sentiment, as our bodies have no use for that fashionable little *cul-de-sac*, you know, though wise men say it once served its purpose, too. . . . Stephen Siward, *what* do you think of me now?"

"I am learning," he replied simply.

"What, if you please?"

"Learning a little about what I am losing."

"You mean—me?"

"Yes."

She bent forward impulsively, balancing her body on the pool's rim with both arms, dropping her knee until her ankles swung interlocked above the water. "Listen," she said in a low, distinct voice: "What you lose is no other man's gain! If I warm and expand in your presence—if I say clever things sometimes—if I am intelligent, sympathetic, and amusing—it is because of *you*. You inspire it in me. Normally I am the sort of girl you first met at the station. I tell you that I don't know myself now—that I have not known myself since I knew you. Qualities of understanding, ability to appreciate, to express myself without employing the commonplaces, subtleties of intercourse—all, maybe, were latent in me, but sterile, until you came into my life. . . . And when you go, then, lacking impulse and incentive, the new facility, the new sensitive alertness, the unconscious self-confidence, all will smoulder and die out in me. . . . I know it; I realise that it was due to you—part of me that I should never have known, of which I should have remained totally ignorant, had it not blossomed suddenly, stimulated by you alone."

Slowly the clouded seriousness of her blue eyes cleared, and the smile began to glimmer again. "That is your revenge; you recommit me to my commonplace self; you restore me to my tinsel career, practically a dolt. Shame on you, Stephen Siward, to treat a poor girl so! . . . But it's just as well. Blunted perceptions, according to our needs, you know; and so life is tempered for us all, else we might not endure it long. . . . A pleasantly morbid suggestion for a day like this, is it not? . . . Shall we take a farewell plunge, and dress? You know we say good-bye to-morrow."

"Where do you go from here?"

"To Lenox; the Claymores have asked us for a week; after that, Hot Springs for another two weeks or so; after that, to Oyster Bay. . . . Mr. Quarrier opens his house on Sedge Point," she added demurely, "but I don't think he expects to invite you to 'The Sedges.'"

"How long do you stay there?" asked Siward irritably.

"Until we go to town in December."

"What will you find to do all that time in Oyster Bay?" he asked more irritably.

"What a premature question! The yacht is there. Besides, there's the usual neighbourhood hunting, with the usual packs and inevitable set; the usual steeple-chasing; the usual exchange of social amenities; the usual driving and riding; the usual, my poor friend, the usual, in all its uncompromising certainty. . . . And what are you to do?"

"When?"

"After you leave here?"

"I don't know."

"You don't know where you are going?"

"I'm going to town."

"And then?"

"I don't know."

"Oh, but haven't you been asked somewhere? You have, of course."

"Yes, and I have declined."

"Matters of business," she inferred. "Too bad!"

"Oh, no."

"Then," she concluded, laughing, "you don't care to tell me where you are going."

"No," he said thoughtfully, "I don't care to tell you."

She laughed again carelessly, and, placing one hand on the tiled pavement, sprang lightly to her feet.

"A last plunge?" she asked, as he rose at her side.

"Yes, one last plunge together. Deep! Are you ready?"

She raised her white arms above her head, finger-tips joined, poised an instant on the brink, swaying forward; then, at his brief word, they flashed downward together, cutting the crystalline sea-water, shooting like great fish over the glass-tiled bed, shoulder to shoulder under the water; and opening their eyes, they turned toward one another with a swift outstretch of hands, an uncontrollable touch of lips, the very shadow of contact; then cleaving upward, rising to the surface to lie breathlessly floating, arms extended, and the sun filtering down through the ground-glass roof above.

"We are perfectly crazy," she breathed. "I'm quite mad; I see that. On land it's bad enough for us to misbehave; but submarine sentiment! We'll be growing scales and tails presently. . . . Did you ever hear of a Southern bird—a sort of hawk, I think—that almost never alights; that lives and eats and sleeps its whole life away on the wing? and even its courtship, and its honeymoon? Grace Ferrall pointed one out to me last winter, near Palm Beach—a slender bird, part black, part snowy white, with long, pointed, delicate wings like an enormous swallow; and all day, all night, it floats and soars and drifts in the upper air, never resting, never alighting except during its brief nesting season. . . . Think of the exquisite bliss of drifting one's life through in mid-air—to sleep, balanced on light wings, upborne by invisible currents flowing under the stars—to sail dreamily through the long sunshine, to float under the moon! . . . And at last, I suppose, when its time has come, down it whirls out of the sky, stone dead! . . . There is something thrilling in such a death —something magnificent. . . . And in the exquisitely spiritual honeymoon, vague as the shadow of a rainbow, is the very essence and aroma of that impalpable Paradise we women prophesy in dreams! . . . More sentiment! Heigho! My brother is the weeping crocodile, and the five winds are my wits. . . . Shall we dress? Even with a maid and the electric air-blast it will take time to dry my hair and dress it."

. . . . .

When he came out of his dressing-room she was apparently still in the hands of the maid. So he sauntered through the house as far as the library, and drawing a cheque-book from one pocket, fished out a memorandum-book from another, and began to cast up totals with a view to learning something about the various debts contracted at Shotover.

He seemed to owe everybody. Fortune had smitten him hip and thigh; and, a trifle concerned, he began covering a pad with figures until he knew where he stood. Then he drew a considerable cheque to Major Belwether's order, another to Alderdene. Others followed to other people for various amounts; and he was very busily at work when, aware of another presence near, he turned around in his chair. Sylvia Landis was writing at a desk in the corner, and she looked up, nodding the little greeting that she always reserved for him even after five minutes' separation.

"I'm writing cheques," she said. "I suppose you're writing to your mother."

"Why do you think so?" he asked curiously.

"You write to her every day, don't you?"

"Yes," he said, "but how do you know?"

She looked at him with unblushing deliberation. "You wrote every day. . . . If it was to a woman, I wanted to know. . . . And I told Grace Ferrall that it worried me. And then Grace told me. Is there any other confession of my own pettiness that I can make to you."

"Did you really care to whom I was writing?" he asked slowly.

"Care? I—it worried me. Was it not a pitifully common impulse? 'Sisters under our skin,' you know —I and the maid who dresses me. She would have snooped; *I* didn't; that's the only generic difference. I wanted to know just the same. . . . But—that was before——"

"Before what?"

"Before I—please don't ask me to say it. . . . I did, once, when you asked me."

"Before you cared for me. Is that what you mean?"

"Yes. You are so cruelly literal when you wish to punish me. . . . You are interrupting me, too. I owe that wretched Kemp Ferrall a lot of money, and I'm trying to find out how much seven and nine are, to close accounts with Marion Page."

Siward turned and continued his writing. And when the little sheaf of cheques was ready he counted them, laid them aside, and, drawing a flat packet of fresh bank-notes from his portfolio, counted out the tips expected of him below stairs. These arranged for, he straightened up and glanced over his shoulder at Sylvia, but she was apparently absorbed in counting something on the ends of her fingers, so he turned smilingly to his desk and wrote a long letter to his mother—the same tender, affectionately boyish letter he had always written her, full of confidences, full of humour, gaily anticipating his own return to her on the heels of the letter.

In his first letter to her from Shotover he had spoken casually of a Miss Landis. It seemed the name was familiar enough to his mother, who asked about her; and he had replied in another letter or two, a trifle emphatic in his praise of her, because from his mother's letters it was quite evident that she knew a good deal concerning the very unconventional affairs of Sylvia's family.

Of his swift and somewhat equivocal courtship he had had nothing to say in his letters; in fact recently he had nothing to say about Sylvia at all, reserving that vital confidence for the clear sympathy and understanding which he looked forward to when he should see her, and which, through dark days and bitter aftermaths, through struggle and defeat by his master-vice, had never failed him yet, never faltered for an instant.

So he brought his letter to a close with a tender and uneasy inquiry concerning her health, which, she had intimated, was not exactly satisfactory, and for that reason she had opened the house in town in order to be near Dr. Grisby, their family doctor.

Sealing and directing the letter, he looked up to see Sylvia standing at his elbow. She dropped a light hand on his shoulder for a second, barely touching him—a fugitive caress, delicate as the smile hovering on her lips, as the shy tenderness in her eyes.

"More letters to your sweetheart?" she asked, abandoning her hand to him.

"One more—the last before I see her. . . . I wish you could see her, Sylvia."

"I wish so, too," she answered simply, seating herself on the arm of his chair as though it were a side-saddle.

They sat there very silent for a few moments, curiously oblivious to the chance curiosity of any one who might enter or pass.

" Would she—care for me—do you think? " asked the girl in a low voice.

" I think so,—for your real self."

" I know. She could only feel contempt for me—as I am."

" She is old-fashioned," he said reverently.

" That means all that is best in a woman. . . . The old fashion of truth and faith; the old fashion of honour, and faith in honour; the old, old fashion of—love. . . . All that is best, Stephen; all that is worth the love of a man. . . . Some day somebody will revive those fashions."

" Will you? "

" Dear, they would not become me," she said, the tenderness in her eyes deepening a little; and she touched his head lightly in humourous caress.

" What shall we do with the waning daylight? " she asked. " It is my last day with you. I told Howard it was my last day with you, and I did not care to be disturbed."

" You probably didn't say it that way," he commented, amused.

" I did."

" How much of that sort of thing is he prepared to stand? " asked Siward curiously.

" How much? I don't know. I don't believe he cares. It is my uncle, Major Belwether, who is making things unpleasant for me. I had to tell Howard, you know."

" What! " exclaimed Siward incredulously.

" Certainly. Do you think my conduct has passed without protest? "

"You *told* Quarrier!" he repeated.

"Did you imagine I could do otherwise?" she asked coolly. "I have that much decency left. Certainly I told him. Do you suppose that, after what we did—what I admitted to you—that I could meet him as usual? Do you think I am afraid of him?"

"I thought you were afraid of losing him," muttered Siward.

"I was, dreadfully. And the morning after you and I had been imprudent enough to sit up until nearly daylight—and do what we did—I made him take a long walk with me, and I told him plainly that I cared for you, that I was too selfish and cowardly to marry you, and that if he couldn't endure the news he was at liberty to terminate the engagement without notice."

"What did he say?" stammered Siward.

"A number of practical things."

"You mean to say he stands it!"

"It appears so. What else is there for him to do, unless he breaks the engagement?"

"And he—hasn't?"

"No. I was informed that he held me strictly and precisely to my promise; that he would never release me voluntarily, though I was, of course, at liberty to do what I chose. . . . My poor friend, he cares no more for love than do I. I happen to be the one woman in New York whom he considers absolutely suitable for him; by race, by breeding, by virtue of appearance and presence, eminently fitted to complete the material portion of his fortune and estate."

Her voice had hardened as she spoke; now it rang a little at the end, and she laughed unpleasantly.

"It appears that I was a little truer to myself than you gave me credit for—a little truer to you—a little

"'It seems that I am capable of love; but I am incapable of its degradation.'"

less treacherous, less shameless, than you must have thought me. But I have gone to my limit of decency; . . . and, were I ten times more in love with you than I am, I could not put away the position and power offered me. But I will not lie for it, nor betray for it. . . . Do you remember, once you asked me for what reasons I dropped men from my list? And I told you, because of any falsehood or treachery, any betrayal of trust—and for no other reason. You remember? And did you suppose that elemental standard of decency did not include women—even such a woman as I?"

She dropped one arm on the back of his chair and rested her chin on it, staring at space across his shoulders.

"That's how it had to be, you see, when I found that I cared for you. There was nothing to do but to tell him. I was quite certain that it was all off; but I found that I didn't know the man. I knew he was sensitive, but I didn't know he was sensitive to personal ridicule only, and to nothing else in all the world that I can discover. I—I suppose, from my frankness to him, he has concluded that no ridicule could ever touch him through me. I mean, he trusts me enough to marry me. . . . He will be safe enough, as far as my personal conduct is concerned," she added naïvely. "It seems that I am capable of love; but I am incapable of its degradation."

Siward, leaning heavily forward over his desk, rested his head in both hands; and she stooped from her perch on the arm of the chair, pressing her hot cheeks against his hands—a moment only; then slipping to her feet, she curled up in a great arm-chair by the fire, head tipped back, blue gaze concentrated on him.

"The thing for you to do," she said, "is to ambush me some night, and throw me into a hansom, and drive us both to the parson's. I'd hate you for it as much as I'd love you, but I'd make you an interesting wife."

"I may do that yet," he said, lifting his head from his hands.

"You've a year to do it in," she observed. . . . By the way, you're to take me in to dinner, as you did the first night. Do you remember? I asked Grace Ferrall then. I asked her again to-day. Heigho! It was years ago, wasn't it, that I drove up to the station and saw a very attractive and perplexed young man looking anxiously about for somebody to take him to Shotover. Ahem! the notorious Mr. Siward! Dear, . . . I didn't mean to hurt you! You know it, silly! Mayn't I have my little joke about your badness—your redoubtable badness of reputation? There! You had just better smile. . . . How dare you frighten me by making me think I had hurt you! . . . Besides, you are probably unrepentant."

She watched him closely for a moment or two, then, "*Are* you unrepentant?"

"About what?"

"About your general wickedness? About—" she hesitated—"about that girl, for example."

"What girl?" he asked coldly.

"That reminds me that you have told me absolutely nothing about her."

"There is nothing to tell," he said, in a tone so utterly new to her in its finality that she sat up as though listening to an unknown voice.

Tone and words so completely excluded her from the new intimacy into which she had imperceptibly drifted that both suddenly developed a significance from sheer contrast. Who was this girl, then, of whom he had absolutely nothing to say? What was she to him? What could she be to him—an actress, a woman of common antecedents?

She had sometimes idly speculated in an indefinitely innocent way as to just what a well-born man could find to interest him in such women; what he could have to talk about to persons of that sort, where community of tastes and traditions must be so absolutely lacking.

Gossip, scandal of that nature, hints, silences, innuendoes, the wise shrugs of young girls oversophisticated, the cool, hard smiles of matrons, all had left her indifferent or bored, partly from distaste, partly from sheer incredulity; a refusal to understand, an innate delicacy that not only refrains from comprehension, but also denies itself even the curiosity to inquire or the temptation of vaguest surmise on a subject that could not exist for her.

But now, something of the uncomfortable uneasiness had come over her which she had been conscious of when made aware of Marion Page's worldly wisdom, and which had imperceptibly chilled her when Grace Ferrall spoke of Siward's escapade, coupling this woman and him in the same scandal.

She took it for granted that there must be, for men, an attraction toward women who figured publicly behind the foot-lights, though it appeared very silly to her. In fact it all was silly and undignified—part and parcel, no doubt, of that undergraduate foolishness which seemed to cling to some men who had otherwise attained discretion.

But it appeared to her that Siward had taken the matter with a seriousness entirely out of proportion in his curt closure of the subject, and she felt a little irritated, a little humiliated, a little hurt, and took refuge in a silence that he did not offer to break.

Early twilight had fallen in the room; the firelight grew redder.

"Sylvia," he said abruptly, reverting to the old, light tone hinting of the laughter in his eyes which she could no longer see, "Suppose, as you suggested, I did ambush you—say after the opera—seize you under the very nose of your escort and make madly for a hansom?"

"I know of no other way," she said demurely.

"Would you resist, physically?"

"I would, if nobody were looking."

"Desperately?"

"How do I know? Besides, it couldn't last long," she said, thinking of his slimly powerful build as she had noticed it in his swimming costume. Smiling, amused, she wondered how long she could resist him with her own wholesome supple activity strengthened to the perfection of health in saddle and afoot.

"I should advise you to chloroform me," she said defiantly. "You don't realise my accomplishments with the punching-bag."

"So you mean to resist?"

"Yes, I do. If I were going to surrender at once, I might as well go off to church with you now."

"Wenniston church!" he said promptly. "I'll order the Mercedes."

She laughed, lazily settling herself more snugly by the fire. "Suppose it were *our* fire?" she smiled. "There would be a dog lying across that rug, and a comfortable Angora tabby dozing by the fender, and—you, cross-legged, at my feet, with that fascinating head of yours tipped back against my knees."

The laughter in her voice died out, and he had risen, saying unsteadily: "Don't! I—I can't stand that sort of thing, you know."

She had made a mistake, too; she also had suddenly become aware of her own limits in the same direction.

"Forgive me, dear! I meant no mockery."

"I know. . . . After a while a man finds laughter difficult."

"I was not laughing at—anything. I was only pretending to be happy."

"Your happiness is before you," he said sullenly.

"My future, you mean. You know I am exchanging one for the other. . . . And some day you will awake to the infamy of it; you will comprehend the depravity of the monstrous trade I made. . . . And then—and then——"

She passed one slim hand over her face—"then you will shake yourself free from this dream of me; then, awake, my punishment at your hands will begin. . . . Dear, no man in his right senses can continue to love a girl such as I am. All that is true and ardent and generous in you has invested my physical attractiveness and my small intellect with a magic that cannot last, because it is magic; and you are the magician, enmeshed for the moment in the mists of your own enchantment. When this fades, when you unclose your eyes in clear daylight, dear, I dread to think what I shall appear to you—what a dreadful, shrunken, bloodless shell, hung with lace and scented, silken cerements—a jewelled mummy-case—a thing that never was! . . . Do you understand my punishment a little, now?"

"If it were true," he said in a dull voice, "you will have forgotten, too."

"I pray I may," she said under her breath.

And, after a long silence: "Do you think, before the year is out, that you might be granted enough courage?" he asked.

"No. I shall not even pray for it. I *want* what is offered me! I desire it so blindly that already it has become part of me. I tell you the poison is in every vein; there is nothing else but poison in me. I am what I tell you, to the core. It is past my own strength of will to stop me, now. If I am stopped, another must do it. My weakness for you, being a treachery if not confessed, I was obliged to confess, horribly frightened as I was. He might have stopped me; he did not. . . . And now, what is there on earth to halt me? Love cannot. Common decency and courage cannot. Fear of your unhappiness and mine cannot. No, even the certitude of your contempt, some day, is powerless to halt me now. I could not love; I am utterly incapable of loving you enough to balance the sacrifice. And that is final."

. . . . .

Grace Ferrall came into the room and found a duel of silence in progress under the dull fire-glow tinting the ceiling.

"Another quarrel," she commented, turning on the current of the drop-light above the desk from which Siward had risen at her entrance. "You quarrel enough to marry. Why don't you?"

"I wish we could," said Sylvia simply.

Grace laughed. "What a little fool you are!" she said tenderly, seating herself in Siward's chair and dropping one hand over his where it rested on the arm. "Stephen, can't you make her—a big, strong fellow like you? Oh, well; on your heads be it! My conscience is now clear for the first time, and I'll never meddle again." She gave Siward's hand a perfunctory pat and released him with a discreetly stifled yawn. "I'm disgracefully sleepy; the wind blew like fury along the coast. Sylvia, *have* you had a good time at Shotover—the time of your life?"

Sylvia raised her eyes and encountered Siward's.

"I certainly have," she said faintly.

"*C'est bien, chérie.* Can you be as civil, Stephen—conscientiously? Oh, that is very nice of you! But there's one thing: *why* on earth didn't you make eyes at Marion? Life might be one long, blissful carnival of horse and dog for you both. Oh, dear! there, I'm meddling again! Pinch me, Sylvia, if I ever begin to meddle again! How did you come out at Bridge, Stephen? What—bad as that? Gracious! this is disgraceful—this gambling the way people do! I'm shocked and I'm going up to dress. Are you coming, Sylvia?"

. . . . .

The dinner was very gay. The ceremony of christening the Shotover Cup, which Quarrier had won, proceeded with presentation speech and a speech of acceptance faultlessly commonplace, during which Quarrier wore his smile—which was the only humorous thing he contributed.

The cup was full. Siward eyed it, perplexed, deadly afraid, yet seeing no avenue of escape from what must appear a public exhibition of contempt for Quarrier if he refused to taste its contents. That meant a bad night for him; yet he shrank more from the certain misinterpretation of a refusal to drink from the huge loving-cup with its heavy wreath of scented orchids, now already on its way toward him, than he feared the waking struggle so sure to follow.

Marion received the cup, lifted it in both hands, and said distinctly, "Good Hunting!" as she drank to Quarrier. Her brother Gordon took it, and drank entirely too much. Then Sylvia lifted it, her white hands half buried among the orchids: "To *you*!" she murmured for Siward's ear alone; then drank gaily, mischievously, "To the best shot at Shotover!" And Siward took the cup: "I salute victory," he said, smiling, "always, and everywhere! To him who takes the fighting chance and wins out! To the *best* man! Health!" And he drank as a gentleman drinks, with a gay bow to Quarrier, and with death in his heart.

Later, the irony of it struck him so grimly that he laughed; and Sylvia, beside him, looked up, dismayed to see the gray change in his face.

"What is it?" she faltered, catching his eye; "why do you—why are you so white?"

But he only smiled, as though he had misunderstood, saying:

"The survival of the fittest; that is the only test, after all. The man who makes good doesn't whine for justice. There's enough of it in the world to go round, and he who misses it gets all that's due him just the same."

Later, at cards, the aromatic odour from Alderdene's decanter roused him to fierce desire, but he fought it down until only the deadened, tearing ache remained to shake and loosen every nerve. And when Ferrall, finishing his usual batch of business letters, arrived to cut in if needed, Siward dropped his cards with a shudder, and rose so utterly unnerved that Captain Voucher, noticing his drawn face, asked him if he were not ill.

He was leaving on an earlier train than the others, having decided to pass through Boston and Deptford, at which latter place he meant to leave Sagamore for the winter in care of the manager of his mother's farm. So he took a quiet leave of those to whom the civility might not prove an interruption—a word to Alderdene and

Voucher as he passed out, a quick clasp for Ferrall and for Grace, a carefully and cordially formal parting from the Page boys, which pleased them ineffably.

Eileen and Rena, who had never had half a chance at him, took it now, delighted to discipline their faithful Pages; and he submitted in his own engagingly agreeable way, and so skilfully that both Eileen and Rena felt sorry that they had not earlier understood how civilly anxious he had been to devote himself to them alone. And they looked at the Pages, exasperated.

In the big hall he passed Marion, and stopped to take his leave.

No, he would do no hunting this season either at Carysford or with the two trial packs at Eastwood. Possibly at Warrenton later, but probably not; business threatened to detain him in town more or less. . . . Of course he'd come to see her when she returned to town. . . . And it *had* been a jolly party, and it was a shame to sound "lights out" so soon! Good-bye. . . . Good night. And that was all.

And that was all, unless he disturbed Sylvia, seated at cards with Quarrier and Major Belwether and Leila Mortimer—and very intent on the dummy, very still, and a trifle pallid with the pallor of concentration.

So—that was all, then.

Ascending the stairs, a servant handed him a letter bearing the crest of the Lenox Club. He pocketed it unopened and continued his way.

In the darkness of his own room he sat down, the devil's own clutch on his shrinking nerves, a deathly desire tearing at his very vitals, and every vein a tiny trail of fire run riot. He had been too long without it, too long to endure the craving aroused by that gay draught from Quarrier's loving-cup.

The awakened fury of his desire appalled him, and for a while that occupied him, enabling him to endure. But fear and dismay soon passed in the purely physical distress; he walked the floor, haggard, the sweat starting on his face; he lay with clenched hands, stiffened out across the bed, deafened by the riotous clamour of his pulses, conscious that he was holding out, unconscious how long he could hold out.

Crisis after crisis swept him; sometimes he found his feet and moved blindly about the room.

Strange periods of calm intervened; sensation seemed deadened; and he stood as a man who listens, scarcely daring to breathe lest the enemy awake and seize him.

He turned on the light, later, to look for his pipe, and he caught a glimpse of himself in the mirror. It was a sick man who stared back at him out of hollow eyes, and the physical revulsion shocked him into something resembling self-command.

"Damn you!" he said fiercely, setting his teeth and staring back at his reflected face, "I'll kill you yet before I've finished with you!"

Then he filled his pipe, and opening his bedroom window, sat down, resting his arm on the sill. A splendid moon silvered the sea; through the intense stillness he heard the surf, magnificently dissonant among the reefs, and he listened, fascinated, loathing the tides as he feared and loathed the inexorable tides that surged and ebbed with his accursed desire.

Once he said to himself, weakly—for he was deadly tired—"What am I making the fight for, anyway?" And "*Who* are you making the fight for?" echoed his heavy pulses.

He had asked that question and received that answer

before. After all, it had been for his mother's sake alone. And now—and now?—his heart beat out another answer; and before his eyes two other eyes seemed to open, fearlessly, sweetly, divinely tender. But they were no longer his mother's grave, gray eyes.

After the second pipe he remembered his letter. It gave him something to do, so he opened it and tried to read it, but for a long while, in his confused physical and mental condition, he could make no sense of it.

Little by little he began to comprehend its purport: that his resignation was regretfully requested by the governors of the Lenox Club for reasons unassigned.

The shock of the thing came to him after a while, like a distant, dull report long after the flash of the explosion. Well, the affair, bad enough at first, was turning worse, that was all. How much of that sort of discredit could a man stand and keep his balance? . . . And what would his mother say?

Confused from his own physical suffering, the blow had fallen with a deadened force on nerves already numbed; but his half-stupefied acquiescence had suddenly become a painful recoil when he remembered where the brunt of the disgrace would fall—where the centre of suffering must always be, and the keenest grief concentrated. Roused, appalled, almost totally unnerved, he stood staring at the letter, beginning to realise what it would mean to his mother. A passion of remorse and resentment swept him. She *must* be spared that! There must be some way—some punishment for his offence that could not strike her through him! It was wicked, it was contemptible, insane, to strike her! What were the governors of the Lenox about—a lot of snivelling hypocrites, pandering to the horrified snobbery at the Patroons! Who were they, anyway, to discipline him!

Scarce one in fifty among the members of the two clubs was qualified to sit in judgment on a Siward!

But that tempest of passion and mortification passed, too, leaving him standing there, dumb, desperate, staring at the letter crushed in his shaking hand.

He must see somebody, some member of the Lenox, and do something—*something!* Ferrall! Was that Ferrall's step on the landing?

He sprang to the door and opened it. Quarrier, passing the corridor, turned an expressionless visage toward him, and passed on with a nod almost imperceptible.

"Quarrier!" he called, swept by a sudden impulse.

Quarrier halted and turned.

"Could you give me a moment—here in my room? I won't detain you."

The faint trace of surprise faded from Quarrier's face; he quietly retraced his steps, and, entering Siward's room, stood silently confronting its pallid tenant.

"Will you sit down a moment?"

Quarrier seated himself in the arm-chair by the window, and Siward found a chair opposite.

"Quarrier," said the younger man, turning a tensely miserable face on his visitor, "I want to ask you something. I'll not mince matters. You know that the Patroons have dropped me, and you know what for."

"Yes, I know."

"When I was called before the Board of Governors to explain the matter, if I could, you were sitting on that Board."

"Yes."

"I denied the charge, but refused to explain. . . . You remember?"

Quarrier nodded coldly.

"And I was dropped by the club!"

A slight inclination of Quarrier's symmetrical head corroborated him.

"Now," said Siward, slowly and very distinctly, "I shall tell *you* unofficially what I refused to tell the other governors officially." And, as he began speaking, Quarrier's face flushed, then the features became immobile, set, and inert, and his eyes grew duller and duller, as though, under a smooth surface the soul inside of him was shrinking back into some dark corner, silent, watchful, suspicious, and perhaps defiant.

"Mr. Quarrier," said Siward quietly, "I did not take that girl to the Patroons Club—and you know it."

Quarrier was *all* surface now; he had drawn away internally so far that even his eyes seemed to recede until they scarcely glimmered through the slits in his colourless mask. And Siward went on:

"I knew perfectly well what sort of women I was to meet at that fool supper Billy Fleetwood gave; and you must have, too, for the girl you took in was no stranger to you. . . . Her name is Lydia Vyse, I believe."

The slightest possible glimmer in the elder man's eyes was all the answer he granted.

"What happened," said Siward calmly, "was this: She bet me she could so disguise herself that I could safely take her into any club in New York. I bet her she couldn't. I never dreamed of trying. Besides, she was your—dinner partner," he added with a shrug.

His concentrated gaze seemed at length to pierce the expressionless surface of the other man, who moved slightly in his chair and moistened his thin lips under the glossy beard.

"Quarrier," said Siward earnestly, "What happened in the club lobby I don't exactly know, because I was not in a condition to know. I admit it; that was the trouble with me. When I left Fleetwood's rooms I left with a half dozen men. I remember crossing Fifth Avenue with them; and the next thing I remember distinctly was loud talking in the club lobby, and a number of men there, and a slim young fellow in Inverness and top hat in the centre of a crowd, whose face was the face of that girl, Lydia Vyse. And that is absolutely all. But I couldn't do more than deny that I took her there unless I told what I *knew;* and of course that was not possible, even in self-defence. But it was for *you* to admit that I was right. And you did not. You dared not! You let another man blunder into your private affairs and fall a victim to circumstantial evidence which you could have refuted; and it was up to you to say something! And you did not! . . . And now—what are you going to do? The Lenox Club has taken this thing up. A man can't stand too much of that sort of thing. What am I to do? I can't defend myself by betraying my accidental knowledge of your petty, private affairs. So I leave it to you. I ask you what are you going to do?"

"Do you mean"—Quarrier's voice was not his own, and he brought it harshly under command—"do you mean that you think it necessary for me to say I knew her? What object would be attained by that? I did not take her to the Patroons'."

"Nor did I. Ask her how she got there. Learn the truth from her, man!"

"What proof is there that I ever met her before I took her into supper at Fleetwood's?"

"Proof! Are you mad? All I ask of you is to say to the governors what I cannot say without using your name."

"You wish me," asked Quarrier icily, "to deny that you made that wager? I can do that."

"You *can't* do it! I *did* make that bet."

"Oh! Then, what is it you wish me to say?"

"Tell them the truth. Tell them you *know* I did not take her to the club. You need not tell them why you know it. You need not tell them how much you know about her, whose brougham she drove home in. I can't defend myself at your expense—intrench myself behind your dirty little romance. What could I say? I denied taking her to the club. Then Major Belwether confronted me with my wager. Then I shut up. And so did you, Quarrier—so did you, seated there among the governors, between Leroy Mortimer and Belwether. It was up to you, and you did not stir!"

"Stir!" echoed the other man, exasperated. "Of course I did not stir. What did I know about it? Do you think I care to give a man like Mortimer a hold on me by admitting I knew anything?—or Belwether—do you think I care to have that man know anything about my private and personal business? Did you expect me to say that I was in a position to prove anything one way or another? And," he added with increasing harshness, "how do you know what I might or might not prove? If she went to the Patroons Club, I did not go with her; I did not see her; I *don't* know whether or not you took her."

"I have already told you that I did not take her," said Siward, turning whiter.

"You told that to the governors, too. Tell them again, if you like. I decline to discuss this matter with you. I decline to countenance your unwarranted intrusion into what you pretend to believe are my private affairs. I decline to confer with Belwether or Mortimer.

It's enough that you are inclined to meddle—" His cold anger was stirring. He rose to his full, muscular height, slow, menacing, his long, pale fingers twisting his silky beard. "It's enough that *you* meddle!" he repeated. "As for the matter in question, a dozen men, including myself, heard you make a wager; and later I myself was a witness that the terms of that wager had been carried out to the letter. I know absolutely nothing except that, Mr. Siward; nor, it appears, do you, for you were drunk at the time, and you have admitted it to me."

"I have asked you," said Siward, rising, and very grave, "I have asked you to do the right thing. Are you going to do it?"

"Is that a threat?" inquired Quarrier, showing the edges of his well-kept teeth. "Is this intimidation, Mr. Siward? Do I understand that you are proposing to bespatter others with scandal unless I am frightened into going to the governors with the flimsy excuse you attempt to offer me? In other words, Mr. Siward, are you bent on making me pay for what you believe you know of my private life? Is it really intimidation?"

And still Siward stared into his half-veiled, sneering eyes, speechless.

"There is only one name used for this kind of thing," added Quarrier, taking a quick involuntary step backward to the door as the blaze of fury broke out in Siward's eyes.

"Good God! Quarrier," whispered Siward with dry lips, "what a cur you are! What a cur!"

And long after Quarrier had passed the door and disappeared in the corridor, Siward stood there, frozen motionless under the icy waves of rage that swept him.

He had never before had an enemy worth the name;

he knew he had one now. He had never before hated; he now understood something of that, too. The purely physical craving to take this man and crush him into eternal quiescence had given place to a more terrible mental desire to punish. His brain surged and surged under the first flood of a mortal hatred. That the hatred was sterile made it the more intense, and, blinded by it, he stood there or paced the room minute after minute, hearing nothing but the wild clamour in his brain, seeing nothing but the smooth, expressionless face of the man whom he could not reach.

Toward midnight, seated in his chair by the window, a deathly lassitude weighing his heart, he heard the steps of people on the stairway, the click of the ascending elevator, gay voices calling good night, a ripple of laughter, the silken swish of skirts in the corridor, doors opening and closing; then silence creeping throughout the house on the receding heels of departure—a stillness that settled like a mist through hall and corridor, accented for a few moments by distant sounds, then absolute, echoless silence. And for a long while he sat there listening.

The cool wind from the ocean blew his curtains far into the room, where they bellied out, fluttering, floating, subsiding, only to rise again in the freshening breeze. He sat watching their silken convolutions, stupidly, for a while, then rose and closed his window, and raised the window on the south for purposes of air.

As he turned to adjust his transom, something white thrust under the door caught his eye, and he walked over and drew it across the sill. It was a sealed note. He opened it, reading it as he walked back to the drop-light burning beside his bed:

"Did you not mean to say good-bye? Because it

is to be good-bye for a long, long time—for all our lives—as long as we live—as long as the world lasts, and longer. . . . Good-bye—unless you care to *say* it to me."

He stood studying the note for a while; presently, lighting a match, he set fire to it and carried it blazing to the grate and flung it in, watching the blackened ashes curl up, glow, whiten, and fall in flakes to the hearth. Then he went out into the corridor, and traversed the hall to the passage which led to the bay-window. There was nobody there. The stars looked in on him, twinkling with a frosty light; beneath, the shadowy fronds of palms traced a pale pattern on the glass roof of the swimming pool. He waited a moment, turned, retraced his steps to his own door and stood listening. Then, moving swiftly, he walked the length of the corridor, and, halting at her door, knocked once.

After a moment the door swung open. He stepped forward into the room, closing the door behind him, and confronted the tall girl standing there silhouetted against the lamp behind her.

"You are insane to do this!" she whispered. "I let you in for fear you'd knock again!"

"I went to the bay-window," he said.

"You went too late. I was there an hour ago. I waited. Do you know what time it is?"

"Come to the bay-window," he said, "if you fear me here."

"Do you know it is nearly three o'clock?" she repeated. "And you leave at six."

"Shall we say good-bye here?" he asked coolly.

"Certainly. I dare not go out. And you—do you know the chances we are running? You must be perfectly mad to come to my room. Do you think anybody could have seen—heard you——"

"No. Good night." He offered his hand; she laid both of hers in it. He could scarcely distinguish her features where she stood dark against the brilliant light behind her.

"Good-bye," he whispered, kissing her hands where they lay in his.

"Good-bye." Her fingers closed convulsively, retaining his hands. "I hope—I think that—you——" Her head was drooping; she could not control her voice.

"Good-bye, Sylvia," he said again.

It was quite useless, she could not speak; and when he took her in his arms she clung to him, quivering; and he kissed the wet lashes, and the hot, trembling lips, and the smooth little hands crushed to his breast.

"We have a year yet," she gasped. "Dear, take me by force before it ends. I—I simply cannot endure this. I told you to take me—to tear me from myself. Will you do it? I will love you—truly, truly! Oh, my darling, my darling! Don't—*don't* give me up! Can't you do something for us? Can't you——"

"Will you come with me now?"

"How can——"

"*Will* you?"

A sudden sound broke out in the night—the distant pealing of the lodge-gate bell. Startled, she shrank back; somebody in the adjoining room had sprung to the floor and was opening the window.

"What is it?" she motioned with whitening lips. "Quick! oh, quick, before you are seen! Grace may come! I—I beg of you to go!"

As he stepped into the corridor he heard, below, a sound at the great door, and the stirring of the night watchman on post. At his own door he turned, listening to the movement and whispering. Ferrall, in dressing-gown and slippers, stepped into the corridor; below, the chains were rattling as the wicket swung open. There was a brief parley at the door, sounds of retreating steps on the gravel outside, sounds of approaching steps on the stairway.

"What's that? A telegram?" said Ferrall sharply. "Here, give it to me. . . . Wait! It isn't for me. It's for Mr Siward!"

Siward, standing at his open door, swayed slightly. A thrill of pure fear struck him through and through. He laid one hand on the door to steady himself, and stepped forward as Ferrall came up.

"Oh! You're awake, Stephen. Here's a telegram." He extended his hand. Siward took the yellow envelope, fumbled it, tore it open.

"Good God!" whispered Ferrall; "is it bad?"

And Siward's glazed eyes stared and stared at the scrawled and inky message:

"*YOUR MOTHER IS VERY ILL. COME AT ONCE.*"

The signature was the name of their family physician, Grisby.

CHAPTER VIII

CONFIDENCES

By January the complex social mechanism of the metropolis was whirling smoothly again; the last ultra-fashionable December lingerer had returned from the country; those of the same caste outward bound for a Southern or exotic winter had departed; and the glittering machine, every part assembled, refurbished, repolished, and connected, having been given preliminary speed-tests at the horse show, and a tuning up at the opera, was now running under full velocity; and its steady, subdued whir quickened the clattering pulse of the city, keying it to a sublimely syncopated ragtime.

The commercial reaction from the chaos of the holidays had become a carnival of recovery; shop windows grew brighter and gayer than ever, bursting into gaudy winter florescence; the main arteries of the town roared prosperity; cross streets were packed; Fifth Avenue, almost impassible in the morning, choked up after three o'clock; and all the afternoon through, and late into the night, mounted police of the traffic squad, adrift in the tide of carriages, stemmed the flashing currents pouring north and south from the white marble arch to the gilded bronze battle-horse and its rider on guard at the portals of the richest quarter of the wealthiest city in the world.

So far, that winter, snow had fallen only twice, lasting but a day or two each time; street and avenue remained bone dry where the white-uniformed cleaning squads worked amid clouds of dust; and all day long the flinty asphalt echoed the rattling slap of horses' feet; all day long the big, shining motor-cars sped up town and down town, droning their distant warnings. It was an open winter in New York, and, financially, a prosperous one; and that meant a brilliant social season. Like a set piece of fireworks, with its interdependent parts taking fire in turn, function after function, spectacle after spectacle, glittered, fizzed, and was extinguished, only to give place to newer and more splendid spectacles; separate circles, sets, and groups belonging to the social solar system whizzed, revolved, rotated, with edifying effects on everybody concerned, unconcerned, and not at all concerned; and at intervals, when for a moment or two something hung fire, the twinkle of similar spectacles sputtering away in distant cities beyond the horizon was faintly reflected in the social sky above the incandescent metropolis. For the whole nation was footing it, heel and toe, to the echoes of strains borne on the winds from the social capital of the republic; and the social arbiter at Bird Centre was more of a facsimile of his New York confrère than that confrère could ever dream of even in the most realistic of nightmares.

Three phenomena particularly characterised that metropolitan winter: the reckless rage for private gambling through the mediums of bridge and roulette; the incorporation of a company known as The Inter-County Electric Company, capitalised at a figure calculated to disturb nobody, and, so far, without any avowed specific policy other than that which served to decorate a portion of its charter which otherwise might have remained ornately and comparatively blank; the third phenomenon was the retirement from active affairs of Stanley S. Quarrier, the father of Howard Quarrier, and the election of the son to the presidency of the great Algonquin Loan and Trust Company, with its network system of dependent, subsidiary, and allied corporations.

The day that the newspapers gave this interesting information to the Western world, Leroy Mortimer, on being bluntly notified that he had overdrawn his account with the Algonquin Loan and Trust, began telephoning in every direction until he located Beverly Plank at the Saddle Club—an organisation of wealthy men, and sufficiently exclusive not to compromise Plank's possible chances for something better; in fact, the Saddle Club, into which Leroy Mortimer had already managed to pilot him, was one riser and tread upward on the stair he was climbing, though it was more of a lobby for other clubs than a club in itself. To be seen there was, perhaps, rather to a man's advantage, if he did not loaf there in the evenings or use it too frequently. As Plank carefully avoided doing either, Mortimer was fortunate in finding him there; and he crawled out of his hansom, saying that the desk clerk would pay, and entered the reading-room, where Plank sat writing a letter.

Beverly Plank had grown stouter since he had returned to town from Black Fells; but the increase of weight was evenly distributed over his six feet odd, which made him only a trifle more ponderous and not abdominally fat. But Mortimer had become enormous; rolls of flesh crowded his mottled ear-lobes outward and bulged above his collar; cushions of it padded the backs of his hands and fingers; shaving left his heavy, distended face congested and unpleasantly shiny. But he was as minutely groomed as ever, and he wore that satiated air of prosperity which had always been one of his most important assets.

The social campaign inaugurated by Leila Mortimer in behalf of Beverly Plank had, so far, received no serious reverses. His box at the horse show, of course, produced merely negative results; his box at the opera might mean something some day. His name was up at the Lenox and the Patroons; he had endowed a ward in the new pavilion of St. Berold's Hospital; he had presented a fine Gainsborough—The Countess of Wythe—to the Metropolitan Museum; and it was rumoured that he had consulted several bishops concerning a new chapel for that huge bastion of the citadel of Faith looming above the metropolitan wilderness in the north.

So far, so good. If, as yet, he had not been permitted to go where he wanted to go, he at least had been instructed where not to go and what not to do; and he was as docile as he was dogged, understanding how much longer it takes to shuffle in by way of the mews and the back door than to sit on the front steps and wait politely for somebody to unchain the front door.

Meanwhile he was doggedly docile; his huge house, facing the wintry park midway between the squat palaces of the wealthy pioneers and the outer hundreds, remained magnificently empty save for certain afternoon conferences of very solemn men, fellow directors and associates in business and financial matters—save for the periodical presence of the Mortimers: a mansion immense and shadowy, haunted by relays of yawning, liveried servants, half stupefied under the vast silence of the twilit splendour. He was patient, not only because he was told to be, but also because he had nothing better to do. Society stared at him as blankly as the Mountain confronted Mahomet. But the stubborn patience of the man was itself a strain on the Mountain; he was aware of that, and he waited for it to come to him. As yet, however, he could detect no symptoms of mobility in the Mountain.

"Things are moving all the same," said Mortimer, as he entered the reading room of the Saddle Club. "Quarrier and Belwether have listened a damned sight more respectfully to me since they read that column about you and the bishops and that chapel business."

Plank turned his heavy head with a disturbed glance around the room; for he always dreaded Mortimer's indiscretions of speech—was afraid of his cynical frankness in the presence of others; even shrank from the brutal bonhomie of the man when alone with him.

"Can't you be careful?" he said; "there was a man here a moment ago." He picked up his unfinished letter, folded and pocketed it, touched an electric bell, and when a servant came, "Take Mr. Mortimer's order," he said, supporting his massive head on his huge hands and resting his elbow on the writing-desk.

"I've got to cut out this morning bracer," said Mortimer, eyeing the servant with indecision; but he gave his order nevertheless, and later accepted a cigar; and when the servant had returned and again retired, he half emptied his tall glass, refilled it with mineral water, and, settling back in the padded arm-chair, said: "If I manage this thing as it ought to be managed, you'll go through by April. What do you think of that?"

Plank's phlegmatic features flushed. "I'm more obliged to you than I can say," he began, but Mortimer silenced him with a gesture: "Don't interrupt. I'm going to put you through The Patroons Club by April. That's thirty yards through the centre; d'ye see, you dunderheaded Dutchman? It's solid gain, and it's our ball. The Lenox will take longer; they're a 'holier-than-thou' bunch of nincompoops, and it always horrifies them to have any man elected, no matter who he is. They'd rather die of dry rot than elect anybody; it shocks them to think that any man could have the presumption to be presented. They require the spectacle of fasting and prayer—a view of a candidate seated in sackcloth and ashes in outer darkness. You've got to wait for the Lenox, Plank."

"I am waiting," said Plank, squaring his massive jaws.

"You've got to," growled Mortimer, emptying his glass aggressively.

Plank looked out of the window, his shrewd blue eyes closing in retrospection.

"Another thing," continued Mortimer thickly; "the Kemp Ferralls are disposed to be decent. I don't mean in asking you to meet some intellectual second-raters, but in doing it handsomely. I don't know whether it's time yet," he added, with a sidelong glance at Plank's stolid face; "I don't want to push the mourners too hard . . . Well, I'll see about it . . . And if it's the thing to do, and the time to do it"—he turned on Plank with his boisterous and misleading laugh and clapped him on the shoulder—"it will be done, as sure as snobs are snobs; and that's the surest thing you ever bet on. Here's to them!" and he emptied his glass and fell back into his chair, wheezing and sucking at his unlighted cigar.

"I want to say," began Plank, speaking the more slowly because he was deeply in earnest, "that all this you are doing for me is very handsome of you, Mortimer. I'd like to say—to convey to you something of how I feel about the way you and Mrs. Mortimer——"

"Oh, Leila has done it all."

"Mrs. Mortimer is very kind, and you have been so, too. I—I wish there was something—some way to —to——"

"To what?" asked Mortimer so bluntly that Plank flushed up and stammered:

"To be—to do a—to show my gratitude."

"How? You're scarcely in a position to do anything for *us*," said Mortimer, brutally staring him out of countenance.

"I know it," said Plank, the painful flush deepening.

Mortimer, fussing and growling over his cigar, was nevertheless stealthily intent on the game which had so long absorbed him. His wits, clogged, dulled by excesses, were now aroused to a sort of gross activity through the menace of necessity. At last Plank had given him an opening. He recognised his chance.

"There's one thing," he said deliberately, "that I won't stand for, and that's any vulgar misconception on your part of my friendship for you. Do you follow me?"

"I don't misunderstand it," protested Plank, angry and astonished; "I don't——"

"—As though," continued Mortimer menacingly, "I were one of those needy social tipsters, one of those shabby, pandering touts who——"

"For Heaven's sake, Mortimer, don't talk like that! I had no intention——"

"—One of those contemptible, parasitic leeches," persisted Mortimer, getting redder and hoarser, "who live on men like you. Confound you, Plank, what the devil do you mean by it?"

"Mortimer, are you crazy, to talk to me like that?"

"No, I'm not, but you must be! I've a mind to

drop the whole cursed business! I've every inclination to drop it! If you haven't horse-sense enough—if you haven't innate delicacy sufficient to keep you from making such a break——"

"I didn't! It wasn't a break, Mortimer. I wouldn't have hurt you——"

"You did hurt me! How can I feel the same again? I never imagined you thought I was that sort of a social mercenary. Why, so little did I dream that you looked on our friendship in that light that I was—on my word of honour!—I was just now on the point of asking you for three or four thousand, to carry me to the month's end and square my bridge balance."

"Mortimer, you must take it! You are a fool to think I meant anything by saying I wanted to show my gratitude. Look here; be decent and fair with me. I wouldn't offer you an affront—would I?—even if I were a cad. I wouldn't do it now, just when you're getting things into shape for me. I'm not a fool, anyway. This is in deadly earnest, I tell you, Mortimer, and I'm getting angry about it. You've *got* to show your confidence in me; you've got to take what you want from me, as you would from any friend. I resent your failure to do it now, as though you drew a line between me and your intimates. If you're really my friend, show it!"

There was a pause. A curious and unaccustomed sensation had silenced Mortimer, something almost akin to shame. It astonished him a little. He did not quite understand why, in the very moment of success over this stolid, shrewd young man and his thrifty Dutch instincts, he should feel uncomfortable. Were not his services worth something? Had he not earned at least the right to borrow from this rich man who could afford to pay for what was done for him? Why should he feel ashamed? He had not been treacherous; he really liked the fellow. Why shouldn't he take his money?

"See here, old man," said Plank, extending a huge highly coloured hand, "is all square between us now?"

"I think so," muttered Mortimer.

But Plank would not relinquish his hand.

"Then tell me how to draw that cheque! Great Heaven, Mortimer, what is friendship, anyhow, if it doesn't include little matters like this—little misunderstandings like this? I'm the man to be sensitive, not you. You have been very good to me, Mortimer. I could almost wish you in a position where the only thing I possess might square something of my debt to you."

A few minutes later, while he was filling in the cheque, a dusty youth in riding clothes and spurs came in and found a seat by one of the windows, into which he dropped, and then looked about him for a servant.

"Hello, Fleetwood!" said Mortimer, glancing over his shoulder to see whose spurs were ringing on the polished floor.

Fleetwood saluted amiably with his riding-crop; including Plank, whom he did not know, in a more formal salute.

"Will you join us?" asked Mortimer, taking the cheque which Plank offered and carelessly pocketing it without even a nod of thanks. "You know Beverly Plank, of course? What! I thought everybody knew Beverly Plank."

Mr. Fleetwood and Mr. Plank shook hands and resumed their seats.

"Ripping weather!" observed Fleetwood, replacing

his hat and rebuttoning the glove which he had removed to shake hands with Plank. "Lot of jolly people out this morning. I say, Mortimer, do you want that roan hunter of mine you looked over? I mean King Dermid, because Marion Page wants him, if you don't. She was out this morning, and she spoke of it again."

Mortimer, lifting a replenished glass, shook his head, and drank thirstily in silence.

"Saw you at Westbury, I think," said Fleetwood politely to Plank, as the two lifted their glasses to one another.

"I hunted there for a day or two," replied Plank, modestly. "If it's that big Irish thoroughbred you were riding that you want to sell I'd like a look in, if Miss Page doesn't fancy him."

Fleetwood laughed, and glanced amusedly at Plank over his glass. "It isn't that horse, Mr. Plank. That's Drumceit, Stephen Siward's famous horse." He interrupted himself to exchange greetings with several men who came into the room rather noisily, their spurs resounding across the oaken floor. One of them, Tom O'Hara, joined them, slamming his crop on the desk beside Plank and spreading himself over an arm-chair, from the seat of which he forcibly removed Mortimer's feet without excuse.

"Drink? Of course I want a drink!" he replied irritably to Fleetwood—"one, three, ten, several! Billy, whose weasel-bellied pinto was that you were kicking your heels into in the park? Some of the squadron men asked me—the major. Oh, beg pardon! Didn't know you were trying to stick Mortimer with him. He might do for the troop ambulance, *inside*! . . . What? Oh, yes; met Mr. Blank—I mean Mr. Plank—at Shotover, I think. How d'ye do? Had the pleasure of potting your tame pheasants. Rotten sport, you know. What do you do it for, Mr. Blank?"

"What did you come for, if it's rotten sport?" asked Plank so simply that it took O'Hara a moment to realise he had been snubbed.

"I didn't mean to be offensive," he drawled.

"I suppose you can't help it," said Plank very gently; "some people can't, you know." And there was another silence, broken by Mortimer, whose entire bulk was tingling with a mixture of surprise and amusement over his protégé's developing ability to take care of himself. "Did you say that Stephen Siward is in Westbury, Billy?"

"No; he's in town," replied Fleetwood. "I took his horses up to hunt with. He isn't hunting, you know."

"I didn't know. Nobody ever sees him anywhere," said Mortimer. "I guess his mother's death cut him up."

Fleetwood lifted his empty glass and gently shook the ice in it. "That, and—the other business—is enough to cut any man up, isn't it?"

"You mean the action of the Lenox Club?" asked Plank seriously.

"Yes. He's resigned from this club, too, I hear. Somebody told me that he has made a clean sweep of all his clubs. That's foolish. A man may be an ass to join too many clubs but he's always a fool to resign from any of 'em. You ask the weatherwise what resigning from a club forecasts. It's the first ominous sign in a young man's career."

"What's the second sign?" asked O'Hara, with a yawn.

"Squadron talk; and you're full of it," retorted

Fleetwood—"'I said to the major,' and 'The captain told the chief trumpeter'—all that sort of thing—and those Porto Rico spurs of yours, and the ewe-necked glyptosaurus you block the bridle-path with every morning. You're an awful nuisance, Tom, if anybody should ask me."

Under cover of a rapid-fire exchange of pleasantries between Fleetwood and O'Hara, Plank turned to Mortimer, hesitating:

"I rather liked Siward when I met him at Shotover," he ventured. "I'm very sorry he's down and out."

"He drinks," shrugged Mortimer, diluting his mineral water with Irish whisky. "He can't let it alone; he's like all the Siwards. I could have told you that the first time I ever saw him. We all told him to cut it out, because he was sure to do some damfool thing if he didn't. He's done it, and his clubs have cut him out. It's his own funeral. . . . Well, here's to you!"

"Cut who out?" asked Fleetwood, ignoring O'Hara's parting shot concerning the decadence of the Fleetwood stables and their owner.

"Stephen Siward. I always said that he was sure, sooner or later, to land in the family ditch. He has a right to, of course; the gutter is public property."

"It's a damned sad thing," said Fleetwood slowly.

After a pause Plank said: "I think so, too. . . . I don't know him very well."

"You may know him better now," said O'Hara insolently.

Plank reddened, and, after a moment: "I should be glad to, if he cares to know me."

"Mortimer doesn't care for him, but he's an awfully good fellow, all the same," said Fleetwood, turning to Plank; "he's been an ass, but who hasn't? I like him tremendously, and I feel very bad over the mess he made of it after that crazy dinner I gave in my rooms. . . . What? You hadn't heard of it? Why man, it's the talk of the clubs."

"I suppose that is why I haven't heard," said Plank simply; "my club-life is still in the future."

"Oh!" said Fleetwood with an involuntary stare, surprised, a trifle uncomfortable, yet somehow liking Plank, and not understanding why.

"I'm not in anything, you see; I'm only up for the Patroons and the Lenox," added Plank gravely.

"I see. Certainly. Er—hope you'll make 'em; hope to see you there soon. Er—I see by the papers you've been jollying the clergy, Mr. Plank. Awfully handsome of you, all that chapel business. I say: I've a cousin—er—young architect; Beaux Arts, and all that—just over. I'd awfully like to have him given a chance at that competition; invited to try, you see. I don't suppose it could be managed, now——"

"Would you like to have me ask the bishops?" inquired Plank, naïvely shrewd. And the conversation became very cordial between the two, which Mortimer observed, keeping one ironical eye on Plank, while he continued a desultory discussion with O'Hara concerning a very private dinner which somebody told somebody that somebody had given to Quarrier and the Inter-County Electric people; which, if true, plainly indicated who was financing the Inter-County scheme, and why Amalgamated stock had tumbled again yesterday, and what might be looked for from the Algonquin Trust Company's president.

"Amalgamated Electric doesn't seem to like it a little bit," said O'Hara. "Ferrall, Belwether, and Siward are in it up to their necks; and if Quarrier is really the god in the machine, and if he really is doing stunts with Amalgamated Electric, and is also mixing feet with the Inter-County crowd, why, he is virtually paralleling his own road; and why, in the name of common sense, is he doing that? He'll kill it; that's what he'll do."

"He can afford to kill it," observed Mortimer, punching the electric button and making a significant gesture toward his empty glass as the servant entered; "a man like Quarrier can afford to kill anything."

"Yes; but why kill Amalgamated Electric? Why not merge? Why, it's a crazy thing to do, it's a devil of a thing to do, to parallel your own line!" insisted O'Hara. "That is dirty work. People don't do such things these days. Nobody tears up dollar bills for the pleasure of tearing."

"Nobody knows what Quarrier will do," muttered Mortimer, who had tried hard enough to find out when the first ominous rumours arose concerning Amalgamated, and the first fractional declines left the street speechless and stupefied.

O'Hara sat frowning, and fingering his glass. "As a matter of fact," he said, "a little cold logic shows us that Quarrier isn't in it at all. No sane man would ruin his own enterprise, when there is no need to. His people are openly supporting Amalgamated and hammering Inter-County; and, besides, there's Ferrall in it, and Mrs. Ferrall is Quarrier's cousin; and there's Belwether in it, and Quarrier is engaged to marry Sylvia Landis, who is Belwether's niece. It's a scrap with Harrington's crowd, and the wheels inside of wheels are like Chinese boxes. Who knows what it means? Only it's plain that Amalgamated is safe, if Quarrier wants it to be. And unless he does he's crazy."

Mortimer puffed stolidly at his cigar until the smoke got into his eyes and inflamed them. He sat for a while, wiping his puffy eyelids with his handkerchief; then, squinting sideways at Plank, and seeing him still occupied with Fleetwood, turned bluntly on O'Hara:

"See here: what do you mean by being nasty to Plank?" he growled. "I'm backing him. Do you understand?"

"It *is* curious," mused O'Hara coolly, "how much of a cad a fairly decent man can be when he's out of temper!"

"You mean Plank, or me?" demanded Mortimer, darkening angrily.

"No; I mean myself. I'm not that way usually. I took him for a bounder, and he's caught me with the goods on. I've been thinking that the men who bother with such questions are usually open to suspicion themselves. Watch me do the civil, now. I'm ashamed of myself."

"Wait a moment. Will you be civil enough to do something for him at the Patroons? That will mean something."

"Is he up? Yes, I will;" and, turning in his chair, he said to Plank: "Awfully sorry I acted like a bounder just now, after having accepted your hospitality at the Fells. I did mean to be offensive, and I'm sorry for that, too. Hope you'll overlook it, and be friendly."

Plank's face took on the dark-red hue of embarrassment; he looked questioningly at Mortimer, whose visage remained non-committal, then directly at O'Hara.

"I should be very glad to be friends with you," he said with an ingenuous dignity that surprised Mortimer. It was only the native simplicity of the man, veneered and polished by constant contact with Mrs. Mortimer, and now showing to advantage in the grain. And it gratified Mortimer, because he saw that it was going to make many matters much easier for himself and his protégé.

The tall glasses were filled and drained again before they departed to the cold plunge and dressing-rooms above, whence presently they emerged in street garb to drive down town and lunch together at the Lenox Club, Plank as Fleetwood's guest.

Mortimer, very heavy and inert after luncheon, wedged himself into a great stuffed arm-chair by the window, where he alternately nodded over his coffee and wheezed in his breathing, and leered out at Fifth Avenue from half-closed, puffy eyes. And there he was due to sit, sodden and replete, until the fashionable equipages began to flash past. He'd probably see his wife driving with Mrs. Ferrall or with Miss Caithness, or perhaps with some doddering caryatid of the social structure; and he'd sit there, leering with gummy eyes out of the club windows, while servants in silent processional replenished his glass from time to time, until in the early night the trim little shopgirls flocked out into the highways in gossiping, fluttering coveys, trotting away across the illuminated asphalt, north and south to their thousand dingy destinations. And after they had gone he would probably arouse himself to read the evening paper, or perhaps gossip with Major Belwether and other white-haired familiars, or perhaps doze until it was time to summon a cab and go home to dress.

That afternoon, however, having O'Hara and Fleetwood to give him countenance, he managed to arouse himself long enough to make Plank known personally to several of the governors of the club and to a dozen members, then left him to his fate. Whence, presently, Fleetwood and O'Hara extracted him—fate at that moment being personified by a garrulous old gentleman, one Peter Caithness, who divided with Major Belwether the distinction of being the club bore—and together they piloted him to the billiard room, where he beat them handily for a dollar a point at everything they suggested.

"You play almost as pretty a game as Stephen Siward used to play," said O'Hara cordially. "You've something of his cue movement—something of his infernal facility and touch. Hasn't he, Fleetwood?"

"I wish Siward were back here," said Fleetwood thoughtfully, returning his cue to his own rack. "I wonder what he does with himself—where he keeps himself all the while? What the devil is there for a man to do, if he doesn't do anything? He's not going out anywhere since his mother's death; he has no clubs to go to, I understand. What does he do—go to his office and come back, and sit in that shabby old brick house all day and blink at the bum portraits of his bum and distinguished ancestors? Do you know what he does with himself?" to O'Hara.

"I don't even know where he lives," observed O'Hara, resuming his coat. "He's given up his rooms, I understand."

"What? Don't know the old Siward house?"

"Oh! does he live there now? Of course; I forgot about his mother. He had apartments last year, you remember. He gave dinners—corkers they were. I went to one—like that last one you gave."

"I wish I'd never given it," said Fleetwood gloomily. "If I hadn't, he'd be a member here still. . . . *What* do you suppose induced him to take that little gin-drinking cat to the Patroons? Why, man, it wasn't even an undergraduate's trick! it was the act of a lunatic."

For a while they talked of Siward, and of his unfortunate story and the pity of it; and when the two men ceased,

"Do you know," said Plank mildly, "I don't believe he ever did it."

O'Hara looked up surprised, then shrugged. "Unfortunately he doesn't deny it, you see."

"I heard," said Fleetwood, lighting a cigarette, "that he did deny it; that he said, no matter what his condition was, he couldn't have done it. If he had been sober, the governors would have been bound to take his word of honour. But he couldn't give that, you see. And after they pointed out to him that he had been in no condition to know exactly what he did do, he shut up. . . . And they dropped him; and he's falling yet."

"I don't believe that sort of a man ever would do that sort of thing," repeated Plank obstinately, his Delft-blue eyes partly closing, so that all the Dutch shrewdness and stubbornness in his face disturbed its highly coloured placidity. And he walked away toward the wash-room to cleanse his ponderous pink hands of chalk-dust.

"That's what's the matter with Plank," observed O'Hara to Fleetwood as Plank disappeared. "It isn't that he's a bounder; but he doesn't know things; he doesn't know enough, for instance, to wait until he's a member of a club before he criticises the judgment of its governors. Yet you can't help tolerating the fellow. I think I'll write a letter for him, or put down my name. What do you think?"

"It would be all right," said Fleetwood. "He'll need all the support he can get, with Leroy Mortimer as his sponsor. . . . Wasn't Mortimer rather nasty about Siward though, in his rôle of the alcoholic prophet? Whew!"

"Siward never had any use for Mortimer," observed O'Hara.

"I'll bet you never heard him say so," returned Fleetwood. "You know Stephen Siward's way; he never said anything unpleasant about any man. I wish I didn't either, but I do. So do you. So do most men. . . . Lord! I wish Siward were back here. He was a good deal of a man, after all, Tom."

They were unconsciously using the past tense in discussing Siward, as though he were dead, either physically or socially.

"In one way he was always a singularly decent man," mused O'Hara, walking toward the great marble vestibule and buttoning his overcoat.

"How exactly do you mean?"

"Oh, about women."

"I believe it, too. If he did take that Vyse girl into the Patroons, it was his limit with her—and, I believe his limit with any woman. He was absurdly decent that way; he was indeed. And now look at the reputation he has! Isn't it funny? *isn't* it, now?"

"What sort of an effect do you suppose all this business is going to have on Siward?"

"It's had one effect already," replied Fleetwood, as Plank came up, ready for the street. "Ferrall says he looks sick, and Belwether says he's going to the devil; but that's the sort of thing the major is likely to say. By the way, wasn't there something between that pretty Landis girl and Siward? Somebody—some damned gossiping somebody—talked about it somewhere, recently."

"I don't believe that, either," said Plank, in his

heavy, measured, passionless voice, as they descended the steps of the white portico and looked around for a cab.

"As for me, I've got to hustle," observed O'Hara, glancing at his watch. "I'm due to shine at a function about five. Are you coming up-town either of you fellows? I'll give you a lift as far as Seventy-second Street, Plank."

"Tell you what we'll do," said Fleetwood, impulsively, turning to Plank: "We'll drive down town, you and I, and we'll look up poor old Siward! Shall we? He's probably all alone in that God-forsaken red brick family tomb! *Shall* we? How about it, Plank?"

O'Hara turned impatiently on his heel with a gesture of adieu, climbed into his electric hansom, and went buzzing away up the avenue.

"I'd like to, but I don't think I know Mr. Siward well enough to do that," said Plank diffidently. He hesitated, colouring up. "He might misunderstand my going with you—as a liberty—which perhaps I might not have ventured on had he been less—less unfortunate."

Again Fleetwood warmed toward the ruddy, ponderous young man beside him. "See here," he said, "you are going as a friend of mine—if you care to look at it that way."

"Thank you," said Plank; "I should be very glad to go in that way."

The Siward house was old only in the comparative Manhattan meaning of the word; for in New York nothing is really very old, except the faces of the young men.

Decades ago it had been considered a big house, and it was still so spoken of—a solid, dingy, red brick structure, cubical in proportions, surmounted by heavy chimneys, the depth of its sunken windows hinting of the thickness of wall and foundation. Window-curtains of obsolete pattern, all alike, and all drawn, masked the blank panes. Three massive wistaria-vines, the gnarled stems as thick as tree-trunks, crawled upward to the roof, dividing the façade equally, and furnishing some relief to its flatness, otherwise unbroken except by the deep reveals of window and door. Two huge and unsymmetrical catalpa trees stood sentinels before it, dividing curb from asphalt; and from the centres of the shrivelled, brown grass-plots flanking the stoop under the basement windows two aged Rose-of-Sharon trees bristled naked to the height of the white marble capitals of the flaking pillars supporting the stained portico.

An old New York house, in the New York sense. Old in another sense, too, where in a rapid land Time outstrips itself, painting, with the antiquity of centuries, the stone and mortar which were new scarce ten years since.

"Nice old family mausoleum," commented Fleetwood, descending from the hansom, followed by Plank. The latter instinctively mounted the stoop on tiptoe, treading gingerly as one who ventures into precincts unknown but long respected; and as Fleetwood pulled the old-fashioned bell, Plank stole a glance over the façade, where wisps of straw trailed from sparrows' nests, undisturbed, wedged between plinth and pillar; where, behind the lace pane-screens, shadowy edges of heavy curtains framed the obscurity; where the paint had blistered and peeled from the iron railings, and the marble pillars of the portico glimmered, scarred by frosts of winters long forgotten.

"Cheerful monument," repeated Fleetwood with a sarcastic nod. Then the door was opened by a very old man wearing the black "swallow-tail" clothes and choker of an old-time butler, spotless, quite immaculate, but cut after a fashion no young man remembers.

"Good evening, Gumble," said Fleetwood, entering, followed on tiptoe by Plank.

"Good evening, sir." . . . A pause; and in the unsteady voice of age: "Mr. Fleetwood, sir. . . . Mr. ——." A bow, and the dim eyes peering up at Plank, who stood fumbling for his card-case.

Fleetwood dropped both cards on the salver unsteadily extended. The butler ushered them into a dim room on the right.

"How is Mr. Siward?" asked Fleetwood, pausing on the threshold and dropping his voice.

The old man hesitated, looking down, then still looking away from Fleetwood: "Bravely, sir, bravely, Mr. Fleetwood."

"The Siwards were always that," said the young man gently.

"Yes, sir. . . . Thank you. Mr. Stephen—Mr. Siward," he corrected, quaintly, "is indisposed, sir. It was a—a great shock to us all, sir!" He bowed and turned away, holding his salver stiffly; and they heard him muttering under his breath, "Bravely, sir, bravely. A—a great shock, sir! . . . Thank you."

Fleetwood turned to Plank, who stood silent, staring through the fading light at the faded household gods of the house of Siward. The dim light touched the prisms of a crystal chandelier dulled by age, and edged the carved foliations of the marble mantel, above which loomed a tarnished mirror reflecting darkness. Fleetwood rose, drew a window-shade higher, and nodded toward several pictures; and Plank moved slowly from one to another, peering up at the dead Siwards in their crackled varnish.

"This is the real thing," observed Fleetwood cynically, "all this Fourth Avenue antique business; dingy, cumbersome, depressing. Good God! I see myself standing it. . . . Look at that old grinny-bags in a pig-tail over there! To the cellar for his, if this were my house. . . . We've got some, too, in several rooms, and I never go into 'em. They're like a scene in a bum play, or like one of those Washington Square rat-holes, where artists eat Welsh-rabbits with dirty fingers. Ugh!"

"I like it," said Plank, under his breath.

Fleetwood stared, then shrugged, and returned to the window to watch a brand-new French motor-car drawn up before a modern mansion across the avenue.

The butler returned presently, saying that Mr. Siward was at home and would receive them in the library above, as he was not yet able to pass up and down stairs.

"I didn't know he was as ill as that," muttered Fleetwood, as he and Plank followed the old man up the creaking stairway. But Gumble, the butler, said nothing in reply.

Siward was sitting in an arm-chair by the window, one leg extended, his left foot, stiffly cased in bandages, resting on a footstool.

"Why, Stephen!" exclaimed Fleetwood, hastening forward, "I didn't know you were laid up like this!"

Siward offered his hand inquiringly; then his eyes turned toward Plank, who stood behind Fleetwood; and, slowly disengaging his hand from Fleetwood's sympathetic grip, he offered it to Plank.

"It is very kind of you," he said. "Gumble, Mr. Fleetwood prefers rye, for some inscrutable reason. Mr. Plank?" His smile was a question.

" If you don't mind," said Plank, " I should like to have some tea—that is, if——"

" Tea, Gumble, for two. We'll tipple in company, Mr. Plank," he added. " And the cigars are at your elbow, Billy," with another smile at Fleetwood.

" Now," said the latter, after he had lighted his cigar, " what is the matter, Stephen? "

Siward glanced at his stiffly extended foot. " Nothing much." He reddened faintly, " I slipped. It's only a twisted ankle."

For a moment or two the answer satisfied Fleetwood, then a sudden, curious flash of suspicion came into his eyes; he glanced sharply at Siward, who lowered his eyes, while the red tint in his hollow cheeks deepened.

Neither spoke for a while. Plank sipped the tea which Wands, the second man, brought. Siward brooded over his cup, head bent. Fleetwood made more noise than necessary with his ice.

" I miss you like hell! " said Fleetwood musingly, measuring out the old rye from the quaint decanter. " Why did you drop the Saddle Club, Stephen? "

" I'm not riding; I have no use for it," replied Siward.

" You've cut out the Proscenium Club, too, and the Owl's Head, and the Trophy. It's a shame, Stephen."

" I'm tired of clubs."

" Don't talk that way."

" Very well, I won't," said Siward, smiling. " Tell me what is happening—out there," he made a gesture toward the window; " all the gossip the newspapers miss. I've talked Dr. Grisby to death; I've talked Gumble to death; I've read myself stupid. What's going on, Billy? "

So Fleetwood sketched for him a gay cartoon of

events, caricaturing various episodes in the social kaleidoscope which might interest him. He gossiped cynically, but without malice, about people they both knew, about engagements, marriages, and divorces, plans and ambitions; about those absent from the metropolis and the newcomers to be welcomed. He commented briefly on the opera, reviewed the newer plays at the theatres, touched on the now dormant gaiety which had made the season at nearby country clubs conspicuous; then drifted into the hunting field, gossiping pleasantly in the vernacular about horses and packs and drag-hunts and stables, and what people thought of the new English hounds of the trial pack, and how the new M. F. H., Maitland Gray, had managed to break so many bones at Southbury.

Politics were touched upon, and they spoke of the possibility of Ferrall going to the Assembly, the sport of boss-baiting having become fashionable among amateurs, and providing a new amusement for the idle rich.

So city, State, and national issues were run through lightly, business conditions noticed, the stock market speculated upon; and presently conversation died out, with a yawn from Fleetwood as he looked into his empty glass at the last bit of ice.

"Don't do that, Billy," smiled Siward. "You haven't discoursed upon art, literature, and science yet, and you can't go until you've adjusted the affairs of the nation for the next twenty-four hours."

"Art?" yawned Fleetwood. "Oh, pictures? Don't like 'em. Nobody ever looks at 'em except débutantes, who do it out of deviltry, to floor a man at a dinner or a dance."

"How about literature?" inquired Siward gravely. "Anything doing?"

"Nothing in it," replied Fleetwood more gravely still. "It's another feminine bluff—like all that music talk they hand you after the opera."

"I see. And science?"

"Spider Flynn is matched to meet Kid Holloway; is *that* what you mean, Stephen? Somebody tumbled out of an air-ship the other day; is that what you mean? And they're selling scientific jewelry on Broadway at a dollar a quart; is that what you want to know?"

Siward rested his head on his hand with a smile. "Yes, that's about what I wanted to know, Billy—all about the arts and sciences. . . . Much obliged. You needn't stay any longer, if you don't want to."

"How soon will you be out?" inquired Fleetwood.

"Out? I don't know. I shall try to drive to the office to-morrow."

"Why the devil did you resign from all your clubs? How can I see you if I don't come here?" began Fleetwood impatiently. "I know, of course, that you're not going anywhere, but a man always goes to his club. You don't look well, Stephen. You are too much alone."

Siward did not answer. His face and body had certainly grown thinner since Fleetwood had last seen him. Plank, too, had been shocked at the change in him—the dark, hard lines under the eyes; the pallor, the curious immobility of the man, save for his fingers, which were always restless, now moving in search of some small object to worry and turn over and over, now nervously settling into a grasp on the arm of his chair.

"How is Amalgamated Electric?" asked Fleetwood, abruptly.

"I think it's all right. Want to buy some?" replied Siward, smiling.

Plank stirred in his chair ponderously. "Somebody is kicking it to pieces," he said.

"Somebody is trying to," smiled Siward.

"Harrington," nodded Fleetwood. Siward nodded back. Plank was silent.

"Of course," continued Fleetwood, tentatively, "you people need not worry, with Howard Quarrier back of you."

Nobody said anything for a while. Presently Siward's restless hands, moving in search of something, encountered a pencil lying on the table beside him, and he picked it up and began drawing initials and scrolls on the margin of a newspaper; and all the scrolls framed initials, and all the initials were the same, twining and twisting into endless variations of the letters S. L.

"Yes, I must go to the office to-morrow," he repeated absently. "I am better—in fact I am quite well, except for this sprain." He looked down at his bandaged foot, then his pencil moved listlessly again, continuing the endless variations on the two letters. It was plain that he was tired.

Fleetwood rose and made his adieux almost affectionately. Plank moved forward on tiptoe, bulky and noiseless; and Siward held out his hand, saying something amiably formal.

"Would you like to have me come again?" asked Plank, red with embarrassment, yet so naïvely that at first Siward found no words to answer him; then—

"Would you care to come, Mr. Plank?"

"Yes."

Siward looked at him curiously, almost cautiously. His first impressions of the man had been summed up in one contemptuous word. Besides, barring that, what was there in common between himself and such a type as Plank? He had not even troubled himself to avoid him at Shotover; he had merely been aware of him when Plank spoke to him; never otherwise, except that afternoon beside the swimming pool, when he had made one of his rare criticisms on Plank.

Perhaps Plank had changed, perhaps Siward had; for he found nothing offensive in the bulky young man now—nothing particularly attractive, either, except for a certain simplicity, a certain direct candour in the heavy blue eyes which met his squarely.

"Come in for a cigar when you have a few moments idle," said Siward slowly.

"It will give me great pleasure," said Plank, bowing.

And that was all. He followed Fleetwood down the stairs; Wands held their coats, and bowed them out into the falling shadows of the winter twilight.

Siward, sitting beside his window, watched them enter their hansom and drive away up the avenue. A dull flush had settled over his cheeks; the aroma of spirits hung in the air, and he looked across the room at the decanter. Presently he drank some of his tea, but it was lukewarm, and he pushed the cup from him.

The clatter of the cup brought the old butler, who toddled hither and thither, removing trays, pulling chairs into place, fussing and pattering about, until a maid came in noiselessly, bearing a lamp. She pulled down the shades, drew the sad-coloured curtains, went to the mantelpiece and peered at the clock, then brought a wine-glass and a spoon to Siward, and measured the dose in silence. He swallowed it, shrugged, permitted her to change the position of his chair and footstool, and nodded thanks and dismissal.

"Gumble, are you there?" he asked carelessly.

The butler entered from the hallway. "Yes, sir."

"You may leave that decanter."

But the old servant may have misunderstood, for he only bowed and ambled off downstairs with the decanter, either heedless or deaf to his master's sharp order to return.

For a while Siward sat there, eyes fixed, scowling into vacancy; then the old, listless, careworn expression returned; he rested one elbow on the window-sill, his worn cheek on his hand, and with the other hand fell to weaving initials with his pencil on the margin of the newspaper lying on the table beside him.

Lamplight brought out sharply the physical change in him—the angular shadows flat under the cheek-bones, the hard, slightly swollen flesh in the bluish shadows around the eyes. The mark of the master-vice was there; its stamp in the swollen, worn-out hollows; its imprint in the fine lines at the corners of his mouth; its sign manual in the faintest relaxation of the under lip, which had not yet become a looseness.

For the last of the Siwards had at last stepped into the highway which his doomed forebears had travelled before him.

"Gumble!" he called irritably.

A quavering voice, an unsteady step, and the old man entered again. "Mr. Stephen, sir?"

"Bring that decanter back. Didn't you hear me tell you just now?"

"Sir?"

"Didn't you hear me?"

"Yes, Mr. Stephen, sir."

There was a silence.

"Gumble!"

"Sir?"

"Are you going to bring that decanter?"

The old butler bowed, and ambled from the room, and for a long while Siward sat sullenly listening and scoring the edges of the paper with his trembling pencil. Then the lead broke short, and he flung it from him and pulled the bell. Wands came this time, a lank, sandy, silent man, grown gray as a rat in the service of the Siwards. He received his master's orders, and withdrew; and again Siward waited, biting his under lip and tearing bits from the edges of the newspaper with fingers never still; but nobody came with the decanter, and after a while his tense muscles relaxed; something in his very soul seemed to snap, and he sank back in his chair, the hot tears blinding him.

He had got as far as that; moments of self-pity were becoming almost as frequent as scorching intervals of self-contempt.

So they all knew what was the matter with him—they all knew—the doctor, the servants, his friends. Had he not surprised the quick suspicion in Fleetwood's glance, when he told him he had slipped, and sprained his ankle? What if he had been drunk when he fell—fell on his own doorsteps, carried into the old Siward house by old Siward servants, drunk as his forefathers? It was none of Fleetwood's business. It was none of the servants' business. It was nobody's business except his own. Who the devil were all these people, to pry into his affairs and doctor him and dose him and form secret leagues to disobey him, and hide decanters from him? Why should anybody have the impertinence to meddle with him? Of what concern to them were his vices or his virtues?

The tears dried in his hot eyes; he jerked the old-fashioned bell savagely; and after a long while he heard servants whispering together in the passage-way outside his door.

He lay very still in his chair; his hearing had become abnormally acute, but he could not make out what they were saying; and as the dull, intestinal aching grew sharper, parching, searing every strained muscle in throat and chest, he struck the table beside him, and clenched his teeth in the fierce rush of agony that swept him from head to foot, crying out an inarticulate menace on his household. And Dr. Grisby came into the room from the outer shadows of the hall.

He was very small, very meagre, very bald, and clean-shaven, with a face like a nut-cracker; and the brown wig he wore was atrocious, and curled forward over his colourless ears. He wore steel-rimmed spectacles, each glass divided into two lenses; and he stood on tiptoe to look out through the upper lenses on the world, and always bent almost double to use the lower or reading lenses.

Besides that, he affected frilled shirts, and string ties, which nobody had ever seen snugly tied. His loose string tie was the first thing Siward could remember about the doctor; and that the doctor had permitted him to pull it when he had the measles, at the age of six.

"What's all this racket?" said the little old doctor harshly. "Got colic? Got the toothache? I'm ashamed of you, Stephen, cutting capers and pounding the furniture! Look up! Look at me! Out with your tongue! Well, now, what the devil's the trouble?"

"You—know," muttered Siward, abandoning his wrist to the little man, who seated himself beside him. Dr. Grisby scarcely noted the pulse; the delicate pressure had become a strong caress.

"Know what?" he grunted. "How do I know what's the matter with you? Hey? Now, now, don't try to explain, Steve; don't fly off the handle! All right; grant that I *do* know what's bothering you; I want to see that ankle first. Here, somebody! Light that gas. Why the mischief don't you have the house wired for electricity, Stephen? It's wholesome. Gas isn't. Lamps are worse, sir. Do as I tell you!" And he went on loquaciously, grumbling and muttering, and never ceasing his talk, while Siward, wincing as the dressing was removed, lay back and closed his eyes.

Half an hour later Gumble appeared, to announce dinner.

"I don't want any," said Siward.

"Eat!" said Dr. Grisby harshly.

"I—don't care to."

"Eat, I tell you! Do you think I don't mean what I say?"

So he ate his broth and toast, the doctor curtly declining to join him. He ate hurriedly, closing his eyes in aversion. Even the iced tea was flat and distasteful to him.

And at last he lay back, white and unstrung, the momentarily deadened desperation glimmering under his half-closed eyes. And for a long while Dr. Grisby sat, doubled almost in two, cuddling his bony little knees and studying the patterns in the faded carpet.

"I guess you'd better go, Stephen," he said at length.

"Up the river—to Mulqueen's?"

"Yes. Let's try it, Steve. You'll be on your feet in two weeks. Then you'd better go—up the river—to Mulqueen's."

"I—I'll go, if you say so. But I can't go now."

"I didn't say go now. I said in two weeks."

"Perhaps."

"Will you give me your word?" demanded the doctor sharply.

"No, doctor."

"Why not?"

"Because I may have to be here on business. There seems to be some sort of crisis coming which I don't understand."

"There's a crisis right here, Steve, which *I* understand!" snapped Dr. Grisby. "Face it like a man! Face it like a man! You're sick—to your bones, boy—sick! sick! Fight the fight, Steve! Fight a good fight. There's a fighting chance; on my soul of honour, there is, Steve, a fighting chance for you! Now! now, boy! Buckle up tight! Tuck up your sword-sleeve! At 'em, Steve! Give 'em hell! Oh, my boy, my boy, I know; *I* know!" The little man's voice broke, but he steadied it instantly with a snap of his nut-cracker jaws, and scowled on his patient and shook his little withered fist at him.

His patient lay very still in the shadow.

"I want you to go," said the doctor harshly, "before your self-control goes. Do you understand? I want you to go before your decision is undermined; before you begin to do devious things, sly things, cheating things, slinking things—anything and everything to get at the thing you crave. I've given you something to fight with, and you won't take it faithfully. I've given you free rein in tobacco and tea and coffee. I've helped you as much as I dare to weather the nights. Now, *you* help *me*—do you hear?"

"Yes . . . I will."

"You say so; now do it. Do something for yourself. Do anything! If you're sick of reading—and I don't blame you, considering the stuff you read—get people down here to see you; get lots of people. Telephone 'em; you've a telephone there, haven't you? There it is, by your elbow. Use it! Call up people. Talk all the time."

"Yes, I will."

"Good! Now, Steve, we know what's the matter, physically, don't we? Of course we do! Now, then, what's the matter *mentally*?"

"Mentally?" repeated Siward under his breath.

"Yes, mentally. What's the trouble? Stocks? Bonds? Lawsuits? Love?" the slightest pause, and a narrowing of the gimlet eyes behind the lenses. "Love?" he repeated harshly. "Which is it, boy? They're all good to let alone."

"Business," said Siward. But, being a Siward, he was obliged to add "partly."

"Business—*partly*," repeated the doctor. "What's the matter with business—partly?"

"I don't know. There are rumours. Hetherington is pounding us—apparently. That Inter-County crowd is acting ominously, too. There's something underhand, somewhere." He bent his head and fell to plucking at the faded brocade on the arm of his chair, muttering to himself, "somewhere, somehow, something underhand. I don't know what; I really don't."

"All right—all right," said the doctor testily; "let it go at that! There's treachery, eh? You suspect it? You're sure of it—as reasonably sure as a gentleman can be of something he is not fashioned to understand? That's it, is it? All right, sir—all right! Very well—ver-y well. Now, sir, look at me! Business symptoms admitted, what about the 'partly,' Stephen?—what about it, eh? What about it?"

But Siward fell silent again.

"Eh? Did you say something? No? Oh, very well, ver-y well, sir. . . . Perfectly correct, Stephen. You have not earned the right to admit further symptoms. No, sir, you have not earned the right to admit them to anybody, not even to yourself. Nor to—*her*!"

"Doctor!"

"Sir?"

"I have—admitted them."

"To yourself, Steve? I'm sorry. You have no right to—yet. I'm sorry——"

"I have admitted them—admitted them—to *her*."

"That settles it," said the doctor grimly, "that clinches it! That locks you to the wheel! That pledges you. The squabble is on, now. It's your honour that's engaged now, not your nerves, not your intestines. It's a good fight—a very good fight, with no chance of losing anything but life. You go up the river to Mulqueen's. That's the strategy in this campaign; that's excellent manœuvring; that's good generalship! Eh? Mask your purpose, Steve; make a feint of camping out here under my guns; then suddenly fling your entire force up the Hudson and fortify yourself at Mulqueen's! Ho, that'll fix 'em! That's going to astonish the enemy!"

His harsh, dry, crackling laughter broke out like the distant rattle of musketry.

The ghost of a smile glimmered in Siward's haunted eyes, then faded as he leaned forward.

"She has refused me," he said simply.

The little doctor, after an incredulous stare, began chattering with wrath. "Refused *you*! Pah! Pooh! That's nothing! That signifies absolutely nothing! It's meaningless! It's a detail. You get well—do you hear? You go and get well; then try it again! *Then* you'll see! And if she is an idiot—in the event of her irrational persistence in an incredible and utterly indefensible attitude"—he choked up, then fairly barked at Siward—"take her anyway, sir! Run off with her! Dominate circumstances, sir! take charge of events! . . . But you can't do it till you've clapped yourself into prison for life. . . . And God help you if you let yourself escape!"

And after a long while Siward said: "If I should ever marry—and—and——"

"Had children, eh? Is *that* it? Oh, it *is*, eh? Well, I say, marry! I say, have children! If you're a man, you'll breed men. The chances are they may not inherit what you have. It skips some generations—some, now and then. But if they do, good God! I say it's better to be born and have a chance to fight than never to come into the arena at all! By winning out, the world learns; by failure, the world is no less wise. The important thing is birth. The main point is to breed—to produce—to reproduce! but not until you stand, sword in hand, and your armed heel on the breast of your prostrate and subconscious self!"

He jumped up and began running about the room with short little bantam steps, talking all the while.

"People say, 'Shall criminals be allowed to mate and produce young? Shall malefactors be allowed to beget? No!' And I say no, too. Never so long as they remain criminals and malefactors; so long as the evil in them is in the ascendant. Never, until they are cured. That's what I say; that's what I maintain. Crime is a disease; criminals are sick people. No marriage for them until they're cured; no children for them until they're well. If they cure themselves, let 'em marry; let 'em breed; for then, if their children inherit the inclination, they also inherit the grit to cauterise the malady."

He produced a huge handkerchief from the tails of his coat, and wiped his damp features and polished his forehead so violently that his wig took a new and jaunty angle.

"I'm talking too much," he said fretfully; "I'm talking a great deal—all the time—continually. I've other patients—several—plenty! Do you think you're the only man I know who's trying to disfigure his liver and make spots come out all over inside him? *Do* you?"

Siward smiled again, a worn, pallid smile.

"I can stand it while you are here, doctor, but when I'm alone it's—hard. One of those crises is close now. I've a bad night ahead—a bad outlook. Couldn't you——"

"No!"

"Just enough to——"

"No, Stephen."

"—Enough to dull it—just a little? I don't ask for enough to make me sleep—not even to make me doze. You have your needle; haven't you, doctor?"

"Yes."

"Then, just this once—for the last time."

"No."

"Why? Are you afraid? You needn't be, doctor. I don't care for it except to give me a little respite, a little rest on a night like this. I'm so tired of this ache. If I could only have some sleep, and wake up in good shape, I'd stand a better chance of fighting. . . . Wait, doctor! Just one moment. I don't mean to be a coward, but I've had a hard fight, and—I'm tired. . . . If you could see your way to helping me——"

"I dare not help you any more that way."

"Not this once?"

"Not this once."

There was a dead silence, broken at last by the doctor with a violent gesture toward the telephone. "Talk to the girl! Why don't you talk to the girl! If she's worth a hill o' beans she'll help you to hang on. What's she for, if she isn't for such moments? Tell her you need her voice; tell her you need her faith in you. Damn central! Talk out in church! Don't make a goddess of a woman. The men who want to marry her, and can't, will do that! The nincompoop can always be counted on to deify the commonplace. And she *is* commonplace. If she isn't, she's no good! Commend me to sanity and the commonplace. I take off my hat to it! I honour it. God bless it! Good-night!"

Siward lay still for a long while after the doctor had gone. More than an hour had passed before he slowly sat up and groped for the telephone book, opened it, and searched in a blind, hesitating way until he found the number he was looking for.

He had never telephoned to her; he had never written her except once, in reply to her letter in regard to his mother's death—that strange, timid, formal letter, in which, grief-stunned as he was, he saw only the formality, and had answered it more formally still. And that was all that had come of the days and nights by that northern sea—a letter and its answer, and silence.

And, thinking of these things, he shut the book wearily, and lay back in the shadow of the faded curtain, closing his sunken eyes.

CHAPTER IX

CONFESSIONS

In a city in transition, where yesterday is as dead as a dead century, where those who prepare the old year for burial are already taking the ante-mortem statement of the new, the future fulfils the functions of the present. Time itself is considered merely as a by-product of horse-power, discounted with flippancy as the unavoidable friction clogging the fly-wheel of progress.

Memory, once a fine art, is becoming a lost art in Manhattan.

His world and his city had almost ceased to think of Siward.

For a few weeks men spoke of him in the several clubs of which he had lately been a member—spoke of him always in the past tense; and after a little while spoke of him no more.

In that section of the social system which he had inhabited, his absence on account of his mother's death being taken for granted, people laid him away in their minds almost as ceremoniously as they had laid away the memory of his mother. Nothing halted because he was not present; nothing was delayed, rearranged, or abandoned because his familiar presence chanced to be missing. There remained only one more place to fill at a cotillion, dinner, or bridge party; only another man for opera box or week's end; one man the more to be counted on, one more man to be counted out—transferred to the credit of profit and loss, and the ledger closed for the season.

They who remembered him, among those who had not yet lost that old-fashioned art, were very few—a young girl here and there, over whom he had been absent-mindedly sentimental; a débutante or two who had adored him from a distance as a friend of elder sister or brother; here and there an old, old lady to whom he had been considerate, and who perhaps remembered something of the winning charm of the Siwards when the town was young—his father, perhaps, perhaps his grandfather—these thought of him at intervals; the remainder had no leisure to remember even if they had not forgotten how to do it. Several cabmen missed him for a while; now and then a privileged café waiter inquired about him from gay, noisy parties entering some old haunt of his. Mr. Desmond, of art gallery and roulette notoriety, whose business is not to forget, was politely regretful at his absence from certain occult ceremonies which he had at irregular intervals graced with votive offerings. And the list ended there—almost, not quite; for there were two people who had not forgotten Siward: Howard Quarrier and Beverly Plank; and one other, a third, who could not yet forget him if she would—but, as yet, she had not tried very desperately.

The day that Siward left New York to visit everybody's friend, Mr. Mulqueen, in the country, Plank called on him for the second time in his life, and was presently received in the south drawing-room, the library being limited to an informality and intimacy not for Mr. Plank.

Siward, still lame, and using unskilfully two shiny new crutches, came down the stairs and stumped into the drawing-room, which, in spite of the sombre, clustering curtains, was brightly illuminated by the winter sunshine reflected from the snow in the street. Plank was shocked at the change in him—at the ghost of a voice, listlessly formal; at the thin, nerveless hand offered; startled, so that he forgot his shyness, and retained the bony hand tightly in his, and instinctively laid his other great cushion-like paw over it, holding it imprisoned, unable to speak, unconscious, in the impulse of the moment, of the liberty he permitted himself, and which he had never dreamed of taking with such a man as Siward.

The effect on Siward was composite; his tired voice ceased; surprise, inability to understand tinged with instinctive displeasure, were succeeded by humourous curiosity; and, very slowly it became plain to him that this beefy young man liked him, was naïvely concerned about him, felt friendly toward him, and was showing it as spontaneously as a child. Because he now understood something of how it is with a man who is in the process of being forgotten, his perceptions were perhaps the finer in these days, and the direct unconsciousness of Plank touched him more heavily than the pair of heavy hands enclosing his.

"I thought I'd come," began Plank, growing redder and redder as he began to realise the enormity of familiarity committed only on the warrant of impulse. "You don't look well."

"It was good of you to think of me," said Siward. "Come up to the library, if you've a few minutes to spare an invalid. Please go first; I'm a trifle lame yet."

"I—I am sorry," muttered Plank, "very, very sorry."

At first, in the library, Plank was awkward and silent, finding nothing to say, and nowhere to dispose of his hands, until Siward gave him a cigar to occupy his fingers. Even then he continued to sit uncomfortably, his bulk balanced on a rickety, spindle-legged chair, which he stubbornly refused to exchange for another, at Siward's suggestion, out of sheer embarrassment, and with a confused idea that his refusal would somehow ultimately put him at his ease with his surroundings.

Siward, secretly amused, rang for tea, although the hour was early. After a little while, either the toast or the tea appeared to act on Plank as a lingual laxative, for he began suddenly to talk, which is characteristic of bashful men; and Siward gravely helped him on when he floundered and turned shy. After a little, matters went very well with them, and Plank, much more at ease than he had ever dared to hope he could be with Siward, talked and talked; and Siward, his crutches across his knees, lay back in his arm-chair, chatting with that winning informality so becoming to men who are unconscious of their charm.

Watching Plank, it occurred to him gradually that this great, cumbersome creature was not a shrewd, thrifty, self-made and self-finished adult at all; only a big, wistful, lonely boy, without comrades and with nowhere to play. On Plank's round face there remained no trace of shrewdness, of stubbornness, nothing even of the heavy, saturnine placidity of a dogged man who waits his turn.

Plank spoke of himself after a while, sounding the personal note with tentative timidity. Siward gravely encouraged him, and in a little while the outlines of his crude autobiography appeared, embodying his eventless boyhood in a Pennsylvania town; his career at the high school; the dawning desire for college equipment, satisfied by his father, who owned shares in the promising

Deepvale Steel Plank Company; the unhappy years at Harvard—hard years, for he learned with difficulty; solitary years, for he was not sought by those whom he desired to know. Then he ventured to speak of his father's growing interest in steel; the merging and absorbing of independent plants; his own entry upon the scene on the death of his father; and—the rest—material fortune and prosperity, which, perhaps, might stand substitute as a social sponsor for him; stand, perhaps, for something of what he lacked in himself, which only long residence amid the best, long-formed habits for the best, or a long inheritance of the best could give. Did Siward think so? Was the best beyond his reach? Was it hopeless for such a man as he to try? And why?

The innocent snobbery, the abashed but absolute simplicity of this ponderous pilgrim from the smelting pits clambering upward through the high school of the smoky town, groping laboriously through the chilly halls of Harvard toward the outer breastworks of Manhattan, interested Siward; and he said so in his pleasant way, without offence, and with a smiling question at the end.

"Worth while?" repeated Plank, flushing heavily, "it is worth while to me. I have always desired to be a part of the best that there is in my own country; and the best is here, isn't it?"

"Not necessarily," said Siward, still smiling. "The noisiest is here, and some of the best."

"Which *is* the best?" inquired Plank naïvely.

"Why, all plain people, whose education, breeding, and fortune permit them the luxury of thinking, and whose tastes, intelligence, and sanity enable them to express their thoughts. There are such people here, and some of them form a portion of the gaudier and noisier galaxy we call society."

"*That* is what I wish to be part of," said Plank. "Could you tell me what are the requirements?"

"I don't believe I could, exactly," said Siward, amused. "With us, the social system, as an established and finished system, has too recently been evolved from outer chaos to be characteristic of anything except the crudity and energy of the chaos from which it emerged. The balance between wealth, intelligence, and breeding has not yet been established—not from lack of wealth or intelligence. The formula has not been announced, that is all."

"What is the formula?" insisted Plank.

"The formula is the receipt for a real society," replied Siward, laughing. "At present we have its uncombined ingredients in the raw—noisy wealth and flippant fashion, arrogant intelligence and dowdy breeding—all excellent materials, when filtered and fused in the retort; and many of our test tubes have already precipitated pure metal besides, and our national laboratory is turning out fine alloys. Some day we'll understand the formula, and we'll weld the entire mass; and that will be society, Mr. Plank."

"In the meanwhile," repeated Plank, unsmiling, "I want to be part of the best we have. I want to be part of the brightness of things. I mean, that I cannot be contented with an imitation."

"An imitation?"

"Of the best—of what you say is not yet society. I ask no more than your footing among the people of this city. I wish to be able to go where such men as you go; be permitted, asked, desired to be part of what you always have been part of. Is it a great deal I ask? Tell me, Mr. Siward—for I don't know—is it too much to expect?"

"I don't think it is a very high ambition," said Siward, smiling. "What you ask is not very much to ask of life, Mr. Plank."

"But is there any reason why I may not hope to go where I wish to go?"

"I think it depends upon yourself," said Siward, "upon your capacity for being, or for making people believe you to be exactly what they require. You ask me whether you may be able to go where you desire; and I answer you that there is no limit to any journey except the sprinting ability of the pilgrim."

Plank laughed a little, and his squared jaws relaxed; then, after a few moments' thought:

"It is curious that what you cast away from you so easily, I am waiting for with all the patience I have in me. And yet it is always yours to pick up again whenever you wish; and I may never live to possess it."

He was so perfectly right that Siward said nothing; in fact, he could have no particular interest or sympathy for a man's quest of what he himself did not understand the lack of. Those born without a tag unmistakably ticketing them and their positions in the world were perforce ticketed. Siward took it for granted that a man belonged where he was to be met; and all he cared about was to find him civil, whether he happened to be a policeman or a master of fox-hounds.

He was, now that he knew Plank, contented to accept him anywhere he met him; but Plank's upward evolutions upon the social ladder were of no interest to him, and his naïve snobbery was becoming something of a bore.

So Siward directed the conversation into other channels, and Plank, accepting another cup of tea, became very communicative about his stables and his dogs, and the preservation of game; and after a while, looking up confidently at Siward, he said:

"Do you think it beastly to drive pheasants the way I did at Black Fells? I have heard that you were disgusted."

"It isn't my idea of a square deal," said Siward frankly.

"That settles it, then."

"But you should not let me interfere with——"

"I'll take your opinion, and thank you for it. It didn't seem to me to be the thing; only it's done over here, you know. The De Coursay's and the——"

"Yes, I know. . . . Glad you feel that way about it, Plank. It's pretty rotten sportsmanship. Don't you think so?"

"I do. I—would you—I should like to ask you to try some square shooting at the Fells," stammered Plank, "next season, if you would care to."

"You're very good. I should like to, if I were going to shoot at all; but I fancy my shooting days are over, for a while."

"Over!"

"Business," nodded Siward, absently grave again. "I see no prospect of my idling for the next year or two."

"You are in—in Amalgamated Electric, I think," ventured Plank.

"Very much in," replied the other frankly. "You've read the papers and heard rumours, I suppose?"

"Some. I don't suppose anybody quite understands the attacks on Amalgamated."

" I don't—not yet. Do you? "

Plank sat silent, then his shrewd under lip began to protrude.

" I'm wondering," he began cautiously, " how much the Algonquin crowd understands about the matter? "

Siward's troubled eyes were on him as he spoke, watching closely, narrowly.

" I've heard that rumour before," he said.

" So have I," said Plank, " and it seems incredible." He looked warily at Siward. " Suppose it is true that the Algonquin Trust Company is godfather to Inter-County. That doesn't explain why a man should kick his own door down when there's a bell to ring and servants to let him in—and out again, too."

" I have wondered," said Siward, " whether the door he might be inclined to kick down is really his own door any longer."

" I, too," said Plank simply. " It may belong to a personal enemy—if he has any. He could afford to have an enemy, I suppose."

Siward nodded.

" Then, hadn't you better—I beg your pardon! You have not asked me to advise you."

" No. I may ask your advice some day. Will you give it when I do? "

" With pleasure," said Plank, so warmly disinterested, so plainly proud and eager to do a service that Siward, surprised and touched, found no word to utter.

Plank rose. Siward attempted to stand up, but had trouble with his crutches.

" Please don't try," said Plank, coming over and offering his hand. " May I stop in again soon? Oh, you are off to the country for a month or two? I see. . . . You don't look very well. I hope it will benefit you. Awfully glad to have seen you. I—I hope you won't forget me—entirely."

"I am the man people are forgetting," returned Siward, "not you. It was very nice of you to come. You are one of very few who remember me at all."

"I have very few people to remember," said Plank; "and if I had as many as I could desire I should remember you first."

Here he became very much embarrassed. Siward offered his hand again. Plank shook it awkwardly, and went away on tiptoe down the stairs which creaked decorously under his weight.

And that ended the first interview between Plank and Siward in the first days of the latter's decline.

The months that passed during Siward's absence from the city began to prove rather eventful for Plank. He was finally elected a member of the Patroons Club, without serious opposition; he had dined twice with the Kemp Ferralls; he and Major Belwether were seen together at the Caithness dance, and in the Caithness box at the opera. Once a respectable newspaper reported him at Tuxedo for the week's end; his name, linked with the clergy, frequently occupied such space under the column headed "Ecclesiastical News" as was devoted to the progress of the new chapel, and many old ladies began to become familiar with his name.

At the right moment the Mortimers featured him between two fashionable bishops at a dinner. Mrs. Vendenning, who adored bishops, immediately remembered him among those asked to her famous annual *bal poudré*; a celebrated yacht club admitted him to membership; a whole shoal of excellent minor clubs which really needed new members followed suit, and even the rock-ribbed Lenox, wearied of its own time-honoured immobility, displayed the preliminary fidgets which boded well for the stolid candidate. The Mountain was preparing to take the first stiff step toward Mohammed. It was the prophet's cue to sit tight and yawn occasionally.

Meanwhile he didn't want to; he was becoming anxious to do things for himself, which Leila Mortimer, of course, would not permit. It was difficult for him to understand that any effort of his own would probably be disastrous; that progress could come only through his own receptive passivity; that nothing was demanded, nothing required, nothing permitted from him as yet, save a capacity for assimilating such opportunities as sections of the social system condescended to offer.

For instance, he wanted to open his art gallery to the public; he said it was good strategy; and Mrs. Mortimer sat upon the suggestion with a shrug of her pretty shoulders. Well, then, couldn't he possibly do something with his great, gilded ball-room? No, he couldn't; and the less in evidence his galleries and his ball-rooms were at present the better his chances with people who, perfectly aware that he possessed them, were very slowly learning to overlook the insolence of the accident that permitted him to possess what they had never known the want of. First of all people must tire of repeating to each other that he was nobody, and that would happen when they wearied of explaining to one another why he was ever asked anywhere. There was time enough for him to offer amusement to people after they had ceased to find amusement in snubbing him; plenty of time in the future for them to lash him to a gallop for their pleasure. In the meanwhile he was doing very well, because he began to appear regularly in the Caithness-Bonnesdel box, and old Peter Caithness was already boring him at the Patroons; which meant that the thrifty old gentleman considered Plank's millions as a possible underpinning for the sagging house of Caithness, of which his pallid daughter Agatha was the sole sustaining caryatid in perspective.

Yes, he was doing well; for that despotic beauty, Sylvia Landis, whose capricious perversity had recently astonished those who remembered her in her first season as a sweet, reasonable, and unspoiled girl, was always friendly with him. That must be looked upon as important, considering Sylvia's unassailable position, and her kinship to the autocratic old lady whose kindly ukase had for generations remained the undisputed law in the social system of Manhattan.

"There is another matter," said Leila Mortimer innocently, as Plank, lingering after a disastrous rubber of bridge with her, her husband, and Agatha Caithness, had followed her into her own apartments to write his cheque for what he owed. "You've driven with me so much and you come here so often and we are seen together so frequently that the clans are sharpening up their dirks for us. And that helps some."

"What!" exclaimed Plank, reddening, and twisting around in his chair.

"Certainly. You didn't suppose I could escape, did you?"

"Escape! What?" demanded Plank, getting redder.

"Escape being talked about, savagely, mercilessly. Can't you see how it helps? Oh dear, *are* you stupid, Beverly?"

"I don't know," replied Plank, staring, "just how stupid I am. If you mean that I'm compromising you——"

"Oh, please! Why do you use back-stairs words?

Nobody talks about compromising now; all that went out with New Year's calls and brown-stone stoops."

"What *do* they call it, then?" asked Plank seriously.

"Call what? you great boy!"

"What you say I'm doing?"

"*I* don't say it."

"Who does?"

Leila laughed, leaned back in her big, padded chair, dropping one knee over the other. Her dark eyes with the Japanese slant to them rested mockingly on Plank, who had now turned completely around in his chair, leaving his half-written cheque on her escritoire behind him.

"You're simply credited with an affair with a pretty woman," she said, watching the dull colour mounting to his temples, "and that is certain to be useful to you, and it doesn't affect me. What on earth are you blushing about?" And as he said nothing, she added, with a daring little laugh: "You are credited with being very agreeable, you see."

"If—if that's the way you take it—" he began.

"Of course! What do you expect me to do—call for help before I'm hurt?"

"You mean that this talk—gossip—doesn't hurt?"

"How silly!" She looked at him, smiling. "You know how likely I am to require protection from your importunities." She dropped her pretty head, and began plaiting with her fingers the silken gown over her knee. "Or how likely I would be to shriek for it even if"—she looked up with childlike directness—"even if I needed it."

"Of course you can take care of yourself," said Plank, wincing.

"I could, if I wanted to."

"Everybody knows that. I know it, Leroy knows it; only I don't care to figure as that kind of man."

Already he had lost sight of her position in the matter; and she drew a long, quiet breath, almost like a sigh.

"Time enough after you marry," she said deliberately, and lighted a cigarette from a candle, recrossing her knees the other way.

He considered her, started to speak, checked himself, and swung around to the desk again. His pen hovered over the space to be filled in. He tried to recollect the amount, hesitated, dated the cheque and affixed his signature, still trying to remember; then he looked at her over his shoulder.

"I forget the exact amount."

She surveyed him through the haze of her cigarette, but made no answer.

"I forget the amount," he repeated.

"So do I," she nodded indolently.

"But I——"

"Let it go. Besides, I shall not accept it."

He flushed up, astonished. "You can't refuse to take a gambling debt."

"I do," she retorted coolly. "I'm tired of taking your money."

"But you won it."

"I'm tired of winning it. It is all I ever do win . . . from you."

Her pretty head was wreathed in smoke. She tipped the ashes from the cigarette's end, watching them fall to powder on the rug.

"I don't know what you mean," he persisted doggedly.

"Don't you? I don't believe I do, either. There are intervals in my career which might prove eloquent if I opened my lips. But I don't, except to make floating rings and cabalistic signs out of cigarette smoke. Can you read their meaning? Look! There goes one, and there's another, and another—all twisting and uncurling into hieroglyphics. They are very significant; they might tell you a lot of things, if you would only translate them. But you haven't the key—have you?"

There was a heavy, jarring step in the main living-room, and Mortimer's bulk darkened the doorway.

"*Entrez, mon ami,*" nodded Leila, glancing up. "Where is Agatha?"

"I'm going to Desmond's," he grunted, ignoring his wife's question; "do you want to try it again, Beverly?"

"I can't make Leila take her own winnings," said Plank, holding out the signed but unfilled cheque to Mortimer, who took it and scrutinised it for a moment, rubbing his heavy, inflamed eyes; then, gesticulating, the cheque fluttering in his puffy fingers:

"Come on," he insisted. "I've a notion that I can give Desmond a whirl that he won't forget in a hurry. Agatha's asleep; she's going to that ball—where is it?" he demanded, turning on his wife. "Yes, yes; the Page blow-out. You're going, I suppose?"

Leila nodded, and lighted another cigarette.

"All right," continued Mortimer impatiently; "you and Agatha won't start before one. And if you think Plank had better go, why, we'll be back here in time."

"That means you won't be back at all," observed his wife coolly; "and it's good policy for Beverly to go where he's asked. Can't you turn in and sleep, now, and amuse your friend Desmond to-morrow night?"

"No, I can't. What a fool I'd be to let a chance slip when I feel like a winner!"

"You never feel otherwise when you gamble," said Leila.

"Yes, I do," he retorted peevishly. "I can tell almost every time what the cards are going to do to me. Leila, go to sleep. We'll be back here for you by one, or half past."

"Look here, Leroy," began Plank, "there's one thing I can't stand for, and that's this continual loss of sleep. If I go with you I'll not be fit to go to the Pages."

"What a farmer you are!" sneered Mortimer. "I believe you roost on the foot-board of your bed, like a confounded turkey. Come on! You'd better begin training, you know. People in this town are not going to stand for the merry ploughboy game, you see!"

But Plank was shrewdly covering his principal reason for declining; he had too often "temporarily" assisted Mortimer at Desmond's and Burbank's, when Mortimer, cleaned out and unable to draw against a balance non-existent, had plucked him by the sleeve from the faro table with the breathless request for a loan.

"I tell you I can wring Desmond dry to-night," repeated Mortimer sullenly. "It isn't a case of 'want to,' either; it's a case of 'got to.' That old pink-and-white rabbit, Belwether, got me into a game this afternoon, and between him and Voucher and Alderdine I'm stripped clean as a kennel bone."

But Plank shook his head, pretending to yawn; and Mortimer, glowering and lingering, presently went off, his swollen hands thrust into his trousers' pockets, his gross features dark with disgust; and presently they heard the front door slam, and a rattling tattoo of horses' feet on the asphalt; and Leila sprang up impatiently, and, passing Plank, traversed the passage to the windows of the front room.

"He's taken the horses—the beast!" she said calmly, as Plank joined her at the great windows and looked out into the night, where the round, drooping, flower-like globes of the electric lamps spread a lake of silver before the house.

It was rather rough on Leila. The Mortimers maintained one pair of horses only; and the use given them at all hours resulted in endless scenes, and an utter impossibility for Leila to retain the same coachman and footman for more than a few weeks at a time.

"He won't come back; he'll keep Martin and the horses standing in front of Delmonico's all night. You'd better call up the stables, Beverly."

So Plank called up a livery and arranged for transportation at one; and Leila seated herself at a card-table and began to deal herself cold decks, thoughtfully.

"That bit in 'Carmen,'" she said, "it always brings the shudder; it never palls on me, never grows stale." She whipped the ominous spade from the pack and held it out. "*La Mort!*" she exclaimed in mock tragedy, yet there was another undertone ringing through it, sounding, too, in her following laugh. "Draw!" she commanded, holding out the pack; and Plank drew a diamond.

"Naturally," she nodded, shuffling the pack with her smooth, savant fingers and laying them out as she repeated the formula: "*Qui frappe? Qui entre? Qui prend chaise? Qui parle?* Oh, the deuce! it's always the same! *Tiens! je m'ennui!*" There was a flash of her bare arm, a flutter, and the cards fell in a shower over them both.

Plank flipped a card from his knee, laughing uncertainly, aware of symptoms in his pretty vis-à-vis which always made him uncomfortable. For months, now, at certain intervals, these recurrent symptoms had made him wary; but what they might portend he did not know, only that, alone with her, moments occurred when he was heavily aware of a tension which, after a while, affected even his few thick nerves. One of those intervals was threatening now: her flushed cheeks, her feverish activity with her hands, the unconscious reflex movement of her silken knees and restless slippers, all foreboded it. Next would come the nervous laughter, the swift epigram which bored and puzzled him, the veiled badinage he was unequal to; and then the hint of weariness, the curious pathos of long silences, the burnt-out beauty of her eyes from which the fire had gone as though quenched by invisible tears within.

He ascribed it—desired to ascribe it—to her relations with her husband. He had naturally learned and divined how matters stood with them; he had learned considerable in the last month or two—something of Mortimer's record as a burly brother to the rich; something of his position among those who made no question of his presence anywhere. Something of Leila, too, he had heard, or rather deduced from hinted word or shrug or smiling silence, not meant for him, but indifferent to what he might hear and what he might think of what he heard.

He did listen; he did patiently add two and two in the long solitudes of his Louis XV chamber; and if the results were not always four, at least they came within a fraction of the proper answer. And this did not alter his policy or weaken his faith in his mentors; nor did it impair his real gratitude to them, and his real and simple friendship for them both. He was faithful in friendship once formed, obstinately so, for better or for worse; but he was shrewd enough to ignore opportunities for friendships which he foresaw could do him no good on his plodding pilgrimage toward the temple of his inexorable desire.

Lifting, now, his Delft-coloured eyes furtively, he studied the silk-and-lace swathed figure of the young matron opposite, flung back into the depths of her great chair, profile turned from him, her chin imprisoned in her ringed fingers. The brooding abandon of the attitude contrasted sharply with the grooming of the woman, making both the more effective.

"Turn in, if you want to," she said, her voice indistinct, smothered by her pink palm. "You're to dress in Leroy's quarters."

"I don't want to turn in just yet."

"You said you needed sleep."

"I do. But it's not eleven yet."

She slipped into another posture, reaching for a cigarette, and, setting it afire from the match he offered, exhaled a cloud of smoke and looked dreamily through it at him.

"Who is she?" she asked in a colourless voice. "Tell me, for I don't know. Agatha? Marion Page? Mrs. Vendenning? or the Tassel girl?"

"Nobody—yet," he admitted cheerfully.

"Nobody—*yet*," she repeated, musing over her cigarette. "That's good politics, if it's true."

"Am I untruthful?" he asked simply.

"*I* don't know. Are you? You're a man."

"Don't talk that way, Leila."

"No, I won't. What is it that you and Sylvia

Landis have to talk about so continuously every time you meet?"

"She's merely civil to me," he explained.

"That's more than she is to a lot of people. What do you talk about?"

"I don't know—nothing in particular; mostly about Shotover, and the people there last summer."

"Doesn't she ever mention Stephen Siward?"

"Usually. She knows I like him."

"She likes him, too," said Leila, looking at him steadily.

"I know it. Everybody likes him—or did. I do, yet."

"I do, too," observed Mrs. Mortimer coolly. "I was in love with him. He was only a boy then."

Plank nodded in silence.

"Where is he now—do you know?" she asked. "Everybody says he's gone to the devil."

"He's in the country somewhere," replied Plank cautiously. "I stopped in to see him the other day, but nobody seemed to know when he would return."

Mrs. Mortimer tossed her cigarette onto the hearth. For a long interval of silence she lay there in her chair, changing her position restlessly from moment to moment; and at length she lay quite still, so long that Plank began to think she had fallen asleep in her chair.

He rose. She did not stir, and, passing her, he instinctively glanced down. Her cheeks, half buried against the back of the chair, were overflushed; under the closed lids the lashes glistened wet in the lamplight.

Surprised, embarrassed, he halted, as though afraid to move; and she sat up with a nervous shake of her shoulders.

"'What a life!' she said, under her breath; 'what a life for a woman to lead!'"

"What a life!" she said, under her breath; "what a life for a woman to lead!"

"Wh-whose?" he blurted out.

"Mine!"

He stared at her uneasily, finding nothing to say. He had never before heard anything like this from her.

"Can't *anybody* help me out of it?" she said quietly.

"Who? How? . . . Do you mean——"

"Yes, I mean it! I *mean* it! I——"

And suddenly she broke down, in a strange, stammering, tearless way, opening the dry flood-gates over which rattled an avalanche of words—bitter, breathless phrases rushing brokenly from lips that shrank as they formed them.

Plank sat inert, the corroding echo of the words clattering in his ears. And after a while he heard his own altered voice sounding persistently in repetition:

"Don't say those things, Leila; don't tell me such things."

"Why? Don't you *care*?"

"Yes, yes, I care; but I can't do anything! I have no business to hear—to see you this way."

"To whom can I speak, then, if I can not speak to you? To whom can I turn? Where am I to turn, in all the world?"

"I don't know," he said fearfully; "the only way is to go on."

"What else have I done? What else am I doing?" she cried. "Go on? Am I not trudging on and on through life, dragging the horror of it behind me through the mud, except when the horror drags me? To whom am I to turn—to other beasts like him?—

sitting patiently around, grinning and slavering, awaiting their turn when the horror of it crushes me to the mud?"

She stretched out a rounded, quivering arm, and laid the small fingers of the left hand on its flawless contour. "Look!" she said, exasperated, "I am young yet; the horror has not yet corrupted the youth in me. I am fashioned for some reason, am I not?—for some purpose, some happiness. I am not bad; I am human. What poison has soaked into me can be eliminated. I tell you, no woman is capable of being so thoroughly poisoned that the antidote proves useless.

"But I tell you men, also, that unless she find that antidote she will surely reinfect herself. A man can not do what that man has done to me and expect me to recover unaided. People talk of me, and I have given them subjects enough! But—look at me! Straight between the eyes! Every law have I broken except that! Do you understand? That *one*, which you men consider yourselves exempt from, I have not broken—yet! Shall I speak plainer? It is the fashion to be crude. But—I can't be; I am unfashionable, you see."

She laughed, her haunted eyes fixed on his.

"Is there no chance for me? Because I drag his bedraggled name about with me is there no decent chance, no decent hope? Is there only indecency in prospect, if a man comes to care for a married woman? Can't a decent man love her at all? I—I think——"

Her hands, outstretched, trembled, then flew to her face; and she stood there swaying, until Plank perforce stepped to her side and steadied her against him.

So they remained for a while, until she looked up dazed, weary, ashamed, expecting nothing of him; and when it came, leaving her still incredulous, his arms around her, his tense, flushed face recoiling from their first kiss, she did not seem to comprehend.

"I *can't* turn on *him*," he stammered, "I—we are friends, you see. How can I love you, if that is so?"

"Could you love me?" she asked calmly.

"I—I don't know. I did love—I do care for—another woman. I can't marry her, though I am given to understand there is a chance. Perhaps it is partly ambition," he said honestly, "for I am quite sure she has never cared for me, never thought of me in that way. I think a man can't stand that long."

"No; only women can. Who is she?"

"You won't ask me, will you?"

"No. Are you sorry that I am in love with you?"

His arms unclasped her body, and he stepped back, facing her.

"*Are* you?" she asked violently.

"No."

"You speak like a *man*," she said tremulously. "Am I to be permitted to adore you in peace, then—decently, and in peace?"

"Don't speak that way, Leila. I—there is no woman, no friend, I care for as much as I do you. It is easy, I think, for a woman, like you, to make a man care for her. You will not do it, will you?"

"I will," she said softly.

"It's no use; I can't turn on him. I can't! He is my friend, you see."

"Let him remain so. I shall do what I can. Let him remain a monument to his fellow-beasts. What do I care? Do you think I desire to turn you into his image? Do you think I hope for your degradation and mine? Are you afraid I should not recognise love unaccompanied by the attendant beast? I—I don't know;

you had better teach me, if I prove blind. If you can love me, do so in charity before I go blind forever."

She laid one hand on his arm, looked at him, then turned and passed slowly through the doorway.

"If you are going to sleep before we start you had better be about it!" she said, looking back at him from the stairs.

But he had no further need of sleep; and for a long while he stood at the windows watching the lamps of cabs and carriages sparkling through the leafless thickets of the park like winter fire-flies.

At one o'clock, hearing Agatha Caithness speak to Leila's maid, he left the window, and sitting down at the desk, telephoned to Desmond's; and he was informed that Mortimer, hard hit, had signified his intention of recouping at Burbank's. Then he managed to get Burbank's on the wire, and finally Mortimer himself, but was only cursed for his pains and cut off in the middle of his pleading.

So he wandered up-stairs into Mortimer's apartments, where he tubbed and dressed, and finally descended, to find Agatha Caithness alone in the library, spinning a roulette wheel and whistling an air from "La Bacchante."

"That's pretty," he said; "sing it."

"No; it's better off without the words; and so are you," added Agatha candidly, relinquishing the wheel and strolling with languid grace about the room, hands on her hips, timing her vagrant steps to the indolent, wicked air. And,

"'Je rougirais de mon ivresse
Si tu conservais ta raison!'"

she hummed deliberately, pivoting on her heels and advancing again toward Plank, her pretty, pale face delicate as an enamelled cameo under the flood of light from the crystal chandeliers.

"I understand that Mr. Mortimer is not coming with us," she said carelessly. "Are you going to dance with me, if I find nobody better?"

He expressed himself flattered, cautiously. He was one of many who never understood this tall, white, low-voiced girl, with eyes too pale for beauty, yet strangely alluring, too. Few men denied the indefinable enchantment of her; few men could meet her deep-lidded, transparent gaze unmoved. In the sensitive curve of her mouth there was a kind of sensuousness; in her low voice, in her pallor, in the slim grace of her a vague provocation that made men restless and women silently curious for something more definite on which to base their curiosity.

She was wearing, over the smooth, dead-white skin of her neck, a collar of superb diamonds and aquamarines—almost an effrontery, as the latter were even darker than her eyes; yet the strange and effective harmony was evident, and Plank spoke of the splendour of the gems.

She nodded indifferently, saying they were new, and that she had picked them up at Tiffany's; and he mentally sketched out the value of the diamonds, a trifle surprised, because Leila Mortimer had carefully informed him about the condition of the Caithness exchequer.

That youthful matron herself appeared in a few moments, very lustrous, very lovely in her fragrant, exotic brightness, and Plank for the first time thought that she was handsome—the vigorous, youthful incarnation of Life itself, in contrast to Agatha's almost deathly beauty. She greeted him not only without a trace of embarrassment, but with such a friendly, fresh, gay confidence that he scarcely recognised in her the dry-eyed, feverish woman of an hour ago, whose very lips shrank back, scorched by the torrent of her own invective.

And so they drove the three short blocks to the Page's in their hired livery; the street was inadequate for the crush of vehicles; and the glittering pressure within the house was outrageous; all of which confused Plank, who became easily confused by such things.

How they got in—how they managed to present themselves—who took Leila and Agatha from him—where they went—where he himself might be—he did not understand very clearly. The house was large, strange, full of strangers. He attempted to obtain his bearings by wandering about looking for a small rococo reception-room where he remembered he had once talked kennel talk with Marion Page, and had on another occasion perspired freely under the arrogant and strabismic glare of her mother. That good lady had really rather liked him; he never suspected it.

But he couldn't find the rococo room—or perhaps he didn't recognise it. So many people—so many, many people whom he did not know, whom he had never before laid eyes on—high-bred faces hard as diamonds; young, gay, laughing faces; brilliant eyes encountering his without a softening of recognition; clean-cut, attractive men in swarms, all animated, all amused, all at home among themselves and among the silken visions of loveliness passing and repassing, with here an extended gloved arm and the cordial greeting of camaraderie, there a quick smile, a swift turn in passing, a capricious bending forward for a whisper, a compliment, a jest—

all this swept by him, around him, enveloping him with its brightness, its gaiety, its fragrance, and left him more absolutely alone than he had ever been in all his life.

He tried to find Leila, and gave it up. He saw Quarrier talking to Agatha, but the former saluted him so coldly that he turned away.

After a while he found Marion, but she hadn't a dance left for him; neither had Rena Bonnesdel, whom he encountered while she was adroitly avoiding one of the ever-faithful twins. The twin caught up with her in consequence, and she snubbed Plank for his share in the disaster, which depressed him, and he started for the smoking-room, wherever that haven might be found. He got into the ball-room, however, by mistake, and adorned the wall, during the cotillon, as closely as his girth permitted, until an old lady sent for him; and he went and talked about bishops for nearly an hour to her, until his condition bordered on frenzy, the old lady being deaf and peevish.

Later, Alderdene used him to get rid of an angular, old harridan who seemed to be one solid diamond-mine, and who drove him into a corner and talked indelicacies until Plank's broad face flamed like the setting sun. Then Captain Voucher unloaded a frightened débutante on him who tried to talk about horses and couldn't; and they hated each other for a while, until, looking around her in desperation, she found he had vanished—which was quick work for a man of his size.

Kathryn Tassel employed him for supper, and kept him busy while she herself was immersed in a dawning affair with Fleetwood. She did everything to him except to tip him; and her insolence was the last straw.

Then, unexpectedly in the throng, two wonderful

sea-blue eyes encountered his, deepening to violet with pleasure, and the trailing sweetness of a voice he knew was repeating his name, and a slim, white-gloved hand lay in his own.

Her escort, Ferrall, nodded to him pleasantly. She leaned forward from Ferrall's arm, saying, under her breath, "I have saved a dance for you. Please ask me at once. Quick! do you want me?"

"I—I do," stammered Plank.

Ferrall, suspicious, stepped forward to exchange civilities, then turning to the girl beside him: "See here, Sylvia, you've dragged me all over this house on one pretext or another. *Do* you want any supper, or *don't* you? If you don't, it's our dance."

"No, I don't. No, it isn't. Kemp, you annoy me!"

"That's a nice thing to say! Is it your delicately inimitable way of giving me my congé?"

"Yes, thank you," nodded Miss Landis coolly; "you may go now."

"You're spoiled, that's what's the matter," retorted Ferrall wrathfully. "I thought I was to have this dance. You said——"

"I said 'perhaps,' because I didn't see Mr. Plank coming to claim it. Thank you, Kemp, for finding him."

Her nod and smile took the edge from her malice. Ferrall, who really adored dancing, glared about for anybody, and presently cornered the frightened and neglected débutante who had hated Plank.

Sylvia, standing beside Plank, looked up at him with her confident and friendly smile.

"You don't care to dance, do you? Would you mind if we sat out this dance?"

"If you'd rather," he said, so wistfully that she

hesitated; then with a little shrug laid one hand on his arm, and they swung out across the floor together, into the scented whirl.

Plank, like many heavy men, danced beautifully; and Sylvia, who still loved dancing with all the ardour of a schoolgirl, permitted a moment or two of keen delight to sweep her dreamily from her purpose. But that purpose must have been a strong one, for she returned to it in a few minutes, and, looking up at Plank, said very gently that she cared to dance no more.

Her hand resting lightly on his arm, it did not seem possible that any pressure of hers was directing them to the conservatory; yet he did not know where he was going, and she was familiar with the house, and they soon entered the conservatory, where, in the shadow of various palms various youths looked up impatiently as they passed, and various maidens sat up very straight in their chairs.

Threading their dim way into the farther recesses they found seats among thickets of forced lilacs overhung by early wistaria. A spring-like odour hung in the air; somewhere a tiny fountain grew musical in the semi-darkness.

"Marion told me you had been asked," she said. "We have been so friendly; you've always asked me to dance whenever we have met; so I thought I'd save you one. Are you flattered, Mr. Plank?"

He said he was, very pleasantly, perfectly undeceived, and convinced of her purpose—a purpose never even tacitly admitted between them; and the old loneliness came over him again—not resentment, for he was willing that she should use him. Why not? Others used him; everybody used him; and if they found no use for him they let him alone. Mortimer, Fleetwood, Belwether—all, all had something to exact from him. It was for that he was tolerated—he knew it; he had slowly and unwillingly learned it. His intrusion among these people, of whom he was not one, would be endured only while he might be turned to some account. The hospital used him, the clergy found plenty for him to do for them, the museum had room for other pictures of his. Who among them all had ever sought him without a motive? Who among them all had ever found unselfish pleasure in him? Not one.

Something in the dull sadness of his face, as he sat there, checked the first elaborately careless question her lips were already framing. Leaning a little nearer in the dim light she looked at him inquiringly and he returned her gaze in silence.

"What is it, Mr. Plank," she said; "is anything wrong?"

He knew that she did not mean to ask if anything was amiss with him. She did not care. Nobody cared. So, recognising his cue, he answered: "No, nothing is wrong that I have heard of."

"You wear a very solemn countenance."

"Gaiety affects me solemnly, sometimes. It is a reaction from frivolity. I suppose that I am over-enjoying life; that is all."

She laughed, using her fan, although the place was cool enough and they had not danced long. To and fro flitted the silken vanes of her fan, now closing impatiently, now opening again like the wings of a nervous moth in the moonlight.

He wished she would come to her point, but he dared not lead her to it too brusquely, because her purpose and her point were supposed to be absolutely hidden from his thick and credulous understanding. It had taken him some time to make this clear to himself; passing from suspicion, through chagrin and overwounded feeling, to dull certainty that she, too, was using him, harmlessly enough from her standpoint, but how bitterly from his, he alone could know.

The quickened flutter of her fan meant impatience to learn from him what she had come to him to learn, and then, satisfied, to leave him alone again amid the peopled solitude of clustered lights.

He wished she would speak; he was tired of the sadness of it all. Whenever in his isolation, in his utter destitution of friendship, he turned guilelessly to meet a new advance, always, sooner or later, the friendly mask was lifted enough for him to divine the cool, fixed gaze of self-interest inspecting him through the damask slits.

Sylvia was speaking now, and the plumy fan was under savant control, waving graceful accompaniment to her soft voice, punctuating her sentences at times, at times making an emphasis or outlining a gesture.

It was the familiar sequence; topics that led to themes which adroitly skirted the salient point; returned capriciously, just avoiding it—a subtly charming pattern of words which required so little in reply that his smile and nod were almost enough to keep her aria and his accompaniment afloat.

It began to fascinate him to watch the delicacy of her strategy, the coquetting with her purpose; her naïve advance to the very edges of it, the airy retreat, the innocent detour, the elaborate and circuitous return. And at last she drifted into it so naturally that it seemed impossible that fatuous man could have the most primitive suspicion of her premeditation.

And Plank, now recognising his cue, answered her: "No, I have not heard that he is in town. I stopped to see him the other day, but nobody there knew how soon he intended to return from the country."

"I didn't know he had gone to the country," she said without apparent interest.

And Plank was either too kind to terminate the subject, or too anxious to serve his turn and release her; for he went on: "I thought I told you at Mrs. Ferrall's that Mr. Siward had gone to the country."

"Perhaps you did. No doubt I've forgotten."

"I'm quite sure I did, because I remember saying that he looked very ill, and you said, rather sharply, that he had no business to be ill. Do you remember?"

"Yes," she said slowly. "Is he better?"

"I hope so."

"You *hope* so?"—with the controlled emphasis of impatience.

"Yes. Don't you, Miss Landis? When I saw him at his home, he was lame—on crutches—and he looked rather ghastly; and all he said was that he expected to leave for the country. I asked him to shoot next year at Black Fells, and he seemed bothered about business, and said it might keep him from taking any vacation."

"He spoke about his business?"

"Yes, he——"

"What is the trouble with his business? Is it anything about Amalgamated and Inter-County?"

"I think so."

"Is he worried?"

Plank said deliberately: "*I* should be, if my interests were locked up in Amalgamated Electric."

"Could you tell me why that would worry you?" she asked, smiling persuasively across at him.

"No," he said, "I can't tell you."

"Because I wouldn't understand?"

"Because I myself don't understand."

She thought awhile, brushing the rose velvet of her mouth with the fan's edge, then, looking up confidently:

"Mr. Siward is such a boy. I'm so glad he has you to advise him in such matters."

"What matters?" asked Plank bluntly.

"Why, in—in financial matters."

"But I don't advise him."

"Why not?"

"Because he hasn't asked me to, Miss Landis."

"He ought to ask you. . . . He must ask you. . . . Don't wait for him, Mr. Plank. He is only a boy in such things."

And, as Plank was silent:

"You will, won't you?"

"Do what—make his business my business, without an invitation?" asked Plank, so quietly that she flushed with annoyance.

"If you pretend to be his friend is it not your duty to advise him?" she asked impatiently.

"No; that is for his business associates to do. Friendship comes to grief when it crosses the frontiers of business."

"That is a narrow view to take, Mr. Plank."

"Yes, straight and narrow. The boundaries of friendship are straight and narrow. It is best to keep to the trodden path; best not to walk on the grass or trample the flowers."

"I think you are sacrificing friendship for an epigram," she said, careless of the undertone of contempt in her voice.

"I have never sacrificed friendship." He turned, and looked at her pleasantly. "I never made an epigram consciously, and I have never required of a friend more than I had to offer in return. Have you?"

The flush of hot displeasure stained her cheeks.

"Are you really questioning me, Mr. Plank?"

"Yes. You have been questioning me rather seriously—have you not?"

"I did not comprehend your definition of friendship. I did not agree with it. I questioned it, not you! That is all."

Plank rested his head on one big hand and stared at the clusters of dim blossoms behind her; and after a while he said, as though thinking aloud:

"Many have taken my friendship for granted, and have never offered their own in return. I do not know about Mr. Siward. There is nothing I can do for him, nothing he can do for me. If there is to be friendship between us it will be disinterested; and I would rather have that than anything in the world, I think."

There was a pause; but when Sylvia would have broken it his gesture committed her to silence with the dignity one might use in checking a persistent child.

"You question my definition of friendship, Miss Landis. I should have let your question pass, however keenly it touched me, had it not also touched him. Now I am going to say some things which lie within the straight and narrow bounds I spoke of. I never knew a man I cared for as much as I care for Mr. Siward. I know why, too. He is disinterested. I do not believe he wastes very many thoughts on me. Perhaps he will. I want him to like me, if it's possible. But one thing you and I may be sure of: if he does not care to return the friendship I offer him he will never accept anything else from me, though he might give at my request; and *that* is the sort of a man he is; and *that* is why he is every inch a man; and so I like him, Miss Landis. Do you wonder?"

She did not reply.

"Do you wonder?" he repeated sharply.

"No," she said.

"Then—" He straightened up, and the silent significance of his waiting attitude was plain enough to her.

But she shook her head impatiently, saying: "I don't know whose dance it is, and I don't care. Please go on. It is—is pleasant. I like Mr. Siward; I like to hear men speak of him as you do. I like you for doing it. If you should ever come to care for my friendship that is the best passport to it—your loyalty to Mr. Siward."

"No man can truthfully speak otherwise than I have spoken," he said gravely.

"No, not of these things. But—you know w-what is—is usually said when his name comes up among men."

"Do you mean about his habits?" he asked simply.

"Yes. Is it not an outrage to drag in that sort of thing? It angers me intensely, Mr. Plank. Why do they do it? Is there a single one among them qualified to criticise Mr. Siward? And besides, it is not true any more! . . . is it?—what was once said of him with—with some truth? *Is* it?"

The dull red blood mantled Plank's heavy visage. The silence grew grim as he did his slow, laborious thinking, the while his eyes, expressionless and almost opaque in the dim light, never left her's, until, under the unchanging, merciless inspection, the mask dropped for an instant from her anxious face, and he saw what he saw.

He was no fool. What he had come to believe she

at last had only confirmed; and now the question became simple: was she worth enlightening? And by what title did she demand his confidence?

"You ask me if it is true any more. You mean about his habits. If I answer you it is because I cannot be indifferent to what concerns him. But before I answer I ask you this: Would your interest in his fortunes matter to him?"

She waited, head bent; then:

"I don't know, Mr. Plank," very low.

"Did your interest in his fortunes *ever* concern him?"

"Yes, once."

He looked at her sternly, his jaw squaring until his heavy under lip projected. "Within *my* definition of friendship, is he your friend?"

"You mean he——"

"No, I mean *you*! I can answer for him. How is it with you? Do you return what he gives—if there *is* really friendship between you? Or do you take what he offers, offering nothing in return?"

She had turned rather white under the direct impact of the questions. The jarring repetition of his voice itself was like the dull echo of distant blows. Yet it never occurred to her to resent it, nor his attitude, nor his self-assumed privilege. She did not care; she no longer cared what he said to her or thought about her; nor did she care that her mask had fallen at last. It was not what he was saying, but what her own heart repeated so heavily that drove the colour from her face. Not he, but she herself had become the pitiless attorney for the prosecution; not his voice, but the clamouring conscience within her demanded by what right she used the name of friendship to characterise the late relations between her and the man to whom she had denied herself.

Then a bitter impatience swept her, and a dawning fear, too; for she had set her foot on the fallen mask, and the impulse rendered her reckless.

"Why don't you speak?" she said. "Yes, I have a right to know. I care for him as much as you do. Why don't you answer me? I tell you I care for him!"

"Do you?" he said in a dull voice. "Then help me out, if you can, for I don't know what to do; and if I did, I haven't the authority of friendship as my warrant. He *is* in New York. He *did* go to the country; and, at his home, the servants suppose he is still away. But he isn't; he is here, alone, and sick—sick of his old sickness. I saw him, and"—Plank rested his head on his hand, dropping his eyes—"and he didn't know me. I—I do not think he will remember that he met me, or that I spoke. And—I could do nothing, absolutely nothing. And I don't know where he is. He will go home after a while. I call—every day—to see—see what can be done. But if he were there I would not know what to do. When he does go home I won't know what to say—what to try to do. . . . And that is an answer to your question, Miss Landis. I give it, because you say you care for him as I do. Will you advise me what to do?—you, who are more entitled than I am to know the truth, because he has given you the friendship which he has as yet not accorded to me."

But Sylvia, dry-eyed, dry-lipped, could find no voice to answer; and after a little while they rose and moved through the fragrant gloom toward the sparkling lights beyond.

Her voice came back as they entered the brilliant rooms: "I should like to find Grace Ferrall," she said very distinctly. "Please keep the others off, Mr. Plank."

Her small hand on his arm lay with a weight out of all proportion to its size. Fair head averted, she no longer guided him with that impalpable control; it was he who had become the pilot now, and he steered his own way through the billowy ocean of silk and lace, master of the course he had set, heavily bland to the interrupter and the importunate from whom she turned a deaf ear and dumb lips, and lowered eyes that saw nothing.

Fleetwood had missed his dance with her, but she scarcely heard his eager complaints. Quarrier, coldly inquiring, confronted them; was passed almost without recognition, and left behind, motionless, looking after them out of his narrowing, black-fringed eyes of a woman.

Then Ferrall came, and hearing his voice, she raised her colourless face.

"Will you take me home with you, Kemp, when you take Grace?" she asked.

"Of course. I don't know where Grace is. Are you in a hurry to go? It's only four o'clock."

They were at the entrance to the supper-room. Plank drew up a chair for her, and she sank down, dropping her elbows on the small table, and resting her face between her fingers.

"Pegged out, Sylvia?" exclaimed Ferrall incredulously. "*You?* What's the younger set coming to?" and he motioned a servant to fill her glass. But she pushed it aside with a shiver, and gave Plank a strange look which he scarcely understood at the moment.

"More caprices; all sorts of 'em on the programme," muttered Ferrall, looking down at her from where he stood beside Plank. "*O tempora!* O Sylvia! . . . Plank, would you mind hunting up my wife? I'll stay and see that this infant doesn't fall asleep."

But Sylvia shook her head, saying: "Please go, Kemp. I'm a little tired, that's all. When Grace is ready, I'll leave with her." And at her gesture Plank seated himself, while Ferrall, shrugging his square shoulders, sauntered off in quest of his wife, stopping a moment at a neighbouring table to speak to Agatha Caithness, who sat there with Captain Voucher, the gemmed collar on her slender throat a pale blaze of splendour.

Plank was hungry, and he said so in his direct fashion. Sylvia nodded, and exchanged a smile with Agatha, who turned at the sound of Plank's voice. For a while, as he ate and drank largely, she made the effort to keep up a desultory conversation, particularly when anybody to whom she owed an explanation hove darkly in sight on the horizon. But Plank's appetite was in proportion to the generous lines on which nature had fashioned him, and she paid less and less attention to convention and a trifle more to the beauty of Agatha's jewels, until the silence at the small table in the corner remained unbroken except by the faint tinkle of silver and crystal and the bubbling hiss of a glass refilled.

Major Belwether, his white, fluffy, chop-whiskers brushed rabbit fashion, peeped in at the door, started to tiptoe out again, caught sight of them, and came trotting back, beaming rosy effusion. He leaned roguishly over the table, his moist eyes a-twinkle with suppressed mirth; then, bestowing a sprightly glance on

Plank, which said very plainly, "I'm up to one of my irrepressible jokes again!" he held up a smooth, white, and over-manicured forefinger:

"I was in Tiffany's yesterday," he said, "and I saw a young man in there who didn't see me, and I peeped over his shoulder, and what do you think he was doing?"

She lifted her eyes a little wearily:

"I don't know," she said.

"I do," he chuckled. "He was choosing a collar of blue diamonds and aqua marines!—Te-he!—probably to wear himself!—Te-he! Or perhaps he was going to be married!—He-he-he!—next winter—ahem!—next November—Ha-ha! *I* don't know, I'm sure, what he meant to do with that collar. I only——"

Something in Sylvia's eyes stopped him, and, following their direction, he turned around to find Quarrier standing at his elbow, icy and expressionless.

"Oh," said the aged jester, a little disconcerted, "I'm caught talking out in church, I see! It was only a harmless little fun, Howard."

"Do you mean you saw *me*?" asked Quarrier, pale as a sheet. "You are in error. I have not been in Tiffany's in months."

Belwether, crestfallen under the white menace of Quarrier's face, nodded, and essayed a chuckle without success.

Sylvia, at first listless and uninterested, looked inquiringly from the major to Quarrier, surprised at the suppressed feeling exhibited over so trivial a *gaucherie*. If Quarrier had chosen a collar like Agatha's for her, what of it? But as he had not, on his own statement, what did it matter? Why should he look that way at the foolish major, to whose garrulous gossip he was accustomed, and whose inability to refrain from prying was notorious enough.

Turning disdainfully, she caught a glimpse of Plank's shocked and altered face. It relapsed instantly into the usual inert expression; and a queer, uncomfortable perplexity began to invade her. What had happened to stir up these three men? Of what importance was an indiscretion of an old gentleman whose fatuous vanity and consequent blunders everybody was familiar with? And, after all, Howard had not bought anything at Tiffany's; he said so himself. . . . But it was evident that Agatha had chanced on the collar that Belwether thought he saw somebody else examining.

She turned, and looked at the dead-white neck of the girl. The collar was wonderful—a miracle of pale fire. And Sylvia, musing, let her thoughts run on, dreamy eyes brooding. She was glad that Agatha's means permitted her now to have such things. It had been understood, for some years, that the Caithness fortune was in rather an alarming condition. Howard had been able recently to do a favour or two for old Peter Caithness. She had heard the major bragging about it. Evidently Mr. Caithness must have improved the chance, if he was able to present such gems to his daughter. And now somebody would marry her; perhaps Captain Voucher; perhaps even Alderdene; perhaps, as rumour had it now and then, Plank might venture into the arena. . . . Poor Plank! More of a man than people understood. *She* understood. She——

And her thoughts swung back like the returning tide to Siward, and her heart began heavily again, and the slightly faint sensation returned. She passed her ungloved, unsteady fingers across her eyelids and forehead, looking up and around. The major and Howard had disappeared; Plank, beside her, sat staring stupidly into his empty wine-glass.

"Isn't Mrs. Ferrall coming?" she said wearily.

Plank gathered his cumbersome bulk and stood up, trying to see through the entrance into the ball-room. After a moment he said: "They're in there, talking to Marion. It's a good chance to make our adieux."

As they passed out of the supper-room Sylvia paused behind Agatha's chair and bent over her. "The collar is beautiful," she said, "and so are you, Agatha"; and with a little impulsive caress for the jewels she passed on, unconscious of the delicate flush that spread from Agatha's shoulders to her hair. And Agatha, turning, encountered only the stupid gaze of Plank, moving ponderously past on Sylvia's heels.

"If you'll find Leila, I'm ready at any time," she said carelessly, and resumed her tête-à-tête with Voucher, who had plainly been annoyed at the interruption.

Plank went on, a new trouble dawning on his thickening mental horizon. He had completely forgotten Leila. Even with all the demands made upon him; even with all the time he had given to those whose use of him he understood, how could he have forgotten Leila and the recent scene between them, and the new attitude and new relations with her that he must so carefully consider and ponder over before he presented himself at the house of Mortimer again!

Ferrall and his wife and Sylvia were making their adieux to Marion and her mother when he came up; and he, too, took that opportunity.

Later, on his quest for Leila, Sylvia, passing through the great hall, shrouded in silk and ermine, turned to offer him her hand, saying in a low voice:

"I am at home to you; do you understand? Always," she added nervously.

He looked after her with an unconscious sigh, unaware that anything in himself had claimed her respect. And after a moment he swung on his broad heels to continue his search for Mrs. Mortimer.

CHAPTER X

THE SEAMY SIDE

About four o'clock on the following afternoon Mrs. Mortimer's maid, who had almost finished drying and dressing her mistress' hair, was called to the door by a persistent knocking, which at first she had been bidden to disregard.

It was Mortimer's man, desiring to know whether Mrs. Mortimer could receive Mr. Mortimer at once on matters of importance.

"No," said Leila petulantly. "Tell Mullins to say that I can not see anybody," and catching a glimpse of the shadowy Mullins dodging about the dusky corridor: "What is the matter? Is Mr. Mortimer ill?"

But Mullins could not say what the matter might be, and he went away, only to return in a few moments bearing a scratchy note from his master, badly blotted and still wet; and Leila, with a shrug of resignation, took the blotched scrawl daintily between thumb and forefinger and unfolded it. Behind her, the maid, twisting up the masses of dark, fragrant hair, read the note very easily over her mistress' shoulder. It ran, without preliminaries:

"I'm going to talk to you, whether you like it or not. Do you understand that? If you want to know what's the matter with me you'll find out fast enough. Fire that French girl out before I arrive."

She closed the note thoughtfully, folding and

double-folding it into a thick wad. The ink had come off, discolouring her finger-tips; she dropped the soiled paper on the floor, and held out her hands, plump fingers spread. And when the maid had finished removing the stains and had repolished the pretty hands, her mistress sipped her chocolate thoughtfully, nibbled a bit of dry toast, then motioned the maid to take the tray and her departure, leaving her the cup.

A few minutes later Mortimer came in, stood a moment blinking around the room, then dropped into a seat, sullen, inert, the folds of his chin crowded out on his collar, his heavy abdomen cradled on his short, thick legs. He had been freshly shaved; linen and clothing were spotless, yet the man looked unclean.

Save for the network of purple veins in his face, there was no colour there, none in his lips; even his flabby hands were the hue of clay.

"Are you ill?" asked his wife coolly.

"No, not very. I've got the jumps. What's that? Tea? Ugh! it's chocolate. Push it out of sight, will you? I can smell it."

Leila set the delicate cup on a table behind her.

"What time did you return this morning?" she asked, stifling a yawn.

"I don't know; about five or six. How the devil should I know what time I came in?"

Sitting there before the mirror of her dresser she stole a second glance at his marred features in the glass. The loose mouth, the smeared eyes, the palsy-like tremors that twitched the hands where they tightened on the arms of his chair, became repulsive to the verge of fascination. She tried to look away, but could not.

"You had better see Dr. Grisby," she managed to say.

"I'd better see *you*; that's what I'd better do," he retorted thickly. "You'll do all the doctoring I want. And I want it, all right."

"Very well. What is it?"

He passed his swollen hand across his forehead.

"What is it?" he repeated. "It's the limit, this time, if you want to know. I'm all in."

"Roulette?" raising her eyebrows without interest.

"Yes, roulette, too. Everything! They got me upstairs at Burbank's. The game's crooked! Every box, every case, every wheel, every pack is crooked! crooked! crooked, by God!" he burst out in a fever, struggling to sit upright, his hands always tightening on the arms of the chair. "It's nothing but a creeping joint, run by a bunch of hand-shakers! I—I'll——"

Stuttering, choking, stammering imprecations, his hoarse clamour died away after a while. She sat there, head bent, silent, impassive, acquiescent under the physical and mental strain to which she had never become thoroughly hardened. How many such scenes had she witnessed! She could not count them. They differed very little in detail, and not at all in their ultimate object, which was to get what money she had. This was his method of reimbursing himself for his losses.

He made an end to his outburst after a while. Only his dreadful fat breathing now filled the silence; and supposing he had finished, she found her voice with an effort:

"I am sorry. It comes at a bad time, as you know——"

"A bad time!" he broke out violently. "How can it come at any other sort of time? With us, all times are bad. If this is worse than the average it can't be helped. We are in it for keeps this time!"

"*We?*"

"Yes, *we!*" he repeated; but his face had grown ghastly, and his uncertain eyes were fastened on her's in the mirror.

"What do you mean—exactly?" she asked, turning from the dresser to confront him.

He made no effort to answer; an expression of dull fright was growing on his visage, as though for the first time he had begun to realise what had happened.

She saw it, and her heart quickened, but she spoke disdainfully: "Well, I am ready to listen—as usual. How much do you want?"

He made no sign; his lower lip hung loose; his eyes blinked at her.

"What is it?" she repeated. "What have you been doing? How much have you lost? You can't have lost very much; we hadn't much to lose. If you have given your note to any of those gamblers, it is a shame—a shame! Leroy, look at me! You promised me, on your honour, never to do that again. Have you lied, after all the times I have helped you out, stripped myself, denied myself, put off tradesmen, faced down creditors? After all I have done, do you dare come here and ask for more—ask for what I have not got—with not one bill settled, not one servant paid since December——"

"Leila, I—I've got—to tell you——"

"What?" she demanded, appalled by the change in his face. If he was overdoing it, he was overdoing it realistically enough.

"I—I've used Plank's cheque!" he mumbled, and moistened his lips with his tongue.

She stared back at him, striving to comprehend. "Plank's!" she repeated slowly, "Plank's cheque? What cheque? What do you mean?"

"The one he gave you last night. I've used that. Now you know!"

"The one he— But you couldn't! How could you? It was not filled in."

"I filled it."

Her dawning horror was reacting on him, as it always did, like a fierce tonic; and his own courage came back in a sort of sullen desperation.

"*You* . . . You are trying to frighten me, Leroy," she stammered. "You are trying to make me do something—give you what you want—force me to give you what you want! You can't frighten me. The cheque was made out to me—to *my* order. How could you have used it, if I had not indorsed it?"

"I indorsed it. Do you understand that!" he said savagely.

"No, I don't; because, if you did, it's forgery."

"I don't give a damn what you think it is!" he broke in fiercely. "All I'm worried over is what Plank will think. I didn't mean to do it; I didn't dream of doing it; but when Burbank cleaned me up I fished about, and that cursed cheque came tumbling out!"

In the rising excitement of self-defence the colour was coming back into his battered face; he sat up straighter in his chair, and, grasping the upholstered arms, leaned forward, speaking more distinctly and with increasing vigour and anger:

"When I saw that cheque in my hands I thought I'd use it temporarily—merely as moral collateral to flash at Burbank—something to back my I. O. U.'s. So I filled it in."

"For how much?" she asked, not daring to believe him; but he ignored the question and went on: "I filled it and indorsed it, and——"

"How could you indorse it?" she interrupted coolly, now unconvinced again and suspicious.

"I'll tell you if you'll stop that fool tongue a moment. The cheque was made to 'L. Mortimer,' wasn't it? So I wrote 'L. Mortimer' on the back. Now do you know? If you are L. Mortimer, so am I. Leila begins with L; so does Leroy, doesn't it? I didn't imitate your two-words-to-a-page autograph. I put my own fist to a cheque made out to one L. Mortimer; and I don't care what you think about it as long as Plank can stand it. Now put up your nose and howl, if you like."

But under her sudden pallor he was taking fright again, and he began to bolster up his courage with bluster and noise, as usual:

"Howl all you like!" he jeered. "It won't alter matters or square accounts with Plank. What are you staring at? Do you suppose I'm not sorry? Do you fancy I don't know what a fool I've been? What are you turning white for? What in hell——"

"How much have you—" She choked, then, resolutely: "How much have you—*taken?*"

"Taken!" he broke out, with an oath. "What do you mean? I've borrowed about twenty thousand dollars. Now yelp! Eh? What?—no yelps? Probably some weeps, then. Turn 'em on and run dry; I'll wait." And he managed to cross one bulky leg over the other and lean back, affecting resignation, while Leila, bolt upright in her low chair, every curved outline rigid under the flowing, silken wrap, stared at him as though stunned.

"Well, we're good for it, aren't we?" he said threateningly. "If he's going to turn ugly about it, here's the house."

" My—house? "

" Yes, your house! I suppose you'd rather raise something on the house than have the thing come out in the papers."

" Do you think so? " she asked, staring into his bloodshot eyes.

" Yes, I do. I'm damn sure of it! "

" You are wrong."

" You mean that you are not inclined to stand by me? " he demanded.

" Yes, I mean that."

" You don't intend to help me out? "

" I do not intend to—not this time."

He began to show his big teeth, and that nervous snickering " tick " twitched his upper lip.

" How about the courts? " he sneered. " Do you want to figure in them with Plank? "

" I don't want to," she said steadily, " but you can not frighten me any more by that threat."

" Oh! Can't frighten you! Perhaps you think you'll marry Plank when I get a decree? Do you? Well, you won't for several reasons; first, because I'll name other corespondents and that will make Plank sick; second, because Plank wants to marry somebody else and I'm able to assist him. So where do you come out in the shuffle? "

" I don't know," she said, under her breath, and rested her head against the back of the chair, as though suddenly tired.

" Well, I know. You'll come out smirched, and you know it," said Mortimer, gazing intently at her. " Look here, Leila: I didn't come here to threaten you. I'm no black-mailer; I'm no criminal. I'm simply a decent sort of a man, who is pretty badly scared over what he's done in a moment of temptation. You know I had no thought of anything except to borrow enough on my I. O. U.'s to make a killing at Burbank's. I had to show them something big, so I filled in that cheque, not meaning to use it; and before I knew it I'd indorsed it, and was plunging against it. Then they stacked everything on me—by God, they did! and if I had not been in the condition I was in I'd have stopped payment. But it was too late when I realised what I was against. Leila, you know I'm not a bad man at heart. Can't you help a fellow?"

His manner, completely changed, had become the resentful and fretful appeal of the victim of plot and circumstance. All the savage brutality had been eliminated; the sneer, the truculent attempts to browbeat, the pitiful swagger, the cynical justification, all were gone. It was really the man himself now, normally scared and repentant; the frightened, overfed pensioner on his wife's bounty; not the human beast maddened by fear and dissipation, half stunned, half panic-stricken, driven by sheer terror into a rôle which even he shrank from—had shrunk from all these years. For, leech and parasite that he was, Mortimer, however much the dirty acquisition of money might tempt him in theory, had not yet brought himself to the point of attempting the practice, even when in sorest straits and bitterest need. He didn't want to do it; he wished to get along without it, partly because of native inertia and an aversion to the mental nimbleness that he would be required to show as a law-breaker, partly because the word "black-mail" stood for what he did not dare suggest that he had come to, even to himself. His distaste was genuine; there were certain things which he didn't want to commit, and extortion was one of them. He could, at a pinch, lie to his wife, or try to scare her into giving him money; he could, when necessary, "borrow" from such men as Plank; but he had never cheated at cards, and he had never attempted to black-mail anybody except his wife—which, of course, was purely a family matter, and concerned nobody else.

Now he was attempting it again, with more sincerity, energy, and determination than he ever before had been forced to display. Even in his most profane violence the rage and panic were only partly real. He was, it is true, genuinely scared, and horribly shaken physically, but he had counted on violence, and he stimulated his own emotions and made them serve him, knowing all the while that in the reaction his ends would be accomplished, as usual. This policy of alternately frightening, dragooning, and supplicating Leila had carried him so far; and though it was true that this was a more serious situation than he had ever yet faced, he was convinced that his wife would pull him out somehow; and how that was to be accomplished he did not very much care, as long as he was pulled out safely.

"What this household requires," he said, "is economy." He spread his legs, denting the Aubusson carpet with his boot-heels, and glanced askance at his wife. "Economy," he repeated, furtively wetting his lips with a heavily coated tongue; "that's the true solution; economical administration in domestic matters. Retrenchment, Leila! retrenchment! Fewer folderols. I've a notion to give up that farm, and stop trying to breed those damfool sheep. They cost a thousand apiece, and do you know what I got for those six I sent to Westbury? Just twelve hundred dollars from Fleetwood—the bargaining shopkeeper! Twelve hundred!

Think of that! And along comes Granby and sells a single ram for six thousand plunks!"

Leila's head was lowered. He could not see her expression, but he had always been confident of his ability to talk himself out of trouble, so he rambled on in pretence of *camaraderie*, currying favour, as he believed, ingratiating himself with the coarse bluntness that served him among some men, even among some women.

"We'll fix it somehow," he said reassuringly; "don't you worry, Leila. I've confidence in you, little girl! You've got me out of sticky messes before, eh? Well, we've weathered a few, haven't we?"

Even the horrible parody on wedded loyalty left her silent, unmoved, dark eyes brooding; and he began to grow a little restless and anxious as his jocularity increased without a movement in either response or aversion from his wife.

"You needn't be scared, if I'm not," he said reproachfully. "The house is worth two hundred and fifty thousand, and there's only fifty on it now. If that fat, Dutch skinflint, Plank, shows his tusks, we can clap on another fifty." And as she made no sound or movement in reply: "As far as Plank goes, haven't I done enough for him to square it? What have we ever got out of him, except a thousand or two now and then when the cards went against me? If I took it, it was practically what he owes me. And if he thinks it's too much—look here, Leila! I've a trick up my sleeve. I can make good any time I wish to. I'm in a position to marry that man to the girl he's mad about—stark, raving mad."

Mrs. Mortimer slowly raised her head and looked at her husband.

"Leroy, are *you* mad?"

"I! Not much!" he exclaimed gleefully. "I can make him the husband of the most-run-after girl in New York—if I want to. And at the same time I can puncture the most arrogant, the most cold-blooded, selfish, purse-proud, inflated nincompoop that ever sat at the head of a director's table. O-ho! Now you're staring, Leila. I can do it; I can make good. What are you worrying about? Why, I've got a hundred ways to square that cheque, and each separate way is a winner."

He rose, shook out the creases in his trousers, and adjusted the squat, gold fob which ornamented his protruding waistcoat.

"So you'll fix it, won't you, Leila?" he said, apparently oblivious that he had expressed himself as able to adjust the matter in one hundred equally edifying and satisfactory manners.

She did not answer. He lingered a moment at the door, looking back with an ingratiating leer; but she paid him no attention, and he took himself off, confident that her sulkiness could not result in anything unpleasant to anybody except herself.

Nor did it, as far as he could see. The days brought no noticeable change in his wife's demeanour toward him. Plank, when he met him, was civil enough, though it did occur to Mortimer that he saw very little of Plank in these days.

"Ungrateful beggar!" he thought bitterly; "he's toadying to Belwether now. I can't do anything more for him, so I don't interest him."

And for a while he wore either a truculent, aggrieved air in Plank's presence, or the meeker demeanour of a martyr, sentimentally misunderstood, but patient under the affliction.

Then there came a time when he needed money. During the few days he spent circling tentatively and apprehensively around his wife he learned enough to know that there was nothing to be had from her at present. No doubt the money she raised to placate Plank—if she had placated him in that fashion—was a strain on her resources, whatever those resources were.

One thing was certain: Plank had not remained very long in ignorance of the cheque drawn against his balance, if indeed, as Mortimer feared, the bank itself had not communicated with Plank as soon as the cheque was presented for payment. Theretore Plank must have been placated by Leila; how, Mortimer was satisfied not to know.

"Some of these days," he said to himself, "I'll catch her tripping, and then there'll be a decent division of property, or—there'll be a divorce." But, as usual, Mortimer found such practices more attractive in theory than in execution, and he was really quite contented to go on as things were going, if somebody would see that he had some money occasionally.

One of these occasions when he needed it was approaching. He had made a "killing" at Desmond's, and had used the money to stop up the more threatening gaps in the tottering financial fabric known as his "personal accounts." The fabric would hold for a while, but meantime he needed money to go on with. And Leila evidently had none. He tried everybody except Plank. He had scarcely the impudence to go to Plank just yet; but when, completing the vicious circle, he found his borrowing capacity exhausted, and himself once more face to face with the only hope, Plank, he sat down to consider seriously the possibility of the matter.

Of course Plank owed him more than he could ever pay—the ungrateful parvenu!—but what Plank had thought of that cheque transaction he had never been able to discover.

Somehow or other he must put Plank under fresh obligations; and that might have been possible had not Leila invaded the ground, leaving nothing, now that Plank was secure in club life.

Of course the first thing that presented itself to Mortimer's consideration was the engineering of Plank's matrimonial ambitions. Clearly the man had not changed. He was always at Sylvia's heels; he was seen with her in public; he went to the Belwether house a great deal. No possible doubt but that he was as infatuated as ever. And Quarrier was going to marry her next November—that is, if he, Mortimer, chose to keep silent about a certain midnight episode at Shotover.

It was his inclination, except in theory, to keep silent, partly because of his native inertia and unwillingness to go to the physical and intellectual exertion of being a rascal, partly because he didn't really want to be a rascal of that sort.

Like a man with premonitions of toothache, who walks down to the dentist's just to see what the number of the house looks like, and then walks around the block to think it over, so Mortimer, suffering from lack of money, walked round and round the central idea, unable to bring himself to the point.

Several times he called up Quarrier on the 'phone and made appointments to lunch with him; but these meetings never resulted in anything except luncheons which Mortimer paid for, and matters were becoming desperate.

So one day, after having lunched too freely, he sat down and wrote Plank the following note:

My dear Beverly: You will remember that I once promised you my aid in securing what, to you, is the dearest object of your existence. I have thought, I have pondered, I have given the matter deep and, I may add without irreverence, prayerful consideration, knowing that the life's happiness of my closest friend depended on my judgment and wisdom and intelligence to secure for him the opportunity to crown his life's work by the acquisition of the brightest jewel in the diadem of old Manhattan.

"By George! that's wickedly good, though!" chuckled Mortimer, refreshing himself with his old standby, an apple, quartered, and soaked in very old port. So he sopped his apple and swallowed it, and picked up his pen again, chary of overdoing it.

All I say to you is, be ready! The time is close at hand when you may boldly make your avowal. But be ready! All depends upon the psychological moment. An instant too soon, an instant too late, and you are lost. And *she* is lost forever. Remember! Be faithful; trust in me, and wait. And the *instant* I say, "Speak!" pour out your soul, my dear friend, and be certain you are not pouring it out in vain. L. M.

Writing about "pouring out" made him thirsty, so he fortified himself several times, and then, sealing the letter, went out to a letter-box and stood looking at it.

"If I mail it I'm in for it," he muttered. After a while he put the letter in his pocket and walked on.

"It really doesn't commit me to anything," he reflected at last, halting before another letter-box. And as he stood there, hesitating, he glanced up and saw Quarrier entering the Lenox Club. The next moment he flung up the metal box lid, dropped in his letter, and followed Quarrier into the club.

Then events tumbled forward almost without a push from him. Quarrier was alone in a window corner, drinking vichy and milk and glancing over the afternoon papers. He saw Mortimer, and invited him to join him; and Mortimer, being thirsty, took champagne.

"I've been trying a new coach," said Quarrier, in his colourless and rather agreeable voice; and he went on leisurely explaining the points of the new mail-coach which had been built in Paris after plans of his own, while Mortimer gulped glass after glass of chilled wine, which seemed only to make him thirstier. Meantime he listened, really interested, except that his fleshy head was too full of alcohol and his own project to contain additional statistics concerning coaching. Besides, Quarrier, who had never been over-cordial to him, was more so now—enough for Mortimer to venture on a few tentative suggestions of a financial nature; and though, as usual, Quarrier was not responsive, he did not, as usual, get up and go away.

A vague hope stirred Mortimer that it might not be beyond his persuasive tongue to make this chilly, reticent young man into a friend some day—a helpful friend. For Mortimer all his life had trusted to his tongue; and though poorly enough repaid, the few lingual victories remained in his memory, along with an inexhaustible vanity and hope; while his countless defeats and the many occasions on which his tongue had played him false were all forgotten. Besides, he had been drinking more heavily all day than was his custom.

So Quarrier talked, sparingly, about his new coach, about Billy Fleetwood's renowned string of hunters, about Ashley Spencer's new stable and his chances at Saratoga with Roy-a-neh, for which he had paid a fabulous sum—the sum and the story probably equally fabulous.

Mortimer's head was swimming with ideas; he was also talking a great deal, much more than he had intended; he was saying things he had not exactly intended to say, either, in just that way. He realised it, but he went on, unable to stop his own tongue, the noise of which intoxicated him.

Once or twice he thought Quarrier looked at him rather strangely; but he would show Quarrier that he was nobody's fool; he'd show Quarrier that he was a friend, a good, staunch friend; and that Quarrier had long, long undervalued him. Waves of sentiment spread through and through him; his affection for Quarrier dampened his eyes; and still he blabbed on and on, gazing with brimming eyes upon Quarrier, who sat back silent and attentive as Mortimer circled and blundered nearer and nearer to the crucial point of his destination.

Midway in one of his linguistic ellipses Quarrier leaned forward and caught his arm in a grip of steel. Another man had entered the room. Mortimer, made partly conscious by the pain of Quarrier's vise-like grip, was sober enough to recognise the impropriety of his continuing aloud the veiled story he had been constructing with what he supposed to be a cunning as matchless as it was impenetrable.

Later he found himself up-stairs in a private card-room, facing Quarrier across a table, and still talking and quenching his increasing thirst. He knew now what he was telling Quarrier; he was unveiling the parable; he was stripping metaphor from a carefully precise story. He used Siward's name presently; presently he used Sylvia's name. A moment later—or was it an hour?—Quarrier stopped him, coldly, without a trace of passion, demanding corroborative detail. And Mortimer gave it, wagging his head and one fat forefinger as emphasis.

"You *saw* that?" repeated Quarrier, deadly white of a sudden.

"Yes; an' I——"

"At three in the morning?"

"Yes; an' I want——"

"You saw him enter her room?"

"Yes; an' I wan' tersay thish to you, because I'm your fr'en'. Don' wan' anny fr'en's mine get fooled on women! See? Thash how I feel. I respec' the sect! See! Women, lovely women! See? Respec' sect! Gimme y'han', buzzer—er—brother Quar'er! Your m' fr'en'; I'm your fr'en'. I know how it is. Gotter wife m'own. Rotten one. Stingy! Takes money outter m' pockets. Dam 'stravagant. Ruin me! . . . Say, old boy, what about dividend due 'morrow on Orange County Eclectic—mean Erlextic—no!—mean 'Letric! Damn!—Wasser masser tongue?"

Opening his fond and foggy eyes, and finding himself alone in the card-room, he began to cry; and a little later, attempting to push the electric button, he fell over a lounge and lay there, his shirt-front soiled with wine, one fat leg trailing to the floor; not the ideal position for slumber, perhaps, but what difference do attitudes and postures and poses make when a gentleman, in the sacred seclusion of his own club, is wooing the drowsy goddess with blasts of votive music through his empurpled nose?

In the meantime, however, he was due to dine at the Belwether house; and when eight o'clock approached, and he had not returned to dress, Leila called up Sylvia Landis on the telephone:

"My dear, Leroy hasn't returned, and I suppose he's forgotten about the Bridge. I can bring Mr. Plank, if you like."

"Very well," said Sylvia, adding, "if Mr. Plank is there, may I speak to him a moment?"

So Leila rose, setting the receiver on the desk, and Plank came in from the library and settled himself heavily in the chair:

"Did you wish to speak to me, Miss Landis?"

"Is that you, Mr. Plank? Yes; will you dine with us at eight? Bridge afterward, if you don't mind."

"Thank you."

"And, Mr. Plank, you had a note from me this morning?"

"Yes."

"Please disregard it."

"If you wish."

"I do. It is not worth while." And as Plank made no comment, "I have no further interest in the matter. Do you understand?"

"No," said Plank doggedly.

"I have nothing more to say. I am sorry. We dine at eight," concluded Sylvia hurriedly.

Plank hung up the receiver and sat eyeing it for a while in silence. Then his jaw began to harden and his under lip protruded, and he folded his great hands, resting them in front of him on the edge of the desk, brooding there, with eyes narrowing like a sleepy giant at prayer.

When Leila entered, in her evening wraps, she found him there, so immersed in reverie that he failed to hear her; and she stood a moment at the doorway, smiling to herself, thinking how pleasant it was to come down ready for the evening and find him there, as though he belonged where he sat, and was part of the familiar environment.

Recently she had grown younger in a smooth-skinned, full-lipped way—so much younger that it was spoken of. Something girlish in figure, in spontaneity, in the hesitation of her smile, in the lack of that hard, brilliant confidence which once characterised her, had developed; as though she were beginning her *début* again, reverting to a softness and charm prematurely checked. Truly, her youth's discoloured blossom, forced by the pale phantom of false spring, was refolding to a bud once more; and the harsher tints of the inclement years were fading.

"Beverly," she said, "I am ready."

Plank stood up, dazed from his reverie, and walked toward her. His white tie had become disarranged; she raised her hands, halting him, and pulled it into shape for him, consciously innocent of the intimacy.

"Thank you," he said. "Do you know how pretty you are this evening?"

"Yes; I was very happy at my mirror. Do you know, the withered years seem to be dropping from me like leaves from an autumn sapling. And I feel young enough to say so poetically. . . . Did Sylvia try to flirt with you over the wire?"

"Yes, as usual," he said drily, descending the stairs beside her.

"And really you don't love her any more?" she queried.

"Scarcely." His voice was low and rather disagreeable, and she looked up.

"I wish I knew what you and Sylvia find to talk about so frequently, if you're not in love."

But he made no answer; and they drove away to the Belwether house, a rather wide, old-style mansion of brown stone, with a stoop dividing its ugly façade, and a series of unnecessary glass doors blockading the vestibule.

A drawing-room and a reception-room flanked the marble-tiled hall; behind these the dining-room ran the width of the rear. It was a typical gentlefolk's house of the worst period of Manhattan, and Major Belwether belonged in it as fittingly as a melodeon belongs in a west-side flat. The hall-way was made for such a man as he to patter through; the velvet-covered stairs were as peculiarly fitted for him as a runway is for a rabbit; the suave pink-and-white drawing-room, the discreet, gray reception-room, the soft, fat rugs, the intricacies of banisters and alcoves and curtained cubby-holes—all reflected his personality, all corroborated the *ensemble*. It was his habitat, his distinctly, from the pronounced but meaningless intricacy of the architecture to the studied but unconvincing tints, like a man who suddenly starts to speak, but checks himself, realising he has nothing in particular to say.

There were half a dozen people there lounging informally between the living-room on the second floor and Sylvia's apartments in the rear—the residue from a luncheon and Bridge party given that afternoon by Sylvia to a score or so of card-mad women. A few of these she had asked to remain for an informal dinner, and a desperate game later—the sort of people she knew well enough to lose to heavily or win from without remorse—Grace Ferrall, Marion Page, Agatha Caithness. Trusting to the telephone that morning, she had secured the Mortimers and Quarrier, failing three men; and now the party, with Plank as Mortimer's substitute, was complete, all thorough gamesters—sex mattering nothing in the preparation for such a *séance*.

In Sylvia's boudoir Grace Ferrall and Agatha Caithness sat before the fire; Sylvia, at the mirror of her dresser, was correcting the pallor incident to the unbroken dissipation of a brilliant season; Marion, with her inevitable cigarette, wandered between Sylvia's quarters and the library, where Quarrier and Major Belwether were sitting in low-voiced confab.

Leila, greeted gaily from the boudoir, went in. Plank entered the library, was mauled effusively by the major, returned Quarrier's firm hand shake, and sat down with an inquiring smile.

"Oh, yes, we're out for blood to-night," tittered Major Belwether, grasping Quarrier's arm humourously and shaking it to emphasise his words—a habit that Quarrier thoroughly disliked. "Sylvia had a lot of women here playing for the season score, so I suggested she keep the pick of them for dinner, and call in a few choice ones to make a night of it."

"It's agreeable to me," said Plank, still looking at Quarrier with the same inquiring expression, which that gentleman presently chose to understand.

"I haven't had a chance to look into that matter," he said carelessly. "Some day, when you have time to go over it——"

"I have time now," said Plank; "there's nothing to go over; there's no reason for any secrecy. All I wrote you was that I proposed to control the stock of Amalgamated Electric and that I wished your advice in the matter."

"I could not give you any advice off-hand on such an extraordinary suggestion," returned Quarrier coldly. "If you know where the stock is, you'll understand."

"Do you mean what it is quoted at, or who owns it?" interrupted Plank.

"Who owns it. Everybody knows where it has dropped to, I suppose. Most people know, too, where it is held."

"Yes; I do."

"And who is manipulating it," added Quarrier indifferently.

"Do you mean Harrington's people?"

"I don't mean anybody in particular, Mr. Plank."

"Oh!" said Plank, staring, "I was sure you couldn't have meant Harrington; because," he went on deliberately, "there are other theories floating about that mysterious pool, one of which I've proved."

Quarrier looked at him out of his velvety-lidded eyes:

"What have you proved?"

"I'll tell you, if you'll appoint an interview."

"I'll come too," began Belwether, who had been listening, loose-mouthed and intent; "we're all in it—Howard, Kemp Ferrall, and I——"

"And Stephen Siward," observed Plank, so quietly that Quarrier never even raised his eyes to read the stolid face opposite.

Presently he said: "Do you know anybody who can deliver you any considerable block of Amalgamated Electric at the market figures?"

"I could deliver you several blocks, if you care to bid," said Plank bluntly.

Belwether grew red, then pale. Quarrier stiffened in his chair, but his eyes were only sceptical. Plank's under lip had begun to protrude again; he swung his massive head, looking from Belwether back to Quarrier:

"Pool or no pool," he continued, "you Amalgamated people will want to see the stock climb back into the branches from which somebody shook it out; and I propose to put it there. That is all I had meant to say to you, Mr. Quarrier. I'm not averse to saying it here to you, and I do. There's no secrecy about it. Figure out for yourself how much stock I control, and who let it go. Settle your family questions and put your house in order; then invite me to call, and I'll do it. And I have an idea that we are going to stand on our own legs again, and recover our self-respect and our fighting capacity; and I rather think we'll stop this hold-up business, and that our Inter-County friend will let go the sand-bag and pocket the jimmy, and talk business across the line-fence."

Quarrier's characteristic pallor was no index to his feelings, nor was his icy reticence. All hell might be boiling below.

When anybody gave Quarrier a letter to read he took a long time reading it; but if he was slow he was also minute; he went over every word again and again, studying, absorbing each letter, each period, the conformation of every word. And when he ended he had in his brain a photograph of the letter which he would never forget.

And now, slowly, minutely, methodically, he was going over and over Plank's words, and his manner of saying them, and their surface import, and the hidden one, if any.

If Plank had spoken the truth—and there was no reason to doubt it—Plank had quietly acquired a controlling interest in Amalgamated Electric. That meant treachery in somebody. Who? Probably Siward, perhaps Belwether. He would not look at the latter just

"'I don't mean anybody in particular, Mr. Plank.'"

yet; not for a minute or two. There was time enough to see through that withered, pink-and-white old fraud. But why had Plank done this? And why did Plank suspect him of any desire to wreck his own property? He did suspect him, that was certain.

After a silence, he spoke quietly and without emotion:

"Everybody concerned will be glad to see Amalgamated Electric declaring dividends. This is a shock to *us*," he glanced impassively at the shrunken major, "but a pleasant shock. I think it well to arrange a meeting as soon as possible."

"To-morrow," said Plank, with a manner of closing discussion. And in his brusque ending of the matter Quarrier detected the ringing undertone of an authority he never had and never would endure; and though his pale, composed features betrayed not the subtlest shade of emotion, he was aware that a new element had come into his life—a new force was growing out of nothing to confront him, an unfamiliar shape loomed vaguely ahead, throwing its huge distorted shadow across his path. He sensed it with the instinct of kind for kind, not because Plank's millions meant anything to him as a force; not because this lumbering, red-faced meddler had blundered into a family affair where confidence consisted in joining hands lest a pocket be inadvertently picked; not because Plank had knocked at the door, expecting treachery to open, and had found it, but because of the awful simplicity of the man and his methods.

If Plank suspected him, he must also suspect him of complicity in the Inter-County grab; he must suspect him of the ruthless crushing power that corrupts or annihilates opposition, making a mockery of legislation, a jest of the courts, and an epigram of a people's indignation.

And yet, in the face of all this, careless, fearless, frank to the outer verge of stupidity—which sometimes means the inability to be afraid—this man Plank was casually telling him things which men regard as secrets and as weapons of defence—was actually averting him of his peril, and telling him almost contemptuously to pull up the drawbridge and prepare for siege, instead of rushing the castle and giving it to the sack.

As Quarrier sat there meditating, his long, white fingers caressing his soft, pointed beard, Sylvia came in, greeting the men collectively with a nod, and offering her hand to Plank.

"Dinner is announced," she said; "please go in farm fashion. Wait!" as Plank, following the major and Quarrier, stood aside for her to pass. "No, you go ahead, Howard; and you," to the major.

Left for a moment in the room with Plank, she stood listening to the others descending the stairs; then:

"Have you seen Mr. Siward?"

"Yes," said Plank.

"Oh! Is he well?"

"Not very."

"Is he well enough to read a letter, and to answer one?"

"Oh, yes; he's well enough in that way."

"I supposed so. That is why I said to you, over the wire, not to trouble him with my request."

"You mean that I am *not* to say anything about your offer to buy the hunter?"

"No. If I make up my mind that I want the horse I'll write him—perhaps."

Lingering still, she let one hand fall on the banisters, turning back toward Plank, who was following:

"I understood you to mean that—that Mr. Siward's financial affairs were anything but satisfactory?"—the sweet, trailing, upward inflection making it a question.

"When did I say that?" demanded Plank.

"Once—a month ago."

"I didn't," said Plank bluntly.

"Oh, I had inferred it, then, from something you said, or something you were silent about. Is that it?"

"I don't know."

"Am I quite wrong, then?" she asked, looking him in the eyes.

And Plank, who never lied, found no answer. Considering him for a moment in silence, she turned again and descended the stairs.

The dinner was one of those thoroughly well-chosen dinners of few courses and faultless service suitable for card-players, who neither care to stuff themselves as a preliminary to a battle royal, nor to dawdle through courses, eliminating for themselves what is not good for them. The men drank a light, sound, aromatic Irish of the major's; the women—except Marion, who took what the men took—used claret sparingly. Coffee was served where they sat; the men smoking, Agatha and Marion producing their own cigarettes.

"Don't you smoke any more?" asked Grace Ferrall of Leila Mortimer, and at the smiling negative, "Oh, that perhaps explains it. You're growing positively radiant, you know. You'll be wearing a braid and a tuck in your skirt if you go on getting younger."

Leila laughed, colouring up as Plank turned in his chair to look at her closer.

"No, it won't rub off, Mr. Plank," said Marion

coolly, "but mine will. This," touching a faint spot of colour under her eyes, "is art."

"Pooh! I'm all art!" said Grace. "Observe, Mr. Plank, that under this becoming flush are the same old freckles you saw at Shotover." And she laughed that sweet, careless laugh of an adolescent and straightened her boyish figure, pretty head held high, adding: "Kemp won't let me 'improve' myself, or I'd do it."

"You are perfect," said Sylvia, rising from the table, her own lovely, rounded, youthful figure condoning the exaggeration; "you're sufficiently sweet as you are. Good people, if you are ready, we will go through the ceremony of cutting for partners—unless otherwise you decide. How say you?"

"*I* don't care to enter the scramble for a man," cried Grace. "If it's to choose, I'd as soon choose Marion."

Plank looked at Leila, who laughed.

"All right; choose, then!" said Sylvia. "Howard, you're dying, of course, to play with me, but you're looking very guiltily at Agatha."

The major asked Leila at once; so Plank fell to Sylvia, pitted against Marion and Grace Ferrall.

A few moments later the quiet of the library was broken by the butler entering with decanters and ice, and glasses that tinkled frostily.

Play began at table Number One on a passed make of no trumps by Sylvia, and at the other table on a doubled and redoubled heart make, which sent a delicate flush into Agatha's face, and drove the last vestige of lingering thoughtfulness from Quarrier's, leaving it a tense, pallid, and expressionless mask, out of which looked the velvet-fringed eyes of a woman.

Of all the faces there at the two tables, Sylvia's alone had not changed, neither assuming the gambler's mask nor the infatuated glare of the amateur. She was thoughtful, excited, delighted, or dismayed by turns, but always wholesomely so; the game for its own sake, and not the stakes, absorbing her, partly because she had never permitted herself to weigh money and pleasure in the same balance, but kept a mental pair of scales for each.

As usual, the fever of gain was fiercest in those who could afford to lose most. Quarrier, playing to rule with merciless precision, coldly exacted every penalty that a lapse in his opponents permitted. Agatha, her teeth set in her nether lip, her eyes like living jewels, answered Quarrier's every signal, interpreted every sign, her play fitting in exactly with his, as though she were his subconscious self balancing the perfectly adjusted mechanism of his body and mind.

Now and then lifting her eyes, she sent a long, limpid glance at Quarrier like a pale shaft of light; and under his heavy-fringed lashes, at moments, his level gaze encountered her's with a slow narrowing of lids—as though there was more than one game in progress, more than one stake being played for under the dull rose glow of the clustered lights.

Sylvia, sitting dummy at the other table, mechanically alert to Plank's cards dropping in rapid sequence as he played alternately from his own hand and the dummy, permitted her thoughtful eyes to wander toward Agatha from moment to moment. How alluring her subtle beauty, in its own strange way! How perfect her accord with her partner! How faultless her intelligence, divining the very source of every hidden motive controlling him, forestalling his intent—acquiescent, delicate, marvellous intelligence—the esoteric complement of two parts of a single mind.

The collar of diamonds and aqua marines shimmered like the reflection of shadowy lightning across her throat; a single splendid jewel glowed on her left hand as her fingers flashed among the cards for the make-up.

"A hundred aces," broke in Plank's heavy voice as he played the last trick and picked up the scoring card and pencil.

Sylvia's blue eyes were laughing as Plank cut the new pack. Marion Page coolly laid aside her cigarette, dealt, and made it "without" in the original.

"May I play?" asked Sylvia sweetly.

"Please," growled Plank.

So Sylvia serenely played from the "top of nothing," and Grace Ferrall whisked a wonderful dummy across the green; and Plank's thick under lip began to protrude, and he lowered his heavy head like a bull at bay.

Once Marion, over-intent, touched a card in the dummy when she should have played from her own hand; and Sylvia would have let it pass, had not Plank calmly noted the penalty.

"Oh, dear! It's too much like business," sighed Sylvia. "Can't we play for the sake of the sport? I don't think it good sportsmanship to profit by a blunder."

"Rule," observed Marion laconically. "'Ware barbed wire, if you want the brush."

"I myself never was crazy for the brush," murmured Sylvia.

Grace whispered maliciously: "But you've got it, with the mask and pads," and her mischievous head barely tipped backward in the direction of Quarrier.

"Especially the mask," returned Sylvia, under her breath, and laid on the table the last card of a Yarborough.

Plank scored without comment. Marion cut, and resumed her cigarette. Sylvia dealt with that witchery of rounded wrists and slim fingers fascinating to men and women alike. Then, cards *en règle*, passed the make. Plank, cautiously consulting the score, made it spades, which being doubled, Grace led a "singleton" ace, and Plank slapped down a strong dummy and folded his great arms.

Toward midnight, Sylvia, absorbed in her dummy, fancied she heard the electric bell ringing at the front door. Later, having barely made the odd, she was turning to look at the major, when, beyond him, she saw Leroy Mortimer enter the room, sullen, pasty-skinned, but perfectly sober and well groomed.

"You are a trifle late," observed Sylvia carelessly. Grace Ferrall and Marion ignored him. Plank bade him good evening in a low voice.

The people at the other table, having completed their rubber, looked around at Mortimer in disagreeable surprise.

"I'll cut in, if you want me. If you don't, say so," observed Mortimer.

It was plain that they did not; so he settled himself in an arm-chair, with an ugly glance at his wife and an insolent one at Quarrier; and the game went on in silence; Leila and the major still losing heavily under the sneering gaze of Mortimer.

At last, "Who's carrying you?" he broke out, exasperated; and in the shocked silence Leila, very white, made a movement to rise, but Quarrier laid his long fingers across her arm, pressing her backward.

"You don't know what you're saying," he remarked, looking coldly at Mortimer.

Plank laid down his cards, rose, and walked over to Mortimer:

"May I have a word with you?" he asked bluntly.

"You may. And I'll help myself to a word or two with you," retorted Mortimer, following Plank out of the room, down the stairs to the lighted reception-room, where they wheeled, confronting one another.

"What is the matter?" demanded Plank. "At the club they told me you were asleep in the card-room. I didn't tell Leila. What is wrong?"

"I'm—I'm dead broke," said Mortimer harshly. "Billy Fleetwood took my paper. Can you help me out? It's due to-morrow."

Plank looked at him gravely, but made no answer.

"Can you?" repeated Mortimer violently. "Haven't I done enough for you? Haven't I done enough for everybody? Is anybody going to show me any consideration? Look at Quarrier's manner to me just now! And this very day I did him a service that all his millions can't repay. And there you stand, too, staring at me as though I were some damned importuning shabby-genteel, hinting around for an opening to touch you. Yes, you do! And this very day I have done for you the—the most vital thing—the most sacred favour one man can do for another——"

He halted, stammered something incoherent, his battered eyes wet with tears. The man was a wreck—nerves, stamina, mind on the very verge of collapse.

"I'll help you, of course," said Plank, eyeing him. "Go home, now, and sleep. I tell you I'll help you in the morning. . . . Don't give way! Have you no grit? Pull up sharp, I tell you!"

But Mortimer had fallen into a chair, his ravaged face cradled in his hands. "I've got all that's c-coming to me," he said hoarsely; "I'm all in—all in! God! but I've got the jumps this trip. . . . You'll stand for this, won't you, Plank? I was batty, but I woke up in time to grasp the live wire Billy Fleetwood held—three shocks in succession—and his were queens full to my jacks—aces to kings twice!—Alderdene and Voucher sitting in until they'd started me off hiking hellward!"

He began to ramble, and even to laugh weakly, passing his puffy, shaking hands across his eyes.

"It's good of you, Beverly; I appreciate it. But I've been good to you. You're all to the good, my boy! Understand? All to the good. I fixed it; I did it for you. You can have your innings now. You can have her when you want her, I tell you."

"What do you mean?" said Plank menacingly.

"Mean! I mean what I told you that day at Black Fells, when we were riding. I told you you had a chance to win out. Now the chance has come—same's I told you. Start in, and by the time you're ready to say 'When?' she'll be there with the bottle!"

"I don't think you are perfectly sane yet," said Plank slowly.

"Let it go at that, then," sniggered Mortimer, struggling to his feet. "Bring Leila back; I'm all in; I'm going home. You'll be around in the morning, won't you?"

"Yes," said Plank. "Have you got a cab?"

Mortimer had one. The glass and iron doors clanged behind him, and Plank, waiting a moment, sighed, raised his head, and, encountering the curious gaze of a servant, trudged off up-stairs again.

The game had ended at both tables. Quarrier and

Agatha stood by the window together, conversing in low voices. Belwether, at a desk, sat muttering and fussing with a cheque-book. The others were in Sylvia's apartments.

A few moments later Kemp Ferrall arrived, in the best of spirits, very much inclined to consider the night as still young; but his enthusiasm met with no response, and presently he departed with his wife and Marion in their big Mercedes, wheeling into the avenue at a reckless pace, and streaming away through the night like a meteor run mad.

Leila, in her wraps, emerged in a few moments, looking at Plank out of serious eyes; and they made their brief adieux and went away in Plank's brougham.

When Agatha's maid arrived, Quarrier also started to take his leave; but Sylvia, seated at a card-table, idly arranging the cards in geometrical designs and fanciful arabesques, looked up at him, saying:

"I wanted to say something to you, Howard."

Agatha passed them, going into Sylvia's room for her wraps; and Quarrier turned to Sylvia:

"Well?" he said, with the slightest hint of impatience.

"Can't you stay a minute?" asked Sylvia, surprised.

"Agatha is going in the motor with me. Is it anything important?"

She considered him without replying. She had never before detected that manner, that hardness in a voice always so even in quality.

"What is it?" he repeated.

She thought a moment, putting aside for the time his manner, which she could not comprehend; then:

"I wanted to ask you a question—a rather ignorant

one, perhaps. It's about your Amalgamated Electric Company. May I ask it, Howard?"

After a second's stare, "Certainly," he said.

"It's only this: If the other people—the Inter-County, I mean—are slowly ruining Amalgamated, why don't you stop it?"

Quarrier's eyes narrowed. "Oh! And who have you been discussing the matter with?"

"Mr. Plank," she said simply. "I asked him. He shook his head, and said I'd better ask you. And I do ask you."

For a moment he stood mute; then his lips began to shrink back over his beautiful teeth in one of his rare laughs.

"I'll be very glad to explain it some day," he said; but there was no mirth in his voice or eyes, only the snickering lip wrinkling the pallor.

"Will you not answer now?" she asked.

"No, not now. But I desire you to understand it some day—some day before November. And one or two other matters that it is necessary for you to understand. I want to explain them, Sylvia, in such a manner that you will never be likely to forget them. And I mean to; for they are never out of my mind, and I wish them to be as ineffaceably impressed on yours. . . . Good night."

He took her limp hand almost briskly, released it, and stepped down the stairs as Agatha entered, cloaked, to say good night.

They kissed at parting—"life embracing death"—as Mortimer had sneered on a similar occasion; then Sylvia, alone, stood in her bedroom, hands linked behind her, her lovely head bent, groping with the very ghosts of thought which eluded her, fleeing, vanishing, reappearing, to peep out at her only to fade into nothing ere she could follow where they flitted through the dark labyrinths of memory.

The major, craning his neck in the bay-window, saw Agatha and Quarrier enter the big, yellow motor, and disappear behind the limousine. And it worried him horribly, because he knew perfectly well that Quarrier had lied to him about a jewelled collar precisely like the collar worn by Agatha Caithness; and what to do or what to say to anybody on the subject was, for the first time in his life, utterly beyond his garrulous ability. So, for the first time also in his chattering career, he held his tongue, reassured at moments, at other moments panic-stricken lest this marriage he had engineered should go amiss, and his ambitions be nipped at the very instant of triumphant maturity.

"This sort of thing—in your own caste—among your own kind," his panicky thoughts ran on, "is b-bad form—rotten bad taste on both sides. If they were married—one of them, anyway! But this isn't right; no, by gad! it's bad taste, and no gentleman could countenance it!"

It was plain that he could, however, his only fear being that somebody might whisper something to turn Sylvia's innocence into a terrible wisdom which would ruin everything, and knock the underpinning from the new tower which his inflated fancy beheld slowly growing heavenward, surmounting the house of Belwether.

Another matter: he had violated his word, and had been caught at it by his prospective nephew-in-law—broken his pledged word not to sell his Amalgamated Electric holdings, and had done it. Yet, how could Plank dominate, unless another also had done what he had done? And it made him a little more comfortable to know he was sharing the fault with somebody—probably with Siward, whom he now had the luxury of despising for the very thing he himself had done.

"Drunkard!" he muttered to himself; "he's in the gutter at last!"

And he repeated it unctuously, almost reconciled to his own shortcoming, because it was the first time, as far as he knew, that a Belwether might legitimately enjoy the pleasures of holding the word of a Siward in contempt.

Sylvia had dismissed her maid, the old feeling of distaste for the touch of another had returned since the last mad, crushed embrace in Siward's arms had become a memory. More and more she was returning to old instincts, old habits of thought, reverting to type once more, virgin of lip and thought and desire, save when the old memory stopped her heart suddenly, then sent it racing, touching her face with quick, crimson imprint.

Now, blue eyes dreaming under the bright masses of her loosened hair, she sat watching the last glimmer amid the ashes whitening on the hearth, thinking of Siward and of what had been between them, and of what could never be—never, never be.

One red spark among the ashes—her ambition, deathless amid the ashes of life! When that, too, went out, life must be extinct.

What he had roused in her had died when he went away. It could never awake again, unless he returned to awaken it. And he never would; he would never come again.

One brief interlude of love, of passion, in her life could neither tint nor taint the cool, normal sequence of her days. All that life held for a woman of her caste—all save that—was hers when she stretched out her hand for it—hers by right of succession, of descent; hers by warrant unquestioned, by the unuttered text of the ukase to be launched, if necessary, by that very, very old lady, drowsing, enthroned, as the endless pageant wound like a jewelled river at her feet.

So Siward could never come again, sauntering toward her through the sunlight, smiling his absent smile. She caught her breath painfully, straightening up; a single ash fell in the fire; the last spark went out.

CHAPTER XI

THE CALL OF THE RAIN

THE park was very misty and damp and still that morning.

There was a scent of sap and new buds in the February haze, a glimmer of green on southern slopes, a distant bird note, tentative, then confident, rippling from the gray tangle of naked thickets. Here and there in hollows the tips of amber-tinted shoots pricked the soil's dark surface; here and there in the sparse woodlands a withered leaf still clinging to oak or beech was forced to let go by the swelling bud at its base and fell rustling stiffly in the silence.

Far away on the wooded bridle-path the dulled double gallop of horses sounded, now muffled in a hollow, now louder, jarring the rising ground, nearer, heavier, then suddenly checked to a trample, as Sylvia drew bridle by the reservoir, and, straightening in her saddle, raised her flushed face to the sky.

"Rain?" she asked, as Quarrier, controlling his beautiful, restive horse, ranged up beside her.

"Probably," he said, scarcely glancing at the sky, where, above the great rectangular lagoons, hundreds of sea-gulls, high in the air, hung flapping, stemming some rushing upper gale unfelt below.

She walked her mount, head lifted, watching the gulls; he followed, uninterested, imperturbable in his finished horsemanship. With horses he always appeared to advantage, whether on the box of break or coach, or silently controlling a spike or tandem, or sitting his saddle in his long-limbed, faultless fashion, maintaining without effort the very essence of form. Here he was at his best, perfectly informal, informally perfect.

They had ridden every day since the weather permitted—even before it permitted—thrashing and slashing through the rotting ice and snow, galloping over the frozen, gravelly loam, amid leafless trees and a winter-smitten perspective—drearier for the distant, eastern glimpse of the avenue's marble and limestone façades and the vast cliffs of masonry and brick looming above the west and south.

On these daily rides together it was her custom to discuss practical matters concerning their future; and it was his custom to listen until pressed for a suggestion, an assent, or a reply.

Sparing words—cautious, chary of self-commitment, and seldom offering to assume the initiative—this was the surface character which she had come to recognise and acquiesce in; this was Quarrier as he had been developed from her hazy, preconceived ideas of the man before she had finally accepted him at Shotover the autumn before. She also knew him as a methodical man, exacting from others the orderly precision which characterised his own dealings; a man of education and little learning, of attainments and little cultivation, conversant with usages, formal, intensely sensitive to ridicule, incapable of humour.

This was Quarrier as she knew him or had known him. Recently she had, little by little, become aware of an indefinable change in the man. For one thing, he had grown more reticent. At times, too, his reserve seemed to have something almost surly about it; under his cold composure a hint of something concealed, watchful, and very quiet.

Confidences she had never looked for in him nor desired. It appalled her at moments to realise how little they had in common, and that only on the surface—a communion of superficial interest incident to the fulfilment of social duties and the pursuit of pleasure. Beyond that she knew nothing of him, required nothing of him. What was there to know? what to require?

Now that the main line of her route through life had been surveyed and carefully laid out, what was there more for her in life than to set out upon her progress? It was her own road. Presumptive leader already, logical leader from the day she married—leader, in fact, when the ukase, her future legacy, so decreed; it was a royal road laid out for her through the gardens and pleasant places; a road for her alone, and over it she had chosen to pass. What more was there to desire?

From the going of Siward, all that he had aroused in her of love, of intelligence, of wholesome desire and sane curiosity—the intellectual restlessness, the capacity for passion, the renaissance of the simpler innocence—had subsided into the *laissez faire* of dull quiescence. If in her he had sown, imprudently, subtle, impulsive, unworldly ideas, flowering into sudden brilliancy in the quick magic of his companionship, now those flowers were dead under the inexorable winter of her ambition, where all such things lay; her lonely childhood, with its dimmed visions of mother-love ineffable; the strange splendour of the dreams haunting her adolescence—pageants of bravery and the glitter of the cross, altars of self-denial and pure intent, service and sacrifice and the scorn of wrong; and sometimes, seen dimly with enraptured eyes through dissolving mists—the man! glimmering for an instant, then fading, resolved into the starry void which fashioned him.

. . . .

Riding there, head bent, her pulses timing the slow pacing of her horse, she presently became aware, without looking up, that Quarrier was watching her. Dreams vanished. A perfectly unreasonable sense of being spied upon, of something stealthy about it all, flashed to her mind and was gone, leaving her grave and perplexed. What a strange suspicion! What an infernal inference! What grotesque train of thought could have culminated in such a sinister idea!

She moved slightly in her saddle to look at him, and for an instant fancied that there was something furtive in his eyes; only for an instant, for he quietly picked up the thread of conversation where she had dropped it, saying that it had been raining for the last ten minutes, and that they might as well turn their horses toward shelter.

"I don't mind the rain," she said; "there is a spring-like odour in it. Don't you notice it?"

"Not particularly," he replied.

"I was miles away a moment ago," she said; "years away, I mean—a little girl again, with two stiff yellow braids, trying to pretend that a big arm-chair was my mother's lap and that I could hear her whispering to me. And there I sat, on a day like this, listening, pretending, cuddled up tight, and looking out at the first rain of the year falling in the backyard. There was an odour like this about it all. Memory, they say, is largely a matter of nose!" She laughed, fearing that he might have thought her sentimental, already regretting the familiarity of thrusting such trivial and personal incidents upon his notice. He was probably too indifferent to comment on it, merely nodding as she ended.

Then, without reason, through and through her shot a shiver of loneliness—utter loneliness and isolation. Without reason, because from him she expected nothing, required nothing, except what he offered—the emotionless reticence of indifference, the composure of perfect formality. What did she want, then—companions? She had them. Friends? She could scarcely escape from them. Intimates? She had only to choose one or a hundred attuned responsive to her every mood, every caprice. Lonely? With the men of New York crowding, shouldering, crushing their way to her feet? Lonely? With the women of New York struggling already for precedence in her favour?—omen significant of the days to come, of those future years diamond-linked in one unbroken, triumphant glitter.

Lonely!

The rain was falling out of the hanging mist, something more than a drizzle now. Quarrier spoke of it again, but she shook her head, walking her horse slowly onward. The train of thought she followed was slower still, winding on and on, leading her into half light and shadow, and in and out through hidden trails she should have known by this time—always on, skirting the objective, circling it through sudden turns. And now she was becoming conscious of the familiar way; now she recognised the quiet, still by-ways of the maze she seemed doomed to wander in forever. But, for that matter, all paths of thought were alike to her, for, sooner or later, all ultimately led to *him*; and this she was already aware of as a disturbing phenomenon to consider and account for and to provide against—when she had leisure.

"About that Amalgamated Electric Company," she began without prelude; "would you mind answering a question or two, Howard?"

"You could not understand it," he said, unpleasantly disturbed by her abruptness.

"As you please. It is quite true I can make nothing of what the newspapers are saying about it, except that Mr. Plank seems to be doing a number of things."

"Injunctions, and other matters," observed Quarrier.

"Is anybody going to lose any money in it?"

"Who, for example?"

"Why—you, for example," she said, laughing.

"I don't expect to."

"Then it *is* going to turn out all right? And Mr. Plank and Kemp Ferrall and the major and—the other people interested, are not going to be almost ruined by the Inter-County people?"

"Do you think a man like Plank is likely to be ruined, as you say, by Amalgamated Electric?"

"No. But Kemp and the major——"

"I think the major is out of danger," replied Quarrier, looking at her with the new, sullen narrowing of his eyes.

"I am glad of that. Is Kemp—and the others?"

"Ferrall could stand it if matters go wrong. What *others*?"

"Why—the other owners and stockholders——"

"*What* others? Who do you mean?"

"Mr. Siward, for example," she said in an even voice, leaning over to pat her horse's neck with her gloved hand.

"Mr. Siward must take the chances we all take," observed Quarrier.

"But, Howard, it would really mean ruin for him if matters went badly. Wouldn't it?"

"I am not familiar with the details of Mr. Siward's investments."

"Nor am I," she said slowly.

He made no reply.

Lack of emotion in the man beside her she always expected, and therefore this new, sullen note in his voice perplexed her. Too, at times, in his increasing reticence there seemed to be almost a hint of cold effrontery. She felt it now—an indefinite suggestion of displeasure and the power to retaliate; something evasive, watchful, patiently hostile; and, try as she might, she could not rid herself of the discomfort of it, and the perplexity.

She spoke about other things; he responded in his impassive manner. Presently she turned her horse and Quarrier wheeled his, facing a warm, fine rain, slanting thickly from the south.

His silky, Vandyke beard was all wet with the moisture. She noticed it, and unbidden arose the vision of the gun-room at Shotover: Quarrier's soft beard wet with rain; the phantoms of people passing and repassing; Siward's straight figure swinging past, silhouetted against the glare of light from the billiard-room. And here she made an effort to efface the vision, shutting her eyes as she rode there in the rain. But clearly against the closed lids she saw the phantoms passing—spectres of dead hours, the wraith of an old happiness masked with youth and wearing Siward's features!

She *must* stop it! What was all this crowding in upon her as she rode forward through the driving rain—all this resurgence of ghosts long laid, long exorcised? Had the odour of the rain stolen her senses, awakening memory of childish solitude? Was it that which was drugging her with remembrance of Siward and the rattle of rain in the bay-window above the glass-roofed swimming-pool?

She opened her eyes wide, staring straight ahead into the thickening rain; but her thoughts were loosened now, tuned to the increasing rhythm of her heart: and she saw him seated there, his head buried in his hands as she stole through the dim corridors to her first tryst; saw him look up; saw herself beside him among the cushions; tasted again the rose-petals that her lips had stripped from the blossoms; saw once more the dawn of something in his steady eyes; felt his arm about her, his breath——

Her horse, suddenly spurred, bounded forward through the rain, and she rode breathless, with lips half parted, as if afraid, turning her head to look behind—as though she could outride the phantom clinging to her stirrup, masked like youth, wearing the shadowy eyes of Love!

. . . .

In her drenched habit, standing before her dressing-room fire, she heard her maid soliciting entrance, and paid no heed, the door being locked—as though a spectre could be bolted out of rooms and houses! Pacing the floor, restless, annoyed, and dismayed by turns, she flung her wet skirt and coat from her, piece by piece, and stood for awhile, like some slender youth in riding breeches and shirt, facing the fire, her fingers resting on her hips.

In the dull light of a rainy noon-day the fire reddened the ceiling, throwing her giant shadow across the wall, where it towered, swaying, like a ghost above her. She caught sight of it over her shoulder, and watched it absently; then gazed into the coals again, her chin dropping on her bared chest.

At her maid's repeated knocking she turned, her boots and the single spur sparkling in the firelight, and opened the door.

An hour later, fresh from her bath, luxurious in loose and filmy lace, her small, white feet shod with silk, she lunched alone, cradled among the cushions of her couch.

Twice she strolled through the rooms leisurely, summoned by her maid to the telephone; the first time to chat with Grace Ferrall, who, it appeared, was a victim of dissipation, being still abed, and out of humour with the rainy world; the second time to answer in the negative Marion's suggestion that she motor to Lakewood with her for the week's end before they closed their house.

Sauntering back again, she sipped her milk and vichy, tasted the strawberries, tasted a big black grape, discarded both, and lay back among the cushions, her naked arms clasped behind her head, and dropping one knee over the other, stared at the ceiling.

Restlessness and caprice ruled her. She seldom smoked, but seeing on the table a stray cigarette of the sort she kept for any intimates who might desire them, she stretched out her arm, scratched a match, and lighted it with a dainty grimace.

Lying there, she tried to make rings; but the smoke only got into her delicate uptilted nose and stung her tongue, and she very soon had enough of her cigarette.

Watching the slow fire consume it between her fingers she lay supine, following the spirals of smoke with inattentive eyes. By-and-by the lengthening ash fell, powdering her, and she threw the cigarette into the grate, flicked the ashes from her bare, round arm, and, clasping her hands under her neck, turned over and closed her eyes.

Sleep?—with every pulse awake and throbbing, every heart-beat sending the young blood rushing out through a body the incarnation of youth and life itself! There was a faint flush in the hollow of each upturned palm, where the fingers like relaxed petals curled inward; a deepening tint in the parted lips; and under the lids, through the dusk of the lashes, a glimmer of blue.

Lying there, veiled gaze conscious of the rose-light which glowed and waned on the ceiling, she awaited the flowing tide on which so often she had embarked and drifted out into that golden gloom serene, where, spirit becalmed, Time and Grief faded, and Desire died out upon the unshadowed sea of dreams.

It is long waiting for the tide when the wakeful heart beats loudly, when the pulses quicken at a memory, and the thousand idle little cellules of the brain, long sealed, long unused, and consigned to the archives of What Is Ended, open one by one, releasing each its own forgotten ghost.

And how can the heart rest, the pulse sleep, startled to a flutter, as one by one the tiny cells unclose unbidden, and the dead remembrance, from its cerements freed, brightens to life?

Words he had used, the idle lifting of his head, the forgotten inflection of his voice, the sunlight on his hair and the sea-wind stirring it; his figure as it turned to move away, the half-caught echo of his laugh, faint, faint!—so that her own ears, throbbing, strained to listen; the countless unimportant moments she had thought unmarked, yet carefully stored up, without her knowledge, in the magic cellules of her brain—all, all were coming back to life, more and more distinct, startlingly clear.

And she lay like one afraid to move, lest her stirring waken a vague something that still slept, something she dared not arouse, dared not meet face to face, even in dreams. An interval—perhaps an hour, perhaps a second—passed, leaving her stranded so close to the shoals of slumber that sleep passed only near enough to awaken her.

The room was very still and dim, but the clamour in her brain unnerved her, and she sat up among the cushions, looking vacantly about her with the blue, confused eyes, the direct, unseeing gaze of a child roused by a half-heard call.

The call—low, imperative, sustained—continued softly persistent against her windows—the summons of the young year's rain.

She went to the window and stood among the filmy curtains, looking out into the mist; a springlike aroma penetrated the room. She opened the window a little way, and the sweet, virile odour enveloped her.

A thousand longings rose within her; unnumbered wistful questions stirred her, sighing, unanswered.

Aware that her lips were moving unconsciously, she listened to the words forming automatic repetitions of phrases long forgotten:

"And those that look out of the windows be darkened, And the door shall be shut in the streets."

What was it she was repeating?

"Also they shall be afraid of that which is high, and fear shall be in the way."

What echo of the past was this?

". . . And desire shall fail: because——"

Intent, absorbed in retracing the forgotten sequence

to its source, she stood, breathing the thickening incense of the rain; and every breath was drawing her backward, nearer, nearer to the source of memory. Ah, the cliff chapel in the rain!—the words of a text mumbled deafly—the yearly service for those who died at sea! And she, seated there in the chapel dusk thinking of *him* who sat beside her, and how he feared a heavier, stealthier, more secret tide crawling, purring about his feet!

Enfin! Always, always at the end of everything, He! Always, reckoning step by step, backward through time, He! the source, the inception, the meaning of all!

Unmoored at last, her spirit swaying, enveloped in memories of him, she gave herself to the flood—overwhelmed, as tide on tide rose, rushing over her—body, mind, and soul.

She closed her eyes, leaning there heavily amid the cloudy curtains; she moved back into the room and stood staring at space through wet lashes. The hard, dry pulse in her throat hurt her till her under lip, freed from the tyranny of her small teeth, slipped free, quivering rebellion.

She had been walking her room to and fro, to and fro, for a long time before she realised that she had moved at all.

And now, impulse held the helm; a blind, unreasoning desire for relief hurried into action on the wings of impulse.

There was a telephone at her elbow. No need to hunt through lists to find a number she had known so long by heart—the three figures which had reiterated themselves so often, monotonously insistent, slyly persuasive; repeating themselves even in her dreams, so that she awoke at times shivering with the vision in which she had listened to temptation, and had called to him across the wilderness of streets and men.

. . . .

"Is he at home?"

"———!"

"Would you ask him to come to the telephone?"

"———!"

"Please say to him that it is a—a friend. . . . Thank you."

In the throbbing quiet of her room she heard the fingers of the prying rain busy at her windows; the ticking of the small French clock, very dull, very far away—or was it her heart? And, faintly ringing in the receiver pressed against her ear, millions of tiny stirrings, sounds like instruments of an elfin orchestra tuning, echoes as of steps passing through the halls of fairy-land, a faint confusion of human-like tones; then:

"Who is it?"

Her voice left her for an instant; her dry lips made no answer.

"Who *is* it?" he repeated in his steady, pleasant voice.

"It is I."

There was absolute silence—so long that it frightened her. But before she could speak again his voice was sounding in her ears, patient, unconvinced:

"I don't recognise your voice. Who am I speaking to?"

"Sylvia."

There was no response, and she spoke again:

"I only wanted to say good morning. It is afternoon now; *is* it too late to say good morning?"

"No. I'm badly rattled. Is it *you*, Sylvia?"

"Indeed it is. I am in my own room. I—I thought——"

"Yes, I am listening."

"I don't know what I did think. Is it necessary for me to telephone you a minute account of the mental processes which ended by my calling you up—out of the vasty deep?"

The old ring in her voice hinting of the laughing undertone, the same trailing sweetness of inflection—could he doubt his senses any longer?

"I know you, now," he said.

"I should think you might. I should very much like to know how you are—if you don't mind saying?"

"Thank you. I seem to be all right. Are you all right, Sylvia?"

"Shamefully and outrageously well. What a season, too! Everybody else is in rags—make-up rags! *Isn't* that a disagreeable remark? But I'll come to the paint-brush too, of course. . . . We all do. . . . Doesn't anybody ever see you any more?"

She heard him laugh to himself unpleasantly; then: "Does anybody want to?"

"Everybody, of course! You know it. You always were spoiled to death."

"Yes—to death."

"Stephen!"

"Yes?"

"Are you becoming cynical?"

"I? Why should I?"

"You *are*! Stop it! Mercy on us! If that is what is going on in a certain house on lower Fifth Avenue, facing the corner of certain streets, it's time somebody dropped in to——"

"To—what?"

"To the rescue! I've a mind to do it myself. They say you are *not* well, either."

"Who says that?"

"Oh, the usual little ornithological cockatrice—or, rather, cantatrice. Don't ask me, because I won't tell you. I always tell you too much, anyway. Don't I?"

"Do you?"

"Of course I do. Everybody spoils you and so do I."

"Yes—I am rather in that way, I suppose."

"*What* way?"

"Oh—spoiled."

"Stephen!"

"Yes?"

And in a lower voice: "Please don't say such things—will you?"

"No."

"Especially to me."

"*Especially* to you. No, I won't, Sylvia."

And, after a hesitation, she continued sweetly:

"I wonder what you were doing, all alone in that old house of yours, when I called you up?"

"I? Let me see. Oh, I was superintending some packing."

"Are you going off somewhere?"

"I think so."

"Where?"

"I don't know, Sylvia."

"Stephen, how absurd! You must know where you are going! If you mean that you don't care to tell me——"

"I mean—that."

"I decline to be snubbed. I'm shameless, and I wish to be informed. Please tell me."

"I'd rather not tell you."

"Very well. . . . Good-bye. . . . But don't ring off just yet, Stephen. . . . Do you think that, sometime, you would care to see—any people—I mean when you begin to go out again?"

"Who, for example?"

"Why, anybody?"

"No; I don't think I should care to."

"I wish you would care to. It is not well to let go every tie, drop everybody so completely. No man can do that to advantage. It would be so much better for you to go about a bit—see and be seen, you know; just to meet a few people informally; go to see some pretty girl you know well enough to—to——"

"To what? Make love to?"

"That would be very good for you," she said.

"But not for the pretty girl. Besides, I'm rather too busy to go about, even if I were inclined to."

"Are you really busy, Stephen?"

"Yes—waiting. That is the very hardest sort of occupation. And I'm obliged to be on hand every minute."

"But you said that you were going out of town."

"Did I? Well, I did not say it, exactly, but I am going to leave town."

"For very long?" she asked.

"Perhaps. I can't tell yet."

"Stephen, before you go—if you are going for a very, very long while—perhaps you will—you might care to say good-bye?"

"Do you think it best?"

"No," she said innocently; "but if you care to——"

"Do you care to have me?"

"Yes, I do."

There was a silence; and when his voice sounded again it had altered:

"I do not think you would care to see me, Sylvia. I—they say I am—I have—changed—since my—since a slight illness. I am not over it yet, not cured—not very well yet; and a little tired, you see—a little shaken. I am leaving New York to—to try once more to be cured. I expect to be well—one way or another——"

"Stephen, *where* are you going? Answer me!"

"I can't answer you."

"Is your illness serious?"

"A—it is—it requires some—some care."

Her fingers tightening around the receiver whitened to the delicate nails under the pressure. Mute, struggling with the mounting impulse, voice and lip unsteady, she still spoke with restraint:

"You say you require care? And what care have you? Who is there with you? Answer me!"

"Why—everybody; the servants. I have care enough."

"Oh, the servants! Have you a physician to advise you?"

"Certainly—the best in the world. Sylvia, dea—, Sylvia, I didn't mean to give you an impression——"

"Stephen, I *will* have you truthful with me! I know perfectly well you *are* ill. I—if I could only—if there was something, some way— Listen: I am—I am going to do something about it, and I don't care very much what I do!"

"What sweet nonsense!" he laughed, but his voice was no steadier than hers.

"Will you drive with me?" she asked impulsively, "some afternoon——"

"Sylvia, dear, you don't really want me to do it.

Wait, listen: I—I've got to tell you that—that I'm not fit for it. I've got to be honest with you; I am not fit, not in physical condition to go out just yet. I've really been ill—for weeks. Plank has been very nice to me. I want to get well; I mean to try very hard. But the man you knew—is—changed."

"Changed?"

"Not in *that* way!" he said in a slow voice.

"H-how, then?" she stammered, all a-thrill.

"Nerve gone—almost. Going to get it back again, of course. Feel a million times better already for talking with you."

"Do—does it really help?"

"It's the only panacea for me," he said too quickly to consider his words.

"The *only* one?" she faltered. "Do you mean to say that your trouble—illness—has anything to do with——"

"No, no! I only——"

"*Has* it, Stephen?"

"No!"

"Because, if I thought——"

"Sylvia, I'm not that sort! You mustn't talk to me that way. There's nothing to be sorry for about me. Any man may lose his nerve, and, if he *is* a man, go after it and get it back again. Every man has a fighting chance. You said it yourself once—that a man mustn't ask for a fighting chance; he must take it. And I'm going to take it and win out one way or another."

"What do you mean by 'another,' Stephen?"

"I— Nothing. It's a phrase."

"*What* do you mean? Answer me!"

"It's a phrase," he said again; "no meaning, you know."

"Stephen, Mr. Plank says that you are lame."

"What did he say that for?" demanded Siward wrathfully.

"I asked him. Kemp saw you on crutches at your window. So I asked Mr. Plank, and he said you had discarded your crutches too soon and had fallen and lamed yourself again. Are you able to walk yet?"

"Yes, of course."

"Outdoors?"

"A—no, not just yet."

"In other words, you are practically bedridden."

"No, no! I can get about the room very well."

"You couldn't go down-stairs—for an hour's drive, could you?"

"Can't manage that for awhile," he said hastily.

"Oh, the vanity of you, Stephen Siward! the vanity! Ashamed to let me see you when you are not your complete and magnificently attractive self! Silly, I *shall* see you! I shall drive down on the first sunny morning and sit outside in my victoria until you can't stand the temptation another instant. I'm going to do it. You cannot stop me; nobody can stop me. I desire to do it, and that is sufficient, I think, for everybody concerned. If the sun is out to-morrow, I shall be out too! . . . I am so tired of not seeing you! Let central listen! I don't care. I don't care what I am saying. I've endured it so long—I— There's no use! I am too tired of it, and I want to see you. . . . Can't we see each other without—without—thinking about things that are settled once and for all?"

"I can't," he said.

"Then you'd better learn to! Because, if you think I'm going through life without seeing you frequently you are simple! I've stood it too long at a time. I *won't* go through this sort of thing again! You'd better be amiable; you'd better be civil to me, or—or—nobody on earth can tell what will happen! The idea of you telling me you had lost your nerve! You've got to get it back—and help me find mine! Yes, it's gone, gone, gone! I lost it in the rain, somewhere, to-day. . . . Does the scent of the rain come in at your window? . . . Do you remember— There! I can't say it. . . . Good-bye. *Good*-bye. You *must* get well . . . and I must, too. Good-bye."

. . . .

The fruit of her imprudence was happiness—an excited happiness, which lasted for a day. The rain lasted, too, for another day, then turned to snow, choking the city with such a fall as had not been seen since the great blizzard—blocking avenues, barricading cross-streets, burying squares and circles and parks, and still falling, drifting, whirling like wind-whipped smoke from cornice and roof-top. The electric cars halted; even the great snow-ploughs roared impotent amid the snowy wastes; waggons floundered into cross-streets and stuck until dug out; and everywhere, in the thickening obscurity, battalions of emergency men with pick and shovel struggled with the drifts in Fifth Avenue and Broadway. Then the storm ended at daybreak.

All day long squadrons of white gulls wheeled and sailed in the sky above the snowy expanse of park where the great, rectangular sheets of water glimmered black in their white setting. As she sat at her desk she could see them drifting into and out of the gray squares of sky framed by her window-panes. Two days ago she had seen them stemming the sky blasts, heralding the coming of unfelt tempests, flapping steadily through the fragrant rain. Now, the false phantom which had mimicked spring turned on the world the glassy glare of winter, stupefying hope, stunning desire, clogging the life essence in all young, living things. The first vague summons, the restlessness of awakening aspiration, the first delicate, indrawn breath, were stilled to deathly immobility.

Sylvia, at her escritoire, chin cradled in her hollowed hand, sat listlessly inspecting her mail—the usual pile of bills and advertisements, social demands and interested appeals, with here and there a frivolous note from some intimate to punctuate the endless importunities.

Her housekeeper had come and gone; the Belwether establishment could jog through another day. Various specialists, who cared for the health and beauty of her body, had entered and made their unctuous exits. The major had gone to Tuxedo for the week's end; her maid had bronchitis; two horses required the veterinary, and the kitchen range a new water-back.

Cards had come for the Caithness function; cards for young Austin Wadsworth's wedding to a Charleston girl of rumoured beauty; Caragnini was to sing for Mrs. Vendenning; a live llama, two-legged, had consented to undermine Christianity for Mrs. Pyne-Johnson and her guests.

"Would Sylvia be ready for the inspection of imported head-gears to harmonise with the gowns being built by Constantine?

"When——

"Would she receive the courteous agent of 'The Reigning Beauties of Manhattan,' to arrange for her portrait and biographical sketch?

"When——

"Would she realise that Jefferson B. Doty could turn earth into heaven for any young chatelaine by affixing to the laundry his anti-microbe drying machine emitting sixty sterilised hot-air blasts in thirty seconds, at a cost of one-tenth of one mill per blast?

"And when——"

But she turned her head, looking wearily across the room at the brightly burning fire beside which Mrs. Ferrall sat, nibbling mint-paste, very serious over one of those books that "everybody was reading."

"How far have you read?" inquired Sylvia without interest, turning over a new letter to cut with her paper-knife.

Grace ruffled the uncut pages of her book without looking up, then yawned shamelessly: "She's decided to try living with him for awhile, and if they find life agreeable she'll marry him. . . . Pleasant situation, isn't it? Nice book, very; and they say that somebody is making a play of it. I"— She yawned again, showing her small, brilliant teeth—"I wonder what sort of people write these immoral romances!"

"Probably immoral people," said Sylvia indifferently. "Drop it on the coals, Grace."

But Mrs. Ferrall reopened the book where she had laid her finger to mark the place. "Do you think so?" she asked.

"Think what?"

"That rotten books and plays come from morally rotten people?"

"I don't think about it at all," observed Sylvia, opening another letter impatiently.

"You're probably not very literary," said Grace mischievously.

"Not in that way, I suppose."

Mrs. Ferrall took another bonbon: "Did you see 'Mrs. Lane's Experiment'?"

"I did," said Sylvia, looking up, the pink creeping into her cheeks.

"You thought it very strong, I suppose?" asked Grace innocently.

"I thought it incredible."

"But, dear, it was sheer realism! Why blink at truth? And when an author has the courage to tell facts why not have the courage to applaud?"

"If that is truth, it doesn't concern me," said Sylvia. "Grace, why will you pose, even if you are married? for you have a clean mind, and you know it!"

"I know it," sighed Mrs. Ferrall, closing her book again, but keeping the place with her finger; "and that's why I'm so curious about all these depraved people. I can't understand why writers have not found out that we women are instinctively innocent, even after we are obliged to make our morality a profession and our innocence an art. They all hang their romances to motives that no woman recognises as feminine; they ascribe to us instincts which we do not possess, passions of which we are ignorant—a ridiculous moral turpitude in the overmastering presence of love. Pooh! If they only knew what a small part love plays with us, after all!"

Sylvia said slowly: "It sometimes plays a small part, after all."

"Always," insisted Grace with emphasis. "No carefully watched girl knows what it is, whatever her suspicions may be. When she marries, if she doesn't marry from family pressure or from her own motives of common-sense ambition, she marries because she likes the man, not because she loves him."

Sylvia was silent.

"Because, even if she wanted to love him," continued

Grace, " she would not know how. It's the ingrained innocence which men encounter that they don't allow for or understand in us. Even after we are married, and whether or not we learn to love our husbands, it remains part of us as an educated instinct; and it takes all the scientific, selfish ruthlessness of a man to break it down. That's why I say so few among us ever comprehend the motives attributed to us in romance or in that parody of it called realism. Love is rarer with us than men could ever believe—and I'm glad of it," she said maliciously, with a final snap of her pretty teeth.

" It was on that theory you advised me, I think," said Sylvia, looking into the fire.

" Advised you, child? "

" Yes—about accepting Howard."

" Certainly. Is it not a sound theory? Doesn't it stand inspection? Doesn't it wear? "

" It—wears," said Sylvia indifferently.

Grace looked up from her open book. " Is anything amiss? " she asked.

" I don't know."

" Of course you know, child. What is wrong? Has Howard made himself insufferable? He's a master at it. Has he? "

" No; I don't remember that he has. . . . I'm tired, physically. I'm tired of the winter."

" Go to Florida for Lent."

" Horror! It's as stupid as a hothouse. It isn't that, either, dear—only, when it was raining so deliciously the other day I was silly enough to think I scented the spring in the park. I was glad of a change you know —any excuse to stop this eternal carnival I live in."

" *What* is the matter? " demanded Mrs. Ferrall, withdrawing her finger from the pages and plumping the closed book down on her knee. "You'd better tell me, Sylvia; you might just as well tell me now as later when my persistence has vexed us both. Now, what has happened?"

"I have been—imprudent," said Sylvia, in a low voice.

"You mean,"—Mrs. Ferrall looked at her keenly—"that *he* has been here?"

"No. I telephoned him; and I asked him to drive with me."

"Oh, Sylvia, what nonsense! Why on earth do you stir yourself up by that sort of silliness at this late date? What use is it? *Can't* you let him alone?"

"I— No, I can't, it seems. Grace, I was—I felt so—so strangely about it all."

"About what, little idiot?"

"About leaving him—alone."

"Are you Stephen Siward's keeper?" demanded Mrs. Ferrall, exasperated.

"I felt as though I were, for awhile. He is ill."

"With an illness that, thank God, you are not going to nurse through life. Don't look at me that way, dear. I'm obliged to speak harshly; I'm obliged to harden my heart to such a monstrous idea. You know I love you; you know I care deeply for that poor boy—but do you think I could be loyal to either of you and not say what I do say? He is doomed, as sure as you sit there! He has fallen, and no one can help him. Link after link he has broken with his own world; his master-vice holds him faster, closer, more absolutely, than hell ever held a lost soul!"

"Grace, I cannot endure——"

"You must! Are you trying to drug your silly self with romance so you won't recognise truth when you see it? Are you drifting back into old impulses, unreasoning whims of caprice? Have you forgotten what I know of you, and what you know of yourself? Is the taint of your transmitted inheritance beginning to show in you—the one woman of your race who is fashioned to withstand it and stamp it out?"

"I am mistress of my emotions," said Sylvia, flushing.

"Then suppress them," retorted Grace Ferrall hotly, "before they begin to bully you. There was no earthly reason for you to talk to Stephen. No disinterested impulse moved you. It was a sheer perverse, sentimental restlessness—the delicate, meddlesome deviltry of your race. And if that poison is in you, it's well for you to know it."

"It *is* in me," said Sylvia, staring at the fire.

"Then you know what to do for it."

"No, I don't."

"Well, I do," said Grace decisively; "and the sooner you marry Howard and intrench yourself behind your pride, the better off you'll be. That's where, fortunately enough, you differ from your ancestors; you are unable to understand marital treachery. Otherwise you'd make it lively for us all."

"It is true," said Sylvia deliberately, "that I could not be treacherous to anybody. But I am wondering; I am asking myself just what constitutes treachery to myself."

"Sentimentalising over Stephen might fill the bill," observed Grace tartly.

"But it doesn't seem to," mused Sylvia, her blue gaze on the coals. "That is what I do not understand. I have no conscience concerning what I feel for him."

"What do you feel?"

"I was in love with him. You knew it."

"You *liked* him," insisted Grace patiently.

"No—loved him. *I* know. Dear, your theories are sound in a general way, but what is a girl going to do about it when she loves a man? You say a young girl can't love—doesn't know how. But I do love, though it is true that I don't know how to love very wisely. What is the use in denying it? This winter has been a deafening, stupefying fever to me. The sheer noise of it stunned me until I forgot how I did feel about anything. Then—I don't know—somehow, in the rain out there, I began to wake . . . Dear, the old instincts, the old desires, the old truths, came back out of chaos; that full feeling here"—she laid her fingers on her throat—"the sense of expectancy, the restless hope growing out of torpid acquiescence—all returned; and, dearest, with them all came memories of him. What am I to do? Could you tell me?"

For a long while Mrs. Ferrall sat in troubled silence, her hand shading her eyes. Sylvia, leaning over her desk, idling with pen and pencil, looked around from time to time, as though awaiting the opinion of some specialist who, in full possession of the facts, now had become responsible for the patient.

"If you marry him," said Mrs. Ferrall quietly, "your life will become a hell."

"Yes. But would it make life any easier for him?" asked Sylvia.

"How—to know that you had been dragged down?"

"No. I mean could I do anything for him?"

"No woman ever did. That is a sentimental falsehood of the emotional. No woman ever did help a man in that way. Sylvia, if love were the only question, and if you do truly love him, I—well, I suppose I'd be fool enough to advise you to be a fool. Even then you'd be sorry. You know what your future may be; you know what you are fitted for. What can you do without Howard? In this town your rôle would be a very minor one without Howard's money, and you know it."

"Yes, I know it."

"And your sacrifice could not help that doomed boy."

Sylvia nodded assent.

"Then, is there any choice? Is there any question of what to do?"

Sylvia looked out into the winter sky, through the tops of snowy trees; everywhere the stark, deathly rigidity of winter. Under it, frozen, lay the rain that had scented the air. Under her ambition lay the ghosts of yesterday.

"No," she said, "there is no question of choice. I know what must be."

Grace, seated in the firelight, looked up as Sylvia rose from her desk and came across the room; and when she sank down on the rug at her feet, resting her cheek against the elder woman's knees, nothing was said for a long time—a time of length sufficient to commit a memory to its grave, lay it away decently and in quiet befitting.

Sore doubt assailed Grace Ferrall, guiltily aware that once again she had meddled; and in the calm tenor of her own placid, marital satisfaction, looking backward along the pleasant path she had trodden with its little monuments to love at decent intervals amid the agreeable monotony of content, her heart and conscience misgave her lest she had counselled this young girl wrongly, committing her to the arid lovelessness which she herself had never known.

“Nothing was said for a long time.”

Leaning there, her fingers lingering in light caress on Sylvia's bright hair, for every doubt she brought up argument, to every sentimental wavering within her heart she opposed the chilling reason of common sense. Destruction to happiness lay in Sylvia's yielding to her caprice for Siward. There was other happiness in the world besides the non-essential one of love. That must be Sylvia's portion. And after all—and after all, love was a matter of degree; and it was well for Sylvia that she had the malady so lightly—well for her that it had advanced so little, lest she suspect what its crowning miracles might be and fall sick of a passion for what she had forever lost.

. . . .

For a week or more the snow continued; colder, gloomier weather set in, and the impending menace of Ash Wednesday redoubled the social pace, culminating in the Westervelt ball on the eve of the forty days. And Sylvia had not yet seen Siward or spoken to him again across the wilderness of streets and men.

In the first relaxation of Lent she had instinctively welcomed an opportunity for spiritual consolation and a chance to take her spiritual bearings; not because of bodily fatigue—for in the splendour of her youthful vigour she did not know what that meant.

Saint Berold was a pretty good saint, and his church was patronised by Major Belwether's household. The major liked two things high: his game and his church. Sylvia cared for neither, but had become habituated to both the odours of sanctity and of pheasants; so to Saint Berold's she went in cure of her soul. Besides, she was fond of Father Curtis, who, if he were every inch a priest, was also every foot of his six feet a man—simple, good, and brave.

However, she found little opportunity, save at her brief confession, for a word with Father Curtis. His days were full days to the overbrimming, and a fashionable pack was ever at his heels, fawning and shoving and importuning. It was fashionable to adore Father Curtis, and for that reason she shrank from venturing any demand upon his time, and nobody else at Saint Berold's appealed to her. Besides, the music was hard, commonplace, even blatant at times, and, having a delicate ear, she shrank from this also. It is probable then that what comfort she found under Saint Berold's big, brand-new Episcopal cross she extracted from observing the rites, usages, and laws of a creed that had been accepted for her by that Christian gentleman, Major Belwether. Also, she may have found some solace from the still intervals devoted to an inventory of her sins and the wistful searching of a heart too young for sadness. If she did it was her own affair, not Grace Ferrall's, who went with her to Saint Berold's determined always to confess to too much gambling, but letting it go from day to day so that the penance could not interfere with the next *séance*.

Agatha Caithness was there a great deal, looking like a saint in her subdued plumage; and very devout, dodging nothing—neither confession nor Quarrier's occasionally lifted eyes, though their gaze, meeting, seemed lost in dreamy devotion or drowned in the contemplation of the spiritual and remote.

Plank came docilely from his Dutch Reformed church to sit beside Leila. As for Mortimer, once a vestryman, he never came at all—made no pretence or profession of what he elegantly expressed as " caring a damn " for anything " in the church line," though, he added, there were " some good lookers to be found in a few synagogues." His misconception of the attractions of the church amused the new set of men among whom he had recently drifted, to the unfeigned disgust of gentlemen like Major Belwether; "club" men, in the commoner and more sinister interpretation of the word; unfit men, who had managed to slip into good clubs; men, once fit, who had deteriorated to the verge of ostracism; heavy, over-fed, idle, insolent men in questionable financial situation, hard card players, hard drinkers, hard riders, negative in their virtues, merciless in their vices, and whose cynical misconduct formed the sources of the stock of stories told where such men foregather.

Mortimer had already furnished his world with sufficient material for jests of that flavour; now they were telling a new one: how, as Leila was standing before Tiffany's looking for her carriage, a masher accosted her, and, at her haughty stare, said sneeringly: "Oh, you can't play that game on me; I've seen you with Leroy Mortimer!"

The story was repeated frequently enough. Leila heard it with a shrug; but such things mattered to her now, and she cried over it at night, burning that Plank should hear her name used jestingly to emphasise the depth of her husband's degradation.

Mortimer stayed out at night very frequently now. Also, he appeared to make his money go farther, or was luckier at his "card killings," because he seldom attempted to bully Leila, being apparently content with his allowance.

Once or twice Plank saw him with an unusually attractive girl belonging to a world very far removed from Leila's. Somebody said she was an actress when she did anything at all—one Lydia Vyse, somewhat celebrated for an audacity not too delicate. But Plank was no more interested than any man who can't afford to endanger his prospects by a closer acquaintance with that sort of pretty woman.

Meanwhile Mortimer kept away from home, wife, and church, and Plank frequented them, so the two men did not meet very often; and the less they met the less they found to say to one another.

Now that the forty days had really begun, Major Belwether became restless for the flesh-pots of the south, although Lenten duties sat lightly enough upon the house of Belwether. These decent observances were limited to a lax acknowledgment of fast days, church in moderation, and active participation in the succession of informal affairs calculated to sustain life in those intellectually atrophied and wealthy people entirely dependent upon others for their amusements.

To these people no fear of punishment hereafter can equal the terror of being left to their own devices; and so, though the opera was over, theatres unfashionable, formal functions suspended and dances ended, the pace still continued at a discreet and decorous trot; and those who had not fled to California or Palm Beach, remained to pray and play Bridge with an unction most edifying.

And all this while Sylvia had not seen Siward.

Sylvia was changing. The characteristic amiability, the sensitive reserve, the sweet composure which the world had always counted on in her, had become exceptions and no longer the rules which governed the caprice and impulse always latent. An indifference so pointed as to verge on insolence amazed her intimates at times; a sudden, flushed impatience startled the habitués of her shrine. There was a new, unseeing hardness in her eyes; in her attitude the faintest hint of cynicism.

She acquired a habit of doing selfish things coldly, indifferent to the canons of the art; and true selfishness, the most delicate of all the arts, requires an expert.

That which had most charmed—her unfeigned pleasure in pleasure, her unfailing consideration for all, her gentleness with ignorance, her generous unconsciousness of self—all these still remained, it is true, though no longer characteristic, no longer to be counted on.

For the first time a slight sense of fear tinctured the general admiration.

In public her indifference and growing impatience with Quarrier had not reached the verge of bad taste, but in private she was scarcely at pains to conceal her weariness and inattention, showing him less and less of the formal consideration which had been their only medium of coexistence. That he noticed it was evident even to her who carelessly ignored the consequences of her own attitude.

Once, speaking of the alterations in progress at The Sedges, his place near Oyster Bay, he casually asked her opinion, and she as casually observed that if he had an opinion about anything he wouldn't know what to do with it.

Once, too, she had remarked in Quarrier's hearing to Ferrall, who was complaining about the loss of his hair, that a hairless head was a visitation from Heaven, but a beard was a man's own fault.

Once they came very close to a definite rupture, close enough to scare her after all the heat had gone out of her and the matter was ended. Quarrier had lingered late after cards, and something was said about the impending kennel show and about Marion Page judging the English setters.

" Agatha tells me that you are going with Marion,"

continued Quarrier. "As long as Marion has chosen to make herself conspicuous there is nothing to be said. But do you think it very good taste for you to figure publicly on the sawdust with an eccentric girl like Marion?"

"I see nothing conspicuous about a girl's judging a few dogs," said Sylvia, merely from an irritable desire to contradict.

"It's bad taste and bad form," remarked Quarrier coldly; "and Agatha thought it a mistake for you to go there with her."

"Agatha's opinions do not concern me."

"Perhaps mine may have some weight."

"Not the slightest."

He said patiently: "This is a public show; do you understand? Not one of those private bench exhibitions."

"I understand. Really, Howard, you are insufferable at times."

"Do you feel that way?"

"Yes, I do. I am sorry to be rude, but I do feel that way!" Flushed, impatient, she looked him squarely between his narrowing, woman's eyes: "I do not care for you very much, Howard, and you know it. I am marrying you with a perfectly sordid motive, and you know that, too. Therefore it is more decent—if there is any decency left in either of us—to interfere with one another as little as possible, unless you desire a definite rupture. Do you?"

"I? A—a rupture?"

"Yes," she said hotly; "do you?"

"Do *you*, Sylvia?"

"No; I'm too cowardly, too selfish, too treacherous to myself. No, I don't."

“Nor do I,” he said, lifting his furtive eyes.

“Very well. You are more contemptible than I am, that is all.”

Her voice had grown unsteady; an unreasoning rush of anger had set her whole body a-thrill, and the white heat of it was driving her to provoke him, as though that might cleanse her of the ignominy of the bargain—as though a bargain did not require two of the same mind to make it.

“*What* do you want of me?” she said, still stinging under the angry waves of self-contempt. “What are you marrying me for? Because, divided, we are likely to cut small figures in our tin-trumpet world? Because, united, we can dominate the brainless? Is there any other reason?”

Showing his teeth in that twitching snicker that contracted the muscles of his upper lip: “Children!” he said, looking at her.

She turned scarlet to her hair; the deliberate grossness stunned her. Confused, she stood confronting him, dumb under a retort the coarseness of which she had never dreamed him capable.

“I mean what I say,” he repeated calmly. “A man cares for two things: his fortune, and the heirs to it. If you didn't know that you have learned it now. You hurt me deliberately. I told you a plain truth very bluntly. It is for you to consider the situation.”

But she could not speak; anger, humiliation, shame, held her tongue-tied. The instinctive revolt at the vague horror — the monstrous, meaningless threat — nothing could force words from her to repudiate, to deny what he had dared to utter.

Except as the effrontery of brutality, except as a formless menace born of his anger, the reason he flung at her for his marrying her conveyed nothing to her in its grotesque impossibility. Only the intentional coarseness of it was to be endured—if she chose to endure it; for the rest was empty of concrete meaning to her.

. . . .

Lent was half over before she saw him again. Neither he nor she had taken any steps to complete the rupture; and at the *Mi-carême* dance, given by the Siowa Hunt, Quarrier, who was M. F. H., took up the thread of their suspended intercourse as methodically and calmly as though it had never quivered to the breaking point. He led the cotillon with agreeable precision and impersonal accuracy, favouring her at intervals; and though she wasted no favours on him, she endured his, which was sufficient evidence that matters were still in statu quo.

She returned to town next morning with Grace Ferrall, irritable, sulky, furious with herself at the cowardly relief she felt. For, spite of her burning anger against Quarrier, the suspense at times had been wearing; and she would not make the first move—had not decided even to accept his move if it came—at least, had not admitted to herself that she would accept it. It had come and the tension was over, and now, entering Mrs. Ferrall's brougham which met them at Thirty-fourth Street Ferry, she was furious with herself for her unfeigned feeling of relief.

All hot with self-contempt she lay back in the comfortably upholstered corner of the brougham, staring straight before her, sullen red mouth unresponsive to the occasional inconsequent questions of Grace Ferrall.

"After awhile," observed Grace, "people will begin to talk about the discontented beauty of your face."

Sylvia's eyebrows bent still farther inward.

"A fretful face, but rather pretty," commented Grace maliciously. "It won't do, dear. Your rôle is dignified comedy. O dear! O my!" She stifled a yawn behind her faultlessly gloved hand. "I'm feeling these late hours in my aged bones. It wasn't much of a dance, was it? Or am I disillusioned? Certainly that Edgeworth boy fell in love with me—the depraved creature—trying his primitive wiles there in the conservatory! Little beast! There are no nice boys any more; they're all too young or too sophisticated. . . . Howard does lead well, I admit that. . . . You're on the box seat together again I see. Pooh! I wasn't a bit alarmed."

"*I* was," said Sylvia, curling her lip in biting self-contempt.

"Well, that's a wholesome confession, anyway. O dear, how I do yawn! and Lent only half over. . . . Sylvia, what are you staring at? Oh, I—see."

They had driven south to Washington Square, where Mrs. Ferrall had desired to leave a note, and were now returning. Sylvia had leaned forward to look up at Siward's house, but with Mrs. Ferrall's first word she sank back, curiously expressionless and white; for she had seen a woman entering the front door and had recognised her as Marion Page.

"Well, of all indiscretions!" breathed Grace, looking helplessly at Sylvia. "Oh, no, that sort of thing is sheer effrontery, you know! It's rotten bad taste; it's no worse, of course—but it's bad taste. I don't care what privileges we concede to Marion, we're not going to concede this—unless she puts on trousers for good. It's all very well for her to talk her plain kennel talk, and call spades by their technical names, and smoke all over people's houses, and walk all over people's prejudices; but there's no sense in her hunting for trouble; and she'll get it, sure as scandal is scandal!"

And still Sylvia remained pale and silent, eyes downcast, shrinking close into her upholstered corner, as though some reflex instinct of self-concealment was still automatically dominating her.

"She ought to be spanked!" said Grace viciously. "If she were my daughter I'd do it, too!"

Sylvia did not stir.

"Little idiot! Going into a man's house in the face of all Fifth Avenue and the teeth of decency!"

"She has courage," said Sylvia, still very white.

"Courage! Do you mean fool-hardiness?"

"No, courage—the courage I lacked. I knew he was too ill to leave his room and I lacked the courage to go and see him."

"You mean, alone?"

"Certainly, alone."

"You dare tell me you ever contemplated——"

"Oh, yes. I think I should have done it yet, but—but Marion——"

Suddenly she bent forward, resting her face in her hands; and between the fingers a bright drop ran, glimmered, and fell.

"O Lord!" breathed Mrs. Ferrall, and sank back, nerveless, into her own corner of the rocking brougham.

CHAPTER XII

THE ASKING PRICE

SIWARD, at his desk, over which the May sunshine streamed, his crutches laid against his chair, sat poring over the piles of papers left there by Beverly Plank some days before with a curt recommendation that he master their contents.

Some of the papers were typewritten, some appeared to be engraved certificates of stock, a few were in Plank's heavy, squat handwriting. There were several packages tied in pink tape, evidently legal papers of some sort; and also a pile of scrap-books containing newspaper clippings to which Siward referred occasionally, or read them at length, resting his thin, fatigued face between two bony hands.

The curious persistence of youth in his features seemed unaccountable in view of the heavy marks imprinted there; but they were marks, not lines; bluish hollows under eyes still young, marred contours of the cheek-bone; a hardness about the hollow temples above which his short, bright hair clustered with all its soft, youthful allure undimmed; and in every movement, every turn of his head, there still remained much of that indefinable attractiveness which had always characterised his race—much of the unconscious charm usually known as breeding.

In men of Mortimer's fibre, dissipation produced coarser symptoms—distended veins, and sagging flesh

—where in Siward it seemed to bruise and harden, driving the colour of blood out of him and leaving the pallor of marble, and the bluish shadows of it staining the hollows. Only the eyes had begun to change radically; something in them had been quenched.

That he could never hope to become immune he had learned at last when he had returned, physically wholesome, from his long course of training under the famous Irish specialist on the Hudson. He had expected to be immune, spite of the blunt and forcible language of Mulqueen when he turned him out into the world again:

"Ye'll be afther notin'," said Mr. Mulqueen, "that a poonch in the plexis putts a man out; but it don't kill him. That's *you*! Whin a man mixes it up wid the booze, l'ave him come here an' I'll tache him a thrick. But it's not murther I tache; it's the hook on the jaw that shtops, an' the poonch in the plexis that putts the booze-divil on the bum! L'ave him take the count; he'll niver rise to the chune o' the bell av ye l'ave him lie. But he ain't dead, Misther Sayward; mark that, me son! An' don't ye be afther sayin', 'Th' inimy is down an' out fur good! Pore lad! Sure, I'll shake hands over a dhrink wid him, for he can do me no hurrt anny more!' No, sorr! L'ave him lie, an' l'ave the years av yer life count him out; fur the day *you* die, *he* dies, an' not wan shake o' the mixer sooner! G'wan, now, fur the rub-down. Ye've faught yer lasht round, if ye ain't a fool!"

He had been a fool. He had imagined that he could control himself, and practise the moderation that other men practised when they chose. The puerile restraint annoyed him; his implied inability to master himself humiliated him, the more so because, secretly, he was horribly afraid in the remote depths of his heart.

Exactly how it happened he did not remember, except that he had gone down town on business and had lunched with several men. There was claret. Later he remembered another café, farther up town, and another, more brilliantly lighted. After that there were vague hours—the fierce fever of debauch wrapping night and day in flame through which he moved, unseeing, unheeding, deafened, drenched soul and body in the living fire; or dreaming, feeling the subsiding fury of desire pulse and ebb and flow, rocking him to unconsciousness.

His father's old servants had found him again, this time in the area; and this time the same ankle, not yet strong, had been broken.

Through the waning winter days, as he lay brooding in bitterness, realising that it was all to do over again, Plank's shy visits became gradually part of the routine. But it was many days before Siward perceived in the big, lumbering, pink-fisted man anything to attract him beyond the faintly amused curiosity of one man for another who is in process of establishing himself as the first of a race.

As for reciprocation in other forms except the most superficial, or of permitting a personal note to sound ever so discreetly, Siward tolerated no such idea. Even the tentative advances of Plank hinting on willingness, and perhaps ability, to help Siward in the Amalgamated tangle were pleasantly ignored. Unpaid services rendered by men like Plank were impossible; any obligation to Plank was utterly out of the question. Meanwhile they began to like one another—at least Siward often found himself looking forward with pleasure to a visit from Plank. There had never been any question of the latter's attitude toward Siward.

Plank began to frequent the house, but never informally. It is doubtful whether he could have practised informality in that house even at Siward's invitation. Something of the attitude of a college lower classman for a man in a class above seemed to typify their relations; and that feeling is never entirely eradicated between men, no matter how close their relationship in after-life.

One very bad night Plank came to the house and was admitted by Gumble. Wands, the second man, stood behind the aged butler; both were apparently frightened.

That something was amiss appeared plainly enough; and Plank, instinctively producing a card, dropped it on a table and turned to go. It may have been that the old butler recognised the innate delicacy of the motive, or it may have been a sudden confidence born of the necessities of the case, for he asked Plank to see his young master.

And Plank, looking him in the eyes, considered, until his courage began to fail. Then he went up-stairs.

It was a bad night outside, and it was a bad night for Siward. The master-vice had him by the throat. He sat there, clutching the arms of his chair, his broken leg, in its plaster casing, extended in front of him; and when he saw Plank enter he glared at him.

Hour after hour the two men sat there, the one white with rage, but helpless; the other, stolid, inert, deaf to demands for intercession with the arch-vice, dumb under pleadings for a compromise. He refused to interfere with the butler, and Siward insulted him. He refused to go and find the decanters himself, and Siward deliberately cursed him.

Outside the storm raged all night. Inside that house Plank faced a more awful tempest. There was a sedative on the mantel and he offered it to Siward, who struck it from his hand.

Once, toward morning, Siward feigned sleep, and Plank, heavy head on his breast, feigned it, too. Then Siward bent over stealthily and opened a drawer in his desk; and Plank was on his feet like a flash, jerking the morphine from Siward's fingers.

The doctor arrived at daylight, responding to Plank's summons by telephone, and Plank went away with the morphine and Siward's revolver bulging in the side-pockets of his dinner coat.

He did not come again for a week. A short note from Siward started him toward lower Fifth Avenue.

There was little said when he came into the room:

"Hello, Plank! Glad to see you."

"Hello! Are you all right?"

"All right. . . . Much obliged for pulling me through. Wish you'd pull me through this Amalgamated Electric knot-hole, too—some day!"

"Do—do you mean it?" ventured Plank, turning red with delight.

"Mean it? Indeed I do—if you do. Sit here; ring for whatever you want—or perhaps you'd better go down to the sideboard. I'm not to be trusted with the odour in the room just yet."

"I don't care for anything," said Plank.

"Whenever you please, then. You know the house, and you don't mind my being unceremonious, do you?"

"No," said Plank.

"Good!" rejoined Siward, laughing. "I expect the same friendly lack of ceremony from you."

But that, for Plank, was impossible. All he could do was to care the more for Siward without crossing the border line so suddenly made free; all he could do was to sit there rolling and unrolling his gloves into wads with his clumsy, highly coloured hands, and gaze consciously at everything in the room except Siward.

On that day, at Plank's shy suggestion, they talked over Siward's business affairs for the first time. After that day, and for many days, the subject became the key-note to their intercourse; and Siward at last understood that this man desired to do him a service absolutely and purely from a disinterested liking for him, and as an expression of that liking. Also he was unexpectedly made aware of Plank's serenely unerring business sagacity.

That surface cynicism which all must learn, sooner or later, or remain the victims of naïve credulity, was, in Siward, nothing but an outer skin, as it is in all who acquire wisdom with their cynicism. It was not long proof against Plank's simple attitude and undisguised pleasure in doing something for a man he liked. Under that simplicity no motive, no self-interest could skulk; and Siward knew it.

As for the quid pro quo, Siward had insisted from the first on a business arrangement. The treachery of Major Belwether through sheer fright had knocked the key-stone from the syndicate, and the dam which made the golden pool possible collapsed, showering Plank's brokers who worked patiently with buckets and mops.

The double treachery of Quarrier was now perfectly apparent to Plank. Siward, true to his word, held his stock in the face of ruin. Kemp Ferrall, furious with the major, and beginning to suspect Quarrier, came to Plank for consultation.

Then the defence formed under Plank. Legal machinery was set in motion, meeting followed meeting, until Harrington cynically showed his hand and Quarrier smiled his rare smile; and the fight against Inter-County was on in the open, preceded by a furious clamour of charge and counter-charge in the columns of the daily press.

That Quarrier had been guilty of something or other was the vague impression of that great news-reading public which, stunned by the reiteration of figures in the millions, turns to the simpler pleasures of a murder trial. Besides, whatever Quarrier had done was no doubt done within the chalk-marked courts of the game, though probably his shoes may have become a little dusty.

But who could hope to bring players like Quarrier before the ordinary umpire, or to investigate his methods with the everyday investigations reserved for everyday folk, whose road through business life lay always between State's prison and the penitentiary and whose guide-posts were policemen?

Let the great syndicates join in battle; they could only slay each other. Let the millions bury their millions; the public, though poorer, could never be the wiser.

. . . .

Siward, at his desk, the May sunshine pouring over him, sat conning the heaps of typewritten sheets, striving to see between the lines some sign of fortune for his investments, some promise of release from the increasing financial stringency, some chance of justice being done on those high priests who had been performing marvellous tricks upon their altar so that by miracle, mine and thine spelled "ours," and all the tablets of the law were lettered upside down and hind-side before, like the Black Mass.

Gumble knocked presently. Siward raised his perplexed eyes.

"Miss Page, sir."

"Oh," said Siward doubtfully; then, "Ask Miss Page to come up."

Marion strolled in a moment later, exchanged a vigorous hand shake with Siward, pulled up a chair and dropped into it. She was in riding-habit and boots, faultlessly groomed as usual, her smooth, pale hair sleek in its thick knot, collar and tie immaculate as her gloves.

"Well," she said, "any news of your ankle, Stephen?"

"I inquired about my ankle," said Siward, amused, "and they tell me it is better, thank you."

"Sit a horse pretty soon?" she asked, dropping one leg over the other and balancing the riding-crop across her knee.

"Not for awhile. You have a fine day for a gallop, Marion," looking askance at the sunshine filtering through the first green leaves of the tree outside his window.

"It's all right—the day. I'm trying Tom O'Hara's new mare. They say she's a little devil. I never saw a devil of a horse—did you? There may be some out West."

"Don't break that pretty neck of yours, Marion," he said.

She lifted her eyes; then, briefly, "No fear."

"Yes, there is," he said. "There's no use looking for trouble in a horse. Women who hunt as you hunt take all that's legitimately coming to them. Why doesn't Tom ride his own mare?"

"She rolled on him," said Marion simply.

"Oh. Is he hurt?"

"Ribs."

"Well, he's lucky!"

"Isn't he! He'll miss a few drills with his precious squadron, that's all."

She was looking about her, preoccupied. "Where are your cigarettes, Stephen? Oh, I see. Don't try to move—don't be silly."

She leaned over the desk, her fresh young face close to his, and reached for the cigarettes. The clean-cut head, the sweetness of her youth and femininity, boyish in its allure, were very attractive to him—more so, perhaps, because of his isolation from the atmosphere of women.

"It's all very well, Marion, your coming here—and it's very sweet of you, and I enjoy it immensely," he said; "but it's a deuced imprudent thing for you to do, and I feel bound to say so for your sake every time you come."

She leaned back in her chair and coolly blew a wreath of smoke at him.

"All right," he said, unconvinced.

"Certainly it's all right. I've done what suited me all my life. This suits me."

"It suits me, too," he said, "only I wish you'd tell your mother before somebody around this neighbourhood informs her first."

"Let 'em. You'll be out by that time. Do you think I'm going to tell my mother now and have her stop it?"

"Oh, Marion, you know perfectly well that it won't do for a girl to ignore first principles. I'm horribly afraid somebody will talk about you."

"What would you do, then?"

"I?" he asked, disturbed. "What could I do?"

"Why, I suppose," she said slowly, "you'd have to marry me."

"Then," he rejoined with a laugh, "I should think you'd be scared into prudence by the prospect."

"I am not easily—scared," she said, looking down.

"Not at *that* prospect?" he said jestingly.

She looked up at him; and he remembered afterward the poise of her small head, and the slow, clear colour mounting; remembered that it conveyed to him, somehow, a hint of courage and sincerity.

"I am not frightened," she said gravely.

Gravity fell upon him, too. In this young girl's eyes there was no evasion. For a long while he had felt vaguely that matters were not perfectly balanced between them. At moments, even, he had felt an indefinable uneasiness in her presence. The situation troubled him, too; and though he had known her from childhood and had long ago learned to discount her vagaries of informality, her manners *sans façon*, her careless ignoring of convention, and the unembarrassed terms of her speech, his common-sense could not countenance this defiance of social usage, sure to involve even such a privileged girl as she in some unpleasantness.

This troubled him; and now, partly sceptical, yet partly conscious, too, of her very frank liking for himself, he looked at her, perplexed, apprehensive, unwilling to credit her with any deeper meaning than her words expressed.

She had grown pink and restless under his gaze, using her cigarette frequently, and continually flicking the ashes to the floor, until the little finger of her glove was blackened.

But courage characterised her race. It had required more than he knew for her to come into his house; and now that she was there loyalty to her professed principles—that a man and a woman were by right endowed with equal privileges—forced her to face the consequences of her theory in the practise.

She had, with calm face and quivering heart, given him an opening. That was a concession to her essential womanhood and a cowardice on her part; and, lest she turn utterly traitor to herself, she faced him again, cool, quiet, and terror in her heart:

"I'd be very glad to marry you—if you c-cared to," she said.

"Marion!"

"Yes?"

"Oh—I—it is—of course it's a joke."

"No; I'm serious."

"Serious! Nonsense!"

"Please don't say that."

He looked at her, appalled.

"But I—but you don't love—can't be in love with *me*!" he stammered.

"I am."

Gloved hands tightening on either end of her riding-crop, she bent her knee against it, balancing there, looking straight at him.

"I meant to tell you so," she said, "if you didn't tell me first. So—I was rather—tired waiting. So I've told you."

"It is only a fancy," he said, scarcely knowing what he was saying.

"I don't think so, Stephen."

But he could not meet her candour, and he sat, silent, miserable, staring at the papers on his desk.

After a while she drew a deep, even breath, and rose to her feet.

"I'm sorry," she said simply.

"Marion—I never dreamed that——"

"You should dream truer," she said. There was a suspicion of mist in her clear eyes; she turned abruptly to the window and stood there for a few moments, looking down at her brougham waiting in front of the house. "It can't be helped, can it!" she said, turning suddenly.

He found no answer to her question.

"Good-bye," she said, walking to him with outstretched hand; "it's all in a lifetime, Steve, and that's too short for a good, clean friendship like ours to die in. I don't think I'd better come again. Look me up for a gallop when you're fit. And you might drop me a line to say how you're getting on. Is it all right, Stephen?"

"All right," he said hoarsely.

Their hands tightened in a crushing clasp; then she swung on her spurred heel and walked out, leaving him haggard, motionless. He heard the front door close, and he swayed forward, dropping his face in his hands, arms half buried among the papers on his desk.

Plank found him there, an hour later, fumbling among the papers, and at first feared that he read in Siward's drawn and sullen face a premonition of the ever-dreaded symptoms.

"Quarrier has telephoned asking for a conference at last," he said abruptly, sitting down beside Siward.

"Well," inquired Siward, "how do you interpret that—favourably?"

"I am inclined to think he is a bit uneasy," said Plank cautiously. "Harrington made a secret trip to Albany last week. You didn't know that."

"No."

"Well, he did. It looks to me as though there were going to be a ghost of a chance for an investigation. That is how I am inclined to consider Harrington's trip and Quarrier's flag of truce. But—I don't know. There's nothing definite, of course. You are as conversant with the situation as I am."

"No, I am not. That is like you, Plank, to ascribe to me the same business sense that you possess, but I haven't got it. It's very nice and considerate of you, but I haven't it, and you know it."

"I think you have."

"You think so because you think generously. That doesn't alter the facts. Now tell me what you have concluded that we ought to do and I'll say 'Amen,' as usual."

Plank laughed, and looked over several sheets of the typewritten matter on the desk beside him.

"Suppose I meet Quarrier?" he said.

"All right. Did he suggest a date?"

"At four, this afternoon."

"Do you think you had better go?"

"I think it might do no harm," said Plank.

"Amen!" observed Siward, laughing, and touched the electric button for the early tea, which Plank adored at any hour.

For a while they dropped business and discussed their tea, chatting very comfortably together. Long ago Siward had found out something of the mental breadth of the man beside him, and that he was worth listening to as well as talking to. For Plank had formed opinions upon a great many subjects; and whatever culture he possessed was from sheer desire for self-cultivation.

"You know, Siward," he was accustomed to say with a smile, "you inherit what I am qualifying myself to transmit."

"It will be all one in a thousand years," was Siward's usual rejoinder.

"That is not going to prevent my efforts to become

a good ancestor to my descendants," Plank would say laughingly. "They shall have a chance, every one of them. And it will be up to them if they don't make good."

Sipping their tea in the pleasant, sunny room, they discussed matters of common interest—Plank's recent fishing trip on Long Island and the degeneracy of liver-fed trout; the North Side Club's Experiments with European partridges; Billy Fleetwood's new stables; forestry, and the chance of national legislation concerning it—a subject of which Plank was very fond, and on which he had exceedingly sound ideas.

Drifting from one topic to another through the haze of their cigars, silent when it pleased them to be so, there could be no doubt of their liking for each other upon a basis at least superficially informal; and if Plank's manner retained at times a shade of quaint reserve, Siward's was perhaps the more frankly direct for that reason.

"I think," observed Plank, laying his half-consumed cigar on the silver tray, "that I'd better go down town and see what our pre-glacial friend Quarrier wants. I may be able to furnish him with a new sensation."

"I wonder if Quarrier ever experienced a genuine sensation," mused Siward, arranging the papers before him into divisional piles.

"Plenty," said Plank drily.

"I don't think so."

"Plenty," repeated Plank. "It's your thin-lipped, thin-nosed, pasty-pale, symmetrical brother who is closer to the animal under his mask than any of us imagine. I—" He hesitated. "Do you want to know my opinion of Quarrier? I've never told you. I don't usually talk about my—dislikes. Do you want to know?"

"Certainly," said Siward curiously.

"Then, first of all, he is a sentimentalist."

"Oh! oh!" jeered Siward.

"A sentimentalist of the weakest type," continued Plank obstinately; "because he sentimentalises over himself. Siward, look out for the man with elaborate whiskers! Look out for a pallid man with eccentric hair and a silky beard! He's a sentimentalist of the sort I told you, and is usually utterly remorseless in his dealings with women. I suppose you think me a fool."

"I think Quarrier is indifferent concerning women," said Siward.

"You are wrong. He is a sensualist," insisted Plank.

"Oh, no, Plank—not that!"

"A sensualist. His sentimental vanity he lavishes upon himself—the animal in him on women. His caution, born of self-consideration, is the caution of a beast. Such men as he believe they live in the focus of a million eyes. Part of his vanity is to deceive those eyes and be what he is under the mask he wears; and to do that one must be the very master of caution. That is Quarrier's vanity. To conceal, is his monomania."

"I cannot see how you draw that conclusion."

"Siward, he is a bad man, and crafty—every inch of him."

"Oh, come, now! Only characters in fiction have no saving qualities. You never heard of anybody in real life being entirely bad."

"No, I didn't; and Quarrier isn't. For example, he is kind to valuable animals—I mean, his own."

"Good to animals! The bad man's invariable characteristic!" laughed Siward. "I'm kind to 'em, too. What else is he good to?"

"Everybody knows that he hasn't a poor relation left; not one. He is loyal to them in a rare way; he filled one subsidiary company full of them. It is known down town as the 'Home for Destitute Nephews.'"

"Seriously, Plank, the man must have something good in him."

"Because of your theory?"

"Yes. I believe that nobody is entirely bad. So do the great masters of fiction."

Plank said gravely: "He is a good son to his father. That is perfectly true—kind, considerate, dutiful, loyal. The financial world is perfectly aware that Stanley Quarrier is to-day the most unscrupulous old scoundrel who ever crushed a refinery or debauched a railroad! and his son no more believes it than he credits the scandalous history of the Red Woman of Wall Street. Why, when I was making arrangements for that chapel Quarrier came to me, very much perturbed, because he understood that all the memorial chapels for the cathedral had been arranged for, and he had desired to build one to the memory of his father! His *father*! Isn't it awful to think of!—a *chapel* to the memory of the briber of judges and of legislatures, the cynical defier of law!—this hoary old thief, who beggared the widow and stripped the orphan, and whose only match, as a great unpunished criminal, was that sinister little predecessor of his, who dreamed even of debauching the executive of these United States!"

Siward had never before seen Plank aroused, and he said so, smiling.

"That is true," said Plank earnestly; "I waste little temper over my likes and dislikes. But what I know, and what I legitimately infer concerning the younger Quarrier is enough to rouse any man's anger. I won't tell you what I know. I can't. It has nothing to do with his financial methods, nothing to do with this business; but it is bad—bad all through! The blow his father struck at the integrity of the bench the son strikes at the very key-stone of all social safeguard. It isn't my business; I cannot interfere; but Siward, I'm a damned restless witness, and the old, primitive longing comes back on me to strike—to take a stick and use it to splinters on that man whom I am going down town to politely confer with! . . . And I *must* go now. Good-bye. . . . Take care of that ankle. Any books I can send you—anything you want? No? All right. And don't worry over Amalgamated Electric, for I really believe we are beginning to frighten them badly."

"Good-bye," said Siward. "Don't forget that I'm always at home."

"You must get out," muttered Plank; "you must get well, and get out into the sunshine." And he went ponderously down-stairs to the square hall, where Gumble held his hat and gloves ready for him.

He had come in a big yellow and black touring-car; and now, with a brief word to his mechanic, he climbed into the tonneau, and away they sped down town—a glitter of bull's-eye, brass, and varnish, with the mellow, horn notes floating far in their wake.

It was exactly four o'clock when he was ushered into Quarrier's private suite in the great marble Algonquin Loan and Trust Building, the upper stories of which were all golden in the sun against a sky of sapphire.

Quarrier was alone, gloved and hatted, as though on the point of leaving. He showed a slight surprise at seeing Plank, as if he had not been expecting him;

and the manner of offering his hand subtly emphasised it as he came forward with a trace of inquiry in his greeting.

"You said four o'clock, I believe," observed Plank bluntly.

"Ah, yes. It was about that—ah—matter—ah—I beg your pardon; can you recollect?"

"I don't know what it is you want. *You* requested this meeting," said Plank, yawning.

"Certainly. I recollect it perfectly now. Will you sit here, Mr. Plank—for a moment——"

"If it concerns Inter-County, it will take longer than a moment—unless you cannot spare the time now," said Plank. "Shall we call it off?"

"As a matter of fact I am rather short of time just now."

"Then let us postpone it. I shall probably be at my office if you are anxious to see me."

Quarrier looked at him, then laid aside his hat and sat down. There was little to be done in diplomacy with an oaf like that.

"Mr. Plank," he said, without any emphasis at all, "there should be some way for us to come together. Have you considered it?"

"No, I haven't," replied Plank.

"I mean, for you and me to try to understand each other."

"For *us*?" asked Plank, raising his blond eyebrows. "Do you mean Amalgamated Electric and Inter-County, impersonally?"

"I mean for us, personally."

"There is no way," said Plank, with conviction.

"I think there is."

"You are wasting time thinking it, Mr. Quarrier."

Quarrier's velvet-fringed eyes began to narrow, but his calm voice remained unchanged: "We are merely wasting energy in this duel," he said.

"Oh, no; I don't feel wasted."

"We are also wasting opportunities," continued Quarrier slowly. "This whole matter is involving us in a tangle of litigation requiring our constant effort, constant attention."

"I beg your pardon, Mr. Quarrier, but you take it too seriously. I have found, in this affair, nothing except a rather agreeable mental exhilaration."

"Mr. Plank, if you are not inclined to be serious——"

"I *am*," said Plank so savagely that Quarrier, startled, could not doubt him. "I like this sort of thing, Mr. Quarrier. Anything that is hard to overcome, I like to overcome. The pleasure in life, to me, is to win out. I am fighting you with the greatest possible satisfaction to myself."

"Perhaps you see victory ahead," said Quarrier calmly.

"I do, Mr. Quarrier, I do. But not in the manner you fear I may hope for it."

"Do you mind saying in *what* manner you are already discounting your victory, Mr Plank?"

"No, I don't mind telling you. I have no batteries to mask. I don't care how much you know about my resources; so I'll tell you what I see, Mr. Quarrier. I see a parody of the popular battle between razor-back and rattler. The rattler only strives to strike and kill, not to swallow. Mr. Quarrier, that old razor-back isn't going home hungry; but—*he's going home.*"

"I'm afraid I am not familiar enough with the natural history you quote to follow you," said Quarrier with a sneer, his long fingers busy with the silky point of his beard.

"No, you won't *follow* me home; you'll come *with* me, when it's all over. Now is it very plain to you, Mr. Quarrier?"

Quarrier said, without emotion: "I repeat that it would be easy for you and me to merge our differences on a basis absolutely satisfactory to you and to me—and to Harrington."

"You are mistaken," said Plank, rising. "Good afternoon."

Quarrier rose, too. "You decline to discuss the matter?" he asked.

"It has been discussed sufficiently."

"Then why did you come here?"

"To see for myself how afraid of me you really are," said Plank. "Now I know, and so do you."

"You desire to make it a personal matter?" inquired Quarrier, in a low voice, his face dead white in the late sunlight which illuminated the room.

"Personal? No—impersonal; because there could be absolutely nothing personal between us, Mr. Quarrier; and the only thing in the world that there ought to be between us are a few stout, steel bars. Beg pardon for talking shop. I'm a shopkeeper, and I'm in the steel business, and I lack opportunities for cultivation. Good day."

"Mr. Plank——"

"Mr. Quarrier, I want to tell you something. Never before, in business differences, has private indignation against any individual interfered or modified my course of action. It does now; but it does not dictate my policy toward you; it merely, as I say, modifies it. I am perfectly aware of what I am doing; what social

"'Take your fighting chance—it is the cleanest thing you ever touched!'"

disaster I am inviting by this attitude toward you personally; what financial destruction I am courting in arousing the wrath of the Algonquin Trust Company and of the powerful interests intrenched behind Inter-County Electric. I know what the lobby is; I know what judge cannot be counted on; I know my peril and my chances, every one; and I take them—every one. For it is a good fight, Mr. Quarrier; it will be talked of for years to come, wonderingly; not because of your effrontery, not because of my obstinacy, but because such monstrous immorality could ever have existed in this land of ours. Your name, Harrington's, mine, will have become utterly forgotten long, long before the horror of these present conditions shall cease to be remembered."

He stretched out one ponderous arm, pointing full between Quarrier's unwinking eyes.

"Take your fighting chance—it is the cleanest thing you ever touched; and use it cleanly, or there'll be no mercy shown you when your time comes. Let the courts alone—do you hear me? Let the legislature alone. Keep your manicured hands off the ermine. And tell Harrington to shove his own cold, splay fingers into his own pockets for a change. They'll be warmer than his feet by this time next year."

For a moment he towered there, powerful, bulky, menacing; then his arm dropped heavily—the old stolid expression came back into his face, leaving it calm, bovine, almost stupid again. And he turned, moving slowly toward the door, holding his hat carefully in his gloved hand.

Stepping out of the elevator on the ground floor he encountered Mortimer, and halted instinctively. He had not seen Mortimer for weeks; neither had Leila;

and now he looked at him inquiringly, disturbed at his battered and bloodshot appearance.

"Oh," said Mortimer, "you down here?"

"Have you been out of town?" asked Plank cautiously.

Mortimer nodded, and started to pass on toward the bronze cage of the elevator, but something seemed to occur to him suddenly; he checked his pace, turned, and waddled after Plank, rejoining him on the marble steps of the rotunda.

"See here," he panted, holding Plank by the elbow and breathing heavily even after the short chase across the lobby, "I meant to tell you something. Come over here and sit down a moment."

Still grasping Plank's elbow in his puffy fingers, he directed him toward a velvet seat in a corner of the lobby; and here they sat down, while Mortimer mopped his fat neck with his handkerchief, swearing at the heat under his breath.

"Look here," he said; "I promised you something once, didn't I?"

"Did you?" said Plank, with his bland, expressionless stare of an overgrown baby.

"Oh, cut that out! You know damn well I did; and when I say a thing I make good. D'ye see?"

"I don't see," said Plank, "what you are talking about."

"I'm talking about what I said I'd do for you. Haven't I made good? Haven't I put you into everything I said I would? Don't you go everywhere? Don't people ask you everywhere?"

"Yes—in a way," said Plank wearily. "I am very grateful; I always will be. . . . Can I do anything for you, Leroy?"

Mortimer became indignant at the implied distrust of the purity of his motives; and Plank, failing to stem the maudlin tirade, relapsed into patient silence, speculating within himself as to what it could be that Mortimer wanted.

It came out presently. Mortimer had attended a "killing" at Desmond's, and, as usual, had provided the pièce de résistance for his soft-voiced host. All he wanted was a temporary deposit to tide over matters. He had never approached Plank in vain, and he did not do so now, for Plank had a pocket cheque-book and a stylograph.

"It's damn little to ask, isn't it?" he muttered resentfully. "That will only square matters with Desmond; it doesn't leave me anything to go on with," and he pocketed his cheque with a scowl.

Plank was discreetly silent.

"And that is not what I chased you for, either," continued Mortimer. "I didn't intend to say anything about Desmond; I was going to fix it in another way!" He cast an involuntary and sinister glance at the elevators gliding ceaselessly up and down at the end of the vast marble rotunda; then his protruding eyes sought Plank's again:

"Beverly, old boy, I've got a certain mealy-faced hypocrite where any decent man would like to have him—by the scruff of his neck. He's fit only to kick; and I'm going to kick him good and plenty; and in the process he's going to let go of several things." Mortimer leered, pleased with his own similes, then added rather hastily: "I mean, he's going to drop several things that don't belong to him. Leave it to me to shake him down; he'll drop them all right. . . . One of 'em's yours."

Plank looked at him.

"I told you once that I'd let you know when to step up and say 'Good evening' didn't I?"

Plank continued to stare.

"Didn't I?" repeated Mortimer peevishly, beginning to lose countenance.

"I don't understand you," said Plank, "and I don't think I want to understand you."

"What do you mean?" demanded Mortimer thickly; "don't you want to marry that girl!" but he shrank dismayed under the slow blaze that lighted Plank's blue eyes.

"All right," he stammered, struggling to his fat legs and instinctively backing away; "I thought you meant business. I—what the devil do I care who you marry! It's the last time I try to do anything for you, or for anybody else! Mark that, my friend. I've plenty to worry over; I've a lot to keep me busy without lying awake to figure out how to do kindnesses to old friends. Damn this ingratitude, anyway!"

Plank gazed at him for a moment; the anger in his face had died out.

"I am not ungrateful," he said. "You may say almost anything except that, Leroy. I am not disloyal, no matter what else I may be. But you have made a bad mistake. You made it that day at Black Fells when you offered to interfere. I supposed you understood then that I could never tolerate from anybody anything of such a nature. It appears that you didn't. However, you understand it now. So let us forget the matter."

But Mortimer, keenly appreciative of the pleasures of being misunderstood, squeezed some moisture out of his distended eyes, and sat down, a martyr to his emotions. "To think," he gulped, "that *you*, of all men, should turn on me like this!"

"I didn't mean to. Can't you understand, Leroy, that you hurt me?"

"Hurt hell!" retorted Mortimer vindictively. "You've had sensation battered out of you by this time. I guess society has landed you a few while I was boosting you over the outworks. Don't play that old con game on me! You tried to get her and you couldn't. Now I come along and offer to put you next and you yell about your hurt feelings! Oh, splash! There's another lady, that's all."

"Let it go at that, then," said Plank, reddening.

"But I tell you——"

"Drop it!" snapped Plank.

"Oh, very well! if you're going to take it that way again——"

"I am. Cut it! And now let me ask you a question: Where were you going when I met you?"

"What do you want to know for?" asked Mortimer sullenly.

"Why, I'll tell you, Leroy. If you have any idea of identifying yourself with Quarrier's people, of seeking him at this juncture with the expectation of investing any money in his schemes, you had better not do so."

"Investing!" sneered Mortimer. "Well, no, not exactly, having nothing to invest, thanks to my being swindled into joining his Amalgamated Electric gang. Don't worry. If there's any shaking down to be done, I'll do it, my friend," and he rose, and started toward the elevators.

"Wait," said Plank. "Why, man, *you* can't frighten Quarrier! What did you sell your holdings for? Why didn't you come to us—to me? What's the use of going to Quarrier now, and scolding? You can't scare a man like that."

Mortimer fairly grinned in his face.

"Your big mistake," he sneered, "is in undervaluing others. You don't think I amount to very much, do you, Beverly? But I'm going to try to take care of myself all the same." He laughed, showing his big teeth, and the vanity in him began to drug him. "No, you think I don't know much. But men like you and Quarrier will damn soon find out! I want you to understand," he went on excitedly, forgetting the instinctive caution which in saner moments he was only too certain that his present business required—"I want you to understand a few things, my friend, and one of them is that I'm not afraid of Quarrier, and another is, I'm not afraid of you!"

"Leroy——"

"No, not afraid of *you*, either!" repeated Mortimer with an ugly stare. "Don't try any of your smug, aint-it-a-shame-he-drinks ways on me, Beverly! I'm getting tired of it; I'm tired of it now, by God! You keep a civil tongue in your head after this—do you understand?—and we'll get on all right. If you don't, I've the means to make you!"

"Are you crazy?"

"Not a bit of it! Too damn sane for you and Leila to hoodwink!"

"You *are* crazy!" repeated Plank, aghast.

"Am I? You and Leila can take the matter into court, if you want to—unless *I* do. And"—here he leaned forward, showing his teeth again—"the next time you kiss her, *close the door*!"

Then he went away up the marble steps and entered an elevator; and Plank, grave and pale, went out into the street and entered his big touring-car. But the drive up town and through the sunlit park gave him no pleasure, and he entered his great house with a heavy, lifeless step, head bent, as though counting every crevice in the stones under his lagging feet. For the first time in all his life he was afraid of a man.

. . . .

The man he was afraid of had gone directly to Quarrier's office, missing the gentleman he was seeking by such a small fraction of a minute that he realised they must have passed each other in the elevators, he ascending while Quarrier was descending.

Mortimer turned and hurried to the elevator, hoping to come up with Quarrier in the rotunda, or possibly in the street outside; but he was too late, and, furious to think of the time he had wasted with Plank, he crawled into a hansom and bade the driver take him to a number he gave, designating one of the new limestone basement houses on the upper west side.

All the way up town, as he jolted about in his seat, he angrily regretted the meeting with Plank, even in spite of the cheque. What demon had possessed him to boast—to display his hand when there had been no necessity? Plank was still ready to give him aid at a crisis—had always been ready. Time enough when Plank turned stingy to use persuasion; time enough when Plank attempted to dodge him to employ a club. And now, for no earthly reason, intoxicated with his own vanity, catering to his own long-smouldering resentment, he had used his club on a willing horse—deliberately threatened a man whose gratitude had been good for many a cheque yet.

"Ass that I am!" fumed Mortimer; "now when

I'm stuck I'll have to go at him with the club, if I want any money out of him. Confound him, he's putting me in a false position! He's trying to make it look like extortion! I won't do it! I'm no blackmailer! I'll starve, before I go to him again! No blundering, clumsy Dutchman can make a blackmailer out of *me* by holding hands with that scoundrelly wife of mine! That's the reason he did it, too! Between them they are trying to make my loans from Plank look like blackmail! It would serve them right if I took them up—if I called their bluff, and stuck Plank up in earnest! But I won't, to please them! I won't do any dirty thing like that, to humour them! Not much!"

He lay back, rolling about in the jouncing cab, scowling at space.

"Not much!" he repeated. "I'll shake down Quarrier, though! I'll make him pay for his treachery—scaring me out of Amalgamated! That will be restitution, not extortion!"

He was the angrier because he had been for days screwing up his courage to the point of seeking Quarrier face to face. He had not wished to do it; the scene, and his own attitude in it, could only be repugnant to him, although he continually explained to himself that it was restitution, not extortion.

But whatever it was, he didn't like to figure in it, and he had hung back as long as circumstances permitted. But his new lodgings and his new friends were expensive; and Plank, he supposed, was off somewhere fishing; so he hung on as long as it was possible; then, exasperated by necessity, started for Quarrier's office, only to miss him by a few seconds because he was fool enough to waste his temper and his opportunity in making an enemy out of a friend!

"Oh," he groaned, "what an ass I am!" And he got out of his cab in front of a very new limestone basement house with red geraniums blooming on the window-sills, and let himself in with a latch-key.

The interior of the house was attractive in a rather bright, new, clean fashion. There seemed to be a great deal of white wood-work about, a wilderness of slender white spindles supporting the dark, rich mahogany hand-rail of the stairway; elaborate white grilles between snowy, Corinthian pillars separating the hall from the drawing-room, where a pale gilt mirror over a white, colonial mantel reflected a glass chandelier and panelled walls hung with pale blue silk.

All was new, very clean, very quiet; the maid, too, who appeared at the sound of the closing door and took his hat and gloves was as newly groomed as the floors and wood-work, and so noiseless as to be conspicuous in her swift, silent movements.

Yet there was something about it all—about the bluish silvery half-light, the spotless floors and walls, the abnormally noiseless maid in her flamboyant cap and apron—that arrested attention and fixed it. The soundless brightness of the house was as conspicuous as the contrast between the maid's black gown and her snow-white cuffs. There was nothing subdued about anything, although the long, silvery blue curtains were drawn over the lace window hangings; no shadows anywhere, no half-lights. The very stillness was gay with suspense, like a pretty woman's suppressed laughter glimmering in her eyes.

And into this tinted light, framed in palest blue and white, waddled Mortimer, appropriate as a June-bug scrambling in a Sèvres teacup.

"Anybody here?" he growled, leering into the

drawing-room at a tiny grand piano cased in unvarnished Circassian walnut.

"There is nobody at home, sir," said the maid.

"Music lesson over?"

"Yes, sir, at three."

He began to ascend the stairway, breathing heavily, thud, thud over the deep velvet strip, his fat hand grasping the banister rail.

Somewhere on the second floor a small dog barked, and Mortimer traversed the hall and opened the door into a room hung with gold Spanish leather and pale green curtains.

"Hello, Tinto!" he said affably as a tiny Japanese spaniel hurled herself at him, barking furiously, then began writhing and weaving herself about him, gurgling recognition and welcome.

He sat down heavily in a padded easy-chair. The spaniel sprang into his lap, wheezing, sniffling, goggling its protruding eyes. Mortimer liked the dog, but he didn't like what the owner of the dog said about the resemblance between his own and Tinto's eyes.

"Get down!" he said; "you're shedding black and white hairs all over me." But the dog didn't want to get down, and Mortimer's good nature permitted her to curl up on his fat knees and sleep that nervous, twitching sleep peculiar to overpampered toy canines.

The southern sun was warm in the room; the windows open, but not a silken hanging stirred.

Presently another maid entered, with an apple cut into thin wafers and a decanter of port; and Mortimer lay back in his chair, sopping his apple in the thick, crimson wine, and feeding morsels of the combination to himself and to Tinto at intervals until the apple was all gone and the decanter three-fourths empty.

It was very still in the room—so still, that Mortimer, opening his eyes at longer and longer intervals to peer at the door, finally opened them no more.

The droning gurgle that he made kept Tinto awake. When his lower jaw sagged, and he began to really show what snoring could be, Tinto, very nervous, got up and hopped down.

. . . .

It was still daylight when Mortimer awoke, conscious of people about him. As he opened his eyes, a man laughed; several people seated by the windows joined in. Then, straightening up with an effort, something tumbled from his head to the floor and he started to rise.

"Oh, look out, Leroy! Don't step on my hat!" cried a girl's voice; and he sank back in his chair, gazing stupidly around.

"Hello! you people!" he said, amused; "I guess I've been asleep. Oh, is that you Millbank? Whose hat was that—yours, Lydia?"

He yawned, laughed, turning his heavy eyes from one to another, recognising a couple of young girls at the window. He didn't want to get up; but there is, in the society he now adorned, a stringency of etiquette known as "*re*-finement," and which, to ignore, is to become unpopular.

So he got onto his massive legs and went over to shake hands with a gravity becoming the ceremony.

"How d'ye do, Miss Hutchinson? Thought you were at Asbury Park. How de do, Miss Del Garcia. Have you been out in Millbank's motor yet?"

"We broke down at McGowan's Pass," said Miss Del Garcia, laughing the laugh that had made her so attractive in "A Word to the Wise."

"Muddy gasoline," nodded Millbank tersely—an

iron-jawed, over-groomed man of forty, with a florid face shaved blue.

"We passed Mr. Plank's big touring-car," observed Lydia Vyse, shifting Tinto to the couch and brushing the black and white hairs from her automobile coat. "How much does a car like that cost, Leroy?"

"About twenty-five thousand," he said gloomily. Then, looking up, "Hold on, Millbank, don't be going! Why can't you all dine with us? Never mind your car; ours is all right, and we'll run out into the country for dinner. How about it, Miss Del Garcia?"

But both Miss Del Garcia and Miss Hutchinson had accepted another invitation, in which Millbank was also included.

They stood about, veils floating, leather decorated coats thrown back, lingering for awhile to talk the garage talk which fascinates people of their type; then Millbank looked at the clock, made his adieux to Lydia, nodded significantly to Mortimer, and followed the others down-stairs.

There was something amiss with his motor, for it made a startling racket in the street, finally plunging forward with a kick.

Lydia laughed as the two young girls in the tonneau turned to nod to her in mock despair; then she came running back up-stairs, holding her skirt free from her hurrying little feet.

"Well?" she inquired, as Mortimer turned back from the window to confront her.

"Nothing doing, little girl," he said with a sombre smile.

She looked at him, slowly divesting herself of her light leather-trimmed coat.

"I missed him," said Mortimer.

She flung the coat over a chair, stood a moment, her fingers busy with her hair-pegs, then sat down on the couch, taking Tinto into her lap. She was very pretty, dark, slim, marvellously graceful in her every movement.

"I missed him," repeated Mortimer.

"Can't you see him to-morrow?" she asked.

"I suppose so," said Mortimer slowly. "Oh, Lord! how I hate this business!"

"Hasn't he misused your confidence? Hasn't he taken your money?" she asked. "It may be unpleasant for you to make him unbelt, but you're a coward if you don't!"

"Easy! easy, now!" muttered Mortimer; "I'm going to shake it out of him. I said I would, and I will."

"I should hope so; it's yours."

"Certainly it's mine. I wish I'd held fast now. I never supposed Plank would take hold. It was that drivelling old Belwether who scared me stiff! The minute I saw him scurrying to cover like a singed cat I was fool enough to climb the first tree. I've had my lesson, little girl."

"I hope you'll give Howard his. Somebody ought to," she said quietly.

Then gathering up her hat and coat she went into her own apartments. Mortimer picked up a cheap magazine, looked over the portraits of the actresses, then, hunching up into a comfortable position, settled himself to read the theatrical comment.

Later, Lydia not appearing, and his own valet arriving to turn on the electricity, bring him his White Rock and Irish and the *Evening Telegraph*, he hoisted his legs into another chair and sprawled there luxuriously over his paper until it was time to dress.

About half past eight they dined in a white and pink dining-room furnished in dull gray walnut, and served by a stealthy, white-haired, pink-skinned butler, chiefly remarkable because it seemed utterly impossible to get a glimpse of his eyes. Nobody could tell whether there was anything the matter with them or not—and whether they were only very deep set or were weak, like an albino's, or were slightly crossed, the guests of the house never knew. Lydia herself didn't know, and had given up trying to find out.

They had planned to go for a spin in Mortimer's motor after dinner, but in view of the Quarrier fiasco neither was in the mood for anything.

Mortimer, as usual, ate and drank heavily. He was a carnivorous man, and liked plenty of thick, fat, underdone meat. As for Lydia, her appetite was as erratic as her own impulses. Her table, always wastefully elaborate, no doubt furnished subsistence for all the relatives of her household below stairs, and left sufficient for any ambitious butler to make a decent profit on.

"Do you know, Leroy," she observed, as they left the table and sauntered back into the pale blue drawing-room, "do you know that the servants haven't been paid for three months?"

"Oh, for Heaven's sake," he expostulated, "don't begin that sort of thing! I get enough of that at home; I get it every time I show my nose!"

"I only mentioned it," she said carelessly.

"I heard you all right. It isn't any pleasanter for me than for you. In fact, I'm sick of it; I'm dead tired of being up against it every day of my life. When a man has anything somebody gets it before he can side-step. When a man's dead broke there's nobody in sight to touch."

"You had an opportunity to make Howard pay you back."

"Didn't I tell you I missed him?"

"Yes. What are you going to do?"

"Do?"

"Of course. You are going to do something, I suppose."

They had reached the gold and green room above. Lydia began pacing the length of a beautiful Kermanshah rug—a pale, delicate marvel of rose and green on a ground of ivory—lovely, but doomed to fade sooner than the pretty woman who trod it with restless, silk-shod feet.

Mortimer had not responded to her last question. She said presently: "You have never told me how you intend to make him pay you back."

"What?" inquired Mortimer, turning very red.

"I said that you haven't yet told me how you intend to make Howard return the money you lost through his juggling with your stock."

"I don't exactly know myself," admitted Mortimer, still overflushed. "I mean to put it to him squarely, as a debt of honour that he owes. I asked him whether to invest. Damn him! he never warned me not to. He is morally responsible. Any man who would sit there and nod monotonously like a mandarin, knowing all the while what he was doing to wreck the company, and let a friend put into a rotten concern all the cash he could scrape together, is a swindler!"

"I think so too," she said, studying the rose arabesques in the rug.

There was a little click of her teeth when she ended her inspection and looked across at Mortimer. Something in her expressionless gaze seemed to reassure him, and give him a confidence he may have lacked.

"I want him to understand that I won't swallow that sort of contemptible treatment," asserted Mortimer, lighting a thick, dark cigar.

"I hope you'll make him understand," she said, seating herself and resting her clasped, brilliantly ringed hands in her lap.

"Oh, I will—never fear! He has abused my confidence abominably; he has practically swindled me, Lydia. Don't you think so?"

She nodded.

"I'll tell him so, too," blustered Mortimer, shaking himself into an upright posture, and laying a pudgy, clinched fist on the table. "I'm not afraid of him! He'll find that out, too. I know enough to stagger him. Not that I mean to use it. I'm not going to have him think that my demands on him for my own property resemble extortion."

"Extortion?" she repeated.

"Yes. I don't want him to think I'm trying to intimidate him. I won't have him think I'm a grafter; but I've half a mind to shake that money out of him, in one way or another."

He struck the table and looked at her for further sign of approval.

"I'm not afraid of him," he repeated. "I wish to God he were here, and I'd tell him so!"

She said coolly: "I was wishing that too."

For a while they sat silent, preoccupied, avoiding each other's direct gaze. When she rose he started, watching her in a dazed way as she walked to the telephone.

"Shall I?" she asked quietly, turning to him, her hand on the receiver.

"Wait. W-what are you going to do?" he stammered.

"Call him up. Shall I?"

A dull throb of fright pulsed through him.

"You say you are not afraid of him, Leroy."

"No!" he said with an oath, "I am not. Go ahead!"

She unhooked the receiver. After a second or two her low, even voice sounded. There came a pause. She rested one elbow on the walnut shelf, the receiver tight to her ear. Then:

"Mr. Quarrier, please. . . . Yes, Mr. Howard Quarrier. . . . No, no name. Say it is on business of immediate importance. . . . Very well, then; you may say that Miss Vyse *insists* on speaking to him. . . . Yes, I'll hold the wire."

She turned, the receiver at her ear, and looked narrowly at Mortimer.

"Won't he speak to you?" he demanded.

"I'm going to find out. Hush a moment!" and in the same calm, almost childish voice: "Oh, Howard, is that you? Yes, I know I promised not to do this, but that was before things happened! . . . Well, what am I to do when it is necessary to talk to you? . . . Yes, it is necessary! . . . I tell you it is necessary! . . . I am sorry it is not convenient for you to talk to me, but I really must ask you to listen! . . . No, I shall not write. I want to talk to you to-night—*now!* Yes, you may come here, if you care to! . . . I think you had better come, Howard. . . . Because I am liable to continue ringing your telephone until you are willing to listen. . . . No, there is nobody here. I am alone. What time? . . . Very well; I shall expect you. Good-bye."

She hung up the receiver and turned to Mortimer:

"He's coming up at once. Did I say anything to scare him particularly?"

"One thing's sure as preaching," said Mortimer; "he's a coward, and I'm damned glad of it," he added naïvely, relighting his cigar, which had gone out.

"If he comes up in his motor he'll be here in a few minutes," she said. "Suppose you take your hat and go out. I don't want him to think what he will think if he walks into the room and finds you waiting. You have your key, Leroy. Walk down the block; and when you see him come in, give him five minutes."

Her voice had become a little breathless, and her colour was high. Mortimer, too, seemed apprehensive. Things had suddenly begun to work themselves out too swiftly.

"Do you think that's best?" he faltered, looking about for his hat. "Tell Merkle that nobody has been here, if Quarrier should ask him. Do you think we're doing it in the best way, Lydia? By God, it smells of a put-up job to me! But I guess it's all right. It's better for me to just happen in, isn't it? Don't forget to put Merkle wise."

He descended the stairs hastily. Merkle, of the invisible eyes, held his hat and gloves and opened the door for him.

Once on the dark street, his impulse was to flee—get out, get away from the whole business. A sullen shame was pumping the hot blood up into his neck and cheeks. He strove to find an inoffensive name for what he was proposing to do, but ugly terms, synonym after synonym, crowded in to characterise the impending procedure, and he walked on angrily, half frightened, looking back from moment to moment at the house he had just left.

On the corner he halted, breathing spasmodically, for he had struck a smarter pace than he had been aware of.

Few people passed him. Once he caught a glimmer of a policeman's buttons along the park wall, and an unpleasant shiver passed over him. At the same moment an electric hansom flew noiselessly past him. He shrank back into the shadow of a porte-cochère. The hansom halted before the limestone basement house. A tall figure left it, stood a moment in the middle of the sidewalk, then walked quickly to the front door. It opened, and the man vanished.

The hansom still waited at the door. Mortimer, his hands shaking, looked at his watch by the light of the electric bulbs flanking the gateway under which he stood.

There was not much time in which to make up his mind, yet his fright was increasing to a pitch which began to enrage him with that coward's courage which it is impossible to reckon with.

He had missed Quarrier once to-day when he had been keyed to the encounter. Was he going to miss him again through sheer terror? Besides, was not Quarrier a coward? Besides, was it not his own money? Had he not been vilely swindled by a pretended friend? Urging, lashing himself into a heavy, shuffling motion, he emerged from the porte-cochère and lurched off down the street. No time to think now, no time for second thought, for hesitation, for weakness. He had waited too long already. He had waited ten minutes, instead of five. Was Quarrier going to escape again? Was he going to get out of the house before——"

Fumbling with his latch-key, but with sense enough left to make no noise, he let himself in, passed silently through the reception-hall and up to the drawing-room floor, where for a second he stood listening. Then something of the perverted sportsman sent the blood quivering into his veins. He had him! He had run him down! The game was at bay.

An inrush of exhilaration steadied him. He laid his hand on the banister and mounted, gloves and hat-brim crushed in the other hand. When he entered the room he pretended to see only Lydia.

"Hello, little girl!" he said, laughing, "are you surprised to——"

At that moment he caught sight of Quarrier, and the start he gave was genuine enough. Never had he seen in a man's visage such white concentration of anger.

"Quarrier!" he stammered, for his acting was becoming real enough to supplant art.

Quarrier had risen; his narrowing eyes moved from Mortimer to Lydia, then reverted to the man in the combination.

"Rather unexpected, isn't it?" said Mortimer, staring at Quarrier.

"Is it?" returned Quarrier in a low voice.

"I suppose so," sneered Mortimer. "Did you expect to find me here?"

"No. Did *you* expect to find me?" asked the other, with emphasis unmistakable.

"What do you mean?" demanded Mortimer hoarsely. "What the devil do you mean by asking me if I expected to find *you* here? If I had, I'd not have travelled down to your office to-day to see you; I'd have come here for you. Naturally people suppose that an engaged man is likely to give up this sort of thing."

Quarrier, motionless, white to the lips, turned his eyes from one to the other.

"It doesn't look very well, does it?" asked Mortimer; and he stood there, smiling, danger written all over him. "It's beginning rather early," he continued, with a sneer. "Most engaged men with a conscience wait until they're married before they return to the gay and frivolous. But here you are, it seems, handsome, jolly, and irresistible as ever!"

Quarrier looked at Lydia, and his lips moved: "You asked me to come," he said.

"No; *you* offered to. I wished to talk to you over the wire, but"—her lip curled, and she shrugged her shoulders—"you seemed to be afraid of something or other."

"I couldn't talk to you in my own house, with guests in the room."

"Why not? Did I say anything your fashionable guests might take exception to? Am I likely to do anything of that kind?—you coward!"

Quarrier stood very still, then noiselessly turned and made one step toward the door.

"One moment," interposed Mortimer blandly. "As long as I travelled down town to see you, and find you here so unexpectedly, I may as well take advantage of this opportunity to regulate a little matter. You don't mind our talking shop for a moment, Lydia? Thank you. It's just a little business matter between Mr. Quarrier and myself—a matter concerning a few shares of stock which I once held in one of his companies, bought at par, and tumbled to ten and— *What* is the fraction, Quarrier? I forget."

Quarrier thought deeply for a moment; then he raised his head, looking full at Mortimer, and under his silky beard an edge of teeth glimmered. "Did you wish me to take back those shares at par?" he asked.

"Exactly! I knew you would! I knew you'd see it in that way!" cried Mortimer heartily. "Confound it all, Quarrier, I've always said you were that sort of man—that you'd never let a friend in on the top floor, and kick him clear to the cellar! As a matter of fact, I sold out at ten and three-eighths. Wait! Here's a pencil. Lydia, give me that pad on your desk. Here you are, Quarrier. It's easy enough to figure out how much you owe me."

And as Quarrier slowly began tracing figures on the pad, Mortimer rambled on, growing more demonstrative and boisterous every moment. "It's white of you, Quarrier—I'll say that! Legally, of course, you could laugh at me; but I've always said your business conscience would never let you stand for this sort of thing. 'You can talk and talk,' I've told people, many a time, 'but you'll never convince me that Howard Quarrier hasn't a heart.' No, by jinks! they couldn't make me believe it. And here's my proof—here's my vindication! Lydia, would you mind hunting up that cheque-book I left here before dinn——"

He had made a mistake. The girl flushed. He choked up, and cast a startled glance at Quarrier. But Quarrier, if he heard, made no motion of understanding. Perhaps it had not been necessary to convince him of the conspiracy.

When he had finished his figures he reviewed them, tracing each total with his pencil's point; then quietly handed the pad to Mortimer who went over it, and nodded that it was correct.

Lydia rose. Quarrier said, without looking at her: "I have a blank cheque with me. May I use one of these pens?"

So he had brought a cheque! Had he supposed that

a cheque might be necessary when Lydia called him up? Was he prepared to meet any demand of hers, too, even before Mortimer appeared on the scene?

"As long as you have a cheque with you, Howard," said Lydia quietly, "suppose you simply add to Mr. Mortimer's amount what you had intended to offer me?"

He stared at her without answering.

"That little remembrance for old time's sake. Don't you recollect?"

"No," said Quarrier.

"Why, Howard! Didn't you promise me all sorts of things when I wanted to go to your friend Mr. Siward, and explain that it was not his fault I got into the Patroons Club? Don't you remember I felt dreadfully that he was expelled—that I was simply wild to write to the governors and tell them how I took Merkle's clothes and drove to the club and waited until I saw a lot of men go in, and then crowded in with the push?"

Mortimer was staring at Quarrier out of his protruding eyes. The girl leaned forward, deliberate, self-possessed, the red lips edged with growing scorn.

"*That* was a dirty trick!" said Mortimer heavily. He took the pad, added a figure, passed it to Lydia, and she coolly wrote a total, underscoring it heavily.

"*That* is the amount," she said.

Quarrier looked at the pad which she had tossed upon the desk. Then he slowly wetted his pen with ink, and, laying the loose cheque flat, began to fill it in. Afterward he dried it, and, reading it carefully, pushed it aside and rose.

"It wouldn't be advisable for you to stop payment, you know," observed Mortimer insolently, lying back in his chair and stretching his legs.

"I know," said Quarrier, pausing to turn on them

a deathly stare. Then he went away. After awhile they heard the door close. But there was no sound from the electric hansom, and Mortimer rose and walked to the window.

"He's gone," he said.

Lydia stood at the desk, examining the cheque.

"We ought to afford a decent touring-car now," she suggested—"like that yellow and black Serin-Chanteur car of Mr. Plank's."

CHAPTER XIII

THE SELLING PRICE

The heat, which had been severe in June, driving the last fashionable loiterer into the country, continued fiercely throughout July. August was stifling; the chestnut leaves in the parks curled up and grew brittle; the elms were blotched; brown stretches scarred the lawns; the blazing colour of the geranium beds seemed to intensify the heat, like a bed of living coals.

Nobody who was anybody remained in town—except some wealthy business men and their million odd employés; but the million, being nobodies, didn't count.

Nobody came into town; that is to say that a million odd strangers came as usual, swelling the sweltering, resident population sufficiently to animate the main commercial thoroughfares morning and evening, but they didn't count; the money they spent was, however, very carefully counted.

The fashionable columns of the newspapers informed the fashionable ex-urbanated that the city was empty—though the East Side reeked like a cattle-pen, and another million or two gasped on the hot, tin roofs under the stars, or buried their dirty faces in the parched park grass.

What the press meant to say was that the wealthy section of the city within the shadow of St. Patrick's twin white spires and north of Fifty-ninth Street was as empty and silent as an abandoned gold-mine. Which was true. Miles of elaborate, untenanted dwellings glimmered blank under the moon and stood tomb-like in barren magnificence against the blazing blue of noon. Miles of plate-glass windows, boarded, or bearing between lowered shade and dusty pane the significant parti-coloured placard warning the honest thief, stared out at the heated park or, in the cross streets, confronted each other with inert hauteur, awaiting the pleasure of their absent owners.

The humidity increased; the horses' heads hung heavily under their ridiculously pitiful straw bonnets. When the sun was vertical nobody stirred; when the bluish shadows began to creep out over baked sidewalks, broadening to a strip of superheated shade, a few stirred abroad in the deserted streets; here a policeman, thin blue summer tunic open, helmet in hand, swabbing the sweat from forehead and neck; there a white uniformed street sweeper dragging his rubber-edged mop or a section of wet hose; perhaps a haggard peddler of lemonade making for the Park wall around the Metropolitan Museum where, a little later, the East Side would venture out to sit on the benches, or the great electric tourists' busses would halt to dump out a living cargo—perhaps only the bent figure of a woman, very shabby, very old, dragging her ancient bones along the silent splendour of Fifth Avenue, and peering about the gutters for something she never finds—always peering, always mumbling the endless, wordless, soundless *miserere* of the poor.

Quarrier's huge limestone mansion, looming golden in the sun, was tenantless; its owner, closing even The Sedges, his Long Island house, and driven northward for a breath of air, was expected at Shotover.

The house of Mrs. Mortimer was closed and boarded up; the Caithness mansion was closed; the Ferralls', the Bonnesdels', the Pages', the Shannons', Mrs. Vendenning's, all were sealed up like vaults. A caretaker apparently guarded Major Belwether's house, peeping out at intervals from behind the basement windows. As for Plank's great pile of masonry, edging the outer Hundreds in the north, several lighted windows were to be seen in it at night, and a big yellow and black touring-car whizzed down town from its bronze gateway every morning with perfect regularity.

For there was a fight on that had steadily grown hotter with the weather, and Plank had little time to concern himself with the temperature or to mop his red features over the weather bureau report. Harrington and Quarrier were after him, horse, foot, and dragoons; Harrington had even taken a house at Seabright in order to be near in person; and Quarrier's move from Long Island to Shotover House was not as flippant as it might appear, for he had his private car there and a locomotive at Black Fells Crossing station, and he was within striking distance of Rochester, Utica, Syracuse, and Albany. Which was what Harrington thought necessary.

The vast unseen machinery set in motion by Harrington and Quarrier had begun to grind in May; and, at the first audible rumble, the aspect of things financial in the country changed. A few industrials began to rocket, nobody knew why; but the market's first tremor left it baggy and spineless, and the reaction, already overdue, became a sodden and soggy slump. Nobody knew why.

The noise of the fray in the papers, which had first excited then stunned the outside public, continued in a delirium of rumour, report, forecast, and summing up at the week's end.

Scare heads, involving everybody and everything, from the District-Attorney to Plank's office boy, succeeded one another. Plank's name headed column after column. Already becoming familiar in the society and financial sections, it began to appear in neighbouring paragraphs. Who was Plank? And the papers told people with more or less inaccuracy, humour, or sarcasm. What was he trying to do? The papers tried to tell that, too, making a pretty close guess, with comments good-natured or ill-natured according to circumstances over which somebody ought to have some control. What was Harrington trying to do to Plank—if he was trying to do anything? They told that pretty clearly. What was Quarrier going to do to Plank? That, also, they explained in lively detail. A few clergymen who stuck to their churches began to volunteer pulpit opinions concerning the ethics of the battle. A minister who was generally supposed to make an unmitigated nuisance of himself in politics dealt Plank an unexpected blow by saying that he was a "hero." Some papers called him "Hero" Plank for awhile, but soon tired of it or forgot it under the stress of the increasing heat.

Besides Plank scarcely noticed what the press said of him. He was too busy; his days were full days, brimming over deep into the night. Brokers, lawyers, sycophants, tipsters, treacherous ex-employés of Quarrier, detectives, up-State petty officials, lobbyists from Albany, newspaper men, men from Wall Street, Broad Street, Mulberry Street, Forty-second Street—all these he saw in units, relays, regiments—either at his offices or after dinner—and sometimes after midnight in his own house. And these were only a few, picked from the interested or disinterested thousands who besieged him with advice, importunity, threats, and attempted blackmail. And he handled them all in turn, stolidly but with decision. His obstinate under lip protruded further and further with rare recessions; his heavy head was like the lowered head of a bull. Undaunted, inexorable, slow to the verge of stupidity at times, at times swift as a startled tiger, this new, amazing personality steadily developing, looming higher, heavier, athwart the financial horizon—in stature holding his own among giants, then growing, gradually, inch by inch, dominated his surrounding level sky line.

The youth in him was the tragedy to the old; the sudden silence of the man the danger to the secretive. Harrington was already an old man; Quarrier's own weapon had always been secrecy; but the silence of Plank confused him, for he had never learned to parry well another's use of his own weapon. The left-handed swordsman dreads to cross with a man who fights with the left hand. And Harrington, hoary, seamed, scarred, maimed in onslaughts of long forgotten battles, looked long and hard upon this weird of his own dead youth which now rose towering to confront him, menacing him with the armed point of the same shield behind which he himself had so long found shelter—the Law!

The closing of the courts enforced armed truces along certain lines of Plank's battle front; the adjournment of the legislature emptied Albany. Once it was rumoured that Plank had passed an entire morning with the Governor of the greatest State in the Union and that the conference was to be repeated. A swarm of newspaper men settled about the Governor's summer cottage at Saratoga, but they learned nothing, nor could they find a trace of Plank's tracks in the trodden trails of the great Spa.

Besides, the racing had begun; Desmond, Burbank, Sneed, and others of the gilded guild had opened new club-houses; the wretched, half-starved natives in the surrounding hills were violating the game-laws to distend the paunches of the overfed with five-inch troutlings and grouse and woodcock slaughtered out of season; so there was plenty of copy for newspaper men without the daily speculative paragraph devoted to the doings of Beverly Plank. Some scandal, too—but newspapers never touch that; and after all it was nobody's affair that Leroy Mortimer drove a large yellow and black Serin-Chanteur touring-car, new model, all over Saratoga county. Perhaps the similarity of machines gave rise to the rumour of Plank's presence; perhaps not, because the car was often driven by a tall, slender girl with dark eyes and hair; and nobody ever saw that sort of pretty woman in Plank's Serin, or saw Leroy Mortimer for many days without a companion of that species.

Mortimer's health was excellent. The races had not proved remunerative however, and his new motor-car was horribly expensive. So was Lydia. And he began to be seriously afraid that by the end of August he would be obliged to apply to Quarrier once more for some slight temporary token of that gentleman's goodwill. He told Lydia this, and she seemed to agree with him. This pleased him. She had not pleased him very much recently. For one thing she was becoming too friendly with some of his friends—Desmond in particular.

Plank, it was known, had opened his great house at Black Fells. His servants, gamekeepers, were there; his stables, kennels, greenhouses, model stock-farm—all had been put in immaculate condition pending the advent of the master. But Plank had not appeared; his new sea-going steam yacht still lay in the East River, and, at rare intervals, a significant glimmer of bunting disclosed the owner's presence aboard for an hour or two. That was all, however; and the cliff-watchers at Shotover House and the Fells looked seaward in vain for the big *Siwanoa*, as yacht after yacht, heralded by the smudge on the horizon, turned from a gray speck to a white one, and crept in from the sea to anchor.

The Ferralls were at Shotover with their first instalment of guests. Sylvia was there, Quarrier expected—because Kemp Ferrall's break with him was not a social one, and Grace's real affection for Sylvia blinded neither her nor her husband to the material and social importance of the intimacy. Siward was not invited; neither had an invitation to him been even discussed in view of what Grace was aware of, and what everybody knew concerning the implacable relations existing between him, personally, and Howard Quarrier.

Bridge, yachting, and motoring were the August sports; the shooting set had not yet arrived, of course; in fact there was still another relay expected before the season opened and brought the shooting coterie for the first two weeks. But Sylvia was expected to last through and hold over with a brief interlude for a week's end at Lenox. So was Quarrier; and Grace, always animated by a lively but harmless malice, hoped to Heaven that Plank might arrive before Quarrier left, because she adored the tension of situations and was delightedly persuaded that Plank was more than able to hold his own with her irritating cousin.

"Oh, to see them together in a small room," she

sighed ecstatically in Sylvia's ear; "I'd certainly poke them up if they only turned around sulkily in the corners of the cage and evinced a desire to lie down."

"What a mischief-maker you are," said Sylvia listlessly; and though Grace became very vivacious in describing her plans to extract amusement out of Plank's hoped-for presence Sylvia remained uninterested.

There seemed, in fact, little to interest her that summer at Shotover House; and, though she never refused any plans made for her, and her attitude was one of quiet acquiescence always—she never expressed a preference for anything, a desire to do anything; and, if let alone, was prone to pace the cliffs or stretch her slim, rounded body on the sand of some little, sheltered, crescent beach, apparently content with the thunderous calm of sea and sky.

Her interest, too, in people had seemingly been extinguished. Once or twice she did inquire as to Marion's whereabouts, and learned that Miss Page was fishing in Minnesota somewhere but would return to Shotover when the shooting opened. Somebody, Captain Voucher, perhaps, mentioned to somebody in her hearing that Siward was still in New York. If she heard she made no sign, no inquiry. The next morning she remained abed with a headache, and Grace motored to Wendover without her; but Sylvia spent the balance of the day on the cliffs, and played Bridge with the devil's own luck till dawn, piling up a score that staggered Mr. Fleetwood, who had been instructing her in adversary play a day or two before.

The hot month dragged on; Quarrier came; Agatha Caithness arrived a few days later—scheme of the Ferralls involving Alderdene!—but the *Siwanoa* did not come, and Plank remained invisible. Leila Mortimer arrived from Swan's Harbour toward the middle of the month, offering no information as to the whereabouts of what Major Belwether delicately designated as her "legitimate." But everybody knew he was at last to be crossed off and struck clean out, and the ugly history of the winter, now so impudently corroborated at Saratoga, gave many a hostess the opportunity long desired. Mortimer, as far as his own particular circle was concerned, was down and out; Leila, accepted as a matter of course without him, remained quietly uncommunicative. If the outward physical change in her was due to her marital rupture people thought it was well that it had come in time, for she bloomed like a lovely exotic; and her silences and enthusiasms, and the fragrant freshness of her developing attitude toward the world first disconcerted, then amused, then touched those who had supposed themselves to be so long a buckler for her foibles and a shield for her caprice.

"Gad," said Alderdene, "she's well rid of him if he's been choking her this long—the rank, rotten weed that he is, sapping the life from her so when she hung over toward another fellow's bush we thought she was frail in the stem—God bless us all for a simpering lot of blatherskites!"

And if, in the corner of the gun-room, there was a man among them who had ever ventured to hold Leila's smooth little hand, unrebuked, in days gone by, none the less he knew that Alderdene spoke truth; and none the less he knew that what witness he might be called to bear at the end of the end of all must only incriminate himself and not that young matron who now, before their very eyes, was budding again, reverting to the esoteric charm of youth reincarnated.

"A suit before a referee would settle him," mused

Voucher; "he hasn't a leg to stand on. Lord! The same cat that tripped up Stephen Siward!"

Fleetwood's quick eyes glimmered for an instant in Quarrier's direction. Quarrier was in the billiard-room, out of earshot, practising balk-line problems with Major Belwether; and Fleetwood said: "The same cat that tripped up Stephen Siward. Yes. But who let her loose?"

"It was your dinner; you ought to know," said Voucher bluntly.

"I do know. *He* brought her"—nodding toward the billiard-room.

"Belwether?"

"No," yawned Fleetwood.

Somebody said presently: "Isn't he one of the Governors? Oh, I say, that was rather rough on Siward though."

"Yes, rough. The law of trespass ought to have operated; a man's liable for the damage done by his own live-stock."

"That's a brutal way of talking," said somebody. And the subject was closed with the entrance of Agatha in white flannels on her way to the squash court where she had an appointment with Quarrier.

"A strange girl," said somebody after she had disappeared with Quarrier.

"That pallor is stunning," said a big, ruddy youth, with sunburn on his neck and forehead.

"It isn't healthy," said Fleetwood.

"It attracts *me*," persisted the ruddy young man, voicing naïvely that curious truth concerning the attraction that disease so often exerts on health—the strange curiosity the normal has for the sub-normal—that fascination of the wholesome for the unhealthy. It is, perhaps, more curiosity than anything, unless, deep hidden under the normal, there lie one single, perverted nerve.

Sylvia, passing the hall, glanced in through the gun-room door with an absentminded smile at the men and their laughing greeting, as they rose with uplifted glasses to salute her.

"*The* sweetest of all," observed a man, disconsolately emptying his glass. "Oh irony! What a marriage!"

"Do you know any girl who would not change places with her?" asked another.

Every man there insisted that he knew *one* girl at least who would not exchange Sylvia's future for her own. That was very nice of them; it is to be hoped they believed it. Some of them did—for the moment, anyhow. Then Alderdene, blinking furiously, emitted one of his ear-racking laughs; and everybody, as usual, laughed too.

"You damned cynic," observed Voucher affectionately.

"Somebody," said Fleetwood, "insists that she doubled up poor Siward."

"She never met Siward until she was engaged to Howard," remarked Voucher.

"Well?"

"Oh, don't you consider that enough to squelch the story?"

"Engaged girls," mused Alderdene, "never double up except at Bridge."

"Everybody has been or is in love with Sylvia Landis," said Voucher, "and it's a man's own fault if he's hit. Once she did it, innocently enough, and enjoyed it, never realising that it hurt a man to be doubled up."

Fleetwood yawned again and said: "She can have

me to-morrow. But she won't. She's tired of the sport. Any girl would get enough with the pack at her heels day in and day out. Besides she's done for—unless she looses Quarrier and starts on a duke-hunt over in Blinky's country! . . . Is anybody on for a sail? Is anybody on for anything? No? Oh, very well. Shove that decanter north by west, Billy."

This was characteristic of the dog-days at Shotover. The dog-days in town were very different; the city threw open the parks to the poor at night; horses fell dead in the streets; pallid urchins, stripped naked, splashed and rolled and screeched in the basin of the City Hall fountain under the indifferent eyes of the police.

As for Plank he was too busy to know what the thermometer was about; he had no time for anything outside of his own particular business except to go every day to the big, darkened house in lower Fifth Avenue where the days had been hard on Siward and the nights harder.

Siward, however, could walk now, using his crutches still, but often stopping to gently test his left foot and see how much weight he was able to bear on it—even taking a tentative step or two without crutch support. He drove when he thought it prudent to use the horses in the heat, usually very early in the morning, though sometimes at night with Plank when the latter had time to run his touring-car through the park and out into the Bronx or Westchester for a breath of air.

But Plank wanted him to go away, get out of the city for his convalescence, and Siward flatly declined, demanding that Plank permit him to do his share in the fight against the Inter-County people.

And Plank, utterly unable to persuade him, and the

more hampered because of his anxiety about Siward—though that young man did not know it—wore himself out providing Siward with such employment in the matter as would lightly occupy him without doing any good to the enemy.

So Siward, stripped to his pajamas, pored over reams of typewritten matter and took his brief walking exercise in the comparative cool of the evening and drove when he dared use his horses; or, sitting beside Plank, whizzed northward through the starry darkness of the suburbs.

When it was that he first began to like Plank very much he could not exactly remember. He was not, perhaps, aware of how much he liked him. Plank's unexpected fits of shyness, of formality, often and often amused him. But there was a subtler feeling under the unexpressed amusement, and, beneath all, a constantly increasing sub-stratum of respect. Too, he found himself curiously at ease with Plank, as with one born to his own caste. And this feeling, unconscious, but more and more apparent, meant more to Plank than anything that had ever happened to him. It was a tonic in hours of doubt, a pleasure in his brief leisure, a pride never to be hinted at, never to be guessed, never to be dreamed of by any living soul save Plank alone.

Then, one sultry day toward the last week in August, a certain judge of a certain court, known among some as "Harrington's judge," sent secretly for Plank. And Plank knew that the crisis was over. But neither Harrington nor Quarrier dreamed of such a thing.

Fear sat heavy on that judge's soul—the godless, selfish fear that sends the first coward slinking from the councils of conspiracy to seek immunity from those slowly grinding millstones that grind exceeding fine.

Quarrier at Shotover, with his private car and his locomotive within an hour's drive, strolled with Sylvia on the eve of her departure for Lenox with Leila Mortimer; then, when their conference was ended, he returned to Agatha, calmly unconscious of impending events.

Harrington, at Seabright, paced his veranda, awaiting this same judge, annoyed as two boats came in without the expected guest. And never for one instant did he dream that his creature sat closeted with Plank, tremulous, sallow, nearing the edge of cringing avowal—only held back from utter collapse by the agonising necessity of completing a bargain that might save himself from the degradation of the punishment that had seemed inevitable. All day long he sat with Plank. Nobody except those two knew he was there. And after a very long time Plank consented that nobody else except Siward and Harrington and Quarrier should ever know. So he called up Harrington on the telephone, saying that there was, in the office, somebody who desired to speak to him. And when Harrington caught the judge's first faint, stammered word he reeled where he stood, ashen, unbelieving, speechless. The shaking but remorseless voice went on, dinning horribly in his ear, then ceased, and Plank's heavy voice sounded the curt *coup de grâce*.

Harrington was an old man, a very old man, mortally hurt; but he steadied himself along the wall of his study to the desk and sank into the chair.

There he sat, feeling the scars of old wounds throbbing, feeling his age and the tragedy of it, and the new sensation of fear—fear of the wraith of his own youth, wearing the mask of Plank, and menacing him with the menace he had used on others so long ago—so very long ago.

After a little while he passed a thin hand over his eyes, over his gray head, over the mouth that all men watched with fear, over the shaven jaw now grimly set, but trembling. His hand, too, shook with palsy as he wrote, painfully picking out the words and figures of the cipher from his code-book; but he closed his thin lips and squared his unsteady jaw and wrote his message to Quarrier:

"It is all up. Plank will take over Inter-County. Come at once."

And that was all there was to be done until he could come into Plank's camp with arms and banners, a conquered man, cynical of the mercy he dared not expect and which, in all his life, he had never, never shown to man, to woman, or to child.

Plank slept the sleep of utter exhaustion that night; the morning found him haggard but strong, cool in his triumph, serious, stern faced, almost sad that his work was done, the battle won.

From his own house he telegraphed a curt summons to Harrington and to Quarrier for a conference in his own office; then, finishing whatever business his morning mail required, put on his hat and went to see the one man in the world he was most glad for.

He found him at breakfast, sipping coffee and wrinkling his brows over the eternal typewritten pages. And Plank's face cleared at the sight and he sat down, laughing aloud.

"It's all over, Siward," he said. "Harrington knows it; Quarrier knows it by this time. Their judge crawled in yesterday and threw himself on our mercy; and the men whose whip he obeyed will be on their way to surrender by this time. . . . Well! Haven't you a word?"

"Many," said Siward slowly; "too many to utter, but not enough to express what I feel. If you will take two on account, here they are in one phrase: thank you."

"Debt's cancelled," said Plank, laughing. "Do you want to hear the details?"

They talked for an hour, and, in the telling, even Plank's stolidity gave way sufficient to make his heavy voice ring at moments, and the glimmer of excitement edge his eyes. Yet, in the telling, he scarcely mentioned himself, never hinted of the personal part—the inspiration which was his alone; the brunt of the battle which centred in him; the tireless vigilance; the loneliness of the nights when he lay awake, perplexed with doubt and nobody to counsel him—because men who wage such wars are lonely men and must work out their own salvation. No, nobody but his peers could advise him; and he had thought that his enemy was his peer, until that enemy surrendered.

The narrative exchanged by Plank in return for Siward's intensely interested questions was a simple, limpid review of a short but terrific campaign that only yesterday had threatened to rage through court after court, year after year. In the sudden shock of the cessation from battle, Plank himself was a little dazed. Yet he himself had expected the treason that ended all; he himself had foreseen it. He had counted on it as a good general counts on such things, confidently, but with a dozen plans as substitutes in case that plan failed —each plan as elaborately worked out to the last detail as though it alone existed as the only hope of victory. But if Siward suspected something of this it was not from Plank that he learned it.

"Plank," he said at last, "there is nothing in the world that men admire more than a man. It is a good deal of a privilege for me to tell you so."

Plank turned red with surprise and embarrassment, stammering out something incoherent.

That was all that was said about the victory. Siward, unusually gay for awhile, presently turned sombre; and it was Plank's turn to lift him out of it by careless remarks about his rapid convalescence, and the chance for vacation he so much needed.

Once Siward looked up vacantly: "Where am I to go?" he asked. "I'd as soon stay here."

"But I'm going," insisted Plank. "The Fells is all ready for us."

"The Fells! I can't go *there*!"

"W-what?" faltered Plank, looking at Siward with hurt eyes.

"Can't you—don't you understand?" said Siward in a low voice.

"No. You once promised——"

"Plank, I'll go anywhere except there with you. I'd rather be with you than with anybody. Can I say more than that?"

"I think you ought to, Siward. A—a fellow feels the refusal of his offered roof-tree."

"Man! man! it isn't your roof I am refusing. I want to go; I'd give anything to go. If it were anywhere except where it is, I'd go fast enough. Now do you understand? If—if Shotover House and Shotover people were not next door to the Fells, I'd go. *Now* do you understand?"

Plank said: " I don't know whether I understand. If you mean Quarrier, he's on his way here, and he'll have business to keep him here for the next few months, I assure you. But "—he looked very gravely across at Siward—" if you don't mean Quarrier—" He hesitated, ill at ease under the expressionless scrutiny of the other.

" *Do* you know what's the matter with me, Plank? " he asked at length.

" I think so."

" I have wondered. I wonder now how much you know."

" Very little, Siward."

" *How* much? "

Plank looked up, hesitated, and shook his head: " One infers from what one hears."

" Infers what? "

" The truth, I suppose," replied Plank simply.

" And what," insisted Siward, " have you inferred that you believe to be the truth? Don't parry, Plank; it isn't easy for me, and I—I never before spoke this way to any man. . . . It is likely I should have spoken to my mother about it. . . . I had expected to. It may be weakness—I don't know; but I'd like to talk a little about it to somebody. And there's nobody fit to listen, except you."

" If you feel that way," said Plank slowly, " I will be very glad to listen."

" I feel that way. I've been through—some things; I've been pretty sick, Plank. It tires a man out; a man's head and shoulders get tired. Oh, I don't mean the usual reaction from self-contempt, disgust—the dreadful, aching sadness of it all which lasts even while desire, stunned for the moment, wakens into craving. I don't mean that. It is something else—a deathly, mental solitude that terrifies. I tell you, no man except a man smitten by my malady knows what solitude can be! . . . There! I didn't mean to be theatrical; I had no intention of——"

"Go on," cut in Plank heavily.

"Go on! . . . Yes, I want to. You know what a pillow is to a tired man's shoulders. I want to use your sane intelligence to rest on a moment. It's my brain that's tired, Plank."

Although everybody had cynically used Plank, nobody had ever before found him a necessity.

"Go on," he said unsteadily. "If I can be of use to you, Siward, in God's name let me be, for I have never been necessary to anybody in all my life."

Siward rested his head on one clinched hand: "How much chance do *you* think I have?" he asked wearily.

"Chance to get well?"

"Yes."

Plank considered for a moment, then: "You are not trying, Siward."

"I have been trying since—since March."

"Since March?"

"Yes."

Plank looked at him curiously: "What happened in March?"

"Had I better tell you?"

"You know better than I."

Siward, cheek crushed against his fist, his elbow on the desk, gazed at him steadily:

"In March," he said, "Miss Landis spoke to me. I've made a better fight since."

Plank's serious face darkened. "Is she the only anchor you have?"

"Plank, I am not even sure of her. I have made a better fight since then; that is all I dare say. . . . I know what men think about a man like me; I know they demand character, pride, self-denial. But, Plank, I am driving faster and faster toward the breakers, and these anchors are dragging. For it is not, in my case, the physical failure to obey the will; it is the will itself that has been attacked from the first. *That* is the horror of it. And what is there behind the will-power to strengthen it? Only the source of will-power—the mind. It is the mind that cannot help me. What am I to do?"

"There is a spiritual strength," said Plank timidly.

"I have never dreamed of denying it," said Siward. "I have tried to find it through the accepted sources—accepted by me, too. God has not helped me in the conventional way or through traditional methods; but that has not inclined me to doubt Him as the tribunal of last resort," he added hastily. "I don't for a moment waver in faith because I am ignorant of the proper manner to approach Him. The Arbiter of all knows that I desire to be decent. He must be aware, too, that all anchors save one have failed to hold me."

"You mean—Miss Landis?"

"Yes. It may be weakness; it may be to my shame that the cables of pride and self-respect, even the spiritual respect for the Highest, cannot hold me when this one anchor holds. All I know is that it holds—so far. It held me at Shotover; it holds me again, now. And the rocks were close abeam, Plank—very close—when she spoke to me over the wires, through the rain, that dark day in March."

He moistened his lips feverishly.

"She said that I might see her. I have waited a long time. I have taken my fighting chance again and I've won out, so far."

He looked up at Plank, curiously embarrassed:

"Your body is normal; your intelligence wholesome, balanced, sane; and I want to ask you if you think that perhaps, without understanding how, I have found in her, or through her, in some way, the spiritual source that I think might help me to help myself?"

And, as Plank made no reply:

"Or am I talking sentimental cant? Don't answer, if you think that. I can't trust my own mind any more, anyway; and," with an ugly laugh, "I'll know it all some day—the sooner the better!"

"Don't say that!" growled Plank. "You were sane a moment ago."

Siward looked up sharply, but the other silenced him with a gesture.

"Wait! You asked me a perfectly sane question—so wholesome, so normal, that I'm trying to frame an answer worthy of it! I intimated that after the physical, the mental, the ethical phenomena, there remained always the spiritual instinct. Like a wireless current, if a man can establish communication it is well for him, whatever the method. You assented, I think."

"Yes."

"And you ask me if I believe it possible that she can be the medium?"

"Yes."

Plank said deliberately: "Yes, I do think so."

The silence was again broken by Plank: "Siward, you have asked me what I think. Now you must listen to the end. If you believed that through her—her love, marrying her—you stood the best chance in the world to win out, it would be cowardly to ask her to take the risk. As much as I care for you I had rather see you lose the fight than accept such a risk from her. Now you know what I think—but you don't know all. Siward, I say to you that if you are man enough to take her, take her! And I say that of the two risks she is running to-day, the chance she might take with you is infinitely the lesser risk. For with you, if you continue slowly losing your fight, the mental suffering only will be hers. But if she closes this bargain with Quarrier, selling to him her body, the light will go out of her soul for ever."

He leaned heavily toward Siward, stretching out his powerful arm:

"You marry her; and keep open your spiritual communication through her, if that is the way it has been established, and hang on to your God that way until your body is dead! I tell you, Siward, to marry her. I don't care how you do it; I don't care how you get her. Take her! Yours, of the two, is the stronger character, or she would not be where she is. Does she want what you cannot give her? Cure that desire—it is more contemptible than the craving that shatters you! I say, let the one-eyed lead the blind. Miracles are worked out by mathematics—if you have faith enough."

He rose, striding the length of the room once or twice, turned, holding out his broad hand:

"Good-bye," he said. "Harrington is about due at my office; Quarrier will probably turn up to-night. I am not vindictive; I shall be just with them—as just as I know how, which is to be as merciful as I dare be. Good-bye, Siward. I—I believe you and she are going to get well."

When he had gone, Siward lay back in his chair,

very still, eyes closed. A faint colour had mounted to his face and remained there.

It was late in the afternoon when he went downstairs, using his crutches lightly. Gumble handed him a straw hat and opened the door, and Siward cautiously descended the stoop, stood for a few moments on the sidewalk, looking up at the blue sky, then wheeled and slowly made his way toward Washington Square. The avenue was deserted; his own house appeared to be the only remaining house still open in all that old-fashioned but respectable quarter.

He swung leisurely southward, a slim, well-built young fellow, strangely out of place on crutches. The poor always looked at him; beggars never importuned him, yet found him agreeable to watch. Children, who seldom look up into the air far enough to notice grown people, always became conscious of him when he passed; often smiled, sometimes spoke. As for stray curs and tramp cats, they were for ever making advances. As long as he could remember, there was scarcely a week in town but some homeless dog attached himself to Siward's heels, sometimes trotting several blocks, sometimes following him home—where the outcast was always cared for, washed, fed, and ultimately shipped out to the farm, where scores of these "fresh-air" dogs resided on his bounty and rolled in luxury on his lawns.

Cats, too, were prone to notice him, rising as he passed to hoist an interrogative tail and make tentative observations.

In Washington Square, these, and the ragged children, knew him best of all. The children came from Minetta Lane and the purlieus south and west of it; the cats from the Mews, which Siward always thought most appropriate.

And now, as he passed the marble arch and entered the square, glancing behind him he saw the inevitable cat trotting, and, at his left, a very dirty little girl pretending to trundle a hoop, but plainly enough keeping sociable pace with him.

"Hello!" said Siward. The cat stopped; the child tossed her clustering curls, gave him a rapid but fearless sidelong glance, laughed, and ran on in the wake of her hoop. When she caught it she sat down on a bench opposite the fountain and looked around at Siward.

"It's pretty warm, isn't it?" said Siward, coming up and seating himself on the same bench.

"Are you lame?" asked the child.

"Oh, a little."

"Is your leg broken?"

"Oh, no, not now."

"Is that your cat?"

Siward looked around; the cat was seated on the bench beside him. But he was accustomed to that sort of thing, and he caressed the creature with his gloved hand.

"Are you rich?" asked the child, shaking her blond curls from her eyes and staring up solemnly at him.

"Not very," he answered, smiling. "Why do you ask?"

"You look rich, somehow," said the child shyly.

"What! With these old and very faded clothes?"

She shook her head, swinging her plump legs: "You *look* it, somehow. It isn't the clothes that matter."

"I'll tell you one thing," said Siward, laughing: "I'm rich enough to buy all the hokey-pokey you can eat!" and he glanced meaningly at the pedlar of that staple who had taken station between a vender of peaches and a Greek flower-seller.

The child looked, too, but made no comment.

"How about it?" asked Siward.

"I'd rather have something to remember you by," said the girl innocently.

"What?" he said, perplexed.

"A rose. They are five cents, and hokey-pokey costs that much—I mean, for as much as you can eat."

"Do you really want a rose?" he said amused.

But the child fell shy, and he beckoned the Greek and selected a dozen big, perfumed jacks.

Then, as the child sat silent, her ragged arms piled with roses, he asked her jestingly what else she desired.

"Nothing. I like to look at you," she answered simply.

"And I like to look at you. Will you tell me your name?"

"Molly."

But that is all the information he could extract. Presently she said she was going, hesitated, looked a very earnest good-bye, and darted away across the park, her hoop over one arm, the crimson roses bobbing above her shoulders. Something in her flight attracted the errant cat, for she, too, jumped down and bounded after the little flying feet, but, catlike, halted half-way to scratch, and then forgetting what she was about, wandered off toward the Mews again, whence she had been lured by instinctive fascination.

Siward, intensely amused, sat there in the late sunlight which streamed through the park, casting long shadows from the elms and sycamores. It was that time of the day, just before sunset, when the old square looked to him as he remembered it as a child. Even the marble arch, pink in the evening sun, did not disturb the harmony of his memories. He saw his father once more, walking home from down town, tall, slim, laughingly stopping to watch him as he played there with the other children—the nurses, seated in a row, crocheting under the sycamores; he saw the old-fashioned carriage pass, Mockett on the box, Wands beside him, and his pretty mother leaning forward to wave her hand to him as the long-tailed, long-maned horses wheeled into Fifth Avenue. Little unimportant scenes, trivial episodes, grew in the spectral garden of memory: the first time he ever saw Marion Page, when, aged five, she was attempting to get into the fountain, pursued by a shrieking nurse; and a certain flight across the grass he had indulged in with Leila Mortimer, then Leila Egerton, aged six, in hot pursuit, because she found that it bored him horribly to be kissed, and she was bound to do it. He had a fight once, over by that gnarled, old, silver poplar-tree, with Kemp Ferrall—he could not remember what about, only that they ended by unanimously assaulting their nurses and were dragged howling homeward.

He turned, looking across to where the gray towers of the University once stood. There had been an old stone church there, too; and, south of that, old, old houses with hip-roofs and dormers where now the high white cliffs of modern architecture rose, riddled with tiny windows, every pane glittering in the sun. South, the old houses still remained, now degraded to sordid uses. North, the square, red-brick mansions, with their white pillars and steps, still faced the sunset—the last practically unbroken rank of the old régime, the last of the old guard, standing fast and still confronting, still resisting the Inevitable looming in limestone and granite, story piled on story, aloft in the kindling, southern sky.

A cab, driven smartly, passed through the park, the horses' feet slapping the asphalt till the echoes rattled back from the marble arch. He followed it idly with his eyes up Fifth Avenue; saw it suddenly halt in the middle of the street; saw a woman spring out, stand for a moment talking to her companion, then turn and look toward the square.

She stood so long, and she was so far away, that he presently grew tired of watching her. A dozen ragged urchins were prowling around the fountain, casting sidelong glances at a distant policeman. But it was not hot enough that evening to permit the children to splash in the water, and the policeman drove them off.

"Poor little devils!" said Siward to himself; and he rose, adjusted his crutches, and started through the park with a vague idea of seeing what could be done.

As he limped onward, the sun level in his eyes, he heard somebody speak behind him, but did not catch the words or apply the hail to himself. Then, "Mr. Siward!" came the low, breathless voice at his elbow.

His heart stopped as he did. The sun had dazzled his eyes, and when he turned on his crutches he could not see clearly for a second. That past, he looked at Sylvia, looked at her outstretched hand, took it mechanically, still staring at her with only a dazed unbelief in his eyes.

"I am in town for a day," she said. "Leila Mortimer and I were driving up town from the bank when we saw you; and the next thing that happened was me, on Fifth Avenue, running after you—no, the next thing was my flying leap from the hansom, and my standing there looking down the street and across the square where you sat. Then Leila told me I was probably crazy, and I immediately confirmed her diagnosis by running after you!"

She stood laughing, flushed, sunburned, and breathless, her left hand still in his, her right hand laid over it.

"Oh," she said, with a sudden change to anxiety, "does it tire you to stand?"

"No. I was going to saunter along."

"May I saunter with you for a moment? I mean—I only mean, I am glad to see you."

"Do you think I am going to let you go now?" he asked, astonished.

She looked at him, then her eyes evaded his: "Let us walk a little," she said, withdrawing her hand, "if you think you are strong enough."

"Strong! Look, Sylvia!" and he stood unsupported by his crutches, then walked a little way, slowly, but quite firmly. "I am rather a coward about my foot, that is all. I shall not lug these things about after to-day."

"Did the doctor say you might?"

"Yes, after to-day. I could walk home now without them. I could do a good many things I couldn't do a few minutes ago. Isn't that curious?"

"Very," she said, avoiding his eyes.

He laughed. She dared not look at him. The excitement and impetus of sheer impulse had carried her this far; now all the sadness of it was clutching hard at her throat and for awhile she could not speak—walking there in her dainty, summer gown beside him, the very incarnation of youth and health, with the sea-tan on wrist and throat, and *he*, white, hollow-eyed, crippled, limping, at her elbow!

Yet at that very moment his whole frame seemed to glow and his heart clamour with the courage in it, for he was thinking of Plank's words and he knew Plank had spoken the truth. She *could* not give herself to Quarrier, if he stood firm. His was the stronger will after all; his was the right to interfere, to stop her, to check her, to take her, draw her back—as he had once drawn her from the fascination of destruction when she had swayed out too far over the cliffs at Shotover.

"Do you remember that?" he asked, and spoke of the incident.

"Yes, I remember," she replied, smiling.

"Doctors say" he continued, "that there is a weak streak in people who are affected by great heights, or who find a dizzy fascination drawing them toward the brink of precipices."

"Do you mean me?" she asked, amused.

But he continued serenely: "You have seen those pigeons called 'tumbler pigeons' suddenly turn a cart-wheel in mid-air? Scientists say it's not for pleasure they do it; it's because they get dizzy. In other words, they are not perfectly normal."

She said, laughing: "Well, you never saw me turn a cart-wheel!"

"Only a moral one," he replied airily.

"Stephen, what on earth do you mean? You're not going to be disagreeable, are you?"

"I am going to be so agreeable," he said, laughing, "that you will find it very difficult to tear yourself away."

"I have no doubt of it, but I must, and very soon."

"I'm not going to let you."

"It can't be helped," she said, looking up at him. "I came in with Leila. We're asked to Lenox for the week's end. We go to Stockbridge on the early train to-morrow morning."

"I don't care," he said doggedly; "I'm not going to let you go yet."

"If I took to my heels here in the park would you chase me, Stephen?" she asked with mock anxiety.

"Yes; and if I couldn't run fast enough I'd call that policeman. Now do you begin to understand?"

"Oh, I've always understood that you were spoiled. I'm partly guilty of the spoiling process, too. Listen: I'll walk with you a little way"—she looked at him—"a little way," she continued gently; "then I must go. There is only a caretaker in our house and Leila will be furious if I leave her all alone. Besides, we're going to dine there and it won't be very gay if I don't give a few orders first."

"But you brought your maid?"

"Naturally."

"Then telephone her that you and Leila are dining out."

"Where, silly? Do you want us to dine somewhere with you?"

"Want you! You've got to!"

"Stephen, it isn't best."

"It *is* best."

She turned to him impulsively: "Oh, I *do* want to so much! Do you think I might? It is perfectly delicious to see you again. I—you have no idea——"

"Yes, I have," he said sternly.

They turned, walking past the fountain toward Fifth Avenue again. Furtively she glanced at his hands with the city pallor on them as they grasped the cross-bars of the crutches, then looked up at his worn face. He was much thinner, but now in the softly fading light the shadows under the eyes and cheek-bones seemed less sharp, his face fuller and more boyish; the contour of head and shoulders, the short, crisp hair were as she remembered—and the old charm held her, the old fascination grew, tightening her throat, stealing through every vein, stirring her pulses, awakening imperceptibly once more the best in her. The twilight of a thousand years seemed to slip from the world as she looked out at it through eyes opening from a long, long sleep; the marble arch burned rosy in the evening glow; a fairy haze hung over the enchanted avenue, stretching away, away into the blue magic of the city of dreams.

"There is no use," she said under her breath; "I can't go back to Leila. Stephen, the dreadful part of it is that I—I wish she were in Jericho! I wish the whole world were in Ballyhoo, and you and I alone once more!"

Under their gay laughter quivered the undertone of excitement. Sylvia said:

"I'd like to talk to you all alone. It won't do, of course; but I may say what I'd like—mayn't I? What time is it? If I'm dining with you we've got to have Leila for convention's sake, if not from motives of sheer decency, which you and I seem to lack, Stephen."

"We lack decency," said Siward, "and we're proud of it. As for Leila, I am going to arrange for her very simply but very beautifully. Plank will take care of her. Sylvia! There's not a soul in town and we can be as imprudent as we please."

"No, we can't. Agatha's at the Santa Regina. She came down with us."

"But we are not going to dine at the Santa Regina. We're going where Agatha wouldn't intrude her colourless nose—to a thoroughly unfashionable and selectly common resort overlooking the classic Harlem; and we're going to whiz thither in Plank's car, and remain thither until you yawn for mercy, whence we will return thence——"

"Stephen, you silly! I'm perfectly mad to go with you!"

"You'll be madder when you get there, if the table has not improved."

"Table! As though tables mattered on a night like this!" Then with sudden self-reproach and quick solicitude: "*Am* I making you walk too far? Wouldn't you like to go in now?"

"No, I'm not tired; I'm millions of years younger, and I'm as strong as the nine gods of your friend Porsena. Besides, haven't I waited for this?" and under his breath, fiercely, "Haven't I waited!" he repeated, turning on her.

"Do—do you mean that as a reproach?" she asked, lowering her eyes.

"No. I knew you would not come on 'the first sunny day.'"

"Why did you think I would not come? Did you know me for the coward I am?"

"I did not think you would come," he repeated, halting to rest on his crutches. He stood, balanced, staring dreamily into the dim perspective; and again her fascinated eyes ventured to rest on the worn, white face, listless, sombre in its fixedness.

The tears were very near her eyes; the spasm in her throat checked speech. At length she stammered: "I did not come b-because I simply couldn't stand it!"

His face cleared as he turned quietly: "Child, you must not confuse matters. You must not think of being sorry for me. The old order is passing—ticking away on every clock in the world. All that inverted order of things is being reversed. You don't know what I mean, do you? Ah, well; you will know when I grow into something of what you think you remember in me, and when I grow out of what I really was."

"Truly I don't understand, Stephen. But then—I am out of training since you went—went out of things. Have I changed? Do I seem more dull? I—it has not been very gay with me. I don't see—looking back across all the noise, all the chaos of the winter—I do not see how I stood it alone."

"Alone?"

"N-not seeing you—sometimes."

He looked at her with smiling, sceptical eyes. "Didn't you enjoy the winter?"

"Do you enjoy being drugged with champagne?"

His face altered so quickly that, confused, she only stared at him, the fixed smile stamped on her lips; then, overwhelmed in the revelation:

"Stephen, surely, *surely* you know what I meant! I did not mean *that*! Dear, do you dream for one moment that—that I could——"

"No. You have not hurt me. Besides, I know what you mean."

After a moment he swung forward on his crutches, biting his lip, the frown gathering between his temples.

They were passing the big, old-fashioned hotel with its white façade and green blinds, a lingering landmark of the older city.

"We'll telephone here," he said.

Side by side they went up the great, broad stoop and entered the lobby.

"If you'll speak to Leila, I'll get Plank on the wire. Say that we'll stop for you at seven."

She gave her number; then, at the nod of the operator, entered a small booth. Siward was given another booth in a few moments.

Plank answered from his office; his voice sounded grave and tired but it quickened, tinged with surprise, when Siward made known his plan for the evening.

"Is Mrs. Mortimer in town?" he demanded. "I had a wire from her that she expected to be here and I hoped to see her at the station to-morrow on her way to Lenox."

"She's stopping with Miss Landis. Can't you manage to come?" asked Siward anxiously.

"I don't know. Do you wish it particularly? I have just seen Quarrier and Harrington. I can't quite understand Quarrier's attitude. There's a certain hint of defiance about it. Harrington is all caved in. He is ready to thank us for any mercies. But Quarrier—there's something I don't fancy, don't exactly understand about his attitude. He's like a dangerous man whom you've searched for concealed weapons, and who knows you've overlooked the knife up his sleeve. That's why I've expected to spend a quiet evening, studying up the matter and examining every loophole."

"You've got to dine somewhere," said Siward. "If you could fix it to dine with us— But I won't urge you."

"All right. I don't know why I shouldn't. I don't know why I feel this way about things. I—I rather felt—you'll laugh, Siward!—that somehow I'd better not go out of my own house to-night; that I was safer, better off in my own house, studying this Quarrier matter out. I'm tired, I suppose; and this man Quarrier has come close to worrying me. But it's all right, of course, if you wish it. You know I haven't any nerves."

"If you are tired—" began Siward.

"No, no, I'm not. I'll go. Will you say that we'll stop for them at seven? Really, it's all right, Siward."

"I don't want to urge you," repeated Siward.

"You're not. I'll go. But—wait one moment!—tell me, did Quarrier know that Mrs. Mortimer was to stop with Miss Landis?"

"Wait a moment. Hold the wire."

He opened the door of the booth and saw Sylvia waiting for him, seated by the operator's desk. She rose at once when she saw he wished to speak with her.

"Tell me something," he said in a low voice; "did Mr. Quarrier know that Leila was to stay overnight with you?"

"Yes," she answered quietly, surprised. "Why?"

Siward nodded vaguely, closed the door again, and said to Plank:

"Yes, Quarrier knows it. Do you think he'll be there to-night? I don't suppose Miss Landis and Mrs. Mortimer know he is in town."

Plank's troubled voice came back over the wire: "I don't know. I don't know what to think. I suppose I'm a little, just a trifle, overworked. Somebody once said that I had one nerve in me somewhere, and Quarrier's probably found it; that's all."

"If you think it better not to come——"

"I'll come. I'll stop for you in the motor. Don't worry, old fellow! And—*take your fighting chance!* Good-bye!"

Siward, absorbed in his own thoughts, rose and walked slowly out of the booth, utterly unconscious that he had left his crutches leaning upright in the corner. It was only the surprise dawning into tremulous delight on Sylvia's face that at last arrested him.

"See what *you* have done!" he said, laughing

through his own surprise. "I've a mind to leave them there now, and trust to your new cure."

But she was instantly concerned and anxious, and entering the booth brought out the crutches and forced him to take them.

"No risks now!" she said decisively. "We have too much at stake this evening. Leila is coming. Isn't it perfectly delightful?"

"Perfectly," he said, his eyes full of the old laughing confidence again; "and the most delightful part of it all is that you don't know how delightful it is going to be."

"Don't I? Very well. Only I inform you that I mean to be perfectly happy! And that means that I'm going to do as I please! And *that* means—oh, it may mean anything! What are you laughing at, Stephen? I know I'm excited. I don't care! What girl wouldn't be? And I don't know what's ahead of me at all; and I don't want to know—I don't care!"

Her reckless, little laugh rang sweetly in the old-fashioned, deserted hall; her lovely, daring eyes met his undaunted.

"You won't make love to me, will you, Stephen?"

"Will you promise me the same?"

"I don't know, silly! How do I know what I might say to you, you big, blundering boy, who can't take care of himself? I don't know at all; I won't promise. I'm likely to do anything to-night—even before Leila and Mr. Plank—when you are with me. Shame on you for the shameless girl you've educated!" Her voice fell, tremulously, and for an instant standing there she remembered her education and his part in it.

The slow colour in his face reflected the pink confusion in hers.

"O tongue! tongue!" she stammered, "I *can't* hold you in! I can't curb you, and I can't make you say what you ought to be saying to that boy. There's trouble coming for somebody; there's trouble here already! Call me a cab, Stephen, or I'll be dragging you into that big, old-fashioned parlour and planting you on a chair and placing myself opposite, to moon over you until somebody puts us out! There! Now will you call me a hansom? . . . And I will be all ready at seven. . . . And don't dare to keep me waiting one second! . . . Come before seven. You don't want to frighten me, do you? Very well then, at a quarter to seven—so I shall not be frightened. And, Stephen, Stephen, we're doing exactly what we ought not to do. You know it, don't you? So do I. Nothing can stop us, can it? Good-bye!"

CHAPTER XIV

THE BARGAIN

If a man's grief does not awaken his dignity, then he has none. In that event, grief is not even respectable. And so it was with Leroy Mortimer when Lydia at last turned on him. If you caress an Angora too long and too persistently it runs away. And before it goes it scratches.

Under all the physical degeneration of mind and flesh there had still remained in Mortimer the capacity for animal affection; and that does not mean sensuality alone, but generosity and a sort of routine devotion as characteristic components of a character which had now disintegrated into the simplest and most primitive elements.

Lydia Vyse left Saratoga when the financial stringency began to make it unpleasant for her to remain. She told Mortimer without the slightest compunction that she was going.

He did not believe her and he gave her the new car — the big yellow-and-black Serin-Chanteur. She sold it the same day to a bookmaker—an old friend of hers; withdrew several jewels from limbo—gems which Mortimer had given her—and gathered together everything for which, if he turned ugly, she might not be criminally liable.

She had never liked him—she had long disliked him. Such women have an instinct for their own kind, and no matter how low in the scale a man of the other kind sinks he can never entirely supply the type of running mate that such women require, understand, and usually conceive a passion for.

Not liking him she had no hesitation in the matter; disliking him, whatever unpleasant had occurred during their companionship remained as an irritant to poison memory. She resented a thousand little incidents that he scarcely knew had ever existed, but which she treasured without wasting emotion until the sum total and the time coincided to retaliate. Not that she would have cared to harm him seriously; she was willing enough to disoblige him, however—decorate him, before she left him, with one extra scratch for the sake of auld lang syne. So she wrote a note to the governors of the Patroons Club, saying that both Quarrier and Mortimer were aware that the guilt of her escapade could not be attached to Siward; that she knew nothing of Siward, had accepted his wager without meaning to attempt to win it, had never again seen him, and had, on the impulse of the moment, made her entry in the wake of several men. She added that when Quarrier, as governor, had concurred in Siward's expulsion he knew perfectly well that Siward was not guilty, because she herself had so informed Quarrier. Since then she had also told Mortimer, but he had taken no steps to do justice to Siward, although he, Mortimer, was still a governor of the Patroons Club.

This being about all she could think of to make mischief for two men whose recent companionship had nourished and irritated her, she shipped her trunks by express, packed her jewel-case and valise, and met Desmond at the station.

Desmond had business in Europe; Lydia had as

much business there as anywhere; and, although she had been faithless to Mortimer for a comparatively short time, within that time Desmond already had sworn at her and struck her. So she was quite ready to follow Desmond anywhere in this world or the next. And that, too, had not made her the more considerate toward Mortimer.

When the latter returned from the races to find her gone the last riddled props to what passed for his manhood gave way and the rotten fabric came crashing into the mud.

He had loved her as far as he had been capable of imitating that passion on the transposed plane to which he had fallen; he was stupefied at first, then grew violent with the furniture, then hysterically profane, then pitiable in the abandoned degradation of his grief. And, suspecting Desmond, he started to find him. They put him out of Desmond's club-house when he became noisy; they refused him admittance to several similar resorts where his noise threatened to continue; his landlord lost no time in interviewing him upon the subject of damage to furniture from kicks and to the walls and carpets from the contents of smashed bottles.

Creditors with sharp noses scented the whirlwind afar off and hemmed him in with unsettled accounts, mostly hers. Somebody placed a lien on his horses; a deputy sheriff began to follow him about; all credit ceased as by magic, and men crossed the street to avoid meeting with an old companion in direst need.

Still, alternately stupefied by his own grief and maddened into the necessity for action, he packed a suit-case, crawled out of the rear door, toiled across country and found a farmer to drive him twenty miles over a sandy road to a local railroad crossing, where he managed to board a train for Albany.

At Albany, as he stood panting and sweating on the long, concrete platform which paralleled track No. 1, he saw a private car, switched from a Boston and Albany train, shunted to the rear of the Merchants' Express.

The private car was lettered in gold on the central panel, "Algonquin." He boarded the Pullman coupled to it forward, pushed through the vestibule, shoved aside the Japanese steward and darky cook, forcing his way straight into the private car. Quarrier, reading a magazine, looked up at him in astonishment. For a full moment neither spoke. Then Mortimer dropped his suit-case, sat down in an armchair opposite Quarrier, and leisurely mopped his reeking face and neck.

"Scotch and lithia!" he said hoarsely; the Japanese steward looked at Quarrier; then, at that gentleman's almost imperceptible nod, went away to execute the commission.

He executed a great many similar commissions during the trip to New York. When they arrived there at five o'clock, Quarrier offered Mortimer his hand, and held the trembling, puffy fingers as he leaned closer, saying with cold precision and emotionless emphasis something that appeared to require the full concentration of Mortimer's half-drugged faculties.

And when at length Mortimer drove away in a hansom, Quarrier's Japanese steward went with him—perhaps to carry his suit case—a courtesy that did credit to Quarrier's innate thoughtfulness and consideration for others. He was very considerate; he even called Agatha up on the telephone and talked with her for ten minutes. Then he telephoned to Plank's office, learned that Harrington was already there, telephoned the garage for a Mercedes which he always kept ready in town, and presently went bowling away to a conference on which the last few hours had put an entirely new aspect.

It had taken Plank only a few minutes to perceive that something had occurred to change a point of view which he had believed it impossible for Quarrier to change. Something had gone wrong in his own careful calculations; some cog had slipped, some rivet given way, some bed-plate cracked. And Harrington evidently had not been aware of it; but Quarrier knew it. There was *something* wrong.

It was too late now to go tinkering in the dark for trouble. Plank understood that. Coolly, as though utterly unaware that the machinery might not stand the strain, he started it full speed. And when he stopped it at last Harrington's grist had been ground to atoms, and Quarrier had looked on without comment. There seemed to be little more for them to do except to pay the miller.

"To-morrow," said Quarrier, rising to go. It was on the edge of Plank's lips to say, "to-day!"—but he was silent, knowing that Harrington would speak for him. And the old man did, without words, turning his iron visage on Quarrier with the silent dignity of despair. But Quarrier coldly demanded a day before they reckoned with Plank. And Plank, profoundly disturbed, shrugged his massive shoulders in contemptuous assent.

So Quarrier and Harrington went away—the younger partner taking leave of the older with a sneer for an outworn prop which no man could ever again have use for. Old and beaten—that was all Harrington now stood for in Quarrier's eyes. Never a thought of the past undaunted courage, never a memory of the old victories which had made the Quarrier fortune possible—only contempt for age, a sneer for the mind and body that had failed at last. The old robber was done for, his armour rotten, his buckler broken, his sword blade rusted to the core. The least of his victims might now finish him with a club where he swayed in his loosened saddle, or leave him to that horseman on the pale horse watching him yonder on the horizon.

For now, whether Harrington lived or died, he must be counted as nothing in this new struggle darkly outlining its initial strategy in Quarrier's brain. What was coming was coming between himself and Plank alone; and whatever the result—whether an armed truce leaving affairs indefinitely in statu quo, or the other alternative, an alliance with Plank, leaving Harrington like a king in his mail, propped upon his throne, dead eyes doubly darkened under the closed helmet—the result must be attained swiftly, with secrecy, and with the aid of no man. For he did not count Mortimer a man.

So Quarrier's thin lips twitched and the glimmer of teeth showed under the silky beard as he listened without comment to the old man's hesitating words—a tremulous suggestion for a conference that evening—and he said again, "to-morrow," and left him there alone, groping with uncertain hands toward the door of the hired coupé which had brought him to the place of his earthly downfall; the place where he had met his own weird face to face—the wraith that bore the mask of Plank.

Quarrier, brooding sullenly in his Mercedes, was already far up town on his way to Major Belwether's house.

At the door, Sylvia's maid received him smilingly, saying that her mistress was not at home but that Mrs. Mortimer was—which saved Quarrier the necessity of asking for the private conference with Leila which was exactly what he had come for. But her first unguarded words on receiving him as he rose at her entrance into the darkened drawing-room changed that plan, too—changed it all so utterly, and so much for the better, that he almost smiled to think of the crudity of human combinations and inventions as compared to the masterly machinations of Fate. No need for him to complicate matters when here were pawns enough to play the game for him. No need for him to do anything except give them their initial velocity and let them tumble into one another and totter or fall. Leila said, laughingly: "Oh, you are too late, Howard. We are dining with Mr. Plank at Riverside Inn. What in the world are you doing in town so suddenly?"

"A business telegram. I might have come down with you and Sylvia if I had known. . . . Is Plank dining with you alone?"

"I haven't seen him," smiled Leila evasively. "He will tell us his plans of course when he comes."

"Oh," said Quarrier, dropping his eyes and glancing furtively toward the curtained windows through which he could see the street and his Mercedes waiting at the curb. At the same instant a hansom drove up; Sylvia sprang out, ran lightly up the low steps, and the silent, shrouded house rang with the clamour of the bell.

Leila looked curiously at Quarrier, who sat motionless, head partly averted, as though listening to something heard by him alone. He believed perhaps that he was listening to the voice of Fate again, and it may have been so, for already, for the third time, all his plans were changing to suit this new ally of his—this miraculous Fate which was shaping matters for him as he waited. Sylvia had started up-stairs like a fragrant whirlwind, but her flying feet halted at Leila's constrained voice from the drawing-room, and she spun around and came into the darkened room like an April breeze.

"Leila! They'll be here at a quarter to seven——"

Her breath seemed to leave her body as a shadowy figure rose in the uncertain light and confronted her.

"*You!*"

He said: "Didn't you recognise the Mercedes outside?"

She had not even seen it, so excited, so deeply engaged had she been with the riotous tumult of her own thoughts. And still her hurt, unbelieving gaze widened to dismay as she stood there halted on the threshold; and still his eyes, narrowing, held her under their expressionless inspection.

"When did you come? Why?" she asked in an altered voice.

"I came on business. Naturally, being here, I came to see you. I understand you are dining out?"

"Yes, we are dining out."

"I'm sorry I didn't wire you because we might have dined together. I saw Plank this afternoon. He did not say you were to dine with him. Shall I see you later in the evening, Sylvia?"

"I—it will be too late——"

"Oh! To-morrow then. What train do you take?"

Sylvia did not answer; he picked up his hat, repeating the question carelessly, and still she made no reply.

"Shall I see you to-morrow?" he asked, swinging on her rather suddenly.

"I think—not. I—there will be no time——"

He bowed quietly to Leila, offering his hand. "Who did you say was to dine with you—besides Plank?"

Leila stood silent, then, withdrawing her fingers, walked to the window.

Quarrier, his hat in his gloved hands, looked from one to the other, his inquiring eyes returning and focused on Sylvia.

"Who are you dining with?" he asked with authority.

"Mr. Plank and Mr. Siward."

"Mr. Siward!" he repeated in surprised displeasure, as though he had not already divined it.

"Yes. A man I like."

"A man I dislike," he rejoined with the slightest emphasis.

"I am sorry," she said simply.

"So am I, Sylvia. And I am going to ask you to make him an excuse. Any excuse will do."

"Excuse? What do you mean, Howard?"

"I mean that I do not care to have you seen with Mr. Siward. Have I ever demanded very much of you, Sylvia? Very well; I demand this of you now."

And still she stood there, her eyes wide, her colour gone, repeating: "Excuse? What excuse? What do you mean by 'excuse,' Howard?"

"I have told you. You know my wishes. If he has a telephone you can communicate with him——"

"And say that I—that you forbid me——"

"If you choose. Yes; say that I object to him. Is there anything extraordinary in a man objecting to his future wife dining in the country at a common inn with a notorious outcast from every decent club and circle in New York?"

"What!" she whispered, white as death. "What did you say?"

"Shall I repeat what everybody except you seems to be aware of? Do you care to have me explain to you exactly why decent people have ostracised this man with whom you are proposing to figure in a public resort?"

He turned to Leila, who stood at the window, her back turned toward them: "Mrs. Mortimer, when Mr. Plank arrives, you will be kind enough to explain why Sylvia is unable to accompany you."

If Leila heard she neither turned nor made sign of comprehension.

"We will dine at the Santa Regina," he said to Sylvia. "Agatha is there and I'll find somebody at the club to——"

"Why bother to find anybody?" said Leila, wheeling on him, exasperated. "Why not dine there with Agatha alone? It will not be the first time I fancy!"

"What do you mean?" he said fiercely, under his breath. The colour had left his face, too, and in his eyes Leila saw for the first time an expression that she had never before surprised in any eyes except her husband's. It was the expression of fright; she recognised it. But Sylvia stared, unenlightened, at an altered visage she scarcely knew for Quarrier's.

"What do I mean?" repeated Leila; "I mean what I say; and if you don't understand it you can find the key to it, I fancy. Nor shall I answer to you for my guests. I invite whom I choose. Mr. Siward is one, Mr. Plank is another. Sylvia, if *you* care to come I shall be delighted."

"I do care to come," said Sylvia. Her heart was beating violently, her eyes were on Quarrier.

"If you go," said Quarrier, showing the glimmering edge of teeth under his beard, "you will answer to me for it."

"I will answer you now, Howard; I am going with Mrs. Mortimer. What have you to say?"

"I'll say it to-morrow," he replied, contemplating her in a dull, impassive manner as though absorbed in other things.

"Say what there is to be said now!" she insisted, the hot colour staining her cheeks again. "Do you desire me to free you? Is that all? I will if you wish."

"No. And I shall not free you, Sylvia. This—all this can be adjusted in time."

"As you please," she said slowly.

"In time," he repeated, his passionless voice now under perfect control. He turned and looked at Leila; all the wickedness of his anger was concentrated in his gaze. Then he took his leave of them as formally, as precisely as though he had forgotten the whole scene; and a minute later the big Mercedes ran out into a half-circle, backed, wheeled, and rolled away through the thickening dusk, the glare of the acetylenes sweeping the deserted street.

Into the twilight sped Quarrier, head bent, but his soft, dark-lashed eyes of a woman fixed steadily ahead. Every energy, every thought was now bent to this newest phase of the same question which he and Fate were finding simpler to solve every minute. Of all the luxuries he permitted himself openly or furtively, one—the rarest of them all—his self-denial had practically eliminated from the list: the luxury of punishing where no end was served save that of mere personal satisfaction. The temptation of this luxury now presented itself; and the means of gratification were so simple, so secret, so easy to command, that the temptation became almost a duty.

Siward he had not turned out of his way to injure; Siward had been in the way, that was all, and his ruin was to have been merely an agreeable coincidence with the purposed ruin of Amalgamated Electric before Inter-County absorbed the fragments. But here was a new phase; Mrs. Mortimer, whom he had expected to use, and if necessary sacrifice, had suddenly turned vicious. And he now hated her as coldly as he hated Major Belwether for betraying suspicions of a similar nature. As for Plank, fear and hatred of him was becoming hatred and contempt. He had the means of checking Plank if Mortimer did not drop dead before midnight. There remained Sylvia, whom he had selected as the fittest object attainable to transmit his name. Long ago, whatever of liking, of affection, of passion he had ever entertained for her had quieted to indifference and the unemotional contemplation of a future methodically arranged for. Now of a sudden, this young girl he had bought—he knowing what she sold and what he was paying for—had become exposed to the infection of a suspicion concerning himself and another woman; a woman unmarried, and of his own caste, and numbered among her own friends.

And he knew enough of Sylvia to know that if anybody could once arouse her suspicion nothing on earth could induce her to look into his face again. Suppose Leila should do so this evening?

Certainly Quarrier had several matters to ponder over and provide for; and first and foremost of all to provide for his own security and the vital necessity of preserving his name and his character untainted. In this he had to deal with that miserable judge who had betrayed him; with Mortimer, who had once blackmailed him and who now was temporarily in his service; with Mrs. Mortimer, who—God knew how, when, or where—had become suspicious of Agatha and himself; with Major Belwether, who had deserted him before he could sacrifice the major, and whom he now hated and feared for having stumbled over suspicions similar to Mrs. Mortimer's. He had to deal with Sylvia herself, and with Siward—reckon with Siward's knowledge of matters which it were best that Sylvia should not know.

But first of all, and most important of all, he had to deal with Beverly Plank. And he was going to do it in a manner that Plank could not have foreseen; he was going to stop Plank where he stood, and to do this he was deliberately using his knowledge of the man and paying Plank the compliment of counting on his sense of honour to defeat him.

For he had suddenly found the opportunity to defend himself; he had discovered the joint in Plank's old-fashioned armour—the armour of the old paladins—who placed a woman's honour before all else in the world. Now, through his creature, Mortimer, he could menace Plank with a threat to involve him and Leila in a vile publicity; now he was in a position to demand a hearing and a compromise through his new ambassador, Mortimer, knowing that he could at last halt Plank by threatening Leila with this shameful danger. Plank must sign the truce or face with Leila an action for damages and divorce.

First of all he went to the Lenox Club and dressed. Then he dined sparingly and alone. The Mercedes was waiting when he came out ready to run down to the great Hotel Corona, whither the Japanese steward had conducted Mortimer. Mortimer had dined heavily, but his disorganised physical condition was such that it had scarcely affected him at all.

Again Quarrier went over patiently and carefully the very simple part he had reserved for Mortimer that evening, explaining exactly what to say to Leila and what to say to Plank in case of insolent interruption. Then he told Mortimer to be ready at nine o'clock, turned on his heel with a curt word to the Japanese, descended to the street, entered his motor-car again, and sped away to the Hotel Santa Regina.

Miss Caithness was at home, came the message in exchange for his cards for Agatha and Mrs. Vendenning. He entered the gilded elevator, stepped out on the sixth floor into a tiny, rococo, public reception-room. Nobody was there besides himself; Agatha's maid came presently, and he turned and followed her into the large and very handsome parlour belonging to the suite which Agatha was occupying with Mrs. Vendenning for the few days that they were to stop in town.

"Hello," she said serenely, sauntering in, her long, pale hands bracketed on her narrow hips, her lips disclosing her teeth in a smile so like that nervous muscular recession which passed for a smile on Quarrier's visage that for one moment he recognised it and thought she was mocking him. But she strolled up to him, meeting his eye calmly, and lifted her slim neck, lips passive under his impetuous kiss.

"Is Mrs. Vendenning out?" he asked, laying his hands on the bare shoulders of the tall, pallid girl—tall as he, and as pallid.

"No, Mrs. Ven. is *in*, Howard."

"Now? You mean she is coming in to interrupt——"

"Oh no; she isn't fond of you, Howard."

"You said—" he began almost angrily, but she laid her fingers across his lips.

"I said a very foolish thing, Howard. I said that I'd manage to dispense with Mrs. Ven. this evening."

"You mean that you couldn't manage it?"

"Not at all; I could easily have managed it. But—I didn't care to."

She looked at him calmly at close range as he held her embraced, lifted her arms and, with slender, white fingers patted her hair into place where his arm around her head had disarranged it, watching him all the while out of her pale, haunted eyes.

"You promised me," he said, "that you——"

"Oh Howard! Do men still believe in promises?"

Quarrier's face had colour enough now; his voice, too, had lost its passionless, monotonous precision. Whatever was in the man of emotion was astir; his impatient voice, his lack of poise, the almost human lack of caution in his speech betrayed him in a new and interesting light.

"Look here, Agatha, how long is this going to last? Are you trying to make a fool of me? What is the matter? Is there anything wrong?"

"Wrong? Oh dear no! How could there be anything wrong between you and me——"

"Agatha, what is the matter! Look here; let's settle this thing now and settle it one way or the other! I won't stand it; I—I can't!"

"Very well," she said, releasing herself from his tightening arms and stepping back with another glance at the mirror and another light touch of her finger-tips on her burnished hair. "Very well," she repeated, gazing again into the mirror; "what am I to understand, Howard?"

"You know what to understand," he said in a low voice; "you know what we both understood when—when——"

"When what?"

"When I—when you——"

"Oh what, Howard?" she prompted indolently; and he answered in brutal exasperation, and for the first time so plainly that a hint of rose tinted her strange, pale beauty and between her lips the breath came less regularly as she stood there looking at the dull, silvery rug under her feet.

"Did you ever misunderstand me?" he demanded hotly. "Did I give you any chance to? Were you ignorant of what *that* meant," with a gesture toward the splendid crescent of flashing gems, scintillating where the low, lace bodice met the silky lustre of her skin. "Did you misinterpret the collar? Or the sudden change of fortune in your own family's concerns? Answer me, Agatha, once for all. But you need not answer after all: *I* know you have never misunderstood me!"

"I misunderstood nothing," she said; "you are quite right."

"Then what are you going to do?"

"Do?" she asked in slow surprise. "What am I to do, Howard?"

"You have said that you loved me."

"I said the truth, I think."

"Then——"

"Well?"

"How long are you going to keep me at arm's length?" he asked violently.

"That lies with you," she said, smiling. She looked at him for a moment, then, resting her hands on her hips, she began to pace the floor, to and fro, to and fro, and at every turn she raised her head to look at him. All the strange grace of her became insolent provocation—her pale eyes, clear, limpid, harbouring no delusions, haunted with the mockery of wisdom, challenged and checked him. "Howard," she said, "why should I be the fool you want me to be because I love you? Why should I be even if I wished to be? You desire an understanding? *Voilà!* You have it. I love you; I never misunderstood you from the first; I could not afford to. You know what I am; you know what you arouse in me?"

Slim, pale, depraved in all but body she stood, eyeing him a moment, the very incarnation of vicious perversity.

"You know what you arouse in me," she repeated. "But don't count on it!"

"You have encouraged—permitted me to count—" His anger choked him—or was it the haunting wisdom of her eyes that committed him to silence.

"I don't know," she said, musingly, "what it is in you that I am so mad about—whether it is your brutality, or the utter corruption of you that holds me, or your wicked eyes of a woman, or the fascination of the mask you turn on the world, and the secret visage, naked in its vice, that you reserve for me. But I love you—in my own fashion. Count on that, Howard; for that is all you can surely count on. And now, at last, you know."

As he stood there, it came to him slowly that, deep within him he had always known this; that he had never really counted on anything else though he had throttled his doubts by covering her throat with diamonds. Her strangeness, her pallor, her acquiescence, the delicate hint of depravity in her, the subtle response to all that was worst in him had attracted him, only to learn, little by little, that the taint of corruption was only a taint infecting others, not her; that the promise of evil was only a promise; that he had to deal with a young body but an old intelligence, and a mind so old that at moments her faded gaze almost appalled him with its indolent clairvoyance.

Long since he knew, too, that in all the world he could never again find such a mate for him. This had, unadmitted even to himself, always remained a hidden secret within this secret man—an unacknowledged, undrawn-on reserve in case of the failure which he, even in sanguine moods, knew in his inmost corrupted soul that his quest was doomed to.

And now he had no more need of secrets from himself; now, turning his gaze inward, he looked upon all with which he had chosen to deceive himself. And there was nothing left for self-deception.

"If I marry you!" he said calmly, "at least I know what I am getting."

"I will marry you, Howard. I've got to marry somebody pretty soon. You or Captain Voucher."

For an instant a vicious light flashed in his narrowing eyes. She saw it and shook her head with weary cynicism:

"No, not that. It could not attract me even with you. It is really vulgar—*that* arrangement. Noblesse oblige, mon ami. There is a depravity in marrying you that makes all lesser vices stale as virtues."

He said nothing; she looked at him, lazily amused; then, inattentive, turned and paced the floor again.

"Shall I see you to-morrow?" he demanded.

"If you wish. Captain Voucher came down on the same train with me. I'll set him adrift if you like."

"Is he preparing for a declaration?" sneered Quarrier.

"I think so," she said simply.

"Well if he comes to-night after I'm gone, you wait a final word from me. Do you understand?" he repeated with repressed violence.

"No, Howard. Are you going to propose to me to-morrow?"

"You'll know to-morrow," he retorted angrily. "I tell you to wait. I've a right to that much consideration anyway."

"Very well, Howard," she said, recognising in him the cowardice which she had always suspected to be there.

She bade him good night; he touched her hand but made no offer to kiss her. She laughed a little to herself, watching him striding toward the elevator, then, closing the door, she stood still in the centre of the room, staring at her own reflection, full length, in the gilded pier-glass, her lips edged with a sneer so like Quarrier's that, the next moment she laughed aloud, imitating Quarrier's rare laugh from sheer perversity.

"I think," she said to her reflected figure in the glass, "I think that you are either mentally ill or inherently a kind of devil. And I don't much care which."

And she turned leisurely, her slim hands balanced lightly on her narrow hips, and strolled into the second dressing-room, where Mrs. Vendenning sat sullenly indulging in that particular species of solitaire known as "The Idiot's Delight."

"Well?" inquired Mrs. Vendenning, looking up at

the tall, pale girl she was chaperoning so carefully during their sojourn in town.

"Oh, you know the rhyme to that," yawned Agatha; "let's ring up somebody. I'm bored stiff."

"What did Howard Quarrier want?"

"He knows, I think, but he hasn't yet informed me."

"I'll tell you one thing, Agatha," said Mrs. Vendenning, gathering up the packs for a new shuffle: "Grace Ferrall doesn't fancy Howard's attention to you and she's beginning to say so. When you go back to Shotover you'd better let him alone."

"I'm not going back to Shotover," said Agatha.

"What?"

"No; I don't think so. However, I'll let you know to-morrow. It all depends—but I don't expect to." She turned as her maid tapped on the door. "Oh, Captain Voucher. Are you at home to him?" flipping the pasteboard onto the table among the scattered cards.

"Yes," said Mrs. Vendenning aggressively, "unless you expect him to flop down on his knees to-night. Do you?"

"I don't—to-night. Perhaps to-morrow. I don't know; I can't tell yet." And to her maid she nodded that they were at home to Captain Voucher.

Quarrier had met him, too, just as he was leaving the hotel lobby. They exchanged the careful salutations of men who had no use for one another. On the Englishman's clean-cut face a deeper hue settled as he passed; on Quarrier's, not a trace of emotion; but when he entered his motor he sat bolt upright, stiff-backed and stiff-necked, his long gray-gloved fingers moving restlessly over his pointed beard.

The night was magnificent; myriads of summer stars

spangled the heavens. Even in the reeking city itself a slight freshness grew in the air, although there was no wind to stir the parched leaves of the park trees, among which fire-flies floated—their intermittent phosphorescence breaking out with a silvery, star-like brilliancy.

Plank, driving his big motor northward through the night, Leila Mortimer beside him, twice mistook the low glimmer of a fire-fly for the distant lamp of a motor, which amused Leila, and her clear, young laughter floated back to the ears of Sylvia and Siward, curled up in their corners of the huge tonneau. But they were too profoundly occupied with each other to heed the sudden care-free laughter of the young matron, though in these days her laughter was infrequent enough to set the more merciless tongues wagging when it did sound.

Plank had never seen fit to speak to her of her husband's scarcely veiled menace that day he had encountered him in the rotunda of the Algonquin Trust Company. His first thought was to do so—to talk it over with her, consider the threat and the possibility of its seriousness, and then come to some logical and definite decision as to what their future relations should be. Again and again he had been on the point of doing this when alone with Leila—uncomfortable, even apprehensive, because of their frank intimacy; but he had never had the opportunity to do so without deliberately dragging in the subject by the ears in all its ugliness and implied reproach for her imprudence, and seeing that dreadful, vacant change in Leila's face, which the mere mention of her husband's name was sure to bring, turn into horror unspeakable.

A man not prone to fear his fellows, he now feared Mortimer, but that fear struck him only through Leila—

or had so reached him until the days of his closing struggle with Quarrier. Whether the long strain had unnerved him, whether minutely providing against every possible danger he had been over-scrupulous, over-anxious, morbidly exact—or whether a foresight almost abnormal had evoked a sinister possibility—he did not know; but that threat of Mortimer's to involve Plank with Leila in one common ruin, that boast that he was able to do so could not be ignored as a possible weapon if Quarrier should by any chance learn of it.

In all his life he had taken Leila into his arms but once; had kissed her but once—but that once had been enough to arm Mortimer with danger from head to foot. Some prying servant had either listened or seen—perhaps a glimmer of a mirror had betrayed them. At all events, whoever had seen or heard had informed Mortimer, and now the man was equipped; the one and only man in all the world who could with truth accuse Plank; the only man of whom he stood in honest fear.

And it was characteristic of Plank that never for one moment had it occurred to him that the sheer fault of it all lay with Leila; that it was her imprudence alone that now threatened herself and the man she loved—that threatened his very success in life as long as Mortimer should live.

All this, Plank, in his thorough, painstaking review of the subject, had taken into account; and he could not see how it could possibly bear upon the matters now finally to be adjusted between Quarrier and himself, because Quarrier was in New York and Mortimer in Saratoga, and unless the latter had already sold his information the former could not strike at him through knowledge of it.

And yet a curious reluctancy, a hesitation inexplicable—unless overwork explained it—had come over him when Siward had proposed their dining together on the very eve of his completed victory over Quarrier.

It seemed absurd, and Plank was too stolid to entertain superstitions, but he could not, even with Leila laughing there beside him, shake off the dull instinct that all was not well—that Quarrier's attitude was still the attitude of a dangerous man; that he, Plank, should have had this evening in his room alone to study out the matters he had so patiently plodded through in the long hours while Siward slept.

Yet not for one instant did he dream of shifting the responsibility — if responsibility entailed blame — on Siward, who, against Plank's judgment and desire, had on the very eve of consummation drawn him away from that sleepless vigilance which must for ever be the price of a business man's safety.

Leila, gay and excited as a schoolgirl, chattered on ceaselessly to Plank; all the silence, all the secrecy of the arid years turning to laughter on her red lips, pouring out, in broken phrases of delight, words strung together for the sheer pleasure of speech and the happiness of her lot to be with him unrestrained.

He remembered once listening to the song of a wild bird on the edge of a clearing at night, and how, standing entranced, the low, distant jar of thunder sounded at moments, scarcely audible—like his heart now, at intervals, dully persistent amid the gaiety of her voice.

"And would you believe it, Beverly," she said, "I formed the habit at Shotover of walking across the boundary and strolling into your greenhouses and deliberately helping myself. And every time I did it I was certain one of your men would march me out!"

He laughed, but did not tell her that his men had

reported the first episode and that he had instructed them that Mrs. Mortimer and her friends were to do exactly as they pleased at the Fells. However she knew it, because a garrulous gardener, proud of his service with Plank, had informed her.

"Beverly," she said, "you are a dear. If people only knew what I know!"

He began to turn red; she could see it even in the flickering, lamp-shot darkness. And she teased him for a while, very gently, even tenderly; and their voices grew lower in a half-serious badinage that ended with a quiet, indrawn breath, a sigh, and silence.

And now the river swept into view, a darkly luminous sheet set with reflected stars. Mirrored lights gleamed in it; sudden bright, yellow flashes zigzagged into its sombre depths; the foliage edged it with a deeper gloom over which, on the heights, twinkled the multicoloured lights of Riverside Inn.

Up the broad, gentle grade they sped, curving in and out among the clumps of trees and shrubbery, then on a level, sweeping in a great circle up to the steps of the inn.

Now all about them from the brilliantly lighted verandas the gay tumult broke out like an uproarious welcome after the swift silence of their journey; the stir of jolly people keen for pleasure; the clatter of crockery; the coming and going of waiters, of guests, of hansoms, coupés, victorias, and scores of motor-cars wheeling and turning through the blinding glare of their own headlights.

Somewhere a gipsy orchestra, full of fitful crescendoes and throbbing suspensions of caprice, furnished resonant accompaniment to the joyous clamour; the scent of fountain spray and flowers was in the air.

"I didn't know you had telephoned for a table," said Siward, as a head-waiter came up smiling and bowing to Plank. "I confess, in the new excitement of things, I clean forgot it! What a man you are to think of other people!"

Plank reddened again, muttering something evasive, and went forward with Leila.

Sylvia, moving leisurely beside Siward who was walking slowly but confidently without crutches, whispered to him: "I never really liked Mr. Plank before I understood his attitude toward you."

"He is a man, every inch," said Siward simply.

"I think that generally includes what men of your sort demand, doesn't it?" she asked.

"Men of my sort sometimes demand in others what they themselves are lacking in," said Siward, laughing. "Sylvia, look at this jolly crowd! Look at all those tables! It seems an age since I have done anything of this sort. I feel like a boy of eighteen—the same funny, quickening fascination in me toward everything gay and bright and alive!" He looked around at her, laughingly. "As for you," he said, "you look about sixteen. You certainly are the most beautiful thing this beautiful world ever saw!"

"Schoolboy courtship!" she mocked him, lingering as he made his slow way through the crowded place. The tint of excitement was in her eyes and cheeks; the echo of it in her low, happy voice. "Where on earth is Mr. Plank? Oh, I see them! They have a table by the balcony rail, in the corner; and it seems to be rather secluded, Stephen, so I shall, of course, expect you to say nothing further about beauty of any species. . . . Are you a trifle tired? No? . . . Well, you need not be indignant. *I* don't care whether you tumble. Indeed,

I don't believe there is really anything the matter with you—you are walking with the same old careless saunter. Mr. Plank," as they arrived and seated themselves, " Mr. Siward has just admitted that he uses crutches only because they are ornamental. Leila, isn't this air delicious? All sorts of people, too, aren't there, Mr. Plank? Such curious-looking women, some of them—quite pretty, too, in a certain way. Are you hungry, St—Mr. Siward? "

"*Are* you, St—Mr. Siward? " mimicked Leila promptly.

" I am," said Siward, laughing at Sylvia's significant colour and noting Plank's direct gaze as the waiter filled Leila's slender-stemmed glass. And " nothing but Apollinaris," he said coolly, as the waiter approached him; but though his voice was easy enough, a dull patch of colour came out under the cheek-bones.

" That is all I care for, either," said Sylvia with elaborate carelessness.

Plank and Leila immediately began to make conversation. Siward, his eyes bent on the glass of mineral water at his elbow, looked up in silence at Sylvia questioningly.

There was something in her face he did not quite comprehend. She made as though to speak, looked at him, hesitated, her lovely face eloquent under the impulse. Then, leaning toward him, she said:

" ' And thy ways shall be my ways.' "

" Sylvia, you must not deny yourself, just because I——"

" Let me. It is the happiest thing I have ever done for myself."

" But I don't wish it."

" Ah, but I do," she said, the low excited laughter

scarcely fluttering her lips. "Listen: I never before, in all my life, gave up anything for your sake, only this one little pitiful thing."

"I won't let you!" he breathed; "it is nonsense to——"

"You must let me! Am I to be on friendly terms with—with your mortal enemy?" She was still smiling, but now her sensitive mouth quivered suddenly.

He sat silent, considering her, his restless fingers playing with his glass in which the harmless bubbles were breaking.

"I drink to your health, Stephen," she said under her breath. "I drink to your happiness, too; and—and to your fortune, and to all that you desire from fortune." And she raised her glass in the star-light, looking over it into his eyes.

"*All* I desire from fortune?" he repeated significantly.

"All—almost all——"

"No, all," he demanded.

But she only raised the glass to her lips, still looking at him as she drank.

They became unreasonably gay almost immediately, though the beverage scarcely accounted for the delicate intoxication that seemed to creep into their veins. Yet it was sufficient for Siward to say an amusing thing wittily, for Sylvia to return his lead with all the delightful, unconscious brilliancy that he seemed to inspire in her—as though awaking into real life once more. All that had slumbered in her through the winter and spring, and the long, arid summer now crumbling to the edge of autumn, broke out into a delicate riot of exquisite florescence; the very sounds of her voice, every intonation, every accent, every pause, were charming surprises; her laughter was a miracle, her beauty a revelation.

Leila, aware of it, exchanged glance after glance with Plank. Siward, alternately the leader in it all, then the enchanted listener, bewitched, enthralled, felt care slipping from his shoulders like a mantle, and sadness exhaling from a heart that was beating strongly, steadily, fearlessly—as a heart should beat in the breast of him who has taken at last his fighting chance. He took it now, under her eyes, for honour, for manhood, and for the ideal which had made manhood no longer an empty term muttered in desperation by a sick body, and a mind too sick to control it.

Yes, at last the lifelong battle was on. He knew it. He knew, too, whatever his fate with her or without her, he must always go on with the battle for the safeguarding of that manhood the consciousness of which she had aroused.

All he knew was that, through the medium of his love for her, whatever in him of the spiritual remained, or had been generated, was now awake, alive, strong, vital, indestructible—an impalpable current flowing from a sane intelligence, through medium of her, back to the eternal truth, returning always, always, to the deathless source from whence it came.

Lingering over the fruit, the champagne breaking in the glasses standing on the table between them, rim to rim, Leila and Plank had fallen into a low, desultory, yet guarded exchange of words and silences.

Sylvia sprang up and pushed her chair into the farther corner against the balcony rail, where no light fell except the radiance of the stars. Here Siward joined her, dragging his chair around so that it faced her as she leaned back, tilted against a shadowy column.

"Is *this* Bohemianism, Stephen? If it is, I rather like it. Don't you? You are going to smoke now, aren't you? Ah, that is delightful!" daintily sniffing the aroma from his cigarette. "It always reminds me of you—there on the cliffs, that first day. Do you remember?—the smoke from your cigarette whirling up in my face? . . . You *say* you remember. . . . Oh, of course there's nothing else to say when a girl asks you . . . is there? Oh, I won't argue with you, if you insist that you do remember. You will not be like any other man if you do, that's all. . . . The little things that women remember! . . . And believe that men remember! It is pitiful in a way. There! I am not going to spill over, and I don't care a copper penny whether you really *do* remember or not! . . . Yes, I *do* care! . . . Oh, *all* women care. It is their first disappointment to learn how much a man can forget and still remember to care for them—a little! . . . Stephen, I said *a little*; and that is all that you are permitted to care for me; isn't it? . . . Please, don't. You are deliberately beginning to say things! . . . Stephen, you silly! you are making love to me!"

In the darkness his hand encountered hers on the wooden rail, and the tremor of the contact silenced her. She freed one finger, then let it rest with its slender fellow-prisoners. There was no use in trying to speak just then—utterly useless her voice in the soft, rounded throat imprisoned by the swelling pulses that tightened and hammered and tightened.

Years seemed to fall away from her, slipping back, back into girlhood, into childhood, drawing not her alone on the gliding tide, but carrying him with her. An exquisite languor held her. Through it vague hints of those splendid visions of her lonely childhood rose, shaping themselves in the starry darkness—the old mystery of dreams, the old, innocent desires, the old simplicity of clairvoyance wherein right was right and wrong, wrong—in all the conventional significance of right and wrong, in all the old-fashioned, undisturbed faith of childhood.

Drifting deliciously, her eyes sometimes meeting his, sometimes lost in the magic of her reverie, she lay there in her chair, her unresisting fingers locked in his.

Odd little thoughts came hovering into her reverie—thoughts that seemed distantly familiar, the direct, unconscious impulses of a child. To feel was once more the only motive for expression; to think fearlessly was once more inherent; to desire was to demand—unlock her lips, naïvely, and ask for what she wished.

Under the spell, she turned her blue gaze on him, and her lips parted without a tremor:

"What do you offer for what you ask? And do you still ask it? Is it *me* you are asking me for? Because you love me? And what do you give—love?"

"Weigh it with the—other," he said.

"I have—often—every moment since I have known you. And what a winter!" Her voice was almost inaudible. "*What* a winter—without you!"

"That hell is ended for me, too. Sylvia, I know what I ask. And I ask. I know what I offer. Will you take it?"

"Yes," she said.

He rose, blindly. She stood up, pale, wide-eyed, confronting him, stammering out the bargain:

"I take all—all! every virtue, every vice of you. I give all—all! all I have been, all I am, all I shall be!

Is that enough? Oh, if there were only more to give! Stephen, if there were only more!"

Her hands had fallen into his, and they looked each other in the eyes.

Suddenly, through the hush of the enchanted moment, a sullen sound broke—the sound of a voice they knew, threateningly raised, louder and louder, growling, profanely menacing.

Aghast, they turned in the darkness, peering toward the lighted space beyond. Leroy Mortimer, his face shockingly congested, stood unsteadily balancing there, confronting his wife, who sat staring at him in horror. At the same instant Plank rose and laid a hand on Mortimer's shoulder, but Mortimer shook him off with a warning oath.

"You and I will settle with each other to-morrow!" he said thickly, pointing a puffy finger at Plank. "You'll find me at the Algonquin Trust. Do you hear? That's where you'll settle this matter—in the president's office!" He stood swaying and leering at Plank, repeating loudly: "In Quarrier's office! Understand? That's where you'll settle up! See?"

Leila, white face quivering, shrank as though he had struck her, and he turned on her again, grinning: "As for you, you come home! And that'll be about all for yours."

"Are you insane, to make a scene like this?" whispered Plank.

But Mortimer swung on him insultingly: "That's about all from you, too!" he said. "Leila, are you coming?"

He stepped heavily toward her; but Plank's sudden crushing grip was on his fat arm above the elbow, and he emitted a roar of surprise and pain.

"Don't touch him! Don't, in Heaven's name!" stammered Leila, as Plank, releasing him, stepped back beside her chair. "Can't you see that I must go with him! I—I must go." She cast one terrified glance around her, where scores of strange faces met hers; and at every table people were standing up to see better.

Plank, who had dropped Mortimer's arm as the latter emitted his bellow of amazement, stepped toward him again, dropping his voice as he spoke:

"You go! Do you hear?" he said quietly. "I'll do what you ask me, to-morrow! I will do what you ask, if you'll go *now*!"

"*You* come—do you hear!" snarled Mortimer, turning on his wife, who had already risen. "If you don't I'll make a row here that you'll never hear the end of as long as you live! And there'll be nothing to talk over in Quarrier's office, if I do."

Leila looked at Plank, rose, and moved swiftly toward the veranda steps, her head resolutely lowered, the burning shame flaming in her face. Mortimer cast one triumphant glance at Plank, then waddled unsteadily after his wife.

"Hold on," he growled; "I've a Mercedes here! I'll drive you back—wait! Here it is! Here we are!" And to Quarrier's machinist he said: "You get into the tonneau. I want to show Mrs. Mortimer what night-driving is. Do you hear? I tell you I'm going to drive this machine and show you how!"

Leila scarcely heard him. She obeyed the impulse of his hand on her arm, and mounted to the seat, staring straight ahead of her with dazed and straining eyes that saw nothing.

Then Mortimer clambered to his seat, and, without an instant's warning, opened up and seized the wheel.

Unprepared, the machinist attempted to swing aboard, missed his footing in the uncertain light, and fell sprawling on the gravel. Plank saw him from the veranda and instantly vaulted the rail to the lawn below.

"You damn fool!" yelled Mortimer, looking around, "what in hell do you think you'll do?" And he clapped on full speed as Plank made a leap for the car and missed.

Mortimer laughed, and turned his head to look back, and the next instant something seemed to wrench the steering-wheel from its roots. There was a blinding glare of light, a scream, and the great machine bounded into the air full length, turned completely over, and lay across a flower-bed, partly on one side.

Something was afire, too. Men were rushing from the verandas, women screamed, and stood up wringing their hands; a mounted policeman came galloping through the darkness; people shouted: "Throw sand on it! Get shovels, for God's sake! Lift that tonneau! There's a woman under it."

But they were mistaken, for Leila lay at the foot of the slope, one little bloody hand clutching the dead grass; and Plank knelt beside her, giving his orders quietly to those who came running down the hill from the roadway above, which was now fiercely illuminated by burning gasoline. At last they got sand enough to quench the fire and men sufficient to lift the weight from the dead man's neck, and drag what was left of him onto the grass.

"Don't look," whispered Siward, drawing Sylvia back.

He and she both had put their shoulders to the tonneau along with the others; and now they stood there together in the shifting lantern-light. sickened, shivering under the summer stars, staring at the gathering crowd around that shapeless lump on the grass.

Plank passed them, walking beside an improvised stretcher, calm, almost smiling, as Sylvia sprang forward with a little sob of inquiry.

"There's the doctor, over there; that man is a doctor; *he* knows," repeated Plank with studied deliberation, looking down at Leila's deathly face. "He says it's all right; he says he'll get a candle, and that he can tell by the flame's effect on the pupils of the eyes what exactly is the matter. No," to Siward beside him, pressing forward through the crowd which eddied from the dead man to the stretcher; "no, there is not a bone broken. She is stunned, that's all; she fell in the shrubbery. We'll have an ambulance here pretty quick. Stephen," using his first name unconsciously, "won't you look out for Sylvia? I'm going back on the ambulance. If you'll find somebody to drive my machine, I wish you would take Sylvia back. No, I don't want you to drive, Stephen—if you don't mind. Get that machinist, please. I'm rattled, and I don't want you to drive."

Leila lay on the stretcher, her bloodless face upturned to the stars. Beyond, under a blanket, something else lay very still on the lawn.

Plank beckoned a policeman, and whispered to him.

Then, far away in the darkness, a distant clamour grew on the night air, nearer, nearer.

Plank, standing beside the stretcher, raised his head, listening to the ambulance arriving at full speed.

CHAPTER XV

THE ENEMY LISTENS

In September, her marriage to Siward excitingly imminent, Sylvia had been seized with a passion for wholesale renunciation and rigid self-chastisement. All that had been so materially desirable to her in life, all that she had heretofore worshipped, in and belonging to her own world, she now denied. Down went the miniature golden calf from the altar in her private shrine, its tiny crashing fall making considerable racket throughout her world, and the planets and satellites adjacent to that section of the social system which she had long been expected to dominate.

The spectacle of their youthful ruler-elect in sackcloth as the future bride of a business man had more than disconcerted them. The amazing announcement of Quarrier's engagement to Agatha Caithness stupefied the elect, rendering in one harrowing instant null and void the thousand petty plans and plots, intrigues and schemes, upon which future social constructions on the social structure had been based.

The grief and amazement of Major Belwether, already distracted by his non-participation, through his own fault, in Plank's consolidation of Amalgamated with Inter-County, was pitiable to the verge of the unpleasant. Like panic-stricken rabbits, his thoughts ran in circles, and he skipped in their wake, scurrying from Quarrier to Harrington, from Harrington to Plank, from Plank to Siward, in distracted hope of recovering his equilibrium and squatting safely somewhere in somebody's luxuriantly perpetual cabbage-patch. He even squeezed under the fence and hopped humbly about old Peter Caithness, who suddenly assumed monumental proportions among those who had so long tolerated him.

But Quarrier coldly drove him away and the increasing crowds besieging poor, bewildered old Peter Caithness trod upon the major, and there was nothing for him to do but to scuttle back to his own brush-heap and huddle there, squeaking pitifully.

As for Grace Ferrall, she lost no time in tears, but took Agatha publicly to her bosom, turned furiously on Quarrier in private, and for the first time in her life permitted herself the luxury of telling him exactly what she thought of him.

"You had your chance," she said; "but you are all surface! There's nothing to you but soft beard and manicuring, and the reticence of stupidity! The *one* girl for you—and you couldn't hold on to her! The one chance of your life—and it's escaped you, leaving a tuft of pompadour hair and a pair of woman's eyes protruding from the golden dust-heap your father buried you in. Now you'd better sit there and let it cover your mouth, and try to breathe through your nose. Agatha is looking for a new sensation; she's tried everything, now she's going to try you, that's all. She will be an invaluable leader, Howard, and we shall not yawn, I assure you. But, oh! the chance you've lost, for lack of a drop of red blood, and a barber to give you the beard of a man!"

Which merely deepened the fear and hatred which Quarrier had entertained for his pretty cousin from the depths of his silk-wadded cradle. As for Kemp Ferrall, now third vice-president of Inter-County, he only laughed with the tolerance of a man in safety; and, looking at Quarrier through the pickets of the financial fence, not only forgot how close his escape had been, but, being a busy and progressive young man, began to consider how he might ultimately extract a little profit from the expensive tenant of the enclosure.

Grace made the journey to town to express herself freely for Sylvia's benefit; but when she saw Sylvia, the girl's radiant beauty checked her, and all she could say was: "My dear! my dear, I knew you would do it! I knew you would fling him on his head. It's in your blood, you little jade! you little jilt! you minx of a baggage! I knew you'd behave like all the women of your race!"

Sylvia held Mrs. Ferrall's pretty face impressed between both her hands, and looking her mischievously in the eyes, she whispered:

> "'*Comme vous, maman, faut-il faire?*
> *—Eh! mes petits-enfants, pourquoi,*
> *Quand j'ai fait comme ma grand'mère,*
> *Ne feriez-vous pas comme moi?*'"

"O Lord!" said Mrs. Ferrall, "I'll never meddle again—and the entire world may marry and take the consequences!" Then she drove to the Santa Regina, where Marion was to join her in her return to Shotover; and she was already trying to make up her disturbed mind as to which might prove the more suitable for Marion—Captain Voucher, gloomily recovering from his defeat by Quarrier, or Billy Fleetwood, who didn't want to marry anybody.

In the meanwhile, Siward's new duties as second vice-president of Inter-County had given him scant leisure for open-air convalescence. He was busy with Plank; he was also busy with the private investigation stirred up at the Patroons' Club and the Lenox, and which was slowly but inevitably resulting in clearing him, so that his restoration to good standing and full membership remained now only a matter of formal procedure.

So Siward was becoming a very busy man among men; and Plank, still carrying on his broad shoulders burdens unbearable by any man save such a man as he, shook his heavy head, and ordered Siward into the open. And Siward, who had learned to obey, obeyed.

But September had nearly ended, when Leila, in Plank's private car, attended by Siward and Sylvia and two trained nurses, arrived at the Fells. The nurses —Plank's idea—were a surprise to Leila; and the day after her arrival at the Fells she dismissed them, got out of bed, and dressed and came downstairs all alone, on a pair of sound though faltering legs.

Sylvia and Siward were in the music-room, very busily figuring out the probable cost of a house in that section of the city east of Park Avenue, where the newly married imprudent are forming colonies—a just punishment for those reckless brides who marry for love, and are obliged to drive over two car-tracks to reach their wealthy friends and relatives of the Golden Zone.

And Leila, in her pretty invalid's gown of lace, stood silently at the music-room door, watching them. Her thick, dark hair was braided, and looped up under a black bow behind; and she looked like a curious and impertinent schoolgirl peeping at them there through the crack of the door, bending forward, her joined hands flattened between her knees.

"Oh," she said at length, in a frankly disappointed

voice, "is *that* all you do when your chaperone is abed?"

"Angel!" cried Sylvia, springing up, "how in the world did you ever manage to come downstairs?"

"On the usual number of feet. If you think it's very gay up there—" She laid her hands in Sylvia's, and looked at Siward with all the old mockery in her eyes—eyes which slanted a little at the corners, Japanese-wise: "Stephen, you are growing positively plump. You'd better not do that until Sylvia marries you. Look at him, dear! He's getting all smooth in the cheeks, like a horrid undergraduate boy!"

She released one hand and greeted Siward. "Thank you," she said serenely, replying to his inquiry, "I am perfectly well. You pay me no compliment when you ask me, after you have seen me." And to Sylvia, looking at her white flannels: "What have you been playing? What do you find to do with yourself, Sylvia, with that plump sun-burned boy at your heels all day long? Are there no men about?"

"One's coming to-day," said Sylvia, laughing; and slipping her arm around Leila's waist, she strolled with her out through the tall glass doors to the terrace, with a backward glance of airy dismissal for Siward.

Plank had wired from New York, the night before, that he was coming; in another hour he would be there. Leila knew it perfectly well, and she looked into the wickedly expressive young face of the girl beside her, eyes soft but unsmiling.

"Child, child," she murmured, "*you* do not know how much of a man a man can be!"

"Yes, I do!" said Sylvia hotly.

Leila smiled. "Hush, you little silly! I've talked Stephen and praised Stephen to you for days and days, and the moment I dare mention another man you fly at me, hair on end!"

"Oh, Leila, I know it! I'm perfectly mad about him, that's all. But *don't* you think he *is* looking like himself again? And, Leila, *isn't* he strangely attractive?—I don't mean just because I happen to be in love with him, but give me a perfectly cold and unbiassed opinion, dear, because there is simply no use in a girl's blinding herself to facts, or in ignoring certain fixed laws of symmetry, which it is perfectly obvious that Mr. Siward fulfils in those well-known and established proportions which——"

"Sylvia!"

"What?" she asked, startled.

"Nothing. Only for two solid weeks——"

"Of course, if you are not interested——"

"But I am, child—I am! desperately interested! He *is* handsome! I knew him before you did, and I thought so then!"

"Did you?" said Sylvia, troubled.

"Yes, I did. When I wore short skirts I kissed him, too!"

"Did you? W—what did *he* wear?"

"Knickerbockers, silly! You don't think he was still in the cradle, do you? I'm not as aged as *that*!"

"I missed a great deal in my childhood," said Sylvia naïvely.

"By not knowing Stephen? Pooh! He used to pinch me, and then we'd put out our tongues in mutual derision. Once——"

"Stop!" said Sylvia faintly. "And anyhow, you probably taught him. . . . Look at him as he saunters across the lawn, Leila—*look* at him!"

"Well? I see him."

"*Isn't* he almost an ideal?"

"He *is*. He certainly is, dear."

"Do you think he walks as though he were perfectly well?"

"Well, I don't know," said Leila thoughtfully. "Sometimes people whose walk is a gracefully languid saunter develop adipose tissue after forty."

"Nonsense! Really, Leila, do you think he walks like a perfectly well man?"

"He *may* be coming down with whooping-cough——"

Sylvia rose indignantly, but Leila pulled her back to the sun-warmed marble bench:

"A girl in love loses her sense of humour temporarily. Sit down, you little vixen!"

"Leila, you laugh at everything when I don't feel like it."

"I'm not in love, and *that's* why."

"You *are* in love!"

Leila looked at her, then under her breath: "In love, am I—with the whole young world ringing with the laughter I had forgotten the very sound of? Do you call that love?—with the sea and sky laughing back at me, and the wind in my ears fairly tremulous with laughter? Do *you*, who look out upon the pretty world so seriously through those sea-blue eyes of yours, think that *I* can be in love?"

"Oh, Leila, a girl's happiness is serious enough, isn't it? Dear, it frightens me! I was so close to losing it—once."

"I lost mine," said Leila, closing her eyes for a moment. "I shall not sigh if I find it again."

They sat there in the sun, Leila's hand lying idly in Sylvia's, the soft sea-wind stirring their hair, and in their ears the thunderous undertone of the mounting sea.

"Look at Stephen!" murmured Sylvia, her enraptured eyes following him as he strolled hatless and coatless along the cliff's edge, the sun glimmering on his short hair, a tall, slim, well-coupled, strongly knit shape against the sky and sea.

But Leila's quick ear had caught a significant sound from the gravel drive behind her, and she stood up, a delicious colour tinting her face.

"Are you going in?" asked Sylvia. Then she, too, heard the subdued whirring of a motor from the front of the house, and she looked at Leila as she turned and recrossed the terrace, walking slowly but erect, her pretty head held high.

Then Sylvia faced the sea again and presently descended the terrace, crossing the long lawn toward the headland, where Siward stood looking out across the water.

Leila, from the music-room, watched her; then she heard Plank's voice, and his step on the stair, and she called out to him gaily:

"I am downstairs, thank you. How dared you send me those foolish nurses!"

She was laughing when he came into the room, standing there erect, head high, a brilliant colour in her cheeks; and she offered him both hands which he took between his own, holding them strongly, and looking into her face with steady, questioning eyes.

"Well?" she said, still smiling, but her scarlet underlip trembled a little; then: "Yes, you may say what you wish—what I—I wish you to say. . . . There can be no harm in talking about it. But—will you be very gentle with me? Don't m-make me cry; I h-have—

I am t-trying to remember how it feels to laugh once more."

. . . .

Sylvia, lying in the hot sand on the tiny crescent beach under the cliffs, listened gravely to Siward's figures, as, note-book in hand, he went over the real-estate problem, commenting thoughtfully as he discussed the houses offered.

"Twenty by a hundred and two; good rear, north side of the street—next door to the Tommy Barclays, you know, Sylvia; only they're asking forty-two-five."

"That is an outrage!" said Sylvia seriously; "besides, I remember there was a wretched cellar, and only a butler's pantry extension. I'd much rather have that little house in Sixty-fourth Street, where the Fetherbraynes live—next house on the west, you know. Then we can pull it down and build—when we want to."

"We won't be able to afford to build for a while, you know," said Siward doubtfully.

"What do we care, dear? We'll have millions of things to do, anyway, and what is the use of building?"

"As many things to do as that?" he said, looking over his note-book with a smile.

"More! Are we not just beginning to live, and open our eyes, silly? Listen: Books, books, books, from top to bottom of the house, *that* is what I want first of all—except my piano."

"Do let us have a little plumbing, dear," he said so seriously that for a fraction of a second she was on the verge of taking him seriously.

"Why extravagant plumbing when books furnish sufficient circulation for the flow of soul, dear?" she retorted gravely.

"Nobody we know will ever come to see us, if they think we read books," said Siward.

"Isn't it delightful!" sighed Sylvia. "We're going to become frumps! I mustn't forget the blue stockings for my trousseau, and you mustn't forget the California claret for the cellar, dear. We will need it when we read Henry James to each other."

Siward, resting his weight on one hand, laughed, and looked out at the surf drenching the reefs with silver.

"To think," he said, "that I could ever have been enough afraid of the sea to hate it! After all, at low tide the reef is always there in the same place and none the worse for the drenching. All that surf only shows how strong a rock can be."

He smiled, and turned to look at Sylvia; and she lay there, silent, blue eyes looking back into his. Suddenly they glimmered with tears, and she stretched out both arms, drawing his head down to hers convulsively, her quivering mouth crushed against his lips. Then she rose to her knees, to her feet, dazed, brushing the tears from her eyes.

"To think—to think," she stammered, "that I might have let you face the world alone! Dearest, dearest, we must fight a good fight. The sea is always there—always, always there!"

He looked straight into her eyes, fearlessly, tenderly, and she looked back with the divine, untroubled gaze of a child, laying her slender, sun-tanned hands in his.

And, deep in his body, as he stood there, he heard the low challenge of his soul on guard; and he knew that the Enemy listened.

(7)

THE END